They
For P

Lady Margot Vale—The ravishing Englishwoman defied society, sailing to Tahiti to find the man from the *Medusa* with the fabulous black pearl—to find her great love, and her undoing . . .

"Bully" Jenks—He was evil incarnate, fused to Tom Street by a shipwreck, a lust for pearls, and burning envy. If it took a lifetime, he would have Street's empire and his woman—or destroy them all . . .

David Nasis—The Oriental pearl broker vowed to avenge his love for Margot Vale. Surely he could divide and conquer Tom Street's fortune—with Jenks as his partner in crime . . .

Jessica Street—Child of Tom and Margot, she scandalized Paris with her sizzling memoirs—and then discovered passion in the arms of the only man she was forbidden to love . . .

Mia Da Costa—The beautiful Parisian aristocrat offered a ravaged Tom Street revenge and redemption: Catherine the Great's priceless triple strand of black pearls—and a love that refused to hide in the ruins of the past . . .

Susan Chamblis—She wanted only to forgive the father she'd never known. To offer Tom Street a last, forgotten hope . . .

Lustre

John Maccabee

POCKET BOOKS

New York London Toronto Sydney Tokyo

Another *Original* publication of POCKET BOOKS

 POCKET BOOKS, a division of Simon & Schuster, Inc.
1230 Avenue of the Americas, New York, N.Y. 10020

ISBN: 0-671-61097-X

First Pocket Books printing April 1988

10 9 8 7 6 5 4 3 2 1

POCKET and colophon are trademarks of
Simon & Schuster, Inc.

Printed in the U.S.A.

for Sherry

The liquid drops of tears that you have shed
Shall come again, transformed to orient pearl.

—WILLIAM SHAKESPEARE

Contents

Prologue
Below the Equator

July 1891

FOR A WEEK the ship limped through the doldrums and the sun baked the swollen decks. Below, in the fo'c'sle, where the crew lived, the air itself seemed flammable.

Tom Aspinall lay on his bunk watching Stringy Peele, who was as thin and hairy as a monkey, jabbering away at anyone who would listen.

"Jenks is evil. It's him that brings us all this hellish weather." Stringy was creeping toward Jenks, who was sleeping nearby, an arm covering his eyes. A leather pouch was hanging from his belt. "Jenks has pearls in that pouch. I seen 'em once—white, like the teeth of a death angel."

"Stringy!" Tom whispered. "Leave him alone."

Jenks moved in his sleep, turning toward Stringy.

Stringy reached down.

"Don't do it," Tom hissed. "He'll kill you!"

Prying open the folds of the pouch, Stringy pulled out a pearl necklace. It uncoiled like a white snake—a foot long, smooth and shiny, making the grimy fo'c'sle appear even grimier in comparison.

"Oooh," Stringy cooed. "This here is riches I never seen before," he said, rising to his feet.

Jenks stirred; his arm unfolded from his face and settled on his chest.

"Put it back," Tom said, but Stringy, hollow-eyed and distrustful, turned quickly and fled.

Tom pulled on his boots and ran from the fo'c'sle, looking fore and aft.

Two seamen were fishing nearby on the aft deck.

"You see Stringy Peele just now?" Tom asked.

Both shook their heads.

A hatch that led to the tween decks was open. Lowering himself into the darkness, Tom saw Stringy holding a lighted lantern above the necklace. Stringy stumbled backward over some cable and lifted a hatch that led below to the cargo bays.

"Don' come near me," he was saying. "Don' follow—I'll blow us all the way to hell and back . . ."

"I'm not going to hurt you."

"Don' come near me!" Stringy shouted, then disappeared down the hatch, pulling it shut after himself.

Tom lunged for the hatch and felt a whoosh of hot, dank air as he opened it. Flashes of lantern light darted across the hold. Barrels of kerosene, perhaps a thousand of them, were stacked as high as the rafters for as far as Tom could see.

Jenks appeared behind Tom. His hair was a wild, dark tangle framing skin as pale as sand.

"Let me get him. You'll only scare him off," Tom said to him.

But Jenks pushed Tom out of the way and clambered down into the darkness.

Tom followed.

Stringy was scrambling over barrels, trying to blow out the lantern's flame, but it wouldn't go out and he threw it aside. Laughing a high-pitched wheeze of a laugh, he raced over another aisle of barrels.

Tom followed the sound of the laughter and finally heard feet clambering back up the steps.

First Stringy, then Jenks, then Tom cleared the hatch. Stringy ran on deck, climbing into the rigging, with Jenks at his heels.

"Give it to me, you bastard!" Jenks yelled.

Stringy made it to the lower topsail yard and climbed higher onto the topgallant and then to the royal, where he stared down at Jenks and held the pearls out over the sea.

Jenks had now reached the royal and was inching his way out toward Stringy.

"You drop those pearls, you're a dead man," he hissed.

As the crew surged onto the deck, Tom climbed to the topgallant, directly under Stringy.

"Stop right there," Stringy called out to Jenks as he inched closer.

"Stop or I'll chuck them overboard!"

Jenks stopped, teetering like an aerialist.

Stringy, pleased to finally have this much control over Jenks, smiled a lethal, eerie smile and threw the pearls out beyond the yard. They fell, suddenly insignificant and pale, into the sea.

Stringy giggled and, as Jenks took another step closer, fell from the yard, bouncing off the topgallant. His head split open on the topsail yard, soft, pink brains splattering on the deck as he flipped into the sea. A group of sharks quickly swarmed in, jagged mouths agape, and tore him to pieces.

The crew rushed to the gunwales, and Tom, descending on the main shrouds above them, saw smoke rising from the forward cargo bay hatch.

"Fire!" he called out.

The men turned forward in unison.

"Fire!" someone else screamed as the wisp of smoke became thicker and more smoke rose from below deck. The men began scrambling wildly now, and again the dreaded word rang out but it was splintered by an explosion that came roaring up from the bowels of the ship.

From the mainmast to the deckhouse, the forward deck was a gaping, burning hole; it looked like the entry to hell. Tom had been thrown from the rigging by the blast. He lay on the aft deck, arms covering his head.

Seamen were jumping overboard to save their lives, but as Tom reached the port gunwales he saw that these men had only leaped to their death: kerosene had spread on the water and the surrounding sea was in flames.

The first mate was at the wheel screaming out orders to get the men into the rigging to furl the remaining sails, but no one was listening.

Suddenly Jenks, carrying something tucked under his shirt, rushed from the poop deck, followed by the captain, who was trying to level a pistol at Jenks's head. As the ship began to list to port, the captain was knocked off balance and fired at the sky. Jenks made his way toward a skiff that was lashed down between the lifeboats on top of the deckhouse.

The first mate abandoned the wheel as a haunted chorus of shouts rose up.

"The aft cargo bays are gonna blow!"

"Lower the boats! Lower the boats!"

A moment later a second explosion splintered the air. The captain and mates on the poop deck were enveloped by flames.

Jenks began dragging the skiff forward to the port side.

Another explosion rocked the forward bays, leaving Jenks teetering over the burning sea. He fell, and the little boat toppled after him. Tom, losing his balance, rolled to the port side. Jenks was below in the flames, but he'd gotten into the skiff and was jamming the oars into their locks. Sharks swarmed in, furiously snapping at anything that moved. Men were screaming and the air stank of burning flesh and dense kerosene fumes as the great hulking ship began to list violently.

Forward and aft, flames spat out from the bowels of the cargo bays. Tom, poised between twin hells, his head tucked into his chest, dived through them.

Jenks's skiff was directly above him; the painter, the long rope tied to the bow, was trailing under it. Tom grabbed it to pull himself along the skiff's keel to the bow and turned to see a gray dorsal fin closing in. He kicked out wildly. One of his boots connected with the shark's nose and it turned, momentarily abandoning its attack.

Turning, Jenks saw Tom hanging on to the bow.

"Give me a hand!" Tom shouted up.

But Jenks, whose upper body was badly burned, plucked out one of the oars and began pummeling Tom's hands.

The dorsal fin was coming in again. Tom pulled himself to the skiff's starboard side, his hands again reaching up for the gunwales, but Jenks renewed the beating. Fighting past the pain, Tom swung his body up with one last surge of energy. He rolled into the boat with the painter held tightly in his hands.

Jenks raised the oar over Tom's head and hurled himself forward. He fell, and Tom wrapped the painter around Jenks's throat—once, twice—and jerked him into a sitting position.

"Put the oar back into its lock!" he screamed into Jenks's ear, tightening the rope until Jenks began to choke.

"Was half out of my mind—didn't know who it was!" Jenks gasped.

Behind them a curtain of thick gray smoke wrapped around a nimbus of flames. As the smoke shifted, one of the three masts could be seen, starkly black against the gray sky.

"Circle round the flames; we're not leaving any men behind!" Tom shouted.

"Only enough provisions for two men."

Tom twisted the rope tightly.

"I'll survive alone if you don't obey me."

"You can't survive without me," Jenks said hoarsely. "I know the sea. I know where we are. I've got the captain's compass."

"Circle round the flames!"

Tom lay back against the bow, gripping the rope as Jenks rowed.

From somewhere deep within himself Tom found the strength to keep calling out, "Ahoy, ahoy," but no call came back.

"They're all dead. We're all that's left of her," Jenks said.

Scores of sharks were circling in a frenzy, fighting for whatever remained of the crew.

In the distance Tom could hear the last baleful hissing of the ship in its death throes.

"We've got to clear it or she'll take us under when she goes," Jenks said, slumping forward.

"Get us clear then," Tom said, jerking Jenks into an upright position. "Get us clear!"

Jenks, straining at the rope, continued rowing.

Far enough away from the ship now, they drifted. Jenks fell forward, unconscious. Tom sat shivering with his back against the bow. In the distance the ship was burning like a funeral pyre, spinning slowly in a foamy circle.

Let her go, Tom thought, let her go.

And in one rumbling instant she disappeared, taking his former life with her to the bottom.

Once again the water became calm and flat. The sun burned through the smoke like the lit end of a cigar, and Tom shaded his eyes with his hands.

"The lie survives," he whispered, looking out at the empty sea. "If it survives at all . . ."

I

Black Pearls

Chapter One

JUST TWO MONTHS before, Tom had seen the ship tied up at Old Slip in New York harbor. Three-masted and square-rigged, she had loomed over a floating slum of wide, flat canal boats.

"We should be getting back to the office," Duff St. John called out.

But Tom wanted a closer look at the ship. He was a handsome young man, with regular features, except his eyes, which were particularly intense, so dark that each iris appeared to be as black as the pupil.

"See that ship over there?" he called out over his shoulder, pointing at it with his walking stick. "My mother once took me aboard her."

"She's an unremarkable-looking boat," Duff said, standing at the corner of Fulton and South streets, smoothing a wrinkle on his Prince Albert frock coat. "Good God! It smells to high heaven over here. I don't know why I ever let you talk me into coming here for lunch."

"She's a ship, Duff, not a boat. But I can't remember her name."

"Medusa," Duff said. "It's spelled out in white letters. I don't think the food is very good here, either. I think we may have even been poisoned," he said, burping into his gloved hand. He was tall, thin, and fair, with an open, genial face.

"She had another name," Tom said, trying to remember it.

"I thought it was bad luck to change the name of a boat."

"Ship, Duff, ship. Let's walk over there; I want to ask someone."

Crossing to the pier side of South Street, Tom walked

11

ahead. Above him the bowsprits of a dozen vessels loomed. Yards and masts intersected, crosses upon crosses, a stippled field of them stretched as far as the eye could see up and down the East River.

At Old Slip, Tom stood staring up at the ship's hull. Turning, he smiled quickly at Duff, and again pointed up at her with his walking stick.

"See the notch just under her bowsprit? That's where her figurehead used to be, a big buxom blonde. Her hair blended with a floral design, but her plating is all pitted back to her hawse pipes. Someone's taken her carving off."

"Where on earth did you learn all this jargon?"

"Books, mostly, when I was younger. My grandfather was a ship's captain."

"I thought he was a lawyer with our firm."

"That was my father. My mother's father was a seaman."

"It's all very confusing," Duff said wearily.

Tom's concentration remained focused on the ship and a small shack that stood midway down the pier.

"She's awfully low in the water; I wonder if she's got cargo in her hold," he said.

"She looks deserted to me."

"I wish I could remember her name. The afternoon I spent aboard her was one of the best I ever had with my mother. It was just before she died. I wanted to put out to sea so badly."

"On *that?*"

"You should have seen her then—what an adventure that would have been!"

"My grandfather used to say the only real adventure is making money."

"Do you believe that?"

"No, but thank goodness my grandfather did," Duff said, drawing a gold pocket watch from his vest. He wanted nothing more than to return to the sequestered calm of the law offices of Puddy, Cuddahay, at 71 Wall Street, where he and Tom worked. "We really should be getting back. At any rate, you aren't sure this is your boat, are you?"

"There's one way I can find out. She was hit starboard side stern—she'd have a plate back there," Tom said, walking out on the pier. Duff groaned but followed.

Just then two men appeared in the doorway of the shack on the pier. One was a midget, about as tall and broad as a cargo barrel, with a full moustache and a defiant expression in his eyes. He was wearing a sooty shirt, trousers held up by suspenders, and a bowler on his oversized head. Beside him was a tall man dressed in black, with unkempt thick black hair, broad shoulders, and pale, pale skin, who kept his back to Tom and Duff as they passed by. Picking up the collar of his coat to further obscure his features, he turned and glowered at the two other men like a mongrel protecting a bone from a pack of dogs.

"Not the sort one would invite to the club," Duff whispered.

Tom suddenly stopped and, turning to the two men, called out, "I beg your pardon; are you crew on this ship?"

Without turning, the tall man in black spoke in a guttural north English accent.

"We're talkin'. Bugger off!"

Tom impulsively took a step forward, his hand raising his walking stick.

"Hardly worth it," Duff said, putting a cautionary hand on Tom's arm. "Why ruin a perfectly good walking stick?"

The tall man was jabbing a long, slim index finger down at the top of the midget's bowler.

"It's none of our affair," Duff said.

Grudgingly, Tom turned back to the ship, walking slowly to the end of the pier, inspecting the ship's stern.

"She's the same ship, all right. There's the plate."

"Well, I'm glad you've cleared that up. Now let's walk back to the office."

"Think of all the different waters she's been in since the last time I saw her. I'd put out on her right now."

"What for?"

"Don't you ever want to do anything extraordinary with your life, Duff?"

"Yes. I'd like to eat an extraordinarily good meal for lunch tomorrow, and it *won't* be fish."

"I'm serious."

"I know, and it's most disagreeable. You are a lawyer, Tom, with a decent, albeit boring, job, but one with prospects because you have such an indecently rich father-in-law."

"It's his money, not mine."

"Very noble, I'm sure, but still, there you are. Aside from which you have a perfectly beautiful wife."

"Unfortunately, Jelly's more interested in being her father's daughter than her husband's wife," Tom said, more seriously than Duff had expected.

"He needs a hostess and Jelly is so beautiful and ambitious. I admire people who want to bring themselves up in the world," Duff said with all the assurance of someone who had already been "brought up." "This ball he's throwing next week will make him and Jelly. And if you're smart, you'll allow it to make you, too."

Tom smiled. "You actually believe that a single party will make my fortune?"

"Perhaps you fight your father-in-law too much."

"That's why Jelly married me, Duff. She wanted someone to stand up to him."

"And why did you marry her?" Duff asked ruefully.

"I was in love with her . . . or with the idea of her. She seemed to know what she wanted. I was the thing her father didn't want her to have, so of course she had to have me."

"And your children?"

Tom's tone of voice softened. "They're the reason I stay."

"That's not true. I know you love her, and I've just decided what your problem is; you need a vacation. Think of all the other smelly, dirty ports you can tramp round. Trieste, for instance. The last time I was in Trieste, it was truly rank down by their docks."

Harsh words rang out behind them, and both men turned.

"You give me what's mine!" the tall Englishman threatened, holding the flailing midget at arm's length.

"You bastard, Jenks! Bullyin' bastard!" the midget yelled. The taller man reached down, grabbed the midget by the crotch and shirtfront, and in one furious gesture swooped him over his head and began shaking him violently.

"Give me what's mine! Give me it!"

"Put him down!" Tom called out.

But the tall man ignored him, redoubling his efforts to shake something out of the midget's pockets.

"Put me down, you bullyin' Jenks, you bastard! Put me down!" the midget shrieked, but his voice vibrated, sounding comical, as if he were speaking underwater.

As Tom began running toward them, the tall man turned, holding the midget above his head as if he'd hurl him straight at Tom if Tom took another step.

Tom stopped in his tracks—it was the first time he'd gotten a good look at the man's face. The man called Jenks had a long thin nose and strong chin. His eyelids were red, almost the same color as his lips, and the eyes themselves were as soulless as anything Tom had ever seen: pale and chilly, almost opaque, like a blind man's. If ice had the power to burn, it would have been that color.

"Don' take a step closer!" he yelled. "I only want what's my property. And you, boyzo, have nothin' to do with it!"

The voice was powerful and deep, but the accent was too thickly layed on, as if the man were acting a role in a play. Disregarding the threat, Tom took another step forward.

Holding on to the midget's feet, the man lowered him head first, holding him inches above the ground. The bowler fell off and rolled to the edge of the pier. Again, Jenks shook the little man, who screamed and flailed like a flaccid puppet. Suddenly a pearl necklace slipped out of the midget's trouser pocket and hit the ground. Tom only saw it for a moment because Jenks threw the little man against some barrels, grabbed the necklace from the ground, and took off. Tom raised his walking stick and started after him. The man turned and grabbed the tip of the stick, pulling Tom around with it, his grip matching Tom's tug for tug. His eyes were crazed and he smiled as if he relished the possibility of a fight.

"I'll remember y'ur face, boyzo. I'll get you for this!"

Tom's breath was coming in short gasps and his heart was pounding, but he wasn't afraid; if he could get in closer, he'd have the man where he wanted him. He put one hand over the other, shortening the distance between them. He could hear the hiss of the other man's breath and smell its foul odor: a mixture of stale beer and fish.

"I'll get the police," Duff called out, running down the pier toward the police precinct at Old Slip.

Hearing the word *police*, the tall man's eyes flashed with

fear, and Tom, gaining a tighter hold of the stick, jabbed it into the tall man's chest. The man dropped the stick and spun around, winded and wild-eyed. He tucked his shoulder down and charged Tom, who side-stepped him: the man went flying over the edge of the pier, onto the deck of one of the flat canal boats. Scrambling to his feet, he called, "Will get you back, boyzo. Will do it!" In another moment he fled like a wounded animal from one boat to the other and finally disappeared.

"Are you all right?" Tom called out to the midget, who was standing now, rubbing his right shoulder with a spindly little hand.

"I'm awright. He's as mad as a coot," he spat out.

"My friend's gone to get the police."

"He's *what?*"

"Don't worry, we'll get that necklace back."

"What necklace? I tell you he's as mad as a coot," the little man repeated.

"But I saw it."

"Then you're as mad as him," the midget said. Looking up the pier, he saw Duff running back with two policemen in tow. "Now you've gone and done it. Why don't you rich assholes leave the rest of us in peace?" He jumped like a bulky sprite over the pier onto the deck of a canal boat, then waddled in a bow-legged sprint from one deck to another. He, too, disappeared.

"Tom, you all right?" Duff called out as he ran. Tom stood staring out at the canal boats.

"What happened? Where are they?" Duff asked.

Tom pointed out at the boats. "Gone. The tall one stole the midget's necklace."

"What necklace?"

"You didn't see it? Pearls, large ones."

"The midget was wearing a necklace? Are you quite mad?"

"You gennelmen been ruffed up by some vagran's?" one of the policemen asked politely.

"They were beating each other," Tom said in a distracted tone.

"Just as well. Saves us the bother," the policeman added with a wink.

Tom chuckled, straightening his coat and tie.

"You laugh, but you're positively heedless," Duff said. "You rush off into anything without thinking about the consequences. That man could have killed you."

"Poor Duff, you have had a time of it, and all I wanted was to see the old ship again. Do either of you know how long she's been tied up here?" Tom asked the policemen, pointing at the *Medusa*.

"This tub? Quite a while, I think. They was loadin' her a couple a days ago."

"She had another name. You wouldn't happen to know it?"

"'Fraid not. You wanna report this?"

"No, that's not necessary."

"Watch out round here. All sorts of types. Good day, gennelmen."

The policemen walked off.

"Well, I'm sure you're satisfied," Duff said.

"What's that?"

"All this to-do. This was *extraordinary* enough for you, wasn't it?"

Tom was still trying to remember the name of the ship, but it would not come, and so, somewhat disheartened, he patted Duff's shoulder and the two men began walking back to the office on Wall Street. As to Duff's question—had what had happened that afternoon been extraordinary enough for him?—Tom thought not. Not half as extraordinary as he wished life could be.

Chapter Two

"POOR FLEDGE," TOM whispered broadly as he stood behind Duff St. John's desk, staring out the window at the *Medusa* tied up below at Old Slip.

Duff picked his head up from his writing and looked across at the pilastered screen of colored-glass windows that separated the offices of the senior partners from the offices of the junior partners. At that moment Chauncey Fledge, a tall beak-nosed man with pale red hair, was placing a rather eager hand into the unyielding mitt of Mr. Marcus Puddy, the most senior partner of Puddy, Cuddahay.

"What is so poor about poor Chauncey Fledge? Looks to me as though he's just gotten himself a promotion."

"That's what it's *supposed* to look like," Tom said, his dark eyes flashing with undisclosed knowledge.

The office was not conducive to gossip, though not for the lack of endless speculation on the part of the junior partners on the comings and goings of the more senior partners. It was just that the physical layout did not lend itself to privacy: there were no walls separating desk spaces, only low oak banisters. But there were ways around that. You could take a file to a window or to an associate's desk and leaf through it meaningfully as Tom and Duff were now doing.

"He's being put out to pasture," Tom said, resuming his conversation with Duff after Fledge walked past them.

"How do you know?"

"I found out that several of the partners are setting up bogus companies to buy up the stock of steamship companies listed on the Exchange for one of our clients. If anyone on the Street knew who was doing the buying, the stock prices would go wild."

"Who *is* doing the buying?"

"Someone with whom I am intimately acquainted."

"Your father-in-law."

"Mr. Bridge is attempting to put together a steamship combine that would control every route between America and Europe. He's not only setting up bogus companies, he's renting office space and hiring staff, just so no one will suspect that he is the purchaser."

"How do you know all this?"

"I overheard a conversation last weekend between Mr. Bridge and Mr. Puddy. Chauncey's name was mentioned. The senior partners don't like him any more than we do; they were just waiting to see if his mother was going to have Mr. Puddy administer her estate. Now that she's gone over to Cadwallader, they're making Chauncey president of Nautilus Shipping for a month or two, until Mr. Bridge can buy up the rest of the steamship lines. Then he'll absorb them into his mining company, and all the bogus executives in all the bogus companies will be fired."

"Masterful," Duff said breathlessly.

"If you're an admirer of Attila the Hun, it's masterful," Tom said. "But I think it's an awful thing to do to someone, even someone as awful as Fledge."

"But this is great news for you, Tom—surely you'll be moved up to Chauncey's spot."

Both men looked over at Fledge, who was bent over his desk, scrawling in his illegible handwriting.

"You're next in line," Duff went on, "and you're Bridge's son-in-law. You see, I told you all this would work in your favor if you simply let it happen."

That being decided, both men went back to their respective desks, and fifteen minutes later, when one of Mr. Puddy's clerks asked if Mr. Aspinall would join Mr. Puddy for tea, Duff St. John smiled knowingly and winked a good-luck wink at his friend as Tom made his way to Mr. Puddy's office.

The office was at the end of a long corridor. It was a large room with walls painted forest green and accented with honey-colored oak bookshelves. When Tom walked in, Mr. Puddy remained seated behind a long, glass-topped oak desk, his features somewhat obscured behind a cloud of acrid, blue-white pipe smoke. Behind him the sun was shining through tall windows and the smoke was trapped in shafts of light that fell steeply across a gray-green rug.

"Please sit," Puddy rasped, waving a hand through the smoke as if he were drawing aside a curtain.

His head, large and bald, was immersed in a book that was propped up on several others on his desk. A thick, meerschaum pipe was balanced in his mouth. His eyeglasses had slipped down the slim bridge of his nose and rested on its round, dimpled tip. Closing his book, he stared into space as a clerk poured the tea. When the clerk left them alone, Puddy spoke. "Mr. Aspinall, are you happy practicing the law here at Puddy, Cuddahay?"

"I didn't think happiness had anything to do with the practice of law, Mr. Puddy."

"But it should," Puddy said, lifting his teacup to his mouth and sipping it with a wince. "Your father was extremely happy practicing the law with us. He was a good man, your father; we should have advanced him. There should always be room in a firm for the nose-to-the-grindstone men. We should have seen that. I'm sorry that we didn't."

"I don't think my father minded. It meant the world to him to be associated with as fine a firm as this one."

"Yes, yes," Puddy said distractedly. "It was a terrible tragedy."

"You mean my mother and father's death?"

"Was it true, Aspinall? Had he run after her to try to bring her back?"

The intimate nature of the question surprised Tom, and he shifted in his seat.

"That's what my grandmother said. My mother wasn't happy having my grandmother in charge at our house. She felt stifled."

"Maddening. What more could a woman want than a fine family, a good husband, and devoted son?"

"Apparently more," Tom said stiffly.

Puddy nudged his glasses up the bridge of his nose and regarded Tom with an unrelentingly judgmental stare. Disregarding Tom's tone of voice, he continued, "Lost at sea in the sound, wasn't it? In a ferryboat accident? Tragic, tragic."

A pall as thick as a shroud fell over the office.

"How is your grandmother?"

"She's deceased."

"Is she? I thought she was living with her people in Virginia."

"She was at the time of her death."

"I'm so sorry to hear of it. And how is lovely Angelica?"

"My wife is very well."

"And the children?"

"Very well indeed, Mr. Puddy."

"You know how strenuously I objected to your marriage."

"I remember."

"What a hindrance I thought it might eventually be to your career, while everyone round you must have been telling you the opposite. I'm sure even your dear departed grandmother must have been happy to have lived to see you married so well, and how smart you must think you are to have proved me so wrong."

Puddy's tone was tense with suppressed anger.

"I consider myself not so much smart as fortunate, Mr. Puddy."

"Indeed . . ." Puddy said slowly with a chilly hint of irony. "Well, I can be taught a lesson as eagerly as the next man."

Tom doubted that.

"A position has opened up that I thought an ambitious person such as yourself would appreciate," Puddy said, emphasizing *ambitious* as if it were a word not said in polite company. "A position for which I have personally recommended you."

Puddy leaned forward, rolling his thick hands over and over as if he were lathering them with soap.

"Our Mr. Fledge is entering private enterprise as president of the Nautilus Shipping Company," Puddy said with all the disdain of a priest discussing the departure of a novice from a seminary. "That leaves a vacancy in our little group. We think you are qualified to fill Mr. Fledge's very capable shoes."

21

"Why do you think that?" Tom asked impulsively.

Puddy blinked. "What's that?"

"I wondered aloud why you thought I would be able to fill Mr. Fledge's very capable shoes. What qualities do I have that, let's say, Mr. St. John doesn't have? Or is it that I've just been here longer or that I'm Mr. Bridge's son-in-law?"

"I don't understand your tone."

"Speculative, Mr. Puddy, merely speculative. I am also wondering if my duties will be substantially changed. Will I have more responsibilities? Will I, inasmuch as I have been asking you for it for months, be able to meet directly with my own clients?"

"You will assume Mr. Fledge's responsibilities."

"Am I any closer to a partnership?"

"In our little pecking order you are."

"But am I really being trained for it? Would you mind if I stood?"

"I beg your pardon?"

"I'd like to stretch my legs while I think about this."

Tom stood without waiting for Puddy's reply.

Puddy watched incredulously as Tom walked about inspecting the prints on the wall. As he stood at the window with his back to Puddy, he saw the *Medusa* and suddenly he remembered her original name.

"Albion," he whispered. "Of course, *Albion."*

"What's that?"

"The name of a ship tied up at Old Slip."

"I think you are reacting in a most unorthodox manner," Puddy said.

But Tom ignored Puddy as a memory of his mother rushed back into his mind with such an achingly sweet surge that he didn't want to lose it.

He remembered standing at the helm of the ship beside her and she had said the strangest thing to him: that ships were as large as the whole world, and the reason men ran off to sea was that they could trade one world for another and start fresh and clean. That had been the key to his remembering the name: *Albion,* a clean place.

Refocusing his gaze on Puddy, Tom said, "I cannot accept your offer."

"You what?"

"If you were offering me a partnership or some real responsibility, I might jump at it, but I won't allow myself to spend the rest of my days here dreaming of advancement."

"Well, sir, I don't pretend to understand you at all. You are certainly not your father's son."

"More my mother's, I suppose," he said softly. "I'm sorry to have been so abrupt, Mr. Puddy. Is there anything else?"

"A good deal, I would think. Have you thought what effect your decision will have on your wife and children?"

"No, I haven't."

"Well, perhaps you should," Puddy said, smiling, seeing how his last comment had deflated Tom's enthusiasm. "This affects them as well."

Tom stood motionless, feeling as if Puddy had thrown a bucket of lukewarm water over his head. This is what my father must have felt standing before this stodgy man for all those years.

"There now," Puddy said, taking pleasure in his small victory. "You seem to be yourself again. You take the weekend before coming to any decision. And may I offer another suggestion? Don't mention this to anyone. We'll talk again on Monday. I'm sure you'll have a new perspective on everything."

Standing straight, looking the little man straight in the eye, Tom said, "There is nothing to discuss, Mr. Puddy. Thank you for the offer, but no. Not now. Not Monday. Not ever. Good day, sir."

And turning, he left the room.

Chapter Three

THEY WERE A perfectly matched strand of pearls . . . or were they? Jelly wondered. She had a sinking feeling that on second glance they would appear much less perfectly matched than she had first thought. Some were oblong, some were even a bit flat, but most were round and a decent size. The center pearls were as large as her thumbnail, and size was all anyone ever really noticed anyway. They did not shimmer, and certainly they had never belonged to Marie Antoinette or to Catherine the Great. Jelly had so had her heart set on the black pearl necklace that had once belonged to Catherine the Great. And if only she could get beyond their color, which she could not. It was what she disliked most about them. They were yellowish, with just the slightest blush of pink, and she would have preferred them to be creamy pink or silvery pink, which would have been perfect for her light skin and dark hair. But what was most immediately important was to appear appreciative because her father was holding them out to her.

"Well, here, take them," he said as he handed them to her, looking rather pleased with himself. Bridge had an earnest-looking face, with round eyes and a large nose that was red, veined, and pitted like a new potato.

"They're very nice. Thank you so much. Do you know what they say about pearls? A pearl is the shining sarcophagus of a worm," she said in a modulated voice, almost as if she were offering him instruction.

"Damned expensive ones, too. These cost me twenty thousand."

Hearing the sum, Jelly rushed to a gilt frame mirror to examine them again.

Perhaps they weren't as bad as all that, she thought, roping them around her long slim neck four times. She closed the clasp, which was made of small diamonds in a sunburst pattern. She improved them by wearing them, which was the way it should be.

Jelly turned breathlessly to model them for her father, (she was wearing a square-necked dress trimmed with pressed lace and black velvet piping, which framed the pearls perfectly), but he had walked back to his desk at the other end of his study. A cavernous, dim room done in the Italian Renaissance style, it was filled with overstuffed brocade-covered chairs and couches. The walls were covered from waist level to the ceiling with dark paintings no one ever bothered to look at, all framed in heavily curlicued swirling gilt.

"What do you think?" she said in an impetuous way that made her sound very young and vulnerable.

Before he could answer, there was a knock at the door and a butler walked in holding a calling card.

"A Monsieur Gaston to see you."

"The caterer," Jelly said nervously. "We can't keep him waiting."

"Let him cool his heels in the library," her father said, and the butler left.

"Please, Father, Monsieur Gaston is a very busy man."

"He'll wait. I want to continue our conversation."

"Which conversation?"

"The one we were having before I gave you the pearls," he said sharply.

Jelly's eyes, which were hazel, with sharp flecks of blue at the center, closed slightly, indicating that the conversation would not be a pleasant one to have at just that particular moment.

"Have you made up your mind?" her father asked.

She had five hundred people arriving for a ball in less than a week, a ball she had been planning for almost a year. She had payed double the price to procure the services of M. Gaston, the most exclusive caterer in New York, and now her father seemed determined to make everything difficult.

"I think your asking me this question at this particular

moment, when Monsieur Gaston is waiting to see us, is particularly perverse," she said, looking away from him, bringing a small lace handkerchief up to her mouth.

Mr. Bridge was sweating under his blue serge suit. His chubby, furry hand came down on the leather-topped desk.

"Spare me the dramatics, missy. I'm talking about a deal we agreed to."

"Everything is always in terms of business with you," she said.

"A business deal we agreed to here in this very room not more than a year ago. This ball I'm paying for was part of that deal, so this is as good a time as any to ask you if you've made up your mind."

"I don't wish to talk about it right now," Jelly said, turning to leave the room.

Mr. Bridge rose, planting his two fists in front of himself on the desk, looking like a menacing bulldog straining on its leash.

"Don't push me too far, missy."

"Father, I wish you would develop at least a *semblance* of propriety."

"Don't you dare take that tone with me. You were born in Leadville, Colorado, just like me and just like your ma."

She turned again to face him, as determined now as he was, and almost as ferocious.

"And how hard I've worked to have us rise above it. You may have made the money, but I'm going to make sure there is a place in decent society for myself and my children, and what's more—in less than a week people who wouldn't have so much as given you the time of day will be lining up to kiss your boots."

The bulldog launched himself toward the door.

"I'll show you how much of a damn I care about those people," he said, brushing past her. Then thinking better of leaving her behind, he grabbed her slim wrist, jerked open the door, and dragged her into the main hall. Sixty-five feet long, it was made of the finest carved Caen stone.

As the door was thrown open, footmen in the blood-red Bridge livery, who had been standing at ease, jerked to attention, blinking at the sight of Mr. Bridge pulling Jelly over the marble floors.

"Father, stop it!"

"And don't you call me Father, neither!"

Jelly finally broke away from him.

"What are you doing?" she demanded.

"I'm going to tell the butler to tell Mr. Gasbag or whatever his name is that the party is off."

"You wouldn't dare!"

"Cotter!"

"Yes, sir," the butler said.

"Stop!" Jelly cried out, and ran toward the first gilt-encrusted door on the right.

Bridge followed her inside the morning room and closed the door.

"How could you do that to me in front of all of them?" she said quietly, sitting on a low chair beside a fireplace.

"Because we operate under my rules in this house, and in yours as well, because I payed for both."

"You can't imagine that any of this is *easy* for me. You're asking me to leave my husband!"

"It was your idea. You came to me and told me that you made a mistake marrying Tom. You wanted me to 'launch' you. A deal is a deal."

"I didn't know you hated him this much."

"I don't. I've just got better uses for you," her father said, running his open palm along the cool surface of Italian marble on the mantel above her.

She looked startled. Never before had he stated this fact of her life so clearly.

"I wouldn't have started this at all, Jelly, if you hadn't given me the idea yourself. You told me that you'd grown tired of Tom years ago. You said we were a team, Jelly, not you and Tom. Now I'm in a race against time. J. P. Morgan wants to keep me from expanding my steamship business with those greasy Europeans, and he will if I can't find a way into their houses. You're my way in. You want a position in society, and nothing seems to do that quite like marriage to a European nobleman. We're buying one of the best. Hell's bells, missy, the Vanderbilts and Astors are doing it, and who the hell were they twenty years ago?"

"No better than silver miners from Leadville, Colorado, I imagine. Certainly no worse," she said softly.

"Damn straight! It's what you've said time and time again: that's what money is for. Divorces cost money and remarriages cost money. I know that, Jelly; I'm no piker. I set it up the way you want it. Tell me if it isn't."

She couldn't. Turning, she stared into his eyes coldly. "I don't want to be the one to tell Tom. You take care of it."

"That's my girl. Don't worry; it's all being taken care of."

"What are you going to do with him?"

"Something very nice and comfortable. Think of him as a horse that's done its job and is being put out to pasture. Not a huge pasture, mind you, but a comfortable one."

"And I don't want him initiating the divorce. I don't want to be humiliated."

"Don't worry about a thing. Marcus Puddy is handling everything. We're going to give Tom a nice little raise, then pension him off somewhere."

Jelly laughed quietly. "Marcus must be enjoying that; he asked me to marry him the week before Tom did."

As Mr. Bridge began outlining exactly what steps she had to take, she practiced looking contrite, almost pleased. After all, she was getting most of what she wanted. But as she stood there, she swore her revenge. She'd get even with him for having this much control over her life.

Chapter Four

"PAPA, PAPA, PAPA!" Susan yelled, running down the stairs toward Tom, dressed in a starched white pinafore. "Maman is dressed like a queen. She's trying on her costume for the ball. Have you seen her?"

"I've just walked in the door," Tom said, handing his walking stick to the butler.

"This very minute?"

"This very *second*," he said, bending down. He heard the sharp intake of her breath; she loved smelling things, she'd once told him in confidence.

"Then you haven't seen Maman or Antony and I'm the first to tell you about it."

"Yes, you are," he said, kneeling in front of her. She reached up and patted his hair into place just the way Jelly did.

"She's the most beautiful queen. Her dress is all blue and silver with some gold thread in it, too, and she's wearing a white wig."

"A wig?"

"A tall one with a little tiara on its top."

"Well, then she must be a queen if she's wearing a crown."

"Not a crown, Papa, it's a tiara," she said, then brought her small hands up to her mouth as if she'd made a terrible mistake. "I'm not supposed to say *it's,* I'm supposed to say *it is.* Which do you say?"

"That depends on how much time I have."

"What do you mean?"

"If I have all the time in the world, I say *it is;* if I feel as though I am rushing to say something, that I will simply burst if I don't say it—I say *it's.* It really doesn't matter."

"Oh, Maman says it does—I'm supposed to know all the things that matter. Such as the difference between crowns and tiaras, and *it's* and *it is.* And I'm not supposed to say *I'm,* I'm supposed to say *I am,* but that is the most difficult one."

She was leaning against him, her arms around his legs.

Miss Aberdeen came running down the stairs. The governess was a sturdy little Englishwoman with a round face, ruddy cheeks, and narrow eyes.

"Susan, there you are! What are you doing hanging on to your father that way?"

"It's all right, Miss Aberdeen; we're just having a little chat," Tom said, patting his daughter's head, but Susan had already withdrawn her arms and was standing quietly, looking down at his shoes.

"Now, stand up straight, Susan." Miss Aberdeen pulled

Susan's fragile shoulders back into an unnaturally stiff position. "There, that's better."

"That *is* better," Susan added pointedly. Miss Aberdeen glared at her.

The butler brought Tom his copy of the *Sun,* which had been folded in such a way so that Tom could immediately begin reading Robert Louis Stevenson's account of the South Seas, "Letters from a Leisurely Traveller."

"Thank you, Pierce," he said, taking it from the tray.

"In which room will you be sitting, sir?" Pierce asked.

They were always asking questions like that, Tom thought.

"I think I'll sit . . . no, on second thought, I'm going to stand. Perhaps I'll even walk around," he said with a smile.

"But you must see Maman," Susan said. "You must. She is only trying it on for a fitting; she won't stay dressed that way for long."

Bending over he smoothed the little girl's hair with his open palm.

"Don't worry, I'll see her."

Susan impetuously grabbed his hand and nuzzled the auburn hair that covered the back of it.

"Upstairs now. Your father has his paper to read," Miss Aberdeen said, dragging Susan toward the stairs.

"You will come up to see me before I'm put to bed, Papa?"

"I will."

"Promise?"

"Promise. Miss Aberdeen, where's Antony?"

"I'm looking for him myself, sir. Please send him to me if you find him."

Lucky Antony, Tom thought. He'd escaped from the clutches of the dreaded Aberdeen.

"Where shall I bring you your Scotch and water, sir?" Pierce asked.

"The drawing room. Thank you, Pierce," Tom said. He read the paper as he walked. It brushed a tabletop encrusted with miniature vases stuffed with silk flowers.

Jelly had spared her father no expense having the old stone house on Gramercy Park restored. She wanted large, graceful rooms, and as soon as she had them, she filled them to overflowing. Every shelf (and there were many of them) was heavily carved in mahogany; every mantel and table surface was covered with things that Jelly referred to as "objets d'art:" vases, dragon candlesticks, fans. The floors were covered with fillers and rugs and skins. The radiators were concealed under filigree iron screens, and over them were thrown Persian scarves. There were clocks everywhere; their ticking sounded like the unrelenting pelt of sleet against brittle glass—some were embedded in a Psyche's stomach or held aloft in a Cupid's hand.

Tom was concentrating on the adventures of Robert Louis Stevenson in Samoa. He'd faithfully read the account every day since October. Samoa, Tahiti, the Marquesas . . .

As he was turning the page, he looked up and saw Antony seated in the opposite corner beneath an areca palm, reading quietly. Antony had his father's wide, dark eyes and the same self-possessed, inward sense of being. He was six, a year older than his sister.

"Hello, Antony," Tom said.

"Hello, Papa."

"You reading a good book?"

"Ivanhoe."

"That *is* a good one."

"Have you read it?"

"A long time ago. Miss Aberdeen was looking for you."

"Yes, I know."

Tom smiled. "Escaped, did you?" He sat up, putting the newspaper aside on a footstool.

"Come over here, will you?"

The boy stood up, carefully marked his place before closing the book, and walked slowly across the room with his hands held stiffly at his sides.

As he approached, Tom reached out and touched his son's arm. The boy looked down uncomfortably at his father's hand.

"I saw something wonderful today—a ship I'd once been on when I was fifteen or so, and she was the biggest ship I'd ever seen. I wanted to sail off with her to far-off places; I still feel the same way. Have you ever wanted that?"

31

The boy thought about this for a moment, staring intently at a spot on the floor.

"Would I be alone?"

"You'd be in the company of other seamen, the captain, and the mates."

"People I didn't know."

"Could be."

"Would I be able to see Maman or Susan or Miss Aberdeen?"

The boy was obviously missing the point. Tom sat forward and explained, "Well, I suppose you could if you wanted to, but the whole purpose of the voyage would be for you to be on your own, sailing the sea on a great ship."

"But I've never seen the ship."

"Yes, I know you haven't."

"Has Maman seen it?"

He also said *Maman*, and suddenly the sound of the word irritated Tom beyond reason.

"You don't have to call your mother that—call her Ma or Mother or Mom."

"But Maman wants me to call her Maman."

Just then Pierce walked in with Tom's drink on a tray.

"Will you be sitting *here*, sir?"

"I'm not sure, Pierce, but it's worth a gamble," Tom said, rubbing his eyes, then smiling. "I'm sorry, Pierce, put it down wherever you can find a sliver of space." When he looked at Antony again, the boy was staring at him as though he thought his father was very odd. Tom said, "I'm sorry, Antony, you should call your mother whatever she wishes you to call her."

Miss Aberdeen called out from the hallway.

"Antony Aspinall? Where are you, Antony?"

The boy turned reflexively, but then looked back at his father and blurted out, "I'd like to see that ship with you someday, Papa."

"Would you?"

"There you are!" announced the dreaded Aberdeen. She was poised in the doorway of the drawing room like a lioness about to pounce.

Antony gave his father a sad, sweet smile before turning to run off. Tom sank back in his chair. The overstuffed room was suddenly very quiet and very dark. It was a twilit world of little girls afraid of saying things incorrectly and little boys afraid of dreaming. He wondered if anyone ever escaped alive from this brand of domesticity.

Chapter
Five

WHEN TOM WALKED into her dressing room, Jelly turned quickly from her mirror.

"Thomas!" she said as though he were the last person on earth she had expected to see.

"Why so surprised?" he asked with a smile, taking a seat on a plump love seat. He was rarely inside this female bastion, with its walls swathed in peach silk and curtains of toile de Jouy. Slim-legged satinwood tables were cluttered with perfume bottles and mysterious potions, various porcelain bowls of potpourri and powder.

"Surprised? Panic-stricken. They've sewn rosebuds on the bodice rather than on the skirt of my gown and we don't have much gold thread left," she said, turning back to her mirror while her French maid circled around her on hands and knees, sewing a silk bud on her hem.

Made of woven blue silk, silver and gold thread, the gown looked like a diaphanous, low-hanging cloud, and Jelly was charged and radiant.

"I should have gone to Paris to have the dress made. My father wanted to send me. Your costume arrived. Why don't you try it on?"

"I don't much feel like Prince Metternich tonight," Tom said with a cool smile. There was something so ludicrous about having a conversation with her dressed as Catherine the Great.

"I'd like to talk with you alone," he said, staring at the French maid. The girl claimed not to speak any English, but

33

she looked up sternly at him, her pouting mouth filled with pins.

"Not now, Thomas. Oh, I wish I had some proper jewels for this, something she might have worn," Jelly said, using the word *she* casually, as if Jelly and the Russian empress had been the best of friends.

"Jelly, ask your maid to leave."

"Thomas, stop using that tone."

"And stop calling me Thomas. Tom was the name I used the day we were introduced."

Jelly turned and stared at him as if she were looking at him for the first time.

"Ask her to leave," he said more calmly. He stood and walked over to one of the satinwood tables, picking up a cut-crystal perfume bottle and smelling it. Gardenias: of all her scents, it was his favorite.

Jelly told the maid in French to come back in five minutes. Once she left, Jelly turned to Tom.

"What do you think you are doing, coming into my dressing room, ordering me about . . ."

Tom walked over to her and led her to one of the love seats. The scent of gardenias filled the air between them.

"Do you remember the first day we met?"

"My God! I am giving a ball for five hundred people in less than one week, my gown is not finished, and you want to reminisce . . ." she said, rising.

"Sit," he said, softly patting the seat beside himself.

She sat.

"I remember that day quite well," he said. "I'd come to your father's house to deliver some papers for Mr. Puddy. I'd never been inside a house like it before; I was stunned by your father's wealth. He had me wait for him in that cold library, and there you were curled up in a chair with a book . . . you were always reading. Do you remember what you were reading?"

"No," she said. The stridency had gone out of her voice. She avoided his eyes, as if she were too embarrassed to face him directly.

"Shakespeare."

"I never read Shakespeare. It was Jane Austen—*Emma.*"

"That was it. I had read it, too; you were so surprised.

What's a man doing reading a novel, you wanted to know, and we began talking about money and hypocrisy. You knew all there was to know about money, you said. Your father was as rich as Croesus, money hadn't brought him any real happiness, and it had destroyed your mother."

She looked at him curiously.

"What makes you bring all this up now?"

"It's been a day of memories for me. Do you remember saying those things to me?"

"My mother was destroyed because she didn't know how to live with the money. She knew nothing of the world," she said flatly.

"And you didn't want to live with the money, either. You married me."

"I was a silly, wicked girl and you were too much of a dreamer. What would a man read a novel for anyway," she said as if she were convincing herself. "And I didn't hate rich people. I just didn't understand them. The only reason I may have hated those other rich people was because their money was ten years older than ours and they wanted nothing to do with us. All that will change after next week. This ball at my father's house is going to change everything."

"It's not what I want for myself—or for my children."

"We'll see about that," she said under her breath, standing and turning to the mirror again. She stared at herself like a painter about to put the finishing brushstroke on a canvas.

Tom, standing beside her in his dark brown suit, helped strip away the illusion that she actually was a queen. She was momentarily dazed by the sight of herself overcostumed almost beyond recognition. Turning away from him, she lifted the white wig from her head, placed it on a stand, then released her long, dark hair from the stocking cap that had been holding it in place.

"Puddy offered me a rather dubious promotion today," he said slowly. "He wanted me to take Chauncey Fledge's position as the most senior of the junior partners."

"That doesn't sound dubious to me."

"My father wasted away in that office in service to Marcus Puddy."

"You're not your father."

35

"No, I'm not. I turned Puddy down."

She turned, with a look of disbelief in her eyes.

"But you can't have."

"I have. And I've quit the firm."

"Now you've done it," she said in a low voice, suddenly bewildered—he had just destroyed her father's entire elaborate plan.

"I've given myself a reprieve to think about my life. I don't want to spend the rest of it just putting one foot in front of the other—"

"You haven't even asked me what *I* want."

"But I meant it for both of us—"

"What are you talking about? This is my life."

"We can be free again, Jelly, just the way we were when we first met."

"You don't understand. Everything's changed. I'm not the girl you married."

"Look at me, Jelly, think back. Why did you marry me? Don't you remember?"

She studied his face, which looked pale and serious in the half light of the room.

"I thought you were the most beautiful man I'd ever seen," she said, her eyes filling with tears, "and heedless and impulsive."

"I want you to run away with me."

"I'm not like you anymore."

"Don't say that."

"I'm not that brave or foolish. I've hardened myself. I've made certain choices."

"It's not true," Tom said. He wanted the foolish, brave girl back again. Leaning over, he kissed her neck, his lips trailing down her slim shoulders as if by making love to her he could recapture what they'd once been to each other. He began undoing the buttons in back of her dress.

The maid knocked at the door.

"Don't say a word—she'll go away," he said, easing open the gown, which slipped down her arms.

The maid knocked again and called out, "Madame, madame."

"If she's true to her French blood, she'll disappear," Tom said as the gown opened to her waist. He began untying her crinolines, which dropped to the floor, and in another moment the gown's full skirt deflated.

"It's just that you've gotten lost in all these layers," he was whispering as he continued undoing her clothes, "your corset and your chemise, your slips and petticoats . . ." his voice trailed off as he reached behind her, undoing her stays. Her flesh was released slowly in soft curves, her creased belly jutting out slightly. Her hips were round, ripe, full. He tossed the corset aside and she exhaled a full breath.

"Does it feel good to finally be that free?"

"Yes," she said softly.

"But you don't want to be free of me, do you?"

"What? I . . ."

"You what? You love me?"

"Yes . . . I . . ."

"And you want me to make love to you now."

"Yes, now."

"Here in this room—on the love seat—perfect."

"Please . . . Tom." Her oval face tilted down; all he could see of her eyes were the half moons of her lids.

His fingers moved down her as if they were following her gaze, undoing her chemise, cupping one of her breasts: its nipple was as pink as a blush.

"This is the truth of you, isn't it? Under all these layers."

She said nothing as his slim fingers undid another bow knot. Her silk pants dropped to the floor. Her arms rose as he slipped her chemise over her head. She covered her small breasts with her hands, but he took them away from her body, and she stood, supple and startled. There was a single drop of moisture in the crease of one of her breasts. He brought it up to his lips with the tip of his finger and tasted her: salty gardenias. Jelly stared at him, heavy-lidded, distant, and mysterious.

Although Tom had stripped away all the layers of lace and silk, had touched her and even tasted her, he knew he was no closer to the truth of her—and that edge of not knowing if he could ever possess her and of having her there in front of himself for the taking excited him. She pushed back his coat and undid his tie, then his collar. He sank to the love seat and buried his face in her stomach, his fingers twining in her dark pubic hair as if he were strumming her. She moaned. He undid his trouser buttons; his penis pushed through a jumble of shirt tails and underclothes. Jelly sank slowly into his lap and shivered as he entered her. His hands gripped her firmly under each thigh: raising her, lowering her. Her arms were around his neck now, and her tongue was on his lips, searching eagerly for a trace of herself in his mouth.

Early the next morning while he slept, she crept from his room. Ordering her maid to pack quickly, she had Aberdeen pack up the children's necessary belongings, and after writing Tom a good-bye note, she left the house, taking the children and the servants with her.

Chapter
Six

WITH A BURST of strength and anger, Tom raised the huge iron hoop suspended from the lion's mouth and slammed it against the great oak door of his father-in-law's house on Fifth Avenue. The door shook, but no one opened it. Stepping back, Tom put his hands up to his mouth and shouted.

"Bridge! Damn you! Have them open the door!"

"Stop doing that, sir, or we'll have to call the police," someone called out from a barred entry window.

"Who is that?"

"It's Stevens, sir."

"Stevens, it's Mr. Aspinall."

"Yes, sir, I know."

"Open the door."

"We have instructions not to, sir."

Turning his back to the entry window, Tom quickly wrapped a handkerchief around his hand.

"Stevens, you don't understand—I've injured my hand. I need some assistance," Tom said, holding his bandaged hand up to the iron bars.

There was a moment of silence and then the door opened a sliver. Tom, tucking his elbow into his side, slammed into the door with his shoulder, forcing it open and sending Stevens sprawling to the floor.

"Where are they?" Tom yelled, rushing up the three broad steps into the main hall. Its ceiling was made of stained glass, and Tom stood in the center, in a shaft of purple and yellow light.

Two liveried footmen rushed into the hall to come to Stevens's aid, but Tom ran over to the great oak fireplace and grabbed one of the iron pokers. He held it threateningly in front of himself.

"I have no reason to fight with any of you. I only want to know where my wife and children are."

The footmen said nothing. Tom shouted up at the gallery, which circled the hall twenty feet above.

"Anjelica!"

But there was no answer, and with the poker outstretched in one hand, he climbed the large Caen stone stairway two steps at a time. On the first landing he ran to the left, flinging open a door to the Chinese drawing room, Jelly's favorite room. Inside, the air was heavy with the scent of sandlewood. The room was filled with silk hangings, lattices, pierce-carved frames, and chairs tufted in Chinese stone-blue and black. Pierce was there, staring out through the thick, dim light like a pale apparition.

"Where is she?" Tom asked.

"She's gone."

"Gone where?"

"Out for the day. I don't know where."

"And the children?"

"Gone as well."

"With her?"

"With Mr. Bridge. He's taken them away."

"Was all this planned? Did you know about it?"

"No, sir. I didn't know what to do." Pierce was obviously upset. "Mr. Bridge came to get all of us this morning, and she, Mrs. Aspinall, didn't want me to awaken you; she didn't want to see you at all. I swear, sir, I didn't know anything about it."

Numbed, Tom tossed the poker aside, left the room, and walked slowly down the grand staircase. The footmen in the hall below watched him carefully as he crossed the main hall. They were poised for a fight, but Tom left the house without saying another word.

Outside, he automatically began walking uptown. Carriages passed by: landaus and broughams as slick and shiny as black patent leather.

Ahead, entering the park, was a coaching party; a parade of six four-in-hand coaches, called park drags, were being pulled through the streets by teams of horses. Atop each coach, holding the reins, were men wearing dark green coats with silver buttons and silk toppers. Beside them sat women with corsages the same color as the coaches on which they were riding. A footman on the rear-most coach sounded a long horn, the "yard of tin," and the piercing blast captured Tom's attention. As he looked up, one of the riders, looking back, shouted.

"Tom! Hello! Tom!"

It was Duff St. John holding the reins of his grandfather's royal blue coach. He was driving a party of two women and three men. They'd obviously been drinking; the air was ringing with their inconsequential laughter. Duff waved to Tom to catch up to them. As he came alongside the coach, Duff looked down, one eyebrow arched superciliously.

"My God, Tom, you look awful. No wonder Jelly doesn't want to be seen with you today. Why aren't you dressed?"

"Was Jelly with you?"

"With all of us," Duff said, handing Tom down a silver flask of whiskey. "Take a quick snort. You look as though you need it."

But Tom's eyes were riveted on the other coaches up ahead.

"Where is she, Duff? I have to know."

"She's with Count What'shisname," Duff slurred. He turned to ask his passengers, "What *is* that unctuous little man's name?"

"Victor," someone called out.

"That's right, that Victor fellow. Left all of us in the dust a good hour ago."

"Where to?"

"The Claremont, I suppose. Where else does anyone ever go?"

"Tell your friends to step down," Tom said, offering his hand to one of the ladies. "I'm going after her."

"I can't do that, these are my guests."

"I've got to find her!"

Hearing Tom's tone of voice, Duff's companions began to clamber down.

"What on earth has gotten into you? Reckless fights with vagrants on docks, then storming out of the office yesterday—"

"He's trying to take my children from me," Tom said, climbing aboard, grabbing the reins.

"Who? The count? That greasy little man?"

"It's Bridge! Get down, Duff!"

Duff jumped off the coach. "Do you know how to drive this?"

"I'll find out."

Tom tugged at the reins and the horses sauntered out of line to the right side of the street.

"Follow Riverside Drive!" Duff shouted through cupped hands.

Reaching behind the seat, Tom grabbed the whip and cracked it over the heads of the chestnut team. They bolted forward, hooves pounding the packed earth.

Tom rose from his seat. Unsteady at first, then getting his balance, he spread his feet, squatted, and tucked his elbows into his sides at his waist. The horses were tearing down the park drive now, and Tom held the reins firmly.

As shouts of surprise and alarm rang out from other coaches, Tom drove his team to a gallop.

The drag was creaking, rolling up and down like a ship tossing in a heaving sea.

She thinks I'll play the gentleman, he thought, but I'll be damned if I'll have her leave me.

"Watch out!" someone called out as Tom narrowly missed another coach. He was off the main path now and low-hanging branches swiped him from all sides. Ducking, he wrenched the reins to the left, cutting across a broad lawn, then racing back up the path.

"Hold on!" he told himself, and cracked the whip again.

The coach went flying up the path, and as he reined in with his left hand, the horses turned left across the park at Eighty-sixth Street. They galloped uptown on the riding path, going the wrong way. Some angry riders on horseback turned and followed in hot pursuit, but Tom maintained a good lead.

At 110th Street, he headed west to Riverside Drive, then north.

Crowds of cyclists on the drive began cheering as if they thought a race was in progress, and for a stretch of about ten streets people rushed up to the road from the grassy knoll that sloped down to the river, yelling, their fists pumping wildly in the air.

"Go, get a move, go, go, you'll make it!"

Tom kept his eyes on the road, eventually leaving the crowds and the other riders behind. Finally, he saw the Claremont Inn in the distance. It was a three-story wooden building fronted by arches and a long trellised porch; there was a single coach tied up in back. Tom squatted deeply and pulled the reins back tightly. The horses, confused and winded, threw their heads back and reared, their breath hissing like steam engines.

Tom tossed the reins aside, leaped from the coach, and raced up the steps into the inn, where he was confronted by an officious-looking, pink-faced man in a striped suit.

"May I help you?" the man asked as Tom leaned on the front desk to catch his breath.

"Where . . . are . . . the couple . . . who came in the coach . . . tied up in the back?"

The man sensed trouble.

"Do you have a reservation for this afternoon?" he asked.

"I want to make myself perfectly clear," Tom said, still panting. "I'm in no mood for drivel!"

"Please lower your voice, sir, we have ladies here."

"And one of them is my wife. Where is she?"

The man lowered his voice.

"Second floor, room number two, but they've only just arrived—"

Tom raced up the stairs as the man continued.

"Please, sir, we are a respectable establishment . . ."

Tom stood outside the room listening. When he heard nothing, he stepped back and kicked the door in with his boot.

A woman screamed. Walking into the room, he saw Jelly's silver-gray cape hanging over a chair. Beside it was her black straw hat, dressed with black and white feathers, and beside it, a bouquet of jonquils.

Jelly, dressed in gray silk, appeared in the doorway of the bedroom. Her hair was down around her shoulders, and her pale eyes were wide with surprise.

"Tom!" was all she could say.

A small dark man with a thin moustache and dark close-set eyes appeared beside her.

"My dear," the man said. "Who is this?"

"My husband," Jelly said, and the man stepped forward, studying Tom.

"Your husband? But your father assured me that had been all . . . arranged," he said, then turned to Tom with a nervous little smile, "Surely, sir, you haven't come here to challenge me to a duel."

Tom grabbed the man by his neck and the seat of his trousers and pitched him out the door.

Chapter Seven

"I'M RELIEVED," JELLY said nervously. "Relieved that you're here, to have it out in the open and have it end—"

"Where are the children?"

"My father's taken them," she said, twisting the pearls her father had given her around her fingers. "He didn't want you to see the children until after the divorce."

"Was there supposed to be one?"

"He's arranged to have me marry the count."

"He'll have to change his plans. I think the count is running for his life. Where are they?"

"You can't get to them. But I'm grateful that you've come to get me—I couldn't have gone through with it, and I didn't know what to do. My father needs the count to do business in Europe—"

"He bought you lock, stock, and barrel."

"What was my choice?"

"You had me."

"I did. I was wrong. I couldn't fight him alone, but we can fight him together. We'll get the children. Let's go now."

"How much did he pay for your services?" Tom asked coolly.

"You don't understand anything I'm saying. I was wrong, Tom. I was wrong."

Suddenly the strand of pearls broke and scattered across the floor like beads of milk. Jelly knelt and tried frantically to gather them.

"He bought me for these," she said in a shaky voice, "a mediocre strand of pearls—not at all what I wanted." Her hands skittered along the uneven floorboards, but the pearls rolled this way and that, which only made her talk more nervously. "I wanted the black pearls that had belonged to Catherine the Great—do you know the ones I mean? We were once at a ball and a countess was wearing them: three exquisite strands, perfectly matched, very dark gray-black, with that miraculous halo of rose and green—the color of a buzzing fly in a room on a warm, sultry day—" She stopped suddenly to look up at him. "I've ruined our lives. Ruined everything."

He reached for the door.

"No, don't leave, Tom. Please. No one will know. No one will ever know."

But he'd already made up his mind. As soon as he entered the room and saw her there with that fop, he understood that his own life had been bought with her father's money.

"We'll get the children away from my father. We'll go away. We'll do what you want. We'll travel, be free again."

He opened the door.

"No, don't leave me alone with my father. Please. He'll ruin us all."

He left her alone in the room with her scattered pearls.

Tom sat in Gramercy Park on a bench, wearing yesterday's suit of clothes. He had fifty-six dollars in his pocket, his cufflinks, his shirt studs, a pocket watch his father had left him, and little more of any value. He was feeling hungry, but not desperate for food, knowing it was out there if he wanted it, and he was feeling very much alone as night covered the city. Each sign of its coming—a light in a window, the stifled sound of a dinner bell, a curtain being pulled against the dark sky—hollowed out something inside him.

Walking in the shantytown that stretched all the way from 110th Street to below Fourteenth Street, Tom saw barrooms filling with swaggering, burly men and ruined women. They washed down equal doses of despair and joy with their whiskey.

He wound up at the water, walking south. The thick breeze picked up and he smelled a whiff of Jelly's gardenia perfume that had insinuated itself into the fibers of his coat, overlaid now with the odor of sweat and brine. Ahead was Old Slip and the ship *Albion/Medusa,* brooding, casting a massive dark shadow against the dark sky.

"Ahoy! *Medusa!* Ahoy there!" he shouted.

A man with a lantern unlocked a gate on the gangplank and called out, "Who's that?"

"The name is Tom."

"Tom who?"

Seeing a cargo barrel marked DELIVER TO: 330 WEST 12TH STREET, Tom answered, "Street, Tom Street."

"Do I know you?"

"No."

As the man drew near, carrying the lantern close to his face, Tom began to pick out his features: a scraggly beard, which hung like scant twisted threads from his thin chin and upper lip, pleasant eyes, a broad, broken nose. His trousers were held up by a cardboard belt. His shirt was striped, grimy, and smelly. The man stared with interest once he saw that Tom was dressed like a gentleman.

"Geesus Woolly Christ! What do you want down here this time of night?"

"This ship—was she once called the *Albion?*"

"She was when the Brits owned her. She's American now, registered in Columbia, a tramp."

"Is there cargo in her hold?"

"There is—kerosene."

"Where's she bound?"

"'Round the Horn, then out a bit."

"The South Seas?"

"Tahiti. Why you want to know?"

"She got all her crew?"

The man laughed a rheumy little laugh.

"Geesus Woolly Christ! Gentlemen like yourself don't ever really put out on tubs like this. What'samatta, bub, a fight with the missus?"

Tom turned up his collar and blew into his hands as a breeze came up off the water.

"Go home, bub, sleep it off. She'll be back tomorrow."

"Does *Medusa* have all her crew?" Tom asked again.

"Hmm," the man said, looking down at Tom's shiny shoes, his tightly woven wool suit, and the gold watch chain suspended from his vest to his trouser pocket. "No, she don't. You ever put out on a square-rigger before?"

"No, but I learn fast."

"Geesus Woolly, bub, I'm only ship's keep for the night." He looked at Tom skeptically, then shook his head. "Always got to be a first time. You come back tamarra and speak to the first mate, Mr. Murch. He's the one for you to see."

"May I speak to him tonight?"

"No, I'm the only one here tonight," he said, turning back to the gangplank. "You come back tamarra and see Murch. But take my advice, bub, have a good night's sleep and cut back on the booze; you'll feel better. . . ."

"I've got a problem . . . I've got nowhere to sleep tonight. If you don't have anyone aboard, you think I might be able to sleep here?"

The man rubbed his scant beard with a grimy hand.

"The accommodations are what you call stiff, but it'd give you a taste of what you're in for. Probably cure ya. Geesus Woolly, what the hell! Come on up."

As the man turned, Tom followed him up the steep gangplank, slipping once, then again.

When he stepped aboard, he could just barely make out some stunted shapes through the dim light: barrels, coils of line, winches. The masts rose at least a hundred and forty feet above him. The rigging looped down the yards to the deck like gigantic cobwebs.

As the ship's keep held the lantern up, scoops of light fell on the lifeboats lashed to the top of the deckhouse, and aft, at the helm, the pointed spokes of the wheel rose above the poop rail like a jagged half moon.

Holding the lantern out toward the bow, the man said, "You better sleep with y'ur money under y'ur head. Got another seaman in the fo'c'sle; never seen 'im before. Take the bunk next to 'im. There'll be a blanket, or a poor excuse for one."

"What's your name?"

"Kenny, but everyone calls me Ditty."

"Thanks for the bunk, Ditty."

"Don't thank me too much; see if ya can sleep first. If y'ur still here in the mornin', I'll see you speak to Murch. He'll take care of ya."

"Good night."

"Yeah, good night."

As Ditty walked away, taking the light with him, Tom stood outside the forecastle for a moment, allowing his eyes to adjust to the darkness. The sky was clear; a slice of the brittle moon had risen and was hanging above the foremast. Remembering the names of the masts from the books he'd read as a child, Tom repeated them aloud, "Foremast, mainmast, mizzen."

The forecastle was not large; its walls were made of sheet iron, and it smelled of a mixture of kerosene smoke, soiled clothing, and musty dampness. A table was in the center under a sooty skylight. In the dim light he could make out the shapes of two rows of five double bunks. On the lower berth of the farthest bunk on the port side was the outline of a sleeping man.

Tom walked to the berth nearest the sleeper, who was turned on his side, his face to the wall. Spreading out a coarse, stiff blanket, Tom lay down with a groan of relief. He loosened his shoes, his tie, and his stiff collar. His eyes burned when he closed them. In a state of hyperexcitement and exhaustion, the contents of his mind reeled past his eyes. Opening them, he stared out the smoky skylight above his bunk but saw only shadows. None of this was real. Soon his driver would come to fetch him, the landau his father-in-law had bought for him would be waiting at the edge of the pier to take him back to the house on Gramercy Park, where Pierce would hand him his meticulously folded newspaper.

The man beside him stirred and turned slowly, groaning with each move. His stale breath rattled up from his lungs. Suddenly he jerked his head upward, as if he knew he was being watched.

It was the man in black who had attacked the midget yesterday, a lifetime ago. Jenks, the midget had called him. His eyes focused on Tom.

"It's you," Jenks whispered, a pale, thin finger outstretched toward Tom. "I know you. Got a score to settle with you," he said in a low, grave voice that shook Tom to his very core.

Chapter Eight

JENKS HAD A name on the *Medusa* that he carried with him from other voyages: Bully Jenks, and no one on board ventured close enough to find out why he was called that.

Incredibly dirty, his long hair hung down over his forehead and made him look more animal than human—and always the eyes, pale and chilling, staring out at the others, enjoying the fear he engendered, savoring it the way an actor savored praise for a good performance.

Tom had never known or lived closely to such men as these. Some had deserted other ships, others were in hock to the crimps who had sold them onto this one. At meals they stared out impassively over thick plates piled high with food: potatoes, salted pork, stews as thick as mud, muffins as dense as rocks. There was a Norwegian everyone called Sven, although that was not his name, and a robust, red-haired Jew, Leon, who was the resident intellectual, and whom everyone called the rabbi. There was a strange one named Stringy Peele. A nonstop talker, he jabbed hand-rolled cigarette after hand-rolled cigarette into his mouth like a puffing engine.

And then there was Charley Donkin, nicknamed Donkey. No more than twenty-two or -three, short, with pale hair, pale skin, he had a protruding Adam's apple and one other protrusion, from which he got his name and of which he was so proud that he paraded around the fo'c'sle anytime airing it. His penis was enormous, at least eight inches long, flaccid, with testicles the size of Idaho potatoes tied in a low-hanging pink sack, all framed below a slim row of curly dark hair.

"We need to take a depth readin', all we do is hang Donkey over the side," Stringy Peele said at one mealtime, and Donkey looked up from his food, smiling shamelessly through the haze of blue tobacco smoke, proud of the single accomplishment he possessed.

Mornings began at six. Tom, dressed in stiff new dungarees, stepped into the dank mist of an early morning fog, joining a group of five shivering men on the foredeck. Two men manned a saltwater pump, one handled the hose, while Tom and another crewman scrubbed the decks with stiff brooms. They were finished by seven, when Burt, the Jamaican cook, tooted the breakfast call on an old dented trumpet that he kept around his neck on a tasseled chord. The men clambered to their places, the same seat every meal, hungry as lions although the food was barely edible: stacks of hotcakes called liver pads because they were thick, dark, and clotted; dark, stringy syrup resembling molasses; rancid butter; strips of bacon, pungent and greasy; and dark, thick coffee that seemed to be made from the accumulated spittle of hundreds of men on hundreds of voyages. Sometimes at meals Ditty (who, Tom learned, was an "idler": he did not stand watch at night or go aloft except in emergencies, working instead on carpentry and sail repair) would

close his small, dark eyes, throw his head back, and sing
with a slim, good-natured smile on his lips.

> I hope when we get more fresh meat,
> It'll be of a kind that we can eat.
> I care not whether it be cow or hog,
> Nor would I run from a well-cooked dog—
> So here I now likewise declare
> I never will eat more polar bear,
> And if I find it on my plate,
> I will throw it at the steward's pate.

The men laughed—their poor fortunes acknowledged,
their fates sealed when the Articles of Agreement were
signed, consigning them to a voyage on the *Medusa,* tramp-
ing around the world for twelve dollars a month.

In two days they were under sail, heading out into a gray
expanse of empty water, running south-southwest down the
eastern coast. Tom was seasick, as were several others, but
there was no time for complaint; there was too much work.

Tom was sent aloft with Sven to furl the royal sail.
Bug-eyed, his heart beating so wildly he could see his pulses
throbbing on his wrists, Tom climbed just below the big
Norwegian. They reached a platform that was braced to the
foremast by steel struts on which rope ratlines had been
fastened. There seemed to be two ways of climbing topside:
the easier by climbing through a hole in the platform; the
other, which—goddamn his very skin!—Sven chose, crawling out on the shaky rope ratlines over the edge, leaving
nothing between himself and the deck but air.

Sven called down, "Yu can go through the hole if yu vant,
but it ain't no fit sailor's vay!"

"Bastard!" Tom muttered, reaching up and around the
platform. He grabbed the shaky line with an unsteady hand,
then the other, wobbling dangerously like a man walking on
a loosely strung high wire. The wind was screeching in his
ears. Pulling himself out over the deck below, with no safety
net, no hope, just a quick prayer, he had only his wits, his
sheer strength, and the belief that he wouldn't die, not yet,
not like this. His ass waving in the breeze, he inched out and
up toward the foretop, the very pinnacle of the world, and

in another breathtaking moment he was sitting with his legs dangling over the sides of it, hanging on to the topmast shrouds with both hands, trying to recover his breath.

Sven was doing most of the work, but he stopped for a moment, calling out, "You got balls the size of Donkey's —you'll do fine!"

But this was clear sailing and what was going through Tom's mind—aside from *How in hell do I get down from this perch?*—was the nagging thought of what it would be like to be aloft in all this tangle of wire, rope, and steel at midnight when it was tilted at forty-five degrees and when half the cold Atlantic was sweeping across the decks below.

In two more days the wind changed. A churning sea and blinding, gray sheets of rain washed the ship for days, and everyone, even Ditty, was sent aloft to furl the sails. Blindly, Tom grabbed at the canvas that ripped into his soaked, swollen hands, his eyes trained on Sven, who was the most experienced sailor onboard. One by one they climbed higher, Jenks, Donkey, Stringy Peele, who looked so scared Tom wondered why on earth he had ever put out to sea. Tom wound up on the foreroyal yard, suddenly struck by the sight of a boiling sea.

"Stay on the veather side coming down," Sven called to Tom from the topgallant.

Far below, *Medusa*'s bow was splitting the sea into foaming crescents. Tom's heart sank with each downward plunge and upward sway. The yard creaked ominously as the topmast pitched, its movement exaggerated by the swells, and with each roll Tom thought he'd be pitched into the churning water. His feet slid along the footrope and he nearly fell, but he wrapped his arms around the mast and hugged it with all his strength. Looking down at the topgallant, he saw Sven motioning to him to make another try.

It took Tom several minutes to get up his courage. Finally he managed to get his legs around the mast and reluctantly let go the footrope. Experiencing a feeling of terror he had never before known, he slid down to the tenuous safety of the fore topgallant yard and then climbed down the rest of the way to the deck.

Everyone was clambering about. Sven, much to the chagrin of the greener, seasick men, said something about a bigger storm coming, and one man after the other turned a fearful eye up toward the threatening sky before disappearing into the fo'c'sle. As Tom passed Jenks, he looked into Jenks's eyes with a new feeling of camaraderie because they had hung on to the same lines for their very lives, but Jenks dismissed him, retreating into his glowering silence.

Sven's prediction came true: heavier weather poured down while the starboard watch, under Mr. Murch, was on deck. Tom lay below in his bunk, unable to eat, unable to sleep, what with the ceaseless rolling, the unremitting stench of dank clothing, and the stale, foul odor of ten farting, snoring men.

But when the port watch was called, the weather broke. Clouds raced across the skies as though they were being chased, and dim stars were reflected in the inky water. Tom stumbled onto the deck, bleary-eyed, tired, and confused, and took his trick at the wheel, on the lee side of Stringy Peele, who was a passable helmsman. As always, Stringy was talking nonstop, mostly about Jenks (everyone talked about Jenks when he wasn't in earshot), who was standing below the poop deck on a watch called "police," staring out at the darkness.

"Don't like anything 'bout him," Stringy was saying. "Heard too many stories. Old Leon, the rabbi, shipped out with 'im a year or so ago, said Jenks was evil all the way to Monday. The rabbi says some men put out to sea 'cause they're lookin' for adventure or they're runnin' from the cops or some woman they hate, but the rabbi says Jenks is just runnin' from the whole world 'cause he hates it and everyone in it. Source of all evil on this evil ship. Look at his little pouch he carries everywhere with 'im—sometimes I think he carries all his evil there inside it."

Tom had also noticed the pouch—it was unusual because so few of the men had any private possessions. Jenks wore it on his belt at all times, and at night when he slept he kept his hands around it.

"The first time I saw him," Tom said to Stringy, "he was attacking a midget—said the midget had stolen something from him."

"Timmy? The one with the moustache and the bowler hat? I knows Timmy. He ain't a thief; he's a fence."

"They were arguing over a piece of jewelry."

Stringy eyed the pouch with more interest, his nervous little hands gripping the wheel tightly.

"You say it was jewels? Where would dirt like that get jewels unless he stole it? Wanted Timmy to fence it for him and the little bugger di'nt get his price, so Jenks bops his head and takes it back. It's like him . . . I'd love ta look in that pouch."

Just then Jenks looked up at the helm, leveling Stringy with a baleful gaze as if he had read his mind. Stringy almost jumped back from the wheel.

"Did the rabbi happen to tell you how Jenks got the name Bully?" Tom asked.

"Must've killed a man," Stringy said with an uneasy voice.

"But you don't know that for certain."

"Look at those eyes—they seen men squirm before they died."

Jenks finally looked away, turning his chilling eyes out toward the sea again.

Chapter Nine

ONE NIGHT ON midwatch, sitting on the foredeck (the only place a man could be alone with his thoughts), Tom was thinking about his children. Just before coming on deck, he had looked at the wool suit and leather shoes he'd been wearing the night he'd come aboard. They were mildewed now, and the pocket watch his father had left him, which had been put for safekeeping in an inner coat pocket, had been smashed. It was the first time he fully understood how inextricably lost that part of his life now was.

"Street," Borster, the second mate, called out to him from midship.

"Yes, Mr. Borster."

"Say *aye,* not *yes,* Street."

"Aye, Mr. Borster."

"Take your trick at the wheel."

"Aye, aye, sir."

Jenks was at the wheel, on the weather side, his hands poised gently on the spokes. It was the one thing Jenks did that earned him respect; he was the best helmsman onboard *Medusa.* Under his skillful touch the ship moved through the water like a dancer; agile, responsive, sharply kept on course.

Jenks never talked while he was at the helm, but this night, as he handed the wheel to Tom, he said, "Time you tried your turn at it." He stepped aside and stood in the shadows on the lee side.

Tom took the wheel tentatively, his eyes riveted on the steering compass mounted on a platform in a brass binnacle in front of the wheel.

Fairly soon the ship began to creep off course and Tom overcompensated, wrenching the wheel around, then back again. The royals began to shiver. Jenks relieved Tom just as the captain appeared. He stared into the binnacle and gave Jenks an odd look.

"She's running heavy tonight, cap'n," Jenks said, and the captain walked away.

"Thank you for covering for me," Tom said.

"It wasn't your ass I was covering," Jenks said, staring out at a distant cloud he was using to keep the ship on course.

"You don't scare me, Jenks. If the police hadn't come that day on the pier when you were beating up the midget, I would have had you—I was gaining on you."

Jenks turned slowly, squinting at Tom.

"You surprise me, boyzo, talking at me just like we could be mates."

"It's not friendship I'm after. No one else saw the necklace you shook out of the midget—only I did. The midget wouldn't even admit to it—"

Jenks turned away fiercely.

"You keep your mouth shut about that, boyzo. I don't want to hurt you, but you blabber on about that and I'll kill you. Now go along and don't talk to me again."

"I told you, you don't frighten me, Jenks."

Jenks's head dropped. "Be smart—be scared," he hissed.

Those were the last words he spoke directly to Tom on the ship, although he began singling him out for his special scorn. He set up a little gang of frightened henchmen, taking them into his confidence, playing on their jealousy of Tom's patrician face and refined manners.

A vacant-eyed crewman named Creighton and a fat one with a flabby chest and pig eyes named Brenner were part of this group. Then Stringy Peele, too frightened of Jenks to protest, was pressed into service.

Jenks took special delight in degrading Stringy. He had him help him on and off with his boots or wash his clothes in rainwater while he forced Stringy to wash his own clothes, his face, and hairy body in his own urine.

During dogwatch, or on Sundays, if the weather was calm, Jenks and his men could be seen standing in a tight circle focusing all their pent-up rage at Tom.

"Don't like that man," Jenks would growl, pointing a knife at Tom's gut. "Too uppity refined—laughing at us all. Thinks he's above us. Man could get killed for less!"

Sometimes Stringy was a go-between, rushing frantically like a deranged little monkey from the group above deck to Tom below.

"You should really steer clear of 'im, Tom, you really should."

"Why's he got you jumping so, Stringy? I thought you didn't like him," Tom said, sitting on his bunk.

"Oh, I don't, but I know what's good for me. He's got a black temper, Tom, real black."

"You sure you should be seen talking with me?"

"It's a big chance I'm takin', but I thought that since you and me was once pals, I should tell you 'bout him."

"He doesn't scare me, Stringy. You can tell him that for me."

"Wouldn't dare, Tom. It's bad 'nuf the way things are, but on the day we cross the 'quator, when old King Neptune comes 'board, worse things could happen."

"What things, Stringy?"

"I was on a ship once, a little bark out of 'Frisco, when we crossed the Line and some of the crew forced a shave on a big Negro sailor named Nobbs, and he took out his jack-knife and stabbed two of 'em."

"I'll be sure to have my jackknife ready."

"They could start fights—Creighton or Brenner. Captains like a lot of noise and celebration when old King Nep comes. Things like a stabbin' can happen real fast."

"I'll keep it in mind," Tom said, lying back on his bunk. "Now let me get some sleep."

In two days *Medusa*, riding the northeast trade winds, made smooth sailing toward the equator, then the doldrums of the horse latitudes came, and what Tom came to think of as the barefoot days. Schools of flying fish appeared. It was pleasant to scrub the decks, to swim in patches of calm, or to fish for albacore from the bowsprit or for dolphins from the poop. With milder weather Tom worked with his shirt off; his back, shoulders, and arms, which were now thickly muscled, developed a deep ruddy color. His face had become leaner and was framed by a reddish-brown beard that matched the color of his chest hair.

The morning the ship passed the equator, Tom heard a clambering noise above deck and someone calling out, "Ship ahoy!"

And someone else in a false, deep voice sang out, "Halloo! Give me a rope's end, for I'm coming aboard to see if you have got any of my children there."

The captain called out, "Aye, aye, sir. Heave him a rope there, some of you."

Tom, pulling on a shirt, went above to have a look.

Standing midship was Donkey, nude except for a grass skirt and crown, his pendulous penis swaying in the breeze like a soft pink scepter. His face had been made up with flour and red dye. Beside him was Ditty, also in makeup, in a top hat and long johns, carrying a porpoise fork as a trident.

Everyone was summoned on deck to appear before His Majesty. Tom and another crewman, Smyth, were singled out because they were green, had never before crossed the equator.

Before Tom knew what was happening, he was blindfolded and marched around the deck three times. Hands reached out, playfully grabbing at him, lifting him, passing him forward. He thought he heard Jenks's low snarl coming out through the general laughter, "Be smart, be scared, beware."

Ditty grabbed Tom, pulling him away from the crowd, then sat him on a barrel, asking Tom to repeat his name.

"Tom Street."

"Geesus Woolly Christ! Tom Street, what?"

"Tom Street, sir."

"Tom Street, what?"

"Tom Street, Your Majesty."

"Geesus Woolly! That's more like it. Say hello."

When Tom opened his mouth, a shaving brush covered with tar and grease was shoved inside.

Donkey, His Majesty Old King Neptune, asked Tom to speak up, he couldn't hear him, and a speaking trumpet was held at Tom's mouth.

"Now then," said Donkey. "Say hello!"

When Tom opened his mouth, a bucket of saltwater was thrown at him, leaving him choking, trying to clear his throat, and keep his humor at the same time.

"Will you swear never to walk when you can ride unless you choose to walk?" Donkey asked.

"Yes, Your Majesty," Tom said, and in went another brush of tar and grease, washed down by more saltwater.

"Will you swear never to kiss the maid when you can kiss the mistress when you should prefer the maid to the mistress?"

Tom was no dope, he said nothing—Ditty bent down, whispering, "Geesus Woolly, you get it one way or the other."

Tom responded, tight-mouthed, "Yes, Your Majesty." And in went the brush and another bucket of saltwater.

"Will you keep my laws as long as you live?" Donkey asked.

"Yes, yes."

"Yes what?"

"Yes, Your Majesty," and in went another brush and bucketful. Then Tom was slathered with the greasy stuff, shaved with a long wooden fake razor, and sent head over heels into a barrel of saltwater.

Everyone was laughing uproariously by now. Tom had

managed to take off his blindfold and was busy washing the stuff off his face. When he emerged from the barrel, Donkey, alias King Neptune, embraced Tom, calling him one of his sons.

Tom was treated to a snort of whiskey. Instruments appeared, and Ditty sang a chanty as the crew danced wildly with one another. The captain and the mates were watching all this from the poop deck when suddenly Brenner, Jenks's leading henchman, came rushing on deck holding up Tom's smashed pocket watch.

"Captain!" Brenner shouted. "Street's stolen my watch —he had it hidden in his coat!"

"That's not true," Tom said, breaking away from Donkey and Ditty. He reached over Brenner's flabby shoulder to grab the watch, and the man turned, porcine eyes flashing furiously. He slammed a meaty hand into Tom's shoulder, sending him reeling across the deck, landing near Stringy Peele's dirt-caked feet.

"I told you this would happen!" Stringy whispered nervously.

Tom jumped to his feet and rushed Brenner again to grab the watch, but the captain had already taken it and was inspecting it.

"It's inscribed to James—James was my father's name," Tom said.

"James is my name, too," Brenner whined. Tom could not contain himself; with his left fist poised in front of his face, his right jabbed out, connecting with Brenner's nose dead on the bridge. Something snapped. Blood began pouring down Brenner's thick split lips.

Reeling, Brenner turned his pale, thick back on Tom as Tom circled around him.

"A fair fight, men. I want a fair fight," the captain called down from the poop.

Brenner suddenly turned, charging Tom, and slammed his fists into the side of Tom's head. Tom reached up and yanked down mounds of dank, sweaty flesh as if it were sail, pounding Brenner's kidneys. Brenner staggered backward, releasing him. Then Tom battered Brenner's head, opening deep gashes above each eye. Holding Brenner's face with an open palm, pressing in on the broken nose, Tom threw a right, cutting up from the right side of Brenner's chin to his left cheek with so solid a punch that Brenner sank to the deck and lay there, a flaccid, inert mound.

When Tom looked up, his hand dabbing at the blood that was running down the right side of his face, he saw Jenks standing in the middle of the deck beside Brenner.

"Me mate Brenner, here, needs satisfaction! That man," Jenks said, pointing an angry finger at Tom, "accused Brenner of lyin', and I want to extract that satisfaction!"

All eyes were now focused on the captain, who stood stern-faced, his fingers tapping the taff rail.

"You've been challenged, Street. The man wants satisfaction for his friend," the captain called out.

The blood on Tom's cheek was caking, the wound just above his ear was still open, oozing.

"I accept the challenge," Tom said. Jenks turned around to face him, carefully securing the leather pouch on his belt before he slowly unbuttoned his rumpled black shirt and tossed it aside.

Tom had expected to see a pale, bony chest, but Jenks was powerfully built, with thick corded arms.

Remaining where he stood, Tom waited and watched, his arms in front of his body, his fists poised and ready as Jenks came slowly closer.

The crowd of men was silent. Tom could hear their rapid breathing below his own.

Jenks was close now; Tom side-stepped him, waited just a moment more to throw his first punch. He felt warm blood trickling languidly down his cheek. Jenks suddenly dropped to his knees, his arms clamping around Tom's shins. Tom flew backward, landing squarely on the tar-coated pine decks with a thud; for a second he thought his back had broken. Jenks clambered up Tom's legs to sit astride his chest, then his shoulders, pinning Tom's arms outstretched at his sides with his knees. Jenks was wild-eyed, ecstatic; one cruel fist then the other slashed down at Tom's face. The wound above Tom's ear opened fully, blood gushing with each heartbeat. His legs were flailing, and through his swollen eyes, he saw his move: Jenks's pouch was swinging forward, just short of his grasp. He needed an inch more and all his strength to propel himself forward.

Breathing deeply, spitting blood and bile, Tom rose violently and grabbed the pouch, wrenching it forward. Jenks, startled, moved backward away from Tom's grasping, bloody hand, but it was too late. Jenks scrambled backward as Tom rose, both hands wrenching the pouch from Jenks's grasp. It ripped loose and skidded along the deck, stopping by Stringy Peele's foot. One large steely white pearl was visible through the opened top. Stringy's eyes widened as he bent over to pick it up, but Jenks, who had scrambled to his feet, grabbed the pouch and tucked it into his soiled trousers before Stringy could touch it.

Tom lay on the deck trying to catch his breath as Jenks turned to finish the job. Tom rolled forward, crouching, his hamstrings bouncing on the backs of his feet. His head was held low, as if it were hanging in defeat, but as Jenks approached, Tom sprang, his right fist connecting solidly with Jenks's chin. Jenks was staggered by the strength Tom had held in reserve.

Now the crew was yelling to Tom to finish Jenks off, Ditty rooting most loudly, screaming, "You've got 'im now; you've got 'im!"

Tom bounced on the balls of his feet, his fists pumping, looking for an opening. Jenks dropped to his feet, trying to trip Tom again, but Tom kicked up, his left foot slamming into Jenks's windpipe. Jenks spun away, bug-eyed. Tom charged, with rapid-fire fists pummeling Jenks's torso, then rolling up Jenks's chest to his windpipe again.

Jenks staggered back to hold his ground. Tom was panting. Open up just once, open up, he thought. Charging again, Tom pounded Jenks's torso with all his strength until Jenks began sinking, his arms held tightly to his chest, opening slightly. His hands, blood-spattered, bruised and swollen, hanging close to his face, opened now, wider, wider, and his big, pale head dropped. Tom, seizing his chance, coiled his right fist back behind his hip and came up swiftly to Jenks's jaw, through to the long, thin nose. A gash opened on his chin, blood drenched Tom's hands, and with one final, violent jerk, Jenks fell backward, landing unconscious on the blood-spattered deck with a resounding thud.

Chapter
Ten

THERE WERE SCATTERED fights almost every day. The captain clamped down with new rules: no swearing, no fighting, no long yarns at work. The crew and the officers were restless. The food was terrible: a seaman went after the cook with a knife one night and was brutally beaten by Mr. Murch.

Having run into heavy weather off Pernambuco, where the northeast and southeast trades converged, *Medusa* slumbered back into a calm. The sails, hungry for wind, hung as gaunt as ghosts.

Somewhere between Montevideo and the Falklands, they passed a "P" liner loaded with nitrates; a large, battered steamship bound for Hamburg, it was limping for the doldrums like a battle-weary soldier limping home from the front. Seeing it Stringy Peele became more and more frenzied.

"You can't believe where you are when y'ur rounding the dreaded Horn; it's as if all the weather in the world has wound up in that one place—gales an' rain squalls an' hail . . . sometimes it snows! The galley fire goes out, the fo'c'sle is all but underwater, and it's hell to hold her at the wheel, it's hell. . . ."

"Someone shut him up!" fat Brenner called out, and Stringy, jabbing his cigarette fitfully in and out of his mouth, stood wild-eyed, wheezing at his post.

And still they sailed on, like doomed men racing for the gallows, the Horn looming large in every waking thought. One night Tom awakened with a start. There was a terrific uproar as pots and kettles went crashing in a heap, and crockery from the fo'c'sle cupboard smashed to the deck.

"All hands out!"

Throughout the fo'c'sle there was a confused frenzy of

activity as boots, clothing, and heavy objects slid about in the darkness. At first Tom thought they were sinking, but Stringy called out in his thin, frantic voice,

"We're comin' up on it. The Horn, the Horn!"

The roar of a great wind through the rigging made an unearthly noise. The door flew open, and the men rushed wildly on deck.

Wave after wave crashed over the bulwarks with tremendous force, drenching everything and everyone. Water poured into the fo'c'slehead, and the unforgiving wind swooped down on the ship like a devilish claque of screaming harpies.

Tom rushed to the mizzen and worked desperately at snarled clew and buntlines—first the royals, then the three topgallants. There were shouts and orders issued, heard only faintly above the howl of the wind, and then a burst of noise, like cannons firing, and the big topgallant split down the middle, beating itself to tatters.

Tom, working his way off the yard down the mizzen shrouds, looked around as he then heard someone scream.

"Help me! Help me!"

Looking aft, Tom saw Smyth flailing down the steeply heeled deck, battling to hold on to the gunwales as wave after wave poured over him. Grabbing lines hand over hand, Tom worked his way over to Smyth, close enough to see his panic-stricken eyes as more waves surged over the sides. Then, as Smyth reached out desperately toward Tom, a final wave, larger than all before it, washed him away.

"Man overboard!" Tom screamed out, but no one could hear. Battling his way aft, he called up to Murch, who stood at the wheel, dazed and drenched.

"Man overboard!"

"He's lost!" Murch called down, now lashing himself and Jenks to the wheel. Jenks stared dead ahead while the cruel sea hurled itself violently over the decks.

"Throw him a line, Mr. Murch!" Tom shouted.

"Get below, Street! Get below! He's gone!"

And as Tom looked around for a line, the wind descended again. The ship was tossed like a toy boat in the hand of an angry child, and out of the awful darkness overhead hail rattled down, bouncing off the rigging onto the deck. Then, just as quickly as it had come, it stopped. The sky cleared momentarily, turned a sickly gray, then night rolled in again and the wind dumped sheets of water across the decks.

Tom fought his way forward against the waves and, looking up, saw that the lee door of the fo'c'sle had burst open and all the blankets, pillows, and clothes were floating, like face-down corpses, on rivers of water. Sven and Ditty grabbed what they could. Stringy Peele was chattering behind the lee door, his back to the deckhouse wall, his eyes searching the cruel heavens.

"We're dead and dyin'," he was saying. "We're dead and dyin'."

Although the unjust sea did not choose to send them all to a watery grave that night, the grim episode, which claimed two lives, Smyth's and Creighton's, haunted the ship. The men, cowed now, dazed, limp like rags, prayed silently to the sea and would have offered up more than two sacrifices to have appeased it.

Days later, after they passed around the Horn, through the Humbolt current, then headed west and northwest, the tropic sails were set—barefoot days returned. Land was sighted: Sala y Gomez and Easter Island. Then men from a passing ship told them harrowing tales of having survived a typhoon off Ducie Island, and new rounds of fear returned.

Stringy Peele looked as though something was snapping inside him. He jumped around the ship dogging Jenks, the flesh-and-blood object of his fear and hatred.

"He's done this to us. He's made it worse than it ever was," Stringy babbled. "Tahiti's the dream he won't let us have. He's stolen sleep from us. He's stolen all our very souls."

Jenks, bruised and battered and with no henchmen left, crept away from Stringy rather than confront him. He steered clear of Tom. But he haunted the ship like an avenging angel. He skulked as if he was waiting for another chance. Just one false move, and he'd kill Stringy, then Tom.

Jenks's hatred fueled Stringy's madness—that and the miserable life at sea and the lure of pearls kept hidden away in a leather pouch. All that had conspired to egg Stringy on to steal the pearls and set fire to the ship, so that now only the two of them were left, Tom and Jenks, drifting on an endless sea in a tiny open boat.

The sun was merciless. Tom's skin was cracked and burned. At times it felt as if the only working parts of his body were his eyes, which stared dead ahead, compelling him to stare down his fate. His mind was devoid of all hope or fear. If he was burned, he wondered, why did he feel so cold?

He had taken the rope from around Jenks's neck, keeping it nearby, although there was no possible way for Jenks to summon up enough strength to do Tom any further harm.

Burns covered the left side of Jenks's body from his neck to his hip. The wounds were festering and the surrounding skin was discolored, purple and black, and smelled foul, like death itself. For hours he lay huddled in a ball, naked, shivering.

In the late afternoon that first day, Jenks's eyes cracked open and he recognized Tom.

"So it's you—I thought I dreamed it," he whispered. "Water . . . there's a cask . . . under the sail."

Tom stared blankly at him. I could let him die of thirst or toss him overboard, he was thinking.

"Water!" Jenks said again.

Let him die, Tom thought, and as he thought it, Jenks's eyes challenged him to do it.

Let him die.

"Water," Jenks said again, and when his eyes opened this time, it looked as though weakness had overtaken him completely—there was no defiance or hatred left.

Reaching under the sail, Tom found the cask. He uncorked it and, leaning forward, let a drop of water fall onto Jenks's parched lips.

Chapter Eleven

THEY WERE AT opposite ends of the skiff, chewing their daily allotment of food—a sliver of salted pork, a quarter of a biscuit, and a quarter mug of water.

"What was it you said? Enough food for a week?" Jenks said weakly, shivering.

"Maybe more. Not much more," Tom said.

"And maybe it's a week's sail, north northwest, to the Marquesas, off Tahiti."

Tom sat in the stern, one arm crooked over a makeshift tiller, his legs draped protectively over the compass and what little remained of their supplies.

The sail was up, but there was very little wind. The sea was as flat as a pond.

Jenks's pain was unbearable. Sometimes just talking helped ease it.

"Having second thoughts about me?" he asked Tom.

"What about you?"

"About saving me, or are you too much of a gentleman to say it?"

"You use that word as if it were a curse."

"Me? No, far from it. I envy gentlemen. Always doing the right thing no matter what. Saved my hide, didn't you?"

"We'll see what I've saved you for."

"You're noble is what you are, Tom Street. That your real name?"

"Is Jenks yours?"

"Oh, yes. In my own way I have very little to hide. I'm as low as the place I come from. But you've fallen from someplace quite grand. And it's been my experience, with gentlemen of your sort, who have cut and run, that you cut and run completely—new name, new identity."

Tom thought about his children and heard Jelly pleading with him not to leave them behind with Preston Bridge.

"What was the place you ran from like?" Jenks was asking. "I see a mansion with servants. Horses and women, not necessarily in that order."

"It's been my experience with men of your sort," Tom said, "that you idealize the mansions and women and horses."

"What choice do we on the bottom have? I would have loved to be rich."

"How rich?"

"Absolutely stuffed with money."

"What would you have done with it?"

"Same as you. Controlled people, bought things. I'm no fool. I've got eyes. Rich is on top. Rich wins and rules."

"My father wasn't rich."

"Noble—that's even better. Noble marries rich. Saves you the bother of having to work for it. That's what you and he did, isn't it?"

Tom laughed. Perhaps it was worth having saved him.

"You shouldn't talk so much," Tom said. "You should sleep."

"Talking's all I got left, the only thing that reminds me I'm alive."

"I don't want to talk about the past, the present is bleak, and the future . . . I don't want to talk at all."

"Then let me talk—it helps me."

"You'll sleep now that you've eaten. Conserve your strength."

"Got a soft spot for me, do you?" Jenks asked, grimacing in pain.

"You'll have work to do if the wind picks up. I'll need any strength you can muster."

"We're alike, you and me."

"You don't know me at all."

"We survived. Of a whole ship of souls, just you and me. All survivors are alike."

His eyes closed and he slept.

That night a cool breeze, followed by a squall, blew across the little skiff. Tom opened the water cask and bunched up the tarp to catch it. But it ended as quickly as it had begun.

At sunrise Tom drank his allotment of water and began a new regimen. He chewed his piece of pork ten times, leaving what remained for the evening.

Jenks did not stir all that day, and Tom found himself missing the sound of his voice.

In the evening Tom awakened Jenks and fed him, but Jenks was very weak. He drifted back to sleep, and later he was incoherent, chattering away about someone named Toby.

In the middle of the night Tom, feeling Jenks's hand on the water cask, awakened with a start.

"I'll do it," Tom said, filling a mug, holding it up to Jenks's lips.

"See, I told you you've a soft spot for me," Jenks whispered.

"Did you ever have to watch a man die of thirst? Tongue becomes swollen, then blackens, then the face turns black—"

"Please—I'm burned black enough as it is." Jenks groaned as he shifted positions.

"Were you and Toby mates on some other ship?" Tom asked.

"Who told you about Toby?"

"You did, in your sleep."

"Toby's my grandfather's name—he raised me."

"You sounded angry with him."

"Me? No, it's Toby that's mad at me." Jenks paused, then, looking up at the dark sky, he began talking again. "I'm a real bastard, Tom Street, a real one. Never knew my father. My mother was an actress, a bad one—couldn't hear her past the first row even when she was sober enough to remember her lines. Toby was her father, ran a small theatrical troupe in Great Yarmouth, Norfolk. I even spent my time on the boards. Got accents and mannerisms for all sorts of occasions—I'll show you sometime. But I pinched some money from Toby, and he kicked me out of the company. Sixteen, I was. Saw the whole world. America, North and South, India, Africa, and Tahiti—that's why I was on *Medusa,* to get back there. Got a son, Paul, who's eleven years old. Lives in Tahiti at a church school on the southern end of the island.

"A year ago the boy's mother died. I had nothing, and I didn't want him raised by some queer old priests in an orphanage. So I went back to England to see if times had changed, if Toby would give me some money for the boy. But sixteen years changed nothing, except my mother was dead, and now I was old enough to see that Toby was as poor as me. So I became a thief again, but for big stakes."

"The pearl necklace."

"Beautiful pearl necklace—that's when we met, boyzo."

"In New York."

"Me and the midget, little Timmy, my fence, boyzo—that bastard was holding out on me, wanting the necklace for himself—I'd cut his throat before I let him get it. Needed it for my own boy. For Paul." Jenks suddenly sat up, his eyes focused on the horizon behind Tom.

Tom turned, then leaped to his feet. In the distance was a speck of light, a ship.

"Ahoy! Ship ahoy!" Tom began shouting, waving his hands.

"They won't hear you."

Searching frantically under the tarp, Tom found two matches.

"Burn the tarp."

"No, we'll need it."

"My clothes."

"No, mine," Tom said, and began stripping. He knotted his trousers, then, crouching on the floor, struck one of the matches, which sputtered faintly then burst into flame. He held it close to his trousers, and as they caught fire, waved them overhead.

"Ahoy! Ahoy!"

A glowing ash landed on the tarp and Jenks, using all that was left of his strength, stamped it out. Tom knotted his shirt and lighted it, flailing it over his head.

"Ahoy! Ahoy!"

The distant ship disappeared.

Tom sank down on his haunches, a vacant look in his eyes. He would have cried, but there was no water in his body for tears.

"There'll be another ship—don't worry. There's traffic on this route—you'll see," Jenks said.

"There's not much hope of that," Tom said.

"You'll survive. Nobility always does."

Tom closed his stinging eyes. His neck and back were stiff; there was not an inch of comfort on that little boat.

Days passed, and the week was up. There was enough meat for just two more days—and two drinks of water—but rain clouds were forming and the sea was choppy. Tom was almost as weak as Jenks, who drifted in and out of a fitful sleep. Tom found himself missing Jenks whenever Jenks slept, and when he stirred, Tom would say anything that came into his head, just to hear another voice.

"Have you ever seen black pearls?" Tom, thinking about Jelly, asked him one afternoon.

"In Tahiti . . . if we make it . . . a woman I know has a boat. She dives. She'll take us."

"I once saw an illustration in a newspaper of a native diver holding a large black pearl the size of a robin's egg. The pearl fetched twenty-five thousand in London."

"This woman will take us—we'll dive."

Tom's eyes were closing. The sea was shot through with sparkling rays from the sun. He smiled.

"Think of it, pearls waiting on the bottom for the taking. I'd do it just to take something back from the sea that's caused so much misery—just to take something back."

"I want to die spitting at it."

Tom laughed. "There isn't that much justice in death," he said, then drifted off to sleep.

In two days the meat was gone. There was no line for fishing, no knife or hook. There was no land in sight, no other ships, no water. Shoe leather. Tom chewed it but could not swallow it. Jenks sank into a deep sleep from which he did not emerge, although he was not dead.

Two days later Tom felt close to death himself. Now he knew death would not come as he had thought it would, violently, while rounding the Horn. It would come as a thin, wasting sleep. And he fought it, fought to keep his eyes open as if that would ward off death. And finally, when he was too weak to call out or even to move, he saw land. In the distance he saw the feathery tops of palm trees above a long white stretch of beach.

Chapter Twelve

SITTING IN AN outrigged canoe at the eastern end of the lagoon, the pearl diver, Teva, a young man in his twenties, was staring down at the coral, using a glass-bottom box. He had golden skin, an angular face, and was known among the divers of Turipaoa, his village, for being able to dive seventy-five feet or more and hold his breath for up to three minutes without succumbing to *taravana,* loss of oxygen to the brain. The old women in Turipaoa, which was on the atoll called Manihi, said that Teva's father must have tied stone weights to his umbilical cord and thrown it into the deepest part of the lagoon when he was born: they believed that as far down as the cord sank was as far as you were able to dive in your lifetime.

Raina, Teva's *vahine,* his woman, took her turn staring down through the box. Teva was very superstitious about having her approval. He had a happy disregard of danger, but Raina was more practical. She wanted to judge if the dangers were worth the risk. Directly below them, affixed to the spreading, thorny Acropora coral, were hundreds of mollusks—large ones, twenty centimeters or more. The mother-of-pearl inside would be black-lipped, smooth, and luminous, and would fetch a good price in the village.

Raina sat upright now, her slim, firm back as straight as a stick. She had thick hair that fell in dark waves down her back, fanning out below her tan shoulder blades. Her face would have looked completely innocent if it weren't for her eyes, which were surprisingly incisive as she scanned the horizon line, calculating their position. They were opposite a *hoa*, a break in the coral that bridged the ocean and the lagoon. Although it was late, the light was good enough to try one or two dives. Turning to Teva, she smiled, and he began his deep breathing.

He wrapped a cloth around his left hand, tied a coconut fiber satchel to his waist, then slipped over the side. The water was warm. Nearby were harmless yellow reef sharks with black dorsal fins. Teva paid no attention to them.

Grabbing a pearl shell, Teva took his final breath and tumbled forward, plunging head first, his hands outstretched, guiding himself. It was deeper than he had thought. The pressure was building up inside his head. At this depth he often felt as if his eyes would pop out of his skull.

There were many shells down here. Plunging farther downward, his hands finally felt them. He grabbed the largest one, scraped it with his shell, tugged it back and forth until he dislodged it, stuck it into his satchel, then went on to another. Sometimes he was able to bring up as many as fifteen or twenty, but today he wasn't so sure—he was stirring up the bottom and losing sight of the largest ones. Walking along the bottom on his hands like an acrobat, he found several more.

His heart was beginning to pound in his ears, a sign he took seriously. Righting himself, he looked behind. The water was murky with sand particles trapped in the fading shafts of light. At first he couldn't see the canoe, but a stone weight was jiggling above him. Raina was a smart girl. They were almost the same person inside; she knew he would be looking for a marker—she knew without hearing the pump of his heart or without seeing his startled, swollen eyes. With one great thrust, for the full satchel was weighing him down, he pushed up, grabbed the rope, and, hand over hand, climbed to the choppy surface.

Ooopahhhh!

His breath exploded as he cleared the surface. He lay on his back in the water for a moment, dazed, a thin line of blood trickling down from his left nostril.

Raina was leaning over, her hand outstretched to him. He handed up the satchel, then said he was going to make another dive.

She did not like seeing the blood running down his lips, and she was worried, but he smiled and, after resting for a few minutes, began his deep breathing. He tumbled forward again, head first.

Holding the glass box beside the rope, she watched him descend, his legs fluttering, sending rivulets of bubbles to the surface.

The canoe had turned so that she was facing the *hoa*, and when she lifted her head, she saw something that surprised her. Outside the *hoa*, beyond the barrier reef that circled the atoll, was a sail fluttering limply in a strong wind that was blowing from *maoae tahiri*, the east, a good wind for filling sails. It looked as if whoever was sailing the boat was unmindful of the wind and heading straight into the reef. Had the boat been abandoned? she wondered.

Bending forward again, she stared down and watched Teva creep along the bottom, pulling the shells from their fixed places. He was stirring up the water as he worked, so now, with the fading light, she lost sight of him altogether and waited to feel the tug on the marker rope. She looked up again for a moment and watched the boat drift —abandoned, she decided, and unfamiliar, nothing like the outrigger sail canoes from her village with their L-shaped booms and rounded corners.

Remembering Teva, she looked down and, seeing only a cloud of sand, she jiggled the marker line and waited, but there was no tug on the rope. She would wait a second more, and if there was nothing, she would dive in after him. Feeling no tug, she rose, suddenly terrified that something bad had happened and that she had not paid attention, had wasted time watching the boat. Just as she was about to dive over the side, she felt Teva grab hold and pull himself upward. In a surge of bubbles and sand clouds, he rose, exploding onto the surface with a cry. His breath sputtered out, accompanied by shrill peals of laughter, because he knew that he had scared her and was pleased to show her how much breath he could hold inside even so late in the day.

Coiling the rope, she chided him, but he smiled at her, handing her the full satchel of large shells. He had blood running from one nostril and his left ear.

"Pahi," she said—a ship—and pointed at it.

Scrambling into the canoe, Teva looked intently at the strange boat drifting perilously close to the reef.

Turning, he reached for his paddle, and together they paddled through the *hoa.* The wind whistling around their ears, they headed to the outer reef just as the boat hit it. Its hull snapped with a loud, brittle crack and its mast toppled.

"E ta'ata," Raina called out—It's a man!—and Teva saw him fall forward. He was naked, with reddened, blistered skin. The boat listed. Teva and Raina doubled their strokes.

Navigating carefully through the reef, they were close enough to see the man's face—he had a reddish beard—as he fell forward. Then more water rushed into the boat, and a tarp spread out and drifted, revealing another man with pale skin, half his body blackened with burns.

Teva and Raina dropped over the side of their canoe and swam over to the two men, Raina to the one with the reddish beard and Teva to the burned one.

"Tona mofatu?" Teva asked—His heart?—and Raina, pulling the man toward her, keeping his head above the water, felt for a heartbeat. Feeling a slight tremor within his chest, she shook her head, yes, and Teva did the same. Both men were still alive. Together, Teva and Raina pulled the men into the canoe and brought them inside the lagoon.

_____ *Chapter* _____
Thirteen

RAINA KNELT, HER open hands placed flat on the tops of her thighs, staring down at Tom, who was lying on his back, nude, on a grass mat that Raina had woven from coconut palms. She was watching the steady rise and fall of his chest, studying his face, which was pleasantly formed, with its full lips, now cracked and parched, half open, breathing greedily.

She had bathed him, massaged his burned skin with coconut oil, and then applied a plaster made from the pulp of the *mikimiki* tree that grew near the water, which healed burns. She had bathed Jenks as well and applied the *mikimiki*, but she did not know if he would survive. He lay quietly, shivering, the *mikimiki* hardening on his skin.

Tom's eyes had remained closed the entire time, and she was eager to see them and to see what his face looked like without his red-brown beard. She hoped he was dark-eyed. His body was longer and thinner than Teva's. She liked tall men, and what intrigued her most of all was the hair on his body, which was a deep copper color. None of the men on her island had body hair—she thought Tom must be French, or maybe he was a Mormon missionary from America. Two of them lived in Turipaoa with all their wives.

He stirred and his eyes opened slightly, but his irises were swimming around under his lids, and she could not see their color. As he stretched, she reached out and placed the open palm of her right hand just above his chest so that as his chest rose she could feel the soft prickle of his hair against her palm, then she dropped her hand. Her fingers spread out through the hair just over his heart, and moving her hand from his chest to his belly, where the hair was especially thick, she massaged him. Teva, who was sitting at the water's edge, opening the shells he had found that day, turned to her and giggled. She giggled, too, and she dropped her hand farther, circling Tom's navel lightly, then to the thick wiry hair above his penis, which lay across his thigh pink and veined, lengthening now, thickening.

Suddenly his eyes began to open.

It was as if he was coming out of a dream. He didn't know if he was alive or dead. The first thing he saw was the water, and he assumed that he was still captive on the little skiff, but sprinkled across the water was the brilliant glint of a flame, which illuminated the pale sand. Then he made out the indistinct shape of a hut with a thatched roof, a canoe, and a smiling man, who was sitting on a coconut, his knees up to his chest, his hands clasped between them, his loins covered with a bunched-up piece of cloth.

Tom's eyes pitched up to the sky, which was filled with glittering stars. Alive, he decided. Still on this planet. Out of the corner of his eye he saw another shape, and turning slowly toward it, he saw the most beautiful face—with high full cheekbones, a long thin nose, and lips as dark and lush as berries. One long tapered finger moved down from the lips and came to rest on her thigh. The light was faint and golden where she knelt, her skin matching its warm color tone for tone; pale yellow, burnt orange, deep blue. Her neck was long and thin, and her breasts were perfect —uptilted, with smooth golden brown nipples that stood out tautly as her rib cage rose and fell. Reaching out, she touched his shoulder lightly, her fingers trailing down his arm, twirling the smooth hair on his forearms. And when he looked down and saw that he was lying there naked, with an erection, he gasped and rolled away. Then he groaned because the skin on his side was as raw as an open wound.

She moved toward him and tried rolling him over onto his back again, but he struggled away.

Teva ran over to them and also tried rolling Tom to his back, but Tom broke away from him and stood up on shaky legs. They rose, too, and tried to reason with him, but it hardly seemed like reason—it was too bizarre. He turned and then the world seemed to reel out of his control.

Staggering into the shadows, he called out, "I want some covering—some covering."

Raina approached, but Tom shouted: "No, get back. Not you. Him," he said, pointing at Teva. "I'll only talk to him."

Raina and Teva looked at each other uncomprehending, but finally Teva stepped forward and Tom, thinking he had to shout to be understood, began motioning wildly with one hand while his other cupped his genitals.

"Covering—get me some covering—like yours—like this," he was saying, pointing at Teva's loins, but Teva, turning back to giggle at Raina, did not understand what Tom meant, not completely.

"Thees?" Teva said, pointing to his own loins.

"You speak English?"

"Un peu."

"Parlez-vous français?"

"Un peu."

"Je suis Americain."

"Un Mormon?"

"Quoi?"

"Un Mormon de Utah?"

"No! Get me some covering, man, like yours," Tom said, pointing at Teva's loins again.

Teva thought Tom simply wanted some reassurance, so he undid his loincloth and discarded it to show Tom that he, too, had a penis.

"No, no!"

When Raina stepped closer to see what she could do, Tom grabbed Teva's loincloth and held it up over himself. Then, backing away, he staggered again.

Raina offered him her shoulder—she was so soft, so fragrant—then they helped him onto the mat, and he lay there, tightly and, as far as they were concerned, inexplicably clutching the loincloth.

Sometime later he looked up. Raina was kneeling over him, feeding him. And later still he awakened for a moment and heard the unmistakable sound of their happy love-making.

_____ Chapter _____
Fourteen

"THEY DIVE FOR pearls," Tom whispered in Jenks's ear, watching as Raina and Teva got into their outrigged canoe and set off into the lagoon for the afternoon dive.

Tom was wearing a loincloth, called a *maro*, which Teva had made for him, but Jenks was naked, his body still caked with the *mikimiki*.

Before setting off, Raina, who was nude to the waist, looked back at the hut and smiled at Tom.

"She looks at me with these eyes that stare right through me. She's the most perfect-looking creature."

Jenks tried to speak: "A . . . s . . . k . . ."

"Save your strength," Tom interrupted. "They dive every day. He brings back thirty to fifty shells, then searches for pearls, but I don't know if he finds any. They must sell the shells somewhere. We're near Tahiti. At least they've heard of Tahiti—he points to the west every time I mention the word. Do you speak the language?"

Jenks nodded weakly.

"I know they're onto something here—they seem very excited every time they go out. And they're alone."

Just then Teva and Raina, who had paddled out about fifty yards, stopped, and Teva jumped over the side to begin his dive.

"I'm going to ask them to take me diving with them."

"P . . . o . . . e," Jenks whispered.

"Poe? What's that?"

"P . . . p . . . pearl."

"Leave it to you to know that much. *Poe*—pearl."

Raina stood in the stern of the boat, brushing her long thick hair back from her shoulders.

"You should see her now. Do you hear them at night? Every night! Like rabbits! Her little cries—*yip, yip, yip.*"

"A . . . s . . . k . . . ask," Jenks whispered.

"Ask? Ask what?"

"Ask . . . him."

But Jenks was too tired to continue.

Just then Teva rose to the surface of the water and handed his satchel to Raina.

"He's come up with more of them—big ones. She's stowing them. She's turning to look back at us. She's waving to me. She doesn't seem to care that I'm watching. Maybe she thinks I don't know what they're doing. She's brushing her hair back. Oh, Jenks, it's as if she's preening for me."

Jenks hissed.

"Not now, Jenks, I'm watching. I'm going out of my mind."

"Ask . . . him . . ." Jenks whispered again.

"Ask him what?"

"Ask him . . . for . . . her."

"Ask him for her?"

Jenks nodded.

"That's all there is to it?"

"Tell him . . . she is . . . *purotu roa* . . ."

"Purotu roa."

"Beautiful."

"Purotu roa," Tom repeated, then laughed. "Ask him for her! That's just like you, Jenks. You'll get us kicked off this island yet."

"Ask . . ." Jenks said again, then, turning his head, he drifted back to sleep.

Tom slept all afternoon. It was dark by the time he awakened. Teva was sitting on a coconut near the water beside an open fire pit, studying the pearl shells. Raina was sitting with her back to Tom, placing whole fish on pieces of heated coral in the center of the fire.

Tom, eager to see what was inside the pearl shells, struggled to his feet. He didn't want to scare Teva—to have him run off and hide the shells—so he walked slowly and stayed in the shadows.

Teva had opened the shells, taken out the meat, and was turning them to the fire to study them. There were no pearls in sight.

Teva and Raina, suddenly turning, saw Tom. Both were smiling at him, motioning to him to come near the fire. As he sat, Raina pulled one of the fish from the fire and, wrapping it in a leaf, handed it to him.

"Kahaia," she said.

"Thank you." Eating it, he pointed at one of the shells. *"Poe?"* he asked.

"Parau," Raina answered, laughing at him.

"Nacre," Teva added.

"Nacre—shells."

Teva nodded.

"Do you find pearls? *Poe?"*

Teva and Raina looked at each other, uncomprehending.

"Inside," Tom said, putting his fish aside and reaching for the shell to show them what he meant. It was large, about the size of a salad plate. The outer side was pitted and ugly, but the smooth side was uncommonly beautiful—a halo of pink and green with an outer edge of deep black. "The pearl . . . *poe* . . . inside the *nacre* . . . inside."

"*Eaha?*"

"*Poe . . . nacre poe,*" Tom said.

Raina laughed at him again.

"*Poe rava,*" Teva said, finally understanding, but the introduction of the new word, *rava,* left Tom in the dark.

Teva took back the shell and pointed to the outer lip. "*Rava—rava.*"

"Smooth?"

"*Rava.*"

"Edge."

"*Rava—poe rava,*" Teva said again, pointing at the darkest color on the shell.

"Black! Black pearl. Yes! *Poe rava*—where?"

"*Toau,*" Raina whispered.

"*Toau,*" Teva repeated, pointing at the water.

"The sea."

"*Toau,*" Teva said, pointing again.

"Below. At the bottom of the sea. Yes, exactly."

"*Poe rava—poe motea,*" Teva said, pointing at the shell's silvery black color.

"Yes, fine, *poe motea* is fine, too. Do you have any?"

They didn't understand.

"You own?"

Nothing.

Then, with more gestures and a louder voice, he was finally able to make them understand. Teva shook his head yes, and scrambled back to his hut and brought out a little matchbox, inside of which were two medium-sized silvery black pearls.

"*Hina'aro?*" Teva asked, handing the pearls to Tom.

"No, no, they're yours—you keep them," Tom said, pushing them back, but Teva looked insulted.

"*Hina'aro,*" he said again—a gift.

And Tom, nodding appreciatively, took them and studied

them in the firelight. They were pale cobalt, pitted and uneven—nothing at all like the pearls he'd seen dangling from ladies' necks in New York.

"Poe motea?" he said.

"E," Teva answered. Yes.

"Poe rava?" Tom asked.

Again the two pointed at the sea, and Tom, gesturing wildly until he was understood, asked if they would take him with them to look for the *poe rava.* Teva used the word *ananahi,* which meant tomorrow.

Raina, moving closer to Tom, handed him back his fish. She smelled of coconut oil and jasmine, and Tom reached out and gave the two gray pearls to her.

"A gift for you—for nursing me back to health," he said. "Please take them."

She looked at Teva tentatively. He nodded, and she took the pearls.

"Maururu roa!" she said, holding the pearls in the palm of her hand. Then, patting her chest, she said, "Raina."

"Your name is Raina."

"Teva," she said.

"Yes, Teva and Raina."

Then she pointed at Tom.

"Tom," he said.

And she curled over in a fit of laughter, mimicking eating. *"Tama'a."*

"No, Tom."

Another burst of laughter, from both of them this time. She pointed at a coconut palm. *"Tumu ha'ari?"*

"No, Tom—Tom," he said emphatically. He began laughing with them, and then she leaped to her feet and ran down to the water.

Leaning closer to Teva, Tom whispered, "Raina—*purotu roa.*"

Teva, nodding eagerly, said nothing.

After a while Tom stood, and thanking both of them for the meal, said good night and made his way back to the hut.

Jenks's eyes were open.

"They've got pearls, all right," Tom said, lowering himself to the *tapaku,* the floor mat. "Not good ones, but they're taking me to find more. I'm going to dive with them tomorrow if I'm up to it." Tom stretched and yawned. "I did what you told me to do. I asked him for her. A lot of good it did me."

Jenks smiled.

A half hour later Raina appeared at the hut and lightly touched Tom's shoulder. Taking his hand, she led him outside. As he walked away, he heard Jenks's raspy, salacious laughter.

Chapter Fifteen

Yip, yip, yip . . . As soon as he began touching her, and all night long, she made high-pitched, delighted sounds. She stroked him and he was erect in a second. When he stroked her, her arms and legs opened. She took his penis in both hands and placed it in the soft furrow between her legs, rubbing it gently up and down. Then, spreading her labia, he inserted just the tip of his penis, to wet it and continue rubbing it, and now, leaning over her, allowing the full weight of his body to shift to his forearms, he tilted his hips forward. His penis slid into her.

She licked his neck, ran her hands up his sides, then over his chest, twining her fingers through his copper-colored hair. Burying himself inside her, he paused, then shivered. He pressed in farther to get more of himself inside her, then withdrew to the tip and pressed in again, his penis now slick with her. She quivered as his lips grazed her neck and reached her nipples—licking her over and over again—his penis sliding slowly in and out, now faster, then slowing, and faster still. Then he rose so that her face was buried in his chest, and she licked his chest hair and murmured. He exploded inside her and remained there, feeling his own juices mix with hers.

At daybreak he was asleep in her arms. By morning she was up, helping Teva gather food, laughing with him.

Tom rose, surprised to be alone. When he saw them together, he felt a stab of jealousy, but they were so welcoming, so matter-of-fact, that he wondered whether it had really happened or he had dreamed it.

In the afternoon it happened again. She led him to another part of the lagoon and they made love.

This was not love, he told himself, although he didn't know what to call it: he had not paid for it or spent time courting it.

That night she remained with Teva and made the high-pitched sounds with him.

Jenks, listening to them, whispered, "Next is my turn."

"I'll blacken the rest of you if you take a step near her," Tom said harshly.

"It's like saying hello for them," Jenks said. "Didn't know it meant so much to you."

"It's a shame you've gotten your voice back."

"What do you want to do, marry her?"

"She's married to him, isn't she?"

"She's his *vahine*—woman—they're as good as married."

Yip, yip, yip.

"Damnit all to hell," Tom groaned, curling up.

"They're just being generous—you should be, too. Next is my turn."

Tom uncoiled, holding a threatening fist above Jenks's face.

"I swear to all that's holy, you touch her, you're dead."

Jenks laughed, turned his head, and fell asleep.

Later that night she came back to the hut. Tom kissed her greedily, then ran off down the beach with her.

Two days later he was bobbing on the surface of the shallow water, practicing his deep breathing. Teva was working on the bottom, gathering shells. Taking his final breaths, seeing Raina smiling at him, Tom plunged forward, then down. Seeing the mollusks below, he headed straight for them and ripped one from the coral with great difficulty before losing all his air and racing back to the surface.

"Open it," he panted as he handed it to her.

Using Teva's knife, she cut through the fleshy pink mantle and opened the tightly clamped shell. Inside, the meat was pink, blue-veined like a pulsing heart. She searched for pearls but found none. He repeated his deep breathing and plunged forward again, returning to the bottom.

During the next couple of weeks, Tom began to control his breath, to crawl horizontally along the bottom on his hands and forearms, and to use the shell that Teva had given him to pry the larger shells loose. Most often his mind was numbed by the pressure building up inside his head, and his breath was almost gone by the time he got to the surface. He'd hang on to the canoe, panting, as waves of nausea rolled up his chest and blood trickled from his nose and ears.

At night his head throbbed. Jenks cautioned him not to continue.

"I can't stop. It's like roulette. We're getting closer to the best beds. Teva found another gray pearl today. It's not as dark as pearls I've seen in New York. But we're getting closer."

"Let them work for you. He'll give you whatever he finds. He likes you."

"No, I won't do that to them."

"You don't understand. Rape is a way of life with these people."

"How can you say that after they saved our lives?"

"You're not doing anything bad to them—you're just taking what they offer."

But Tom wouldn't listen. During the next week he dived in deeper and deeper water—and they began moving farther out. Although he was becoming more proficient at diving, most often he felt as if his brain was pressing against the back of his eyeballs.

One afternoon, lying in the bottom of the boat opening his shells, he inserted his finger and felt a bump, then two, then another—

"I've found them!" he yelled, pulling the viscous membrane away, seeing them affixed to the shell. Raina helped him—smoothly, smoothly, she didn't want to damage them—she removed three of them. Giddy and wild-eyed, it took him a moment to really see them. Their color was no better than the ones that Teva had found—in fact, they were worse. Mottled and twisted, they looked like overripe fruit.

Rather than being discouraged, he stared down fiercely through the glass box trying to remember at which end of a large coral outcropping he'd been diving. Locating it, he jumped over the side, took his breaths, then tumbled forward.

He circled the outcropping, losing sight of Teva, who was working nearby. Picking off four large shells, then seeing another, even bigger, one inside a coral fold, Tom stuck his hand in, and a gaping, jagged mouth darted from the fold. Opening wider, exposing double rows of razor teeth, it enveloped Tom's hand up to the wrist. Dropping his satchel, he grabbed its thick slippery body, trying to pull it off, but it was fastened tightly. He could feel its slimy, undulating muscles swallowing more of his arm. Screaming out, he tugged furiously. His air was almost gone. A thick, numb feeling began to spread out from his arm.

Through a mass of silvery bubbles Raina swam toward him, a knife clutched in her left hand. As soon as she reached him, she began hacking away at the animal's head, and it uncoiled from the coral fold: a slippery, gray eel, stretching four, five, almost six feet. Tom grabbed the knife and cut more deeply through its muscle tissue and finally the disembodied head unclamped and fell from his hand. Now Teva was rushing toward them, pulling Tom up. The three of them pushed quickly to the surface and lay on their backs, gasping.

Teva offered to help him into the canoe, but Tom was staring down, seeing his satchel on the bottom. Although his hand was throbbing, all his attention was riveted on those shells. Teva offered to dive down to retrieve them, but Tom said no. Taking two deep breaths, he plunged downward, eyes closed. His right hand, throbbing now, scoured the bottom and grabbed the satchel. Then, turning, he raced back to the surface with his find.

Scrambling into the boat, he began cutting open his shells.

The first shell contained nothing. Neither did the second nor the third. Tom, like a man at a roulette table urging the turn of a wheel, cursing his luck then praying for it, cut into the fourth shell, snapping open its tightly clenched muscle, and inserted his finger along the slippery mantle. He felt something large and round, then something similar. His heart stopped. Looking down, he saw them veiled by the slick membrane. Lifting it, he pushed them out. The first one was large, a brilliant color, black shot through with gray, green, and pink, not perfectly round, more pear-shaped, with a dimple on one side. The next one was perfection. Round, large, it didn't have a cut or a scratch, and the color—what had Jelly called it?—as green-black as a fly —with a rose lustre.

Holding it tightly in his fist, he began laughing uproariously.

"Eaha?" Teva asked, wanting to see it. *"Eaha? Poe?"*

"E! Yes! *Poe rava. Purotu! Purotu roa!"* Tom called out, shaking his fist in the air.

That night they feasted on the meat from the shells, which Teva roasted on the heated corals. Jenks, finally feeling stronger, sat with them. His appetite had returned. He ate ravenously and listened as Tom told about his adventure with the eel.

"And your prize pearls are really as beautiful as all that?" Jenks asked.

"You saw them yourself—one is absolutely perfect."

"Let's see them again," Jenks said eagerly.

Tom held them in his open palm. Jenks inspected them in the firelight, and the old Jenks, Bully Jenks, sly and secretive, looked up at Tom, then back at the pearls, smiling covetously.

II
A Prediction

Chapter
Sixteen

THE TWO WOMEN sitting on the bed in the English country house were a study in contrasts. Madame Duntov, who was dark-skinned and dark-haired, fidgeted, snapping her restless fingers above opened astrology books and a scattered deck of tarot cards. Margot Vale, whose thick hair, lit by the morning sun, was the color of bottled honey, sat quite still, looking completely at ease. Only her eyes, deep set, as mysterious as the sea, were vividly intent. She was staring at her mother's strand of pearls, which she had just draped around Madame Duntov's neck.

The pearls were perfectly round, perfectly matched. Each one, Margot was thinking, told a story of invasion, defense, and beauty. An oyster shell, invaded by a grain of sand or a tiny worm, had protected itself by encasing the intruder in crystalline layers, and a pearl, the most sensual of jewels, had been formed.

Just then a memory of her mother, who had died ten years before, darted to the surface of her consciousness. Margot remembered watching her mother, dressed for the opera, sitting at a vanity table putting on the strand of pearls, transfixed by the sight of them in the mirror. Margot's father had walked up behind his wife and had also stared at the pearls. For an instant their eyes had met and they had smiled peacefully at each other, as if the pearls had calmed them.

"Halfway round the world," Madame Duntov was saying slowly in a thick Russian accent, "there's a man. I see the ocean . . ."

Margot shifted her intent gaze from the pearls to Madame Duntov's round face. The reading, having gone on for almost an hour, had thus far been only about the past.

"Who is he?" Margot asked.

"I'm not sure. A young man with dark eyes. And there's something else coming through—a name from mythology," Madame Duntov said, opening her eyes and rifling through the opened books, the charts, the deck of cards.

Margot, whose startling blue-green eyes brimmed with interest, followed Madame Duntov's busy hands, then she took another of her pearl necklaces and draped it over Madame Duntov's neck, pearl-wearing and the reading being included in one fee.

"One of the three Gorgons," Madame Duntov said finally, "whose head, with snakes for hair, turned all those who looked upon it into stone. Slain by Perseus . . ."

"Medusa," Margot said.

"Yes, Medusa," Madame Duntov said. "The man has something to do with Medusa. He's of importance to you. You cannot avoid him—he's your final love," Madame said, giving the word *final* a chilling flourish.

Margot sat up at the foot of the bed, her arms wrapped around her knees.

"He comes to you with a pearl, a black pearl," Madame Duntov said, fingering the strands around her neck. "This pearl gathers all the love possessed by each of its owners, culminating in the final ownership, and that person receives the accumulated love."

"And am I its final owner?"

There was a knock at the door, and a woman called out. "Margot, good morning. It's Kate."

"Lady Vale, is that the call to lunch? I'm starving."

"No, Madame, I'm sorry."

Madame Duntov's face deflated.

There was another knock.

"Margot, dear, it's Kate. Time to get up."

Margot, running to the door, opened it a crack.

Her sister, Kate, dressed for church and wearing the most ridiculous straw bonnet with purple feathers twisted into the shape of roses, was standing there trying to see into the room over Margot's head.

"My dear, I was calling and calling. Who's in there with you?" Kate said, pushing the door open a bit farther. Then, seeing Madame Duntov sitting in the middle of the bed, ropes of pearls round her neck, her thin, dark hair pulled back severely in a chignon, Kate exclaimed, "Margot! What's that dreadful little woman doing in your bed?"

"Madame Duntov came up from London early this morning to give me a reading," said Margot lightly.

"And what's she doing wearing all your pearls?"

"There is something in her skin that adds lustre to them. Everyone in London has her wearing their pearls."

Kate, seeing the strand she had always coveted, winced. "I hate to see her wearing Mother's pearls."

Kate, at thirty, was younger by two years, and although she and Margot had similar features—both were of medium height, slim-waisted, and full-hipped—Margot was considered the lovelier of the two. Kate's face had a perpetual frown, which was now exaggerated as she said, "We're on our way to church, dear. I thought you'd want to join us."

"No, I don't think so," Margot answered, smoothing a wisp of hair back from her forehead.

"But Lord Breigh was wondering if you were going to join us," Kate said pointedly.

"I'm occupied with my guest," Margot said, indicating Madame Duntov.

"Margot, be serious. He's very interested in you—he told Guy he thought you must be the most willful woman in England."

Margot smiled. "And you took that as a compliment?"

"My dear, coming from him, that *is* a compliment. I think you'd better dress and join us."

"I'll see him at lunch."

"I trust you are not bringing that creature to his lordship's table."

"Madame Duntov is my guest, Kate," Margot said firmly. "I'm not putting her out with the servants."

"It's indecent."

"I met her at the Duchess of Teck's table. She's world-famous."

Kate frowned again. "I worry about you, Margot. I really do."

Margot patted her sister's hand in a maternal way. "Then go to church, Kate, and pray for me," Margot said, easing the door shut.

Margot walked back to the bed and lay down across the foot of it.

"You don't enjoy your sister's company," Madame Duntov said.

"You don't have to be clairvoyant to see that."

"Then what brings you here?"

Margot sighed and stretched. "I was so restless at home." She put her hand on a stack of travel books on the table beside the bed. "I've been looking at these, trying to find a place to go next—on any given day I'm in New Guinea or Australia or Ceylon."

"All this has to do with your husband's death, which, I believe, I predicted."

"Yes, you did, at that dinner party the very first time we met. I thought you were the strangest woman, and I wasn't sure about the value of your predictions; you could see for yourself that James was much older than I. You also told me that I was bound to have the life of an adventurer."

"As opposed to an adventuress."

"Yes, I remember you made the distinction. Well, I'm ready for my adventure."

"Be patient, my dear, everything will start here. I'm sure of it," Madame Duntov said, rummaging through her papers again. "This month, this very week. It's in your chart."

"What does it say?"

"You're ruled by Neptune, aren't you? Or Pluto—my goodness! Of course."

"What?"

"We're entering a Pluto-Neptune conjunction—very powerful for you."

"When?"

"This very week!"

Margot stared down skeptically at the charts, and Madame Duntov looked at her disapprovingly.

"My dear, haven't I told you enough truths? Perhaps you need one more. I know something about you that no one knows. Your husband was—what is the thing you English say?—'making love' to you when he died."

Margot sat bolt upright as though a current had just passed through her. "How on earth did you know that?"

Madame Duntov smiled her purposefully inscrutable smile. "You see, my dear, you are simply not to worry. Adventure is coming."

"The man with the black pearl. Tell me more."

Madame Duntov's eyes closed and she grimaced.

"It's hopeless, my dear, I close my eyes and see black pearls, but they look like caviar to me. Can we have some?"

"Madame Duntov, you're making me so hungry, and it's my future we're talking about."

"Some caviar and eggs and a little onion—ooh, and some wodka or champagne—oh, yes, champagne . . ."

And as Madame Duntov went on creating the menu, Margot sank back on the bed in frustration. She'd have to wait until lunch to learn more.

Chapter
Seventeen

At lunch Madame Duntov ate as if it would be her last meal. With each smack of her lips the other guests shifted uncomfortably in their seats. There were several rather pointed "uh-hmms" and napkins dabbed testily at lips, which Margot thought was infinitely more rude than Madame Duntov's eating habits.

Kate was particularly annoyed, staring meanly at her husband, the Honorable Guy Carneelian, a red-faced, balding man with tufts of strawberry-blond hair growing out of his ears.

"Let me get something straight if I may, Madame Duntov," Lord Breigh said. He was sitting at the head of the table, staring at the pearls wrapped around Madame Duntov's neck. "Am I to understand that your skin actually makes pearls shine?"

"Pearls do not shine, Lord Breigh," Madame Duntov said, taking a partridge bone from her mouth. "They glow.

Pearls have layers and layers of crystals. I happen to have an oil in my skin that keeps them moist."

"You know so much about them."

"Information passed down from my grandmother to my mother to me . . ."

Margot watched as Lord Breigh, Robert to his friends and family—Guy Carneelian was his younger brother—listened to Madame Duntov, and she was pleased that he wasn't being snide or bored; he seemed genuinely interested in what she had to say. Lord Breigh was very much the model English country gentleman—courteous, hospitable, a good sportsman, a model landlord, somewhat vague when it came to artistic, intellectual, and business matters, but that, too, was as it should have been, Margot thought, continuing to stare at him, which was not an unpleasant thing to do. On the contrary. He was very handsome—as thick-haired as his brother was bald, also fair, with wide-set brown eyes and a moustache. Extraordinarily eligible, Kate was always telling Margot.

Kate Carneelian suddenly seized the conversation. "And your skin, Madame Duntov"—she said this word as if it were as distasteful to pronounce as it was to look at—"oils the layers of crystal."

"Many things do. You can 'heal' a pearl by rolling it in the palm of your hand—or you can increase its lustre by feeding it to a goose."

"I don't understand, Madame. If the goose eats the pearls, how ever do you see them again—" She stopped abruptly, a look of horror crossing her face as she guessed Madame's answer.

"Exactly!" Madame exclaimed. "Goose feces are so good for pearls."

Kate put her hand to her chest and looked as if she might be ill, and the rest of the table fell into an uneasy silence, which Margot interrupted.

"Madame Duntov has taught me so much of what I know about pearls. She's quite an expert. Did you know that my name, Margot, means *pearl?* Correct me if I'm wrong, Madame Duntov, but isn't it from the Persian? *Murwari,* "pearl, child of light"? From it come the names Marguerite, Margot, Margherita, Marjorie."

"How very interesting," Lord Breigh said, smiling at Margot. He had been sneaking looks at her all through lunch and was now only too glad to stare unabashedly at her. "And was all *your* information passed down from one generation to another?"

"No. I'm book-taught and tutored. I read as much as I can about pearls."

"There are certain words used in connection with pearls that confuse me. For instance, when you talk about a pearl's orient, what is that?"

"It's the brilliance of a particular pearl—pearls of the best quality come from the Orient, from India and Arabia," Margot said.

"And the word *lustre?*" Lord Breigh asked.

"Lustre," Margot said, drawing out the word as if it had a special meaning for her. "It's also a quality of reflected light, but it's much more sensual. The light from within. Sometimes, in the very best pearls, it looks like a cool, cool fire."

Lord Breigh had turned beet-red. "I think it's wonderful you know this much about them," he said.

"I worship them."

Kate rushed to clarify her sister's statement. "She does not mean that literally, Robert."

"I adore them. I love wearing them, touching them; they're warm, alive—I love just looking at them. I wash my face with them—"

"You what?"

"Seed pearls from Ceylon dissolved in vinegar and lemon juice with a touch of oil of tartar makes a wonderful scrub with spring water."

"That's why you shimmer so," Madame Duntov said.

"Someone told me that a single pearl was just auctioned off at Christie's for thirty thousand pounds," Guy Carneelian said.

"The extraordinary pearls," Margot said, looking radiant, "the large perfectly formed ones, are priceless when you think that men risk their lives to dive for them and that only one dive in a thousand brings up a pearl of any value at all. I'd like to go down to the ocean floor with the divers in Ceylon, a place called Mannar."

"You may yet," Madame Duntov said. "The newspapers

reported that the catch in Ceylon was the biggest ever last year—you'll make yourself a fortune there."

"Will I really, Madame? Do you see that, too?"

"Anything you wish, my dear. I told you. Everything is possible."

"Would you really like to go out there?" Lord Breigh asked.

Kate rushed to explain, "She doesn't mean half of what she says literally, Robert."

"Yes. I like to think that I'm brave, but I have to test myself continually to find out if I really am. I want to push myself to some limit. Adventure is that limit. Don't you think so, Robert?"

But he merely looked at her as if he thought she were some wildly exotic creature that he might one day like to tame.

After the meal Madame Duntov decided that her stay had come to an end. Standing in the great hall, she took Margot's hand to say good-bye. Margot slipped an envelope with cash into her purse.

Before leaving, Madame Duntov turned slowly and spoke in a grave tone.

"Something occurs to me. The man you meet, the one who has something to do with Medusa and the black pearl—I want you to remember. He is the source of love, and also of your undoing."

"But isn't that the way it often is with men, Madame?" Margot said with a smile.

"Yes, of course. Laugh at destiny, my dear Lady Vale, laugh uproariously at it. Good-bye. Thank you for your kindness."

Dinner was remarkable for only two reasons—one was that Margot looked absolutely beautiful, and the other was that Lord Breigh could not take his eyes off her.

Everyone noticed it—most especially Kate Carneelian, who was suddenly of two minds about her brother-in-law's interest in her sister. On the one hand Kate congratulated herself on setting up this most perfect of all possible matches. On the other she was annoyed that it might actually come to pass. Margot so often got what she wanted out of life. More to the point, Margot often got exactly what Kate wanted out of life.

"My dear, Robert is positively mad for you," Kate said after the ladies had retired to the drawing room.

"Don't you think all this is happening too soon?"

"Too soon? I don't understand. You weren't even wearing proper mourning dress for the last three months of your year."

"That's not what I meant—it's too soon to speculate what Robert's feelings are."

"Oh, but that's just the way he is—he's reserved. Nothing could happen too soon as far as Robert and you are concerned, my dear. And there is the other matter to consider," she added.

"What other matter?"

"Margot, my dear, neither of us is getting any younger, and you must try again to have children."

This was a topic of conversation that Kate always pursued and Margot found invasive, too personal, and painful to discuss—her two children had died in childbirth. Margot's smile vanished from her face, and turning away from her sister, she stared into the firelight.

But Kate was unrelenting. "We have an obligation to reproduce ourselves, my dear. After all, ours is the breeding stock that keeps the upper class strong."

Just then the men entered the room and Kate turned, smiling, as if she had been waiting all along for their return, without having moved a muscle or uttered a word.

The women wished to retire early, and the gentlemen were eager to retire to the smoking room.

"Shall we continue our little chat in my bedroom?" Kate asked Margot conspiratorially.

"I'm going to rummage around the library for a good book," Margot replied, grateful that the men had interrupted the discussion.

"Better choose your books wisely. Robert has conservative tastes," Kate said, winking.

As good nights were exchanged, Lord Breigh shook Margot's hand meaningfully, then the men left. Kate lingered for a moment, looking lost and left behind by the men, and finally she went off to her bedroom.

Margot went to the library, chose a book about the South Seas, and studied the engravings in it, which only heightened her sense of wanderlust. Then, walking through the darkened galleries filled with faded paintings of Robert's relatives, she found herself trying to remember the sound of James Vale's voice. But she couldn't. He had told her how much he loved her, and when she was first married to him, she had thought that was what love was—to be told by a man that you were loved. But after the death of her two infants, when her own feelings awakened, she came to realize that his love of her wasn't enough. Passion was what had been missing. She'd never craved him. Even now, thinking of him, she had no real desire to see or touch him again.

Walking down the hallway, she heard low, rude laughter coming from the smoking room. The smell of cigars was thickening the air, and she was about to turn and walk back to the library when her eyes fell on a glass case that was filled with pen-and-ink drawings of people in fancy dress. There was a card that read THE APRIL BALL, DEER HALL, 1881, and in a corner on the second shelf was a sketch of her parents.

Her mother was dressed in billowing crinolines, her father in satin breeches and silk stockings. The expression on their faces was so quintessentially them, the way Margot remembered them. Her father looked as if he had been drinking and as if he was staring at a beautiful woman who was standing behind the artist. Margot's mother looked resigned to be living with a man whose moods she could no longer predict or fathom.

"Handsome couple," Lord Breigh said from behind her.

She turned. He held a brandy snifter in one hand. "Yes, they were," she said, smiling.

"Do you remember those parties? Everyone looked so beautiful."

"You should have parties like that, Robert."

"Not alone. I need a hostess," he said. "I was thinking about what you said at lunch, about having adventures. I want that, too."

"Do you want to travel? I was just thinking about doing that exact same thing."

"I was thinking of something else, actually." He took a sip of cognac as though to fortify himself. "Oh, Margot, you must know how I feel about you."

"I think I do. At least I know what Kate tells me she thinks you feel about me."

"These dreams of yours are all well and good. But once you get them, they're not dreams anymore. Stay here with me, Margot. I love you. I always have, even when we were children. I adored you even then, and this is the life you know. Just like your parents there—look how happy they were, how beautiful they looked. This is where you belong."

She said nothing; she was too busy staring into his sympathetic eyes—he looked so forthright and honest. This is a possibility, she said to herself, just as James Vale had been a possibility.

"I hope you don't mind that I'm not blushing and tongue-tied," she answered finally. "And I don't want to be coy with you, Robert. I thank you for what you've just said, and I take it enough to heart to want to think about it before I give you an answer."

"Yes, of course. I want you to think about all of it. And take all the time you need. I'm honored that you're even considering it."

She brought her hand up to stroke his cheek, and he kissed her palm, held it for a moment, then said good night.

Chapter Eighteen

THE NEXT DAY Margot's good friend Baron Felix Clausen stopped off to see her on his way down to London.

"I'm on a mission involving you," the baron said. "I'm a courier."

"Whose?"

"All in good time," he said, taking her arm.

They were walking in the Italian garden with Lord Breigh, but seeing that the two friends wanted to be alone, Breigh had taken a seat on a stone bench. Pretending to read a book, he was peering over the binding and following every move Margot and Baron Clausen made. The baron steered Margot away from the garden and onto a path in a plantation of pine trees.

Spry and dapper, in his early sixties, Clausen had a long face with inquisitive features, a full, expressive mouth, and dark, busy eyes. A slim, pointed beard framed his face like a carefully sketched pencil line.

Romance did not complicate his friendship with Margot. Twice a widower and once divorced, he had given up on romance altogether and much preferred the passionate goings-on of his young friends.

"Felix, you look as though you'll burst unless you tell me whose courier you are."

"A young acquaintance of mine, someone you met at my house in London six months ago—David Nasis."

The name did not register.

"He'll be upset that you haven't remembered."

"Nasis. What sort of name is that?"

"He's an Oriental Jew, the grandson of Solomon Nasis, the entrepreneur. The old man was quite a colorful character. After leaving Baghdad, he settled in Bombay, and all his life he dressed like a potentate, complete with turban and robes."

"I never met anyone like that at your house."

"No, my dear. His sons and their children are *veddy* British. They sent young David down to London to have him develop a trade. He was floundering when I first met him, but you, my dear, changed his life by providing him with a vocation."

"Pearls," Margot said as the image of an intense, dark-haired young man suddenly came into her mind. He had sat at her feet in the baron's study while she told him all about pearls.

"Apparently the family has given him the backing to go into the pearl business."

Dark eyes, she remembered, and something about his speech—a stammer.

"I don't know what you said to him, but he's heading for the South Seas on the family yacht to purchase black pearls. He wanted me to give you this so that you'd think about him while he was away," Clausen said, reaching into his coat pocket. He brought out a small black velvet box.

Inside was a Medusa-head pendant carved in pink coral within green enamel with pearls and rose-cut diamonds.

Margot was momentarily speechless. "Do you know Madame Duntov?" she finally asked.

"The little Russian? She gives me the shivers every time I see her—predicted my second wife's death."

"She was here yesterday to give me a reading. She told me about a man who has something to do with black pearls and Medusa."

"Well, Nasis will be overjoyed. Unfortunately, I don't think his lordship will like it very much," Clausen said, indicating Lord Breigh, who was now walking on a terraced path directly below them.

"He's asked me to marry him."

"Oh, I see. I had no idea it was this serious. He's a very sensible choice for you."

"You don't make it sound very exciting."

"Marriage doesn't have to be."

"Oh, Felix, please don't be jaded. I have to talk this out with you."

"My dear, I'm not jaded. After three marriages I'm exhausted. This Breigh certainly seems to love you."

"I know, but for the first time in my life I'm asking myself if I feel passionately in love."

"Sometimes that grows."

"Like old age—what an exciting prospect. What I want is an adventure. Madame Duntov said that something extraordinary would happen soon. I think your showing up to deliver this pendant is the beginning."

"What do you mean?"

"I'm expected to marry Lord Breigh. I've always done what I was expected to do, and now, out of the blue, a friend has brought me a gift from a man who has sailed off to Tahiti. Why not seize this opportunity for adventure? What if I sailed off to Tahiti to see him?"

"Nasis would not only be overjoyed, he'd be dazed,"

Clausen said. "And I see your point; that would be an adventure."

"It is so easy for me to talk about doing something exciting with my life. Why not just do it?"

Lord Breigh was approaching them on the path. "This will be the hard part," Margot said, staring at him.

"I know men, my dear," the baron whispered. "You're catching him early in the game; he's more obsessed than in love. And you seem so sure of yourself, he'll know it isn't his fault. You are sure, aren't you?"

"I have no idea. But isn't uncertainty the best part of an adventure?" she said with a smile, and holding the Medusa pendant tightly in her hand, she began walking toward Robert.

September 18, 1891

Dearest Felix,

Your letter was waiting for me when I arrived in Papeete, Tahiti, and the book you sent—Balzac's—*A Harlot High and Low*—you evil-minded man!

David Nasis would not hear of my staying in town on my own. There aren't any good hotels, he said, and although I had found a perfectly adequate guest house, he insisted on moving me lock, stock, and barrel onto his yacht, the *Distant Star,* which is so luxurious I feel as if I've never left home. Actually, I'm feeling a little like a kept woman, although my "keeper" is not pressing the point.

Is love in the air, Felix? Or anticipation? Have I mistaken one for the other? Perhaps that is all love really is.

I wish I had you nearby to talk to. I miss you more than words can express.

Your devoted friend,
Margot

Chapter
Nineteen

DAVID NASIS STOOD on a black sand beach south of the port town of Papeete on Tahiti. His white linen trousers were flapping around his ankles. The shoreline rose steeply like a pitch wall, and beyond it stood the remote and lush mountains. Behind him was the tender that had brought him ashore.

Two Tahitians, wearing pale blue overblouses and white trousers, were walking toward him from the jungle.

"Monsieur Nasis," one of them called out.

David waved, adjusting the wide brim of his Panama hat. The Tahitians looked greedy but would be easy to deal with, David was thinking. The only problem with these people was that they talked too much and didn't have the best pearls.

"Monsieur Nasis, I brought my friend."

"You're t-t-twenty m-m-minutes l-l-late," David called out. His stammer was as much of a surprise to himself as it was to other people. He always thought in fluid sentences, he even practiced saying things in his head before speaking them, but it never came out easily.

"You're an efficient man, Monsieur Nasis," the Tahitian said with a smile.

"And a b-b-busy one, Thierry."

"This is my friend Hugo."

Hugo was tall and blank-faced, with a thick black beard.

Both men were staring out at the white yacht, which was a hundred and twenty feet long, anchored beyond the reef that ringed the island.

"Hugo and me, we thought we'd do our business on the boat. It looks like a comfortable place to work."

"I thought I'd save you the trouble and c-c-come ashore to s-s-see what you and your f-f-friend have."

Thierry smiled, then shrugged—there was no sweet-talking this Englishman.

"It's getting r-r-rather h-h-hot," David said, staring up at the sun. "Why don't you let me s-s-see what you have?"

Hugo brought out a soiled handkerchief, took out five pearls, and held them in the palm of his hand.

Leaning over, folding back the brim of his hat, David inspected them, seeing at once that only one was a good color. It was darker than the rest, pear shaped, useful for a pendant or a drop earring.

"Is this all you've g-g-got?"

"Got one or two others, but I didn't know if you wanted to pay the price for them."

"Show me what you've g-g-got before I s-s-sweat through my shirt."

Thierry reached into his pocket, pulled out a small sack, and, opening it, took out two pearls that were better than the others but still not what Nasis was looking for.

"Is there no p-p-pearl on all th-th-these islands that is even close to p-p-perfect?" he said, inspecting them.

"Place been fished out. Got to go farther and farther to find perfect ones, the out islands maybe. These two come from a place called Manihi, only place left to find good ones."

Thierry pointed to the yacht. "You want a perfect one *pour madame, oui?*"

"N-n-never mind that—I'll g-g-give you five hundred for these two and the d-d-darker one your friend has."

"Five hundred? Each is worth five hundred."

"Bedloe," David called out to one of the crewmen on the tender. "Give them f-f-five hundred."

"But monsieur—"

"Not a *centime* m-m-more, Thierry. It's more than you d-d-deserve. Bring me something p-p-perfect, Thierry. Something p-p-perfect."

Bedloe approached, counting the money, and seeing it, Hugo's eyes bulged. David knew he had won. Reaching over, he took the two pearls from Thierry's hand and the darker one from Hugo, then he turned and walked back to the tender.

Thierry called out, "Maybe next time we do business on the boat. I like to see it. Nothing like it down here."

But David said nothing as he got into the tender. He didn't want them out on the boat ogling Margot. As they moved off into the surf, he called "G-g-good d-d-day, Thierry."

"Good day, monsieur."

As the boat crashed through the waves, the spray hit David's hat before he could duck behind the glass windscreen.

Lifting the hat from his dark hair, he let the sun beat down on his face for a few moments. With his mind's eye he saw Margot sitting on the deck, which looked like a summer veranda, on a white wicker chaise longue, tubs of flowers all around her. Shaded by the pink-and-white striped awnings, she was waiting for him. Opening his eyes, he saw the yacht, looking dire and glamorous, fill the horizon. He decided he would have her that very afternoon. He would, he told himself again—this time he really would.

She'd come up on deck just in time to see the tender cutting through waves. David was sitting behind the windscreen, a serious look on his face.

"Hello," he called up to her.

His eyes were resolute, but seeing her, they melted. He blushed.

"Have you bought something very beautiful?" she asked with a smile, leaning forward at the rail, her strands of white Australian pearls swinging out gently.

"N-n-not as beautiful as you d-d-deserve," he said as he climbed up the gangway.

He was beside her now, standing closer than he usually did. She smiled at him, then turned quickly away as some yellow sharks circling nearby caught her eye.

David stared at her lips, followed the full curve of the lower one to the subtle curve of her jaw, along her slim neck to the strands of white pearls. One was at the base of her neck, the next hung loosely above her soft, full breasts, and the third strand fell below her breasts, emphasizing their curve under the pale yellow fabric of her dress. She turned back quickly, and he looked up, embarrassed to be caught looking.

"They're very beautiful," he said.

"My pearls?" she asked saucily. "They're quite old."

"They d-d-don't appear to be," David added with a smile.

"I usually keep them covered—it isn't good to expose them to too much light."

She moved closer, and he stiffened slightly. "Your p-p-pearls?"

"Well, of course. What else are we talking about?" she added with a laugh.

He moved back, his eyes darting nervously now.

"Is something wrong?" she asked.

"You're l-l-lovely."

"Thank you, but perhaps it would be better if I were less lovely."

"Why?"

"You might think me more . . . approachable."

"N-n-no—I like you as you are. You're s-s-something I've conjured up, like some d-d-dream."

"But I'm here. Don't men like to realize their dreams?"

He looked away from her again. "You d-d-don't understand."

But she did; adoration was what he was after. Perhaps he would like her better if she were on an altar.

"What did you buy today?" she asked, dismissing her thought.

He reached into his trouser pocket and brought out the two mediocre pearls and held them in his palm.

"They're not r-r-right for you. I want s-s-something p-p-perfect for you."

"You don't have to buy me anything, David," she said, and seeing the wounded expression on his very young face, she smiled. "I'm sorry you haven't found the black pearls you're looking for."

"Has a-a-anything I've d-d-done displeased you?" he asked.

"Do I seem displeased? I don't mean to. You've been more than generous."

"We've stayed in Tahiti t-t-too long. I've been told there's another island where they've f-f-found good pearls. Would you like to go there?"

"If you'd like."

"I could have them t-t-take you ashore again. I d-d-don't like touring, but you could go round the island again with B-b-bedloe."

"David, it's nothing you've done."

"It's what I haven't d-d-done," he said now, looking more wounded than ever.

"It's all right. Everything is all right."

And he moved closer, until she could hear the quick intake of his breath.

"I adore you, Margot. I c-c-can't even pretend to cover it up or p-p-play the j-j-jaded lover." His hands came up to touch her but remained poised at her shoulders.

"I'm not made of glass," she whispered.

"You're like the pearls themselves—pure and p-p-perfect."

"Much less perfect than you think."

"And I know that you must care for me—came halfway round the world to be with me."

"Of course I care for you."

"I'm so much in love with you—" he began, but he stopped himself and, leaning over, looking as if he'd mustered up all his resolve, he kissed her.

It was such a soft kiss, like a schoolboy's or the kiss of an aging, grateful lover. Looking at him, seeing the guileless look in his eyes, she brought her hands up to his face and kissed him more urgently.

"You do c-c-care for me," he said, stepping back, holding her hands as if the kiss had been the culmination of his lovemaking. Then, looking around for the steward, he said, "We sh-sh-should have some wine."

"I don't need any wine," she said softly.

"W-w-wouldn't you like that? I would. S-s-some wine," he said, going off to look for the steward. And she was left feeling stranded, half amused and frustrated. Turning, she laughed when she saw *A Harlot High and Low* lying face up on a wicker chaise lounge.

Chapter Twenty

"I'VE DEALT WITH these people before," Jenks was saying. "If you give me a percentage, I'll get you the best price in Papeete for the pearls."

He must be recovering, Tom thought, standing next to Jenks on a spit of land opposite the camp, whittling an *oka paru*, a wooden fishing spear, which Teva had taught him to use.

"I don't want to give a percentage to anyone," Tom said without looking up from his work.

"But I know how to trade with the Chinese dealers in Papeete—my *vahine* was Chinese," Jenks said, rubbing the scabs on the left side of his face with the back of his hand.

"You'll start bleeding again if you keep doing that," Tom said.

"We've been here for months. I've got to get off this island, get to Papara."

"Where's that?"

"On Tahiti. It's where my son lives. If I take your pearls with me, I can get you good money. I know these Chinese merchants. I can help."

"When the time comes, we'll all go."

Jenks shrugged, then took a step or two into the shallow water. The yellow sharks were cruising near his feet like sniffing terriers.

"How many pearls did Teva find yesterday?"

"Three more."

"How much longer do you think this will be kept secret? If we start now, get to Papeete with what we've got, we can get the best prices."

"How do you propose we get there?"

"We'll have Teva take us to his village. They've got ocean-going canoes."

Raina, who was sitting nearby, looked over at Tom, signaling to him with a wave of her hand. It was the same every day, as if her body had a clock in it and at a certain moment the pleasure alarm went off.

Jenks snickered. "But you've got more important things to think about than making a good price for your pearls."

"What do I need money for? I've got everything I need."

"Please, boyzo, paradise lasts for a month, maybe two, four at the outside, but we've been here five months."

Raina, giggling, began walking toward their clearing.

"What do you talk about with her?" Jenks asked.

"Who talks?"

"That should keep you interested for as long as you can maintain your erection."

"I rest my case," Tom said lightly, and although he still eagerly ran after her every time she waved at him, he was not oblivious to what Jenks was saying.

She turned to look back at him, dropped her sarong, then started running down the beach, her tight buttocks bouncing gently with each step.

"You're thinking with your cock," Jenks said. "Roosters do that, bulls in the field do that."

But Tom had dropped the fishing spear and had already taken off after her.

That afternoon they were diving in deeper water. It was their largest catch in a single afternoon, almost fifty shells. At night they sat in a line, Teva opening the shells, then passing them to Raina, who scooped out the meat. Then she gave them to Tom, who searched both the meat and the shell for pearls. They had finished scooping out Tom's catch —nothing tonight—and they were working on Teva's when Jenks suddenly got to his feet.

"What did I tell you, boyzo? Company!"

Raina ran down to the water.

"Hopu i raro," she called out to Teva.

"Divers, she's saying," Jenks said.

In the distance were specks of light as tiny as fireflies.

"How many do you think there are?"

"What difference does it make? They'll see your haul, and the place will be overrun."

Tom began making plans. He would hide his pearls somewhere behind the clearing, then he'd categorize the shells, separating them by size and color so that if merchants were accompanying the divers, they could see at a glance which were the best. First thing tomorrow morning he and Teva would head west in the canoe to scout more beds, to get the jump on the divers.

But by midmorning the next day, it became apparent that the beds they had been fishing were the best. That afternoon they returned to them. Tom made more dives than he ever had, and by the end of the day his nose and right ear were bleeding badly and the pain inside his head would not stop.

The first canoes showed up early the following morning. In them were friends of Teva's and Raina's, two young men from Turipaoa. Before the diving began, Tom told all four of them that he would give them the pick of his shells if they would share their catch with him fifty-fifty.

"Now you're talking," Jenks called out, walking down to the water to hear their conversation.

Tom was motioning with his hands, first to the shells, then to Teva and Raina and the other two.

"Aufau," Jenks said, then winked at Tom, "means pay."

Then Jenks went on explaining the situation in his pidgin Tahitian.

Teva and Raina looked dismayed at first, but then went along with it, and the four went off to dive.

"God only knows what you told them."

"Just what you wanted me to tell them," Jenks said.

"First thing I'm going to do when we get to Papeete is learn the language."

"Don't you trust me, boyzo?" Jenks asked with a smile.

That afternoon and the following day more and more boats showed up—about a dozen divers in all and Tom made separate deals with six of them; for a percentage he would personally negotiate the sale of the shells to the merchants.

By the third day the western section of the lagoon opposite the camp was filled with divers, and then the first of the merchants showed up—two Chinese men from Turipaoa, looking for pearls and mother-of-pearl shells. Tom disposed of all the shells, clearing two francs more per kilo than the divers usually got.

"The white man prevails," Jenks said, eyeing the money.

Tom made thirty francs on the deal and gave Jenks five for acting as interpreter.

"I'll need more than this to get to Papeete."

"Then you'll have to be patient," Tom said, loading the catch onto the Chinamen's canoe.

The next day the hordes descended. More divers than Tom would have believed existed on the little atoll all staked out sites and began diving, and at night they overran the camp, sleeping on every available inch of sand.

Two days later Thierry, with blank-faced, bearded Hugo in tow, arrived from Tahiti, guiding a fat, bug-eyed Frenchman named Thibeau, who was dressed in creased gray linen. Thierry was surprised and slightly intimidated by Tom's and Jenks's presence. He'd obviously told Thibeau that he would be the only white man there. As soon as Thibeau came ashore, he began poking around the camp, seeing if there were any pearls for sale.

Tom, following a hunch, decided to hold back his pearls, but he told Thibeau that his diver, Teva, had found some, and Teva went off to fetch them.

Thibeau was fanning off the flies under a coconut tree at one end of the encampment, and Thierry and Hugo were talking with the other divers, trying to make side deals, when suddenly Teva came running out of his hut with his empty matchbox and told Tom that his pearls were missing.

"Any of them could have stolen those pearls," Jenks whispered into Tom's ear, staring at the circle of divers and Thierry and Hugo, who were skulking on the edge of the crowd, looking suspicious.

But suddenly Thierry looked up and, seeing something startling, ran down to the water's edge. In a moment everyone was running into the water.

"My God!" Jenks said.

Tom's eyes widened. Coming toward them from the eastern end of the lagoon was the largest yacht he had ever seen, the *Distant Star.*

Chapter
Twenty-one

"THAT YOUNG, STUTTERING Jew," Thibeau said, staring as the yacht dropped anchor. "He throws too much money around."

"Who is he?" Jenks called out.

"David Nasis, son of a Jew banker."

"Is he a pearl-buyer?" Tom asked.

"Fancies himself that."

"There's a woman on deck with him."

"*Oui*—always," Thierry called out over his shoulder. "Keeps her locked up out there. Doesn't want anyone to see her."

"I've seen her," Thibeau said with a sniff. "Her name is Lady Margot Vale."

"You can keep your Chinese pearl merchants in Papeete," Tom said to Jenks, "I think our limey friend out there and the Frenchman are about to provide me with a killing."

He and Jenks watched as the tender was lowered into the water. The man got in first, then held his hand up for the woman, and when she was settled, the crew began rowing for shore. Tom walked into the water to get a better look at her. Jenks was close behind.

She was holding a lace parasol above her head. It being midday, the sun was directly above, throwing shadowy lines over her face.

Tom held his hands up over his eyes and saw her reddish golden hair, her clear, flushed skin, and deep-set eyes.

"She's a beauty," he said. "What in the world is she doing out here?"

"She takes one look at the two of us in our loincloths, with our beards and tangled hair, she'll run."

The tender was pulled ashore by the crewmen.

"Monsieur Nasis," Thierry called out, and David turned, offering him a stiff nod.

"Ahoy, *Distant Star,*" Tom called out, waving his hand in the air.

Nasis was startled to hear an American accent, and Margot lowered her parasol and stared at Tom.

Tom suddenly felt ashamed of his appearance. He thought she'd look away, but she continued staring at him.

Walking toward Nasis with his hand outstretched, Tom called out, "Hello, Mr. Nasis. My name is Tom Street."

Nasis came ashore and shook Tom's hand. When Tom turned to help Margot from the tender, her eyes widened. She didn't know where to look, or more precisely, where not to look first, so her eyes remained fixed on his.

"We'd heard there were only Tahitians on these atolls," she said.

"I apologize for the costume, or lack of one. It's just that I have nothing else."

David Nasis also extended his hand to help Margot down from the boat.

"D-d-do you live here?" he asked.

"Our ship was blown up—we were saved by these people," Tom said, pointing at Teva and Raina. Teva smiled, but Raina was busy appraising Margot.

"You're lucky to be alive," Margot said.

"Yes," he said distractedly. Her presence suddenly made him feel sad; his mind was filled with memories of Jelly.

"Have you been alone all this time?"

"No, I've been with another crewman from our ship, Jenks," he said, looking over his shoulder, but Jenks had disappeared.

Thibeau, fanning himself with a lace-trimmed handkerchief, sniffed a good day to both Nasis and Margot as they walked up to the huts and began inspecting the camp.

"Have we b-b-beaten the m-m-middlemen to the source?" Nasis asked Thierry.

"Too late, Monsieur Nasis."

"Everything's g-g-gone?"

"The Chinamen from Turipaoa took the best shells."

"And the pearls?" Margot asked.

"Nothing worth your time—what little there was has been stolen, madame."

"Not entirely," Tom suddenly said. "I have some pearls that may be of interest to you."

"Did you buy them from the divers?" Margot asked.

"Oh, no, Lady Vale. I've also been diving. I have three pearls for sale."

Tom took out only two of them, holding back the perfect one.

Nasis, Thierry, Margot, and Thibeau huddled around him inspecting the pearls, each holding them for a moment. Thibeau took out his loupe and stared at them.

"Very nice," he said.

"I'll t-t-take them," Nasis said sharply.

"But he hasn't set a price," Thibeau sniffed.

"How much will you pay?" Tom asked Nasis.

"T-t-two hundred for the pair."

Thierry moved close next to Tom and whispered, "That's what he paid for two I sold him that weren't as nice—let me handle this."

But Tom disregarded him, speaking instead to Thibeau. "And you, monsieur?"

Thibeau's lips were screwed up skeptically, but his bulging eyes remained riveted on the pair of pearls. Smirking at Nasis, he said, "Two-fifty."

"Three," Nasis countered.

"Three-fifty."

"F-f-five and be done with it," Nasis said, then turning to one of his crewmen, called out, "Bedloe, b-b-bring me the money."

"Monsieur Thibeau?" Tom asked, disregarding Nasis.

Thibeau, nibbling on his lower lip, finally exhaled disgustedly.

"Monsieur Nasis, in this business the object is not to come in and buy everything in sight for whatever you wish to pay."

Nasis, to his credit, Tom thought, did not answer him.

"Sold to Mr. Nasis," Tom said.

"You s-s-said there were th-th-three pearls."

"The last one is very special."

"I w-w-would have th-th-thought as much."

Reaching inside a small satchel, Tom pulled out the prize, holding it up between his index finger and thumb.

There was a dead silence, then Margot stepped forward to look at it.

"May I?" she asked. He placed it in the palm of her hand. "It's the most beautiful black pearl I've ever seen," she said.

Nasis and Thibeau eyed it covetously.

"Where did you find it?" she asked.

"Nearby, in the lagoon."

"No one's owned it before?"

Tom laughed. "The sea."

"Yes, I like that," Margot said, thinking of the black pearl in Madame Duntov's prediction.

"This one, gentlemen, has a starting price. One thousand."

"Absurd!" Thibeau cried, then brought out his loupe and inspected it again.

"That's r-r-rather steep."

"I'll give you a thousand," Thibeau sniffed.

"T-t-twelve hundred."

"Fifteen, not a *centime* more."

"T-t-two."

Thibeau, turning away, groaned, then muttered, "Twenty-five, my final offer."

"Th-th-three," Nasis said with a smile.

"Four," Margot said.

Nasis blanched.

"You, Lady Vale?"

"Yes, I'd like to buy it," she said. Then, looking at Nasis, "David, is three your final bid?"

"B-b-but it was to be f-f-for you."

"Thank you, but I want to buy it for myself."

"Please let me b-b-buy it for you."

"No, David, I insist. My bid is four."

"Going once . . . twice . . . sold to Lady Vale," Tom said, handing her the pearl.

"My money is on the boat. Will you join us this evening for dinner, and I'll give it to you then—David, dinner is all right, isn't it?"

Nasis nodded.

"I haven't eaten with anything but my hands in a long time."

"Amazing how fast it comes back to you," Margot said with a smile. "At dinner, then," she said, walking away, clutching the pearl tightly in her left hand.

Nasis, watching her carefully, had Bedloe count out the five hundred he owed Tom, then he took the pearls and followed after Margot.

Tom walked them to the tender, then looked down at himself. "I haven't any clothes for dinner."

"David, will you lend him some?" Margot asked.

"Y-y-yes, of c-c-course, if you'd l-l-like."

"Everything I had was blown to smithereens on the ship."

"Which ship was it?"

"Medusa," Tom said, and hearing the name, Margot looked at him with as startled an expression as he had ever seen.

_____ *Chapter* _____
Twenty-two

THAT NIGHT TOM appeared in the yacht's mahogany-paneled dining room clean-shaven, wearing one of David's white linen suits. Margot tried splitting her attention equally between the two men, but she could not. She was fascinated by Tom, and Nasis was jealous.

"I've always w-w-wondered what makes a m-m-man put out to s-s-sea," Nasis was saying. "What sort of l-l-life did you leave b-b-behind, Mr. Street?"

Tom hesitated for a moment, placing his soup spoon beside the blue and white Canton tureen in front of him.

"I was a lawyer."

"Where?"

"In New York."

"Wh-wh-which firm?"

Tom's fist tightened. "It was another life," he said offhandedly.

"Th-th-that sounds suspiciously vague. D-d-did you v-v-vanish to the South Seas with the f-f-funds?" Nasis asked with a contrived laugh.

"Nothing that dramatic," Tom said tensely. "I was a junior partner about to be made a slightly less junior partner. I decided to walk away from it."

Margot changed the subject. "What's the law compared with pearl diving? Have you actually done it?"

"I found that very one," Tom said, pointing at the pearl Margot had bought from him, which she'd placed on a silk handkerchief next to her plate.

"There's no other place on earth that produces a pearl this color," she said, studying it.

"I'd like to learn about the different pearl-producing regions and the different colors. The ones around your neck, for instance," he said, indicating a choker of rosé pearls.

"From the Persian Gulf; a creamy, pinkish color—similar to Ceylon pearls."

"And which are the whitest?"

"From Australia—although even there the colors vary. The Shark's Bay pearl from northwest Australia has a yellowish tint. The Thursday Island pearls are the purest white."

"Margot has t-t-taught me a great deal of what I know about p-p-pearls," Nasis interrupted.

"Venezuelan pearls are creamy, sometimes mistaken for the Oriental," Margot said to Tom. "Disreputable jewelers will often try to blend them."

"But you can spot the difference," Tom said, egging her on.

"It's an acquired skill, like a wine taster's. And one must have a certain flair for knowing the deep lustre that radiates from the very heart of an Oriental that can be found in no other," she said as her index finger rolled over the luminous surface of the black pearl.

Nasis drummed his fingers on the table, unable to hide his anxiety.

117

"Please continue," Tom said to Margot.

"I'll do better than that," she said, rising. "I'll fetch my jewel case. Please don't get up."

Leaving the table, she went back to her stateroom.

Nasis was staring appraisingly at Tom, as Tom, amazed to be surrounded by so much luxury, took in the ornate room; candlelight sparkled weblike from etched crystal globes on the sterling silver chandelier and was reflected, like smoldering flames, in the dark red walls. There were sterling silver wall sconces in a seashell design and Georgian silver candelabras and table service. The damask tablecloth was embroidered with a seashell pattern, and in the center was a large embroidered *N*.

"So, Mr. Street, you w-w-were a c-c-clerk in a law f-f-firm," David said in a superior tone.

"No, sir, a junior partner."

"Which f-f-firm was it?"

"Puddy, Cuddahay," Tom said quickly.

"On Wall Street. My uncles have d-d-dealt with them."

Tom stared at Nasis with more interest. "How long will you be staying in the South Seas, Mr. Nasis?"

"Now I've g-g-gone and d-d-done it, asked t-t-too many p-p-personal questions. Now you can't wait for us to l-l-lift anchor."

"Perhaps it's you who can't wait to leave."

"Whatever do you m-m-mean?"

"How long have you known Lady Vale?"

"What sort of q-q-question is that?" Nasis asked, red-faced.

"Is there a Lord Vale?"

"He's d-d-deceased," Nasis said, flustered.

"She's lovely."

"Th-th-that's obvious. I'm a very l-l-lucky m-m-man," Nasis began, but he stopped because Margot had come back into the room.

"This is my finest strand," she said as she approached them, opening a velvet case from which she took a long strand of creamy pink pearls. "They belonged to my mother. They're from the Persian Gulf." Standing beside Tom's chair, she took out several other strands. "These are also rare—Madras pearls."

A steward brought in the fish course.

"The Madras are like Persian Gulf pearls but have an added metallic quality," she was saying, reaching down to touch them, grazing Tom's hand, then retracting her own.

"This one is beautiful," Tom said, holding up a large single pearl fashioned as a drop pendant capped with diamonds.

"What a good eye you have. It's from Panama—parti-colored. See how the colors shade into one another?"

"Like a sunset," Tom said, placing it in her hand, grazing her arm with his hand.

Nasis coughed. "The fish is g-g-getting c-c-cold," he said.

Margot took her seat, continuing her instruction as she ate, and Nasis stared suspiciously at Tom from the head of the table.

After dinner they sat in the main saloon, which also had mahogany walls and silver sconces. As a steward poured brandy into cut-crystal snifters, Margot continued talking about pearls and Nasis asked more prying questions.

Tom was attentive, defending himself against Nasis's subtle jibes; he had not lost his social skills altogether. In fact, he found himself missing his former life.

"Will you stay on this atoll?" Margot was asking.

"I'm not sure."

"Because if you'd like, we're heading for Tahiti tomorrow."

"Margot, I d-d-don't th-th-think Mr. Street n-n-needs rescuing."

Margot turned away from Nasis and faced Tom directly. "I don't mean to pry, Mr. Street, but could you actually spend the rest of your life out here?"

"Is that so extraordinary?"

"Yes."

"But it's something you'd admire."

Her eyes and hair were catching the play of the candle-light and the glint of the silver. She was radiant.

"Yes."

"Why?"

"Because it is extraordinary, I suppose," she said.

"An extraordinary life is what I'm after."

"I've always thought that to choose such a life, one would

have to pay an extraordinary price," she said tentatively, waiting to see how what she said had affected him.

Thinking about his children, he smiled sadly, then rose and said that he should be getting back to the camp.

Nasis said good night stiffly, then Margot gave Tom the money she owed him for the black pearl and, taking his arm, leaving Nasis behind, walked Tom out to the deck.

"I apologize for Mr. Nasis and myself; we spent the evening prying."

"It was interesting being in the world again."

"You must miss it."

"Not entirely," Tom said, staring out at the fires burning on shore.

"Why don't you miss it? I really don't mean to pry. I need to know for myself."

"This world," Tom said staring at her, then back at the richly lighted saloon, "is so exquisitely tense."

"But it's your world. I saw how you handled yourself. How could you have turned your back on it?"

"Is that what you want to do, Lady Vale?"

"I'm not that brave," she said.

Smiling at her, he said good night.

When he reached the shore, Raina was waiting for him, looking a little frightened of him as she stroked his smooth face. He held her, but his eyes were riveted on the yacht.

Damn all civilized women, he said to himself as Raina began pulling him toward their clearing. But this time he held back, and she broke away and ran up the beach toward Teva's hut.

Drunken laughter rang out nearby.

Thibeau and Thierry were sitting around a fire, swapping shots of cognac. Thibeau stared up drunkenly as Tom approached, then reached into his pocket and pulled out a handful of pearls.

"They're not up to your standards, monsieur, but at least I'm not leaving paradise empty-handed," Thibeau said.

"Where'd you get these?" Tom asked, inspecting them.

"Paid good money for them."

"Not to Teva," Tom said, pulling Thierry up by the scruff of his neck. "You stole these."

"No, monsieur!" Thierry screamed out.

"Like hell he did."

"Where'd you get them?"

"From the Englishman."

"What Eng—from Jenks? Jenks! Jenks!" Tom called out, letting drop Thierry to the sand.

"Won't do you any good, monsieur—he's gone."

"Gone where?"

"Paid Hugo to take him to Turipaoa, from there to Tahiti."

Tom stood at the water's edge, his anger rising. He cupped his hands around his mouth and shouted, "Jenks! Come back here you bloody bastard!"

"Left hours ago."

Tom whirled around, pointing at Thierry. "You've got a canoe."

"We'll never catch him."

Then, turning back toward the yacht, Tom said, "Don't worry, I'll catch him."

_____ *Chapter* _____
Twenty-three

JENKS, ILL-KEMPT AND unshaven, moved cautiously but quickly through the streets of Papeete. The French officers who sat drinking in the treehouse bar off the Avenue Bruat, the broad, central tree-lined street of town, turned to look at him, wondering if he was a vagrant or a troublemaker. First things first, Jenks was thinking. Get rid of the clothes, become less conspicuous.

Walking up the Rue de Rivoli, past a government house, he turned abruptly, thinking he was being followed, but it was only a line of silent native women, wearing broad-brimmed hats and oversized dresses, making their way to the church.

On the Rue de la Petite Pologne, a narrow dirt street darkened by the thick growth of intertwining tree limbs overhead, Jenks went into a dry-goods store, S. Drollet's. He bought a proper pair of trousers, a coat and shirt, some shoes, and a tightly woven straw hat. Then, paying M. Drollet an extra ten francs, he was shown upstairs to a tiny apartment, where he bathed and where Mme. Drollet, a languid, sloe-eyed mixed Chinese Polynesian, shaved him and cut his hair.

Afterward he walked more casually down the Avenue Bruat. He could have been a plantation owner in town for the day or a ship's broker. The French officers in the treehouse bar nodded when he walked by. He tipped his hat, sat down, and ordered beer after beer, then switched to something heartier. The afternoon wore on slowly.

Papeete was a melancholy place, neither French nor Polynesian, a backwash. Natives carrying bushels of coconuts walked by, followed by French ladies clutching their parasols or their skirts or their small children. Jenks found that suddenly he wasn't so eager to see his son. The boy expected Jenks to take him away. Jenks had filled his head with stories of England, but now Jenks couldn't take him anywhere.

By late afternoon Jenks was drunk, but not too drunk to know that he was incurring suspicion. He had been sitting in the same chair for hours, and two gendarmes were circling the bar. After paying for his drinks, he slipped out, then vanished down a side street.

On the Boulevard Pomare, a street that curved along the harbor, he hired a horse and carriage to take him to Papara, a village near the church school where Paul lived.

On the bumpy ride Jenks became more melancholy. He had no home and could not provide his son with one. The only money he'd made, he'd spent.

It was dark by the time the driver stopped beside a whitewashed church. Beside it were several thatched huts. Jenks gave the driver a franc and lumbered into the church. A tall priest with pale skin and black hair was reading by candlelight. He looked up without surprise as Jenks walked in.

"You've come back," the priest said.

"To see my son," Jenks answered sullenly.

"He's still with us."

"That's why I left him here—you're the only ones I trust to keep him."

"After you left the last time, he ran off. He kept running off till we convinced him that you weren't in Papeete any longer and that his mother was indeed dead."

"But you get him back every time, don't you? Once you've got them, you never lose them."

"The truth of it is, where else does he have to go? Her people don't want him because he looks too much like you. He's western in their eyes. He thinks you're coming to take him home to England. But you haven't come to take him back to England, have you?"

Jenks looked down and stared at his mud-splattered new shoes, then shook his head. "I've got some money for you," he muttered, "to keep him awhile longer, till I can collect him."

"I see. Of course we'll keep him. And he doesn't run off anymore. He's a smart boy."

"Do you hate me, Father?" Jenks asked, looking up at the priest with a baleful gaze.

"I don't find you hateful. I find you unregenerate."

"Then will you hear my confession?" Jenks asked, moving over to the priest.

"Are you Catholic, Monsieur Jenks?"

Jenks knelt beside the priest and blew out the candle.

"I'll make my confession anyway—in the dark. Isn't that the way? In the dark and I say, 'Hail Mary, mother of God, forgive me for I know not what I do.'"

"Monsieur Jenks, I can't hear your confession—" the priest began, but Jenks covered the priest's mouth roughly with his hands.

"You heard the rumors that I killed the boy's mother," he hissed. "The courts said no. My greatest crime is that I am my own creation, and I despise the world that forced me to be what I am . . ." Then, more quietly, he added, "Hating myself and the world isn't the worst of crimes, is it?" And after a while he withdrew his hands and hung his head, feeling, as the priest had described him, unregenerate.

Sighing, he reached inside his coat, took out his remaining francs, and dropped them to the floor.

"I want to see him, but I don't want him to know I'm here. Tell him you got a letter, that I'm getting more money and I'll come to take him away as soon as I have it."

The priest walked Jenks down a low corridor to the kitchen. Opening the door a crack, Jenks, his face pressed against the doorjamb, looked in and saw a row of boys sitting at a long wooden table. Some were native boys with dark eyes and brown skin, and one or two were European. At the end of the table was Paul, who was fair-skinned but had Eurasian features—high, sculpted cheekbones, almond-shaped dark eyes, dark hair, and Jenks's full mouth. He looked sullen.

A native boy to his right made a grab for the last piece of bread on the tray, but Paul, without looking up from his plate, grabbed the boy's wrist and applied just the right amount of pressure with his thumb and middle finger to make the boy release the bread. Then Paul took the bread for himself.

"Bully Jenks's other creation," Jenks said dispiritedly, then he closed the door and, without acknowledging the priest, left the church.

The next morning he awakened in a nearby village called Mataiea, in a house that was owned by a native woman who had many "daughters," whom she rented out to visitors. Jenks had arrived in the middle of the night, demanding booze and a woman, whom he mistreated. He covered her face with a sack, which he tied tightly around her neck so that he didn't have to look at her, and took her from the rear. Her compliance made him want to abuse her.

Now he was alone on a woven mat, the sun slanting in through the open window above him. His eyes were throbbing, and his head felt as if it were swollen to twice its normal size.

Pulling on his clothes, he wandered out onto the wide veranda, which overlooked a small lagoon. Sitting on the floor was a sailor with a grizzled, puffy face and a coat of black hair covering his chest, back, and shoulders. Staring dull-eyed into the sun, he sipped from a bottle.

"You buying for the house or do you want to drink alone?" Jenks asked, sitting down beside him.

The man passed Jenks his bottle. "You made quite a racket last night," the sailor said—he was an American. "What ship you off?"

"It was a long time ago—don't even remember her name. And you?"

"A pearling fleet owned by a Brit named Hard-cross."

"Ah, pearls," Jenks said, looking down at the deep, clear water. "Not an easy way to make a living."

"Not in these waters. It's all fished out here. Pity, too, 'cause the beds was plentiful ten years ago, when I first come here."

"Where you heading next?"

"Hardcross is tight of money. We're here lookin' for some. Supposed to be a rich Jew around with a yacht. Hardcross is goin' to try 'n' cut him in to get us under way again. You interested in shippin' out?"

"Maybe, but tell me. What's his proposition to the rich Jew? What's he selling him?"

"We heard some reports comin' out of Ceylon. Last year had the biggest fishery they ever held, and this year the beds is supposed to be better."

"Ceylon's far away."

"But if the beds're as rich as they say, makes the trip worthwhile. Hardcross wants to use Tahitian divers—more honest than the Arabs you find in Ceylon and sure as hell the deepest divers. Wants to bring a bunch of 'em—with their women to keep 'em happy—let 'em dive in Ceylon. Hell, water's water, right?"

Jenks's looked at the sailor with more interest.

"What sort of a man is Hardcross? What's he like to work under?"

"He's like the rest of 'em, maybe a bit better. He's not above swappin' a drink or two with the crew."

Of course not, Jenks thought. That's why he's so hard up for money.

"I'll put in a good word for you if you want to sign on. What's y'ur name?"

Jenks stood up, his head clearing.

"Y'ur name. I mean, if you want me to put in a good word with Hardcross, I got to know y'ur name."

"Lucifer," Jenks called out as he walked back into the hut.

"Lucifer? That's one hell of a name, you don't mind me saying."

"It's a hard name to live up to, but I try," Jenks said with a cackle, quickening his pace, a plan forming.

Chapter
Twenty-four

THAT AFTERNOON JENKS watched as the *Distant Star* put in at Papeete. When Margot and Tom were brought ashore in a tender, Jenks, hiding behind some cargo barrels, heard Tom order a carriage to take them to Papara.

After they left, Jenks stole a skiff from the dock and rowed out to the yacht.

Nasis was sprawled out on one of the wicker chaise longues on the aft deck, refilling his champagne glass.

Jenks appraised the situation in one glance; Margot had run off with Tom and Nasis was drinking himself into coma.

Looking up suddenly, Nasis was startled. "Who are you?"

"Jenks."

"Street's Jenks? But he's gone off looking for you." Getting to his feet, Nasis rushed to the rail. "If you hurry, you can catch them," he said, trying to pick out the carriage on the west road.

"If I could just talk with you a moment, Nasis."

"But if you hurry, you can catch them." He looked frantic. "I'll have my man row you to shore."

"She's run off with him?"

"D-d-don't put it like that. She's taking him to find you."

"She's a beautiful woman."

"Oh, she's the l-l-loveliest woman in all the w-w-world,

126

and so unpredictable. Came halfw-w-way round the world to s-s-see me."

"She's in love with you."

Nasis turned to Jenks with a brooding but hopeful expression in his eyes. "What I thought, t-t-too—why else would a w-w-woman travel halfway r-r-round the w-w-world . . ."

Here is a very spoiled bugger, Jenks was thinking, susceptible to encouragement and advice. "She loves adventure," he said, "and I'd think you were in the perfect business to give her a life of it. There are plenty of opportunities around."

"N-n-not out here."

"No, but plenty of other places. Arabia, Ceylon."

"She wants to g-g-go to Ceylon. To a place there called M-m-mannar."

"Said that, did she? There's plenty of opportunities there if you have the right business idea."

Just then a voice boomed up at them from the port side of the boat. Jenks saw a middle-aged man standing in a small rowboat.

"Mr. Nasis?"

"Who wants him?"

"Lavelle Hardcross."

Jenks thought quickly as Nasis came up beside him.

"Are you Mr. Nasis?"

"Yes."

Jenks turned away from the rail and whispered into Nasis's ear. "I know this man—let me handle it for you."

"Why? Who is he?"

"He's no one you should know," Jenks said, then seized the conversation. "Go sober up before you come calling on English gentlemen."

"How dare you talk to me that way!" Hardcross yelled, shaking his fist at Jenks.

"I've known this man for years," Jenks said to Nasis. "He's made a profession of business partnerships with unsuspecting souls."

"What? Come down here and say that to my face."

"Hardcross, do you deny that you rowed all the way out here to tap Mr. Nasis for a loan?"

"Well . . ."

"Well? Can you deny it?"

"I have a business proposition for him . . ."

"Need we be bothered with this man any longer? Would you like me to get rid of him? I hate to have your crew trouble themselves."

"Th-th-that's what they're paid for. Bedloe!"

As Jenks popped open another bottle of champagne, the sounds of a scuffle reached the deck, then Hardcross rowed away from the yacht and headed to shore.

"Where were we before he came by?" Jenks asked, handing Nasis his glass. "Ceylon. I have sources in Ceylon who tell me that last year's catch was the biggest on record. They're expecting the same this year."

"Margot mentioned this."

Jenks pointedly watched Hardcross row to shore. "Devious old Hardcross once had a first-rate pearling operation. Used Tahitian divers—they're the best, and they don't rob you blind," he said over his shoulder. Then turning, he added, "You know, I just had an idea that could help you. Why should the Hardcrosses of the world always be the ones to profit?" And he proceeded to outline Hardcross's idea of using Tahitian divers in Ceylon. "You'd wind up controlling the catch out there, and Tom Street is friendly with some of the best divers on Manihi . . ."

Hearing the name, Nasis flinched.

"And there's another thing I'm thinking," Jenks said, putting his arm protectively around Nasis's shoulder. "If you have Street come along with the divers, you've got him under your own roof, where you can watch him—and nothing wipes out romantic notions as quickly as familiarity."

Nasis began to look hopeful. "But can we get her back before anything more happens?"

Hearing the word *we*, Jenks breathed easily for the first time since he'd come onboard. "Of course we can. You leave it all to me, David. I may call you David, mayn't I?" Jenks asked, but Nasis was fixated elsewhere.

"Can you get her back here before nightfall?"

"David, I tell you she's as good as here," Jenks said, looking down at the western end of the Boulevard Pomare.

"... AND YOU'RE SURE we're talking about the same man —burns on his face, my height, dark hair," Tom said to the priest as they stood outside the whitewashed church.

"I know who Jenks is, monsieur. You are a friend of his?"

"We were onboard a ship together," Tom said, looking back at Margot, who was sitting in the carriage. Their eyes met, and she held his gaze.

"I'm sorry, monsieur. By this time Jenks is probably back in Papeete."

"Did he take the boy with him?"

"Monsieur?"

"I know about his son. Jenks gave you money for the boy. The money wasn't his to give."

"I don't ask Jenks too many questions about things like this. I am sorry if he has stolen money from you, monsieur."

"Not from me—from one of the natives."

"This is unfortunate but not unexpected. He didn't leave that much money, and what he did leave I've already spent. I'm sorry I can't help you. I don't think he'll be back. Good-bye."

Margot continued to stare at Tom as he walked back to the carriage, and she was smiling. She had, Tom thought, the most knowing smile, both reassuring and daunting.

"Any luck?"

"No, he's gone back to Papeete."

"Should we hurry back?"

"It doesn't matter now," he said, looking up the road. As he got into the carriage, he told the driver to take them back to Papeete, but slowly.

Sitting close to her now, he smelled her fresh, perfumed scent—gardenias, Jelly's scent. He wondered how much like Jelly she was.

"Something's made you smile," she said.

"Have you known Nasis long?"

"No, not very long."

"Are you in love with him?"

"That's a very personal question."

"Well, here we are on a carriage ride on a tropical island. I suppose we could talk about the weather."

"No, I'm not in love with him. We're friends."

"He seems to be in love with you."

"I'd say you were right."

"Women pride themselves on getting men to fall in love with them."

"Not all women," she said.

"Only those of a certain class who have no real power over their lives."

"Has that been your experience, Mr. Street?"

"My experience tells me that men are quite susceptible to romance and women are actually very practical about it."

He was curious to see her reaction to this, but Margot merely looked uncertain as to where his conversation was leading.

"Perhaps I've just been out on that island too long." Moving closer, he brought his hand up to her hair. "A woman like you wouldn't want me to be too civilized, would you? Which do you prefer, Lady Vale? The man in the linen suit or the man in the loincloth?"

"There's a grotto," she said, somewhat flustered, pointing to a cave hollowed out at the base of a mountain. "Would you like to look at it?"

"Yes, of course."

The carriage stopped, and climbing down, he went around to take her arm.

"I can manage," she said, but she let him help her down.

"I've made you angry."

"Not at all," she said, walking past him into the grotto, where water dripped into a shallow, clear pool and everything was green, vividly alive. "But as long as we're talking in generalities, why is it men think they can change a woman's mood with a single word? I'm stronger than that, Mr. Street."

"I'm acting like a boor," he said, walking up beside her. "Especially when I consider the trouble you've gone to."

"Trouble? What trouble?" she said, turning toward him.

"To have us be alone. It was obvious that Mr. Nasis wanted to join us, but you persuaded him not to. I understand your situation."

"Do you?" she said wryly.

"You're not in love with Nasis. He's mad for you, keeps you in wonderful style—"

"Keeps me? How do you explain my having enough money to purchase the black pearl from you?"

"That just proves how smart you are—you have him thinking you're independent and don't need his money."

"I see," she said, and turned away from him. But not before Tom caught the beginnings of a smile.

"And this carriage ride is risky for you." He persisted. "I know that. He saw how interested you were in being alone with me. But there's no harm done. You can go back to the boat with a perfectly clear conscience."

"Oh, thank you very much."

"You see, I do understand your position. A woman like you can afford just so much independence."

"*A woman like you,*" Margot said, suddenly turning around to face him again. "You keep using that phrase. You'd like to see me safely put in some category or other. But I warn you—I don't stay put that easily."

"Now I *have* made you angry."

"You're making inroads," she said crisply. "Mr. Street, I wanted to take this ride with you because I thought it might be interesting to talk with you."

"You thought I'd be exotic."

"Not so much exotic as interesting. It isn't every day I meet a man who's been stranded on an island."

"I imagine you'd need some of that after a dose of Nasis."

"Please leave David out of this."

"Not that I think he isn't a perfectly nice man. But he's like a puppy—just follows your every move with his big, sad eyes. But a woman like you would want a man like that, wouldn't you?"

"Let's go look at a ruin," she said abruptly and started to walk back toward the carriage.

Tom did not utter another word. He felt as if Jelly had come back into his life. Although Margot was more beautiful, and had a far better mind and was by far more spirited, she was still like Jelly—pampered, suspended somewhere between a desire for freedom and her tepid, enslaving love affairs.

The ruin, called a *marae,* consisted of several carved wood totems, their happy, stolid faces and genitalia intact, scattered here and there amid black, crusty volcanic rock. There was also an altar made of rocks that looked like either skulls or cannonballs.

Although they stood a distance apart, the air between Tom and Margot was charged—sizzling, in fact—and without the refuge of their banter, they both seemed uncomfortable.

Turning back toward the carriage, Margot was startled to see a man with the most sinister and sensual face she'd ever seen. He was standing beside one of the short statues, his hand lightly resting on one of its pendulous breasts.

"That's the scoundrel we've been on this carriage ride looking for," Tom called out.

"Jenks at your service, your ladyship," he said, eyeing her so crudely, she blushed.

"I can't wait to hear your excuse," Tom was saying.

"You always think the worst of me, boyzo," Jenks said, "but I have been busy taking care of all of us."

"As well as you've taken care of Teva and Raina? You stole the only thing of value they owned."

"A necessary evil," Jenks said, tossing Tom's remark aside. "Your ladyship, you be the judge. Do the ends justify the means? I'm in the process of taking care of Teva and Raina for life."

"What was in the food they served you on that ship? The two of you are the strangest men I've ever encountered," Margot said, and began to walk off, but Jenks moved to block her way.

"My plan is to take care of you as well, Lady Vale," Jenks purred. "We can all make our fortunes in Mannar."

"What do you know about Mannar?"

"First things first," he said, walking over to Tom. "You want me to pay back Teva and Raina. With your help, I can. It's no secret that the beds are drying up out here. But what if I came up with a way to keep Teva and Raina working year-round on the richest beds in the world?"

"Where?"

"The Ceylon beds at Mannar," Margot said.

Jenks outlined his plan, explaining Tom's, Teva's, Raina's, and Nasis's roles.

"How big a catch of pearls are we talking about?" Tom asked.

"Millions, Mr. Street," Margot said, "if this year's catch is as big as last year's. The colonial government organizes an inspection tour in the fall to check on the beds."

"That doesn't leave us much time."

"We don't know that Teva and Raina or any of the other divers will want to leave their homes," Tom said skeptically.

"They'd do it for you," Jenks said, "if you told them you were going to feed and shelter them for a diving season, then split profits with them."

"What about David?" Margot interrupted. "Is he going along with all this?"

"There is a condition," Jenks said slowly, looking from Margot to Tom. "He wants the lady back by nightfall."

Margot laughed. "Did he say that? To vouchsafe my honor?"

"He will not sail without you," Jenks said, meaning to compliment her.

"And this is how you plan to take care of me, Mr. Jenks?" Margot said ruefully.

He smiled evenly at her, then turned to Tom. "Do we have a deal?"

"Three equal shares," Tom said.

"Exactly—it was my idea. You provide the divers and Nasis, the transportation."

"Oh, that's good, very good," Margot said irritably. "You men are not only insufferable, you're so predictable. Gentlemen, it will be four equal shares if I am to be the condition on which he sails."

Both men turned to gape at her.

"Please spare me the patronizing looks. We agree on my

133

participation, or I sabotage this entire scheme. I have considerable influence with Mr. Nasis," she added, unnecessarily.

Jenks smiled. "I like a woman who knows her own mind," he said smoothly.

Margot turned to Tom, who was staring at her quizzically. "What do you say, Mr. Street?"

"Four shares it is," he said.

III

Ceylon

Chapter
Twenty-six

AFTER PICKING UP Teva and Raina and six other native couples in Manihi, the *Distant Star* set sail for Ceylon. It moved from Pago Pago to Fiji to Erromanga to Port Moresby, then into the Arafura Sea.

The Tahitians were given the aft deck and remained segregated from the crew and the four partners.

Margot felt surrounded by the men. Nasis, as much in love with her as ever, fell over himself whenever she was nearby, and she and Tom were like two puppets who had gotten their wires tangled. Whenever she walked out on deck, Tom stood and walked to a rail, trying to avoid looking at her, but compelled to try and read her thoughts. When she sat, he stood. When she stood, he sat. It was like a dance, except no one was leading.

Jenks was another story, a mystery; he was alternately aloof, then leering, following her every move with his sinister eyes.

One night he appeared at her stateroom door, shaved, brushed, and dressed to the nines.

"I've pinched these for you from the mess," he whispered, prying open the cover of a tin of raspberries.

His tone of voice was playful, but the look in his eyes was almost cruel. It infused everything he did with an edge, she was thinking.

"How many ships have you been on, Jenks?" she asked, sitting down on a chaise longue.

"I lost count—been at sea since I was sixteen. Never before on a ship like this. Oh, it's not whole raspberries, it's jam."

"I'll ring for a spoon."

"Our fingers will do," he said, scooping some up with his

137

index and middle fingers. "I don't have to teach you how to do this, do I?"

She laughed. "No, I had a normal childhood."

Passing the tin to her, he smiled, his pale eyes darting from her eyes to her breasts, to the thick folds of her aqua silk robe, then up to her lips, his interest so obvious, it excited her.

She dipped her index finger into the tin, then into her mouth.

"You do that very well," he whispered.

"You don't have to whisper—we won't be tried for our crimes."

His fingers scooped up more jam, and he continued watching her as he ate.

"You're a constant source of surprise to me," he said.

"And you to me. I never know what to expect from you."

"You're so . . . human. I thought you'd be distant."

"It's you who've been distant," she said, taking more jam.

"People like you and me would never have talked back at home. Oh, maybe I'd have been your driver or mucked your stables, but we wouldn't have talked like this."

Reaching out suddenly—his hand as pale and strong as marble, the veins standing out like blue silk cords—he touched her cheek. "You've got jam on your face."

Her breath caught in her throat, and turning to a mirror, her face now out of his reach, she wiped her cheek with a handkerchief.

"Don't want me touching you, do you?"

The stateroom suddenly felt cool and dim.

And he was on his feet, towering over her. "I'm not used to talking to women like you."

"You were doing very well," she said slowly.

"Then can I touch you again?" Without waiting for her reply, he cupped the side of her face with his hand, his index finger resting in the hollow of her left temple.

"You're a cool goddess, aren't you? But I make you feel human."

Standing up, she smelled the odor of his sweat under the scent of lemon water. His beard looked blue-black under his pale skin. "Mr. Jenks, if you'd take some time—"

"You'd what?" he said with a thin smile. "You're all alike.

You're just a woman." His other hand slipped around her waist.

"I am my own woman," she said, backing away from him.

His grip tightened. "I see what I see. You're interested in me. Look at your eyes—you don't know where to look first."

She reached the stateroom door and, grasping the handle, pushed it open.

He dropped his hands.

Standing in the hall, she pressed her back against the port windows.

He leaned against the doorframe, his sullen mouth drawn back in a tight smile.

"Come back inside," he whispered, holding out his hand to her.

Footsteps sounded in the hall.

"Mr. Street," she called out.

As Tom approached, Jenks walked into the hall, and she was momentarily wedged between them.

Jenks stepped aside.

"Is everything all right?" Tom asked, staring into the open stateroom.

"Yes, fine, thank you. Everything's fine. Good night," she said, stepping back into her room, easing the door shut.

"What have you been up to?" Tom asked Jenks.

"She couldn't get the porthole closed," he said, walking away. Damn it to hell, he was thinking—I almost had her.

When Ceylon was first sighted, everyone rushed onto the deck. The country rose on the horizon like an enormous South Sea island—wide, sandy beaches, tall stands of coconut palms; in the distance remote plateaus, and beyond them, mountains.

At Ahamgama they saw stilt-fishermen. Each man was perched on a pole embedded in the surf, casting out his line.

Traveling north, they passed Unawatuna, a wide curving bay with a golden sweep of beach, and Galle, a large, older city, colonized by the Dutch. Margot said it was thought to have been the biblical town of Tarshish, where King Solomon had mined gems. Further north they passed Hikkaduwa, with its vast coral outcroppings.

Teva had told them these would be rich pearl beds, but Margot disagreed.

"Northern Ceylon is where we'll find the richest beds —near the Gulf of Mannar."

"Maybe we should find out, send the Tahitians into the water," Jenks said.

"Wh-wh-what harm could it do?" Nasis added.

Margot stared out at the darkening sky. "We've got to push on to Colombo, where the government offices are. We'll find all the information we need about the richest beds in the north."

"Damn Colombo," Jenks said. "I say we drop one or two of the Tahitians over the side and see what they come up with."

"Look at those clouds in the west," Margot said. "That's a monsoon, Mr. Jenks."

"Damn woman," Jenks muttered under his breath.

Within fifteen minutes the monsoon swept up from the southwest, buffeting the yacht. Margot sat in the bay window of the main saloon following their course on her maps and charts. The coast, from Ambalangoda to Bentota, was obscured by the downpour.

By mid-afternoon, when the rain subsided, they reached Colombo. A familiar argument sprang up among the three men—how best to find out about the pearl beds. Tom wanted to head straight up the coast to Mannar to see them for himself. Jenks wanted to steal government reports. Nasis wanted to bribe officials.

Margot had her own ideas. Dressed in a crisp white linen suit and broad-brimmed white straw hat, she asked Bedloe to lower the tender.

"Wh-wh-where are you g-g-going?" Nasis asked.

"Ashore," she said, putting on a pair of cotton mesh gloves.

"You have a plan?" Tom asked.

"Yes, I do," she said, turning to check her hair in one of the saloon windows.

"Well, don't k-k-keep us in s-s-suspense."

"I have my calling cards—I'm going calling."

"You d-d-don't know anyone here."

"I'm going to present myself at Queen's House, the home

of the colonial governor. I'll have all the information we require by this evening," she said. With Bedloe's help, she stepped into the tender.

Before Bedloe cast off, David called out, "M-m-margot, I sh-sh-should go with you."

"You needn't trouble yourself, David. I can manage," she said.

"But M-m-margot . . ." David pleaded.

"Don't embarrass yourself, Nasis, let her go," Jenks hissed.

"Tell Bedloe to bring the tender back after he's dropped her on shore," Tom said, watching her.

"You think I-I-I should f-f-follow her, don't you, Street?"

"I think we should all follow her," Tom said.

Chapter
Twenty-seven

HALF AN HOUR later the three men arrived on shore. It was hot in the town, which was called Fort, a throbbing commercial center where one saw such disparate characters as Englishmen in linen suits and pith helmets, Buddhist monks in saffron robes, apprentice snake charmers, and innocent-eyed schoolgirls in pale blue uniforms being shuttled through the streets by stern-looking nuns.

"Imagine M-m-margot finding her way through all of th-th-this," Nasis said as they stood under the clock tower at the junction of Chatham and Queen streets.

"We take this road to something called the Galle Road and follow that to Queen's House," Tom said, looking at the map.

"You aren't following her, are you?" Jenks snarled.

"She seemed more sure of herself than we did."

"Th-th-that's what I think we should d-d-do."

Jenks draped his arm around Nasis's shoulder. "I hate to

see you make a fool of yourself over her. She's told you she doesn't want you following her. That's not the way to keep her interest."

"I know it's g-g-good to show her I won't cave in every t-t-time she acts willfully."

"Of course it is. We're going to find ourselves an English club and ask the right people the right questions. You've got money on you, don't you, Nasis?"

"Of course."

"Of course you do—let's go. Driver!" Jenks called out, and a carriage stopped in front of the tower.

"Sure you w-w-won't j-j-join us, Street?" Nasis called out as Jenks pulled him aboard and the carriage took off.

Tom hailed his own carriage.

An hour later he was pacing outside the gates of Queen's House, wondering what on earth she was doing inside.

When she finally emerged, it was on the arm of an elderly man, who was tall, pear-shaped, and had a fringe of whiskers and thin, neatly parted hair. He took her hand and kissed it warmly, then she said good-bye and got into her carriage.

As it approached the gate, Tom stepped into the road.

"Lady Vale," he whispered, but she did not hear him.

The gates opened and the carriage pulled through them and into the narrow street.

"Your ladyship!"

When she saw him, her blue-green eyes widened with excitement. "What are you doing here?"

"I thought you were on the most promising trail."

"Where are the others?"

"They've gone off to some club. May I get into your carriage?"

She turned to look back. "Quickly—I don't want anyone to see. They thought it was odd enough, my showing up unannounced."

As he got in beside her, he asked, "What have you found out?"

Rather than answering, she looked over her shoulder at the white mansion.

"You're not talking."

142

"I may not have that much to say as yet."

"You haven't found out anything. Damn! I knew we should go straight up to Mannar."

"Please, Mr. Street, it hasn't been a total loss. I've come up with two invitations to a ball at Queen's House tonight . . ."

A ball? he was thinking. Is that all these women ever think about?

"The minister of fisheries will be there. He sends out diving teams that scout the beds for the winter fishery. Mr. Nasis and I will go tonight and find out something more."

"You're taking Nasis? You'd do better with Jenks—at least he'd steal something."

They didn't exchange another word as they rode back to the harbor. When they arrived, the tender was waiting for them. Jenks was missing, and Nasis, who was a shade lighter green than a mango skin, was very, very drunk.

"Oh, Margot, I f-f-feel awful."

"I'm sure you do, David. You look awful."

"Where's Jenks?" Tom asked.

"The m-m-man's powers of consumption are m-m-mind-boggling. I'm going to be s-s-sick. You'd better have B-b-bedloe help me aboard the t-t-tender."

"So much for your dancing partner," Tom said with a smile.

"I think the job has fallen to you, Mr. Street. But I wonder if you can be trusted to behave," she said over her shoulder as Bedloe helped her board.

"I'll have Bedloe put a sharp crease in my loincloth," he called out after her.

Chapter
Twenty-eight

TOM, WEARING NASIS'S evening clothes, was pacing up and down the main saloon of the *Distant Star*, sipping whiskey. He couldn't decide if he was nervous or excited or both. Stopping in front of a gold French clock on the mantel, he wondered how long Margot would keep him waiting.

Five minutes ahead of schedule she walked to the doorway at the other end of the saloon and stood busily looking for something in her evening bag.

She didn't see him at first, so he could just stare at her. She was wearing a beautiful dress of pale, pale orchid-colored silk chiffon, with a high waist and low neckline. Ropes and ropes of her finest pearls were knotted around her throat and twined in her hair. Something in her expression made him see that he had been wrong. She was not at all like Jelly, or what Jelly had become. Margot had somehow escaped; she still seemed brave.

Now finding a small crystal flacon, she applied perfume to her neck, then closed her bag and entered the saloon. Looking up, she was as startled by him as he had been by her.

They stood motionless for a moment; he, rapt with his new insight, she, taken with his elegant looks and the new, warmer expression in his eyes.

At Queen's House introductions went well, Tom thought, noticing the satisfied smile on Margot's face when he addressed the colonial governor and his wife, Sir Arthur and Lady Havelock, as Your Excellency. He found himself wanting to please Margot. He loved being in league with her; they were like spies on a mission—and besides, she was so terrifically beautiful.

The house was grand, with large pillared halls and fine airy reception rooms filled with Oriental furniture. Sinhalese servants, almost a hundred of them, in a fanciful livery of starched jackets and long skirts, were padding around barefoot. They had maroon-black skin, aquiline features, and shiny, oiled hair.

"The person we're here to find is named Bainbridge —Ellis Bainbridge," Margot was whispering. "Sir Arthur pointed him out to me."

Bainbridge was the dour, goat-faced man with thinning hair who was standing by himself in a corner. Margot took a deep breath, preparing herself to walk over to him.

"Another conquest in the making?" Tom asked.

"We can only hope."

"You make Mr. Bainbridge crack a smile, and his mortician will never speak to you again."

Laughing, she walked off.

Tom plucked a glass of champagne from a passing tray and watched as Margot began talking with Bainbridge. In no time Bainbridge succumbed. He was smiling a bit lamely, but cheerfully enough. Their conversation went on until dinner was announced, then Bainbridge took Margot's arm and escorted her into the dining hall.

At the table Margot managed to position herself next to Bainbridge, and throughout the meal, to her credit, she appeared unflappable, talking to Bainbridge when it looked as if there was no talk left in her.

Afterward, when the ladies left and the gentlemen enjoyed their port and cigars, Tom noticed that Bainbridge had disappeared. Excusing himself, Tom searched the house for him, but couldn't find either Bainbridge or Margot.

Walking outside, he suddenly had the strangest feeling. It was the way the English must feel, he decided, whenever they leave their houses. Inside, except for the servants and the presence of curry in some of the dishes, there wasn't a trace of another culture and yet out here there was dense jungle and thick animal smells.

Walking away from the house on a path that snaked through the jungle, he heard the roar of an elephant. In a clearing was a huge pen in which five or six elephants were kept. Margot was standing near it with Bainbridge, who had his back to Tom and was talking in a raspy monotone.

"Every large house has a *kraal,* a pen for the elephants. The elephants do all the heavy work on the plantations up in the mountains. They're not dangerous, except when the males are in musk. They're kept by boys called *mahouts.*"

Tom started to move closer to the pen, but Margot, seeing him, signaled to him to remain in the shadows.

"Anything wrong, Lady Vale?"

"Just a chill," she answered.

"Should we walk back to the house?"

"No, I like it out here."

"Would you like me to fetch a shawl?"

"Would you mind terribly?"

"Not at all."

When he left, Tom walked back onto the trail. Margot had the most animated expression in her eyes, as if she were relishing her role as spy.

"I'm beginning to formulate a plan," she said quickly. "He's sending out an inspection fleet to look at the beds this week. Some of the European divers haven't arrived. He went to great pains, need I say lengths, to tell me that he's never met the European divers, who are arriving tomorrow."

"I'm three steps ahead of you. I dive."

"And he hasn't been introduced to you."

"He doesn't look curious, either—I'm sure he hasn't even seen me."

"But there's a problem. What about the real divers? What do we do with them?"

"We'll deal with that later. What else did he say?"

"They mark off diving areas that are called pars and bring up samples from each."

"What an edge to know which pars produce the most pearls."

There was the sound of a branch snapping on the trail. Margot jumped.

"Get the names," Tom was saying.

"Whose names?"

"The divers'."

She began walking toward the house.

"Where are you going?" he whispered.

"To head off Bainbridge before he comes back and sees you," she said, taking off in a run.

Chapter
Twenty-nine

"I'M NOT SAYING I've changed my mind. I just think we should be more cautious," Margot was saying as she and Tom left the tender and walked up the gangway to the deck of the *Distant Star*.

"Remember, I was the one who wanted to rush straight up to Mannar, but you were right. If we have the best information, we stand to make the most money. What was it you said? Millions?"

"But to impersonate European divers! There are so many risks."

On the aft deck the Tahitians were sleeping in twos and threes on their *tapaku*. "And what about them?"

Teva and Raina were curled up together near where Tom and Margot were standing.

"We dress Teva in European clothes and say he's my assistant. We'll get away with it just because it's so eccentric."

"We still don't know what to do with the real divers," she said, walking to the foredeck.

"I admit it—that's the most troublesome part," Tom said, leaning on the rail with his elbows, drumming his fingers. "What do we do with the divers?"

"You sandbag 'em," a deep voice behind them called out.

Jenks was hidden in the shadows, sprawled out on a deck chair.

"Sandbag? Is that one of Bully Jenks's old tricks?" Tom asked.

"It's an old first mate's trick when he's desperately lookin' for crew for his ship."

Jenks sat up, bleary-eyed with drink. "Sandbag is sometimes known as the old shanghai."

"You clobber them and send them packing."

"No, you get 'em good and drunk and you keep 'em on ice, then you pack 'em off on the next boat out."

"When did Bainbridge say the inspection fleet was heading up to Mannar?" Tom asked Margot.

"The end of the week."

"We'll need a drug," Jenks said, rising. "Drugs work better than booze. We could keep them out here, then drop them off on another boat."

"But Bainbridge is expecting them—he'll be there to meet them," Margot said.

"We've got to make the switch before Bainbridge sees them," Tom said to Jenks. "And we have to make sure Nasis will go along with the plan."

The two men began walking off together, plotting. Margot didn't like being excluded.

"You can leave Bainbridge and Nasis to me," she called out.

"You?" Jenks asked skeptically.

"I've come this far. I don't know why I should miss all the fun."

At twelve-thirty the next day Margot was waiting in a carriage near Bainbridge's house, in a part of town called the Cinnamon Gardens, which had once been a spice plantation and was now the most fashionable residential area in Colombo.

The ship was due in at one. Bainbridge was still inside the house, and she waited until twelve forty-five before making her next move—having the driver move the carriage into Bainbridge's compound.

Bainbridge, who was preparing to leave for the docks, was surprised and delighted to see her. She turned on all her charms, inching her way into the vestibule, holding him there until he was forced to say that while he would love to continue this conversation, he had a very important engagement.

Seeing that he was such an unquestioning sort of man, she did what had worked for generations of women before her: she dropped to his feet in a perfect, pale-faced swoon.

Meanwhile, across town at the harbor, the *Ebersole*, the ship carrying the divers, docked and began unloading passengers.

Tom positioned himself at the base of the gangway, searching the crowd for likely twosomes. Next to him was Teva, dressed in his first pair of trousers, at which he kept tugging and pulling in the most inappropriate places and at the most inappropriate times. Tom kept calling out the names that Margot had given him.

"Mr. Donnell? Mr. Troop?"

No one responded.

Suddenly two likely characters emerged on deck carrying their own duffels: a stocky Irishman with a wide, pale face and premature gray hair, and beside him, a short man with a moustache, which he kept compulsively twirling.

"Donnell and Troop?" Tom called up to them.

"I'm Donnell," the Irishman called down. The short one, parroting the Irishman, called out, "He's Donnell."

Just then Bainbridge pulled into the Galle Road. Margot was with him.

Tom, knocking over people in his way, surged up the gangway and grabbed the duffels. Turning, he raced back down. Donnell and Troop came tumbling after.

"Sorry to be so rushed!" Tom shouted over his shoulder.

"Who in hell are you?" Donnell called out.

"Yeah, who in hell are you?" Troop added.

"Mr. Bainbridge's secretary," Tom said, seeing Bainbridge's carriage turn into the harbor road. "This way, if you don't mind. There's been a change of plans. But you'll be filled in on all the new details once you get out to the yacht."

"Bainbridge's yacht?" Donnell said greedily. "Didn't know he had a yacht."

"Didn't know he had one," Troop said.

"Just this way if you will," Tom panted, breaking into a run. The two divers followed at a clip.

"What's the rush?" Donnell called out.

"Yeah, what's the rush?" Troop squeaked.

Tom, seeing Jenks emerge from the tender with a worried look on his face, kept rushing and called out to Jenks, "We're all here now, sir!"

"Is that Mr. Bainbridge?" Donnell asked as he ran.

"You've never met Bainbridge?"

Donnell shook his head.

"No, we haven't," Troop concurred.

"That's him."

Jenks looked ready for introductions, but Tom intervened.

"You can get acquainted in the tender," he said pointedly, pushing Donnell and Troop forward into the long boat. "Offer the men a drink on your way out. I'm sure they're thirsty."

"Something to drink would be most appreciated," Donnell said with a wink.

"*Most* appreciated," Troop said.

Tom took off.

Margot saw him running back to the *Ebersole* and realized that she'd have to stall Bainbridge. As the carriage stopped, she tugged on his arm.

"Thank you so much for everything you've done," she began.

"It was nothing, my dear—just glad you're feeling better."

But Tom was only halfway between the tender and the ship, and as Bainbridge was about to step down from the carriage, Margot crumpled on the floor in a dead faint for the second time that afternoon.

"My word!" Bainbridge called out, stooping, trying to revive her.

She counted to one hundred very slowly before allowing her eyes to flutter open.

By that time Tom was standing at the foot of the gangway, panting, waiting to greet Bainbridge.

That evening Tom borrowed a skiff from a local fisherman and went out to the yacht to make sure everything was going smoothly.

Donnell and Troop had passed out before they got on the yacht and were still sleeping. Nasis and Jenks were ashore, putting the finishing touches on the plan, booking return passage to London for the two on a ship that was leaving early tomorrow morning.

Margot was pacing. "We've committed at least five crimes at last count," she was saying.

"With what Nasis is paying those two, I don't think they'll be complaining. They'll wake up with a fortune in their billfolds. Probably think they stopped in Colombo, did their job, and left."

In the distance the tender with Nasis and Jenks was returning.

"You were wonderful this afternoon," Tom said to her.

"I was, wasn't I?"

"Her ladyship has a real touch for larceny."

"The entire time I kept thinking I was spiting my sister. She has a very sour, disapproving face."

Tom stroked her cheek lightly. "It doesn't run in the family. You have one of the loveliest faces I've ever seen."

"Are you romancing me?"

"I don't know what came over me—it must be the soft light or the larceny or something. . . ."

"I think you should go."

"I won't see you for a while."

Nasis, standing in the tender now, saw them on deck.

"S-s-street, what are you doing here? Everything all r-r-right?"

Tom stepped between Margot and Nasis and Jenks, his back to the tender.

"Tell me quickly before they come aboard that you'll miss me. Quickly, before Nasis can hear you."

"I say, S-s-street, what's g-g-going on?"

"Say it."

"Yes, yes, I will. Now, go."

"You mean it?"

"Yes, I mean it—go!" she said, and Tom turned to reassure Nasis, who was staring up at them suspiciously.

Chapter
Thirty

Tom and Teva were assigned to a schooner-rigged ship, a hundred-tonner called the *Sea Forth*. The other diving teams aboard were mostly Tamils, from northern Ceylon, and Arabs. Everyone was suspicious of Tom and most especially of Teva, because they'd never seen a Tahitian before. Cut off from his friends and so far from home, Teva was growing confused and listless.

"You miss Raina?" Tom asked him the first night out.

"She bring me luck on dives. I bring up lots of *parau.*"

"We won't be keeping the ones we bring up this time, only going down to see how many there are."

"Why for we do that?"

"So we know where to dive when we come back in February."

"Fepuare? Without Raina until *Fepuare?"*

"No, you'll be seeing her in a few weeks."

"We go Manihi in *Fepuare?"*

"In *Mati*, March, or April—I don't know how to say April."

"Eperera—long time. Don't think I ever get home again."

"Don't say that. You'll get home in *Eperera.*"

Teva, having the Polynesian's sense of time, which did not extend much beyond the present, didn't look convinced.

The fleet traveled up the coast slowly, anchoring in clusters of two or three boats at the end of the day. Calls to evening prayer rang out, and at night the smell of curry from the Tamil cookstoves permeated the air.

The first inspection dives took place fifty miles north of Colombo, at Chilaw, inside a protected bay.

The Arabs and Tamils worked in pairs, using a rope weighted with a single diving stone.

Tom, getting his bearings again under water, depended on Teva to bring up most of the shells.

The pars at Chilaw were not good ones because sea snakes and starfish had eaten the oysters—the Ceylon mollusks were called Avicula (Meleagrina) Margaratifera. And in some areas the sand currents had obviously shifted, burying beds that had been sighted the year before.

But up at Portuguese Bay the pars called Muttivaratti, Alanturai, Mudalaikuli, and Talavillimondal were rich with oysters. The divers brought up a thousand or more shells, which were opened and searched for pearls, and word quickly spread about the biggest finds. Tom made detailed maps and kept notes on everything he saw and heard.

The Ceylonese pearls were smaller than the Tahitian blacks, but a surprising number of them were round and their lustre was remarkable, even in an unwashed, untreated state. The color varied from silvery white to pinkish white, although some were called black—a slate color, really—and others were yellowish and brown. The smallest, called *masi-tul,* were used as powder for chewing with betel, the substance that the Tamils and Arabs were constantly mashing in their mouths like chewing tobacco and which stained their mouths, lips, and teeth red. The larger of this variety, called *tul,* were used as sacrament—placed in the mouths of wealthy dead Hindus. Every pearl and scrap of pearl dust, Tom learned, had a price and a market.

Before moving on to other pars, the divers put markers in the water—clumsy iron coal drums—but Teva, going ashore to gather materials, fashioned one from bamboo, wood, and stone that was much easier to position. This, unfortunately, caused more trouble for him with the Arabs and Tamils, who didn't like changes in their work habits.

As the ship made its way north, Tom spotted elephants and leopards on long stretches of beach, and as the land became drier, more forbidding, the pars became richer. Finally they reached the dry, desertlike landscape of Mannar and the richest of the pars—beds of oysters that stretched in every direction for as far as the eye could see—Karkukalai, Madragam, Kondachichi, Challe, Arippu, and Anaivilundun.

On each dive Tom stared down at his impending fortune.

153

It would take a larger diving team than a handful of Tahitians to harvest all this. He would need bands of divers, and he began planning for the winter, trying to hire the best Tamils and Arabs for the season.

"Aren't you ever going to forgive me?" Jenks said to Margot as soon as Nasis had left the table.

The three were having dinner in the cavernous ballroom of the Galle Face Hotel.

"But I have forgiven you," Margot said. A Sinhalese waiter with a turban folded in the shape of a cockscomb was beside her, pouring tea.

"You don't like being alone with me," Jenks said.

"We're alone now."

"In a room full of people, and Nasis will be back in a minute. But the other night, when we were alone in your room, I wanted to show you how I felt. You encouraged me."

"You misinterpreted. We're working very closely. We're partners."

"Business is all it is?"

"Yes, we're in business," she said.

The room was filled with hundreds of guests, most of them British military men and their dutiful, attentive wives. How much safer it would have been to be that, she was thinking.

"I felt something more between us," he said.

"Yes, you may have. It doesn't matter. Do you want to be forgiven? I forgive you," she said quickly, not wanting to think about how attracted to him she may have been.

He was leaning closer to her now. Even wearing a freshly pressed suit of clothes and with his hair slicked back, there was something unctuous and threatening about him, she thought. He was unpredictable, and while that made him exciting, it was also unsettling, as if he could, without provocation, suddenly wipe all the crystal and porcelain from the table with the back of his hand or stand and begin shooting at the dozens of fans whirring overhead.

"You've got to tell me what you want from me," he was whispering. "I'm not used to you."

He frightened her, but she knew she couldn't let him see that. "And just the other night you were saying I was like all other women, you knew what I wanted," she said lightly.

And leaning closer still, so that one or two of the military wives turned to stare at them, he persisted. "You know what you want. Whisper it to me. I saw you staring at my hands." He placed them on the table in front of her. They were pale and cruel. "You want me to put my hands on you. Where? Tell me? Whisper it. On your neck? Your legs? The backs of your legs . . ."

Just then Nasis appeared at the table looking ill. "M-m-must have been something I ate," he said. "I'm going b-b-back to the boat. But I insist you t-t-two stay and finish your d-d-dinners."

Margot, pulling an aqua silk shawl around her shoulders, quickly began to rise.

"David, if you're not feeling well, we'll go back with you."

"You're s-s-sweet to th-th-think of me, but I won't hear of it. Jenks, you'll be sure t-t-to see she has a good time."

"But David—"

"I'll see to it," Jenks said.

"—I'm coming with you."

"Abs-s-solutely not," he said, turning to leave.

Jenks reached out, holding his hand on her arm until she sat.

"Frightened?"

"You think too much of yourself."

"It's the fear that excites you. Don't know what I'll do next. You like that."

"You don't frighten me. You want me to tell you what I want? A seduction, but not from you. All you can muster is some rude talk tinged with cruelty. Not much of an accomplishment."

"Don't talk to me like that. I'm not your servant. You think you can 'handle' me the way you handle a fop like Nasis."

She got to her feet again.

"I won't be handled. You never met anyone like me—I excite you, admit it."

She walked off after Nasis, leaving Jenks alone, seething.

Chapter Thirty-one

WITHIN TWO WEEKS Tom was back in Colombo, and the four partners were sitting around Nasis's dining table making plans for the February fishery, which had not, as yet, been announced.

"It's larger than anything we dreamed possible," Tom was saying. "During the dives at Challe and Madragam, we hauled up thousands of shells day after day. At least one in forty contained pearls."

"Wh-wh-what size?"

"Smaller than you'd think, but many were perfectly round."

"The average size in Ceylon is anywhere from two to ten grains, and they were pink-white?" Margot asked.

"Pink-white and silvery-white."

"I got more information from Bainbridge while you were away," she began, and outlined her strategy.

Jenks sat up, watching Tom and Margot, noticing how warmly they smiled at each other, how charged the air was between them. So it was Tom who would be her choice, Jenks was thinking. Bloody noble Tom. So clean and fair. Hatred knotted Jenks's gut. We'll see how clean and fair. I'll send them both to bloody hell.

"We have to be patient," Tom was saying. "We don't know which pars the government will choose to fish."

"Or how much we'll have to pay for the pearls we bring up," Margot said. "The price has been rising."

"Although we don't know that it will continue to rise."

Listen to their overlapping thoughts and words, Jenks was thinking. His hatred was fueled with each word. Calm, he cautioned himself, be calm. Watch. Sit and watch. They'll hang themselves. He began watching Nasis, who was rolling a cigar nervously between his thumb and index finger. Jenks began formulating a plan . . .

"It's good that we have Teva and Raina and the others," Margot began.

"But we have to hire many more."

"We could do that when we go up to the fishery."

"Or start hiring now," Tom added.

"You're right, we can't wait too long. The best divers will be snapped up," she said, racing ahead with their plans.

Nasis stood abruptly.

"P-p-perhaps we sh-sh-should continue this conversation t-t-tomorrow, when we have had time to d-d-digest all this inf-f-formation."

Margot saw the uneasy look in his eyes. How smart was it to arouse his jealousy just now? she wondered. She stood up and said, "I think I'll get some air."

When she left the room, Tom excused himself and followed her out to the deck.

Nasis, looking edgy, began to follow after him, but Jenks called out, "Nasis, I think we should talk."

Nasis, standing by the door, reluctantly turned to Jenks. "Can't it w-w-wait?"

"It's about our two partners."

"What about th-th-them?"

"Some observations you may find interesting," Jenks said slowly, pulling over a chair for Nasis.

Outside, Margot was willing her hands to be steady. But her entire body was vibrating.

"I think we've scared them," she said.

"I don't care. I had to be alone with you. Quickly, come with me," he said, urging her away from the dining room windows, which were showering the deck with pale yellow light.

He pulled her into the shadows beside the deck chairs.

She started to say something, not even sure what it would be, but he kissed her words away. Feeling the soft, pliant touch of his lips, she pressed against him. His hands came up and held her face, and she exhaled as if for the first time in weeks.

She concentrated on his scent, which she could not define, only feel. Her pulse raced.

He drew her farther into the shadows, pressed her back against a wall. His lips were firm, his touch more deliberate. She quivered as his index finger lightly grazed the side of her neck. And as a breeze blew across the deck, his scent washed over her, familiar and mysterious.

Somewhere nearby Raina began to moan in a low voice, then her *yip yip* cries began.

Tom laughed.

"What is it?"

"They're making love."

He kissed her again.

"When I sit next to you at Nasis's table, I feel as if I have to tie my hands to my sides to keep them from touching you."

This time she reached out and drew him closer.

"I wish we were somewhere else. Anywhere else," he whispered.

"What difference does it make?"

"It's his boat. I want to be somewhere that's ours."

She kissed him again like someone who had been starved and, seeing a banquet table, wanted to eat everything in sight all at once—she wanted to feel every possible feeling all at once: passion, confusion, fear, her desire to be overcome, her desire to remain untouched—

"Where can we see each other?" he whispered, his arm encircling her neck, his tongue wetting her lips. "When can I have you?"

Hearing the sound of the opening dining room door, she reflexively sprang away from him, but he pulled her back.

"Where can we meet?"

Nasis, his back to them, walked out onto the deck with Jenks, who had thrown his arm around David's shoulder.

"Where?" Tom whispered fiercely.

"We'll think of something," she said finally, her heart beating so loudly it drowned out every other sound.

Chapter
Thirty-two

THE FIRST WEEK in December the fishery was announced by the government in the Colombo newspaper.

"'Notice is hereby given that a pearl fishery will take place at Marichchukkaddi,'" Margot read aloud.

"Where on e-e-earth is that?"

"At Mannar. 'On or about February 20, 1892—'"

"Get to the good part," Tom said.

"'The banks to be fished ... Karativu, Madragam, Alabturai, containing twenty-one million oysters, sufficient to employ one hundred boats for twenty-one days, average loads of ten thousand each day. Muttuyarato Par—fifteen million oysters, one hundred boats. Challe—ten million oysters. Arripu—twenty million. Koopay—another ten million.'" She dropped the paper. "This is the largest one in history."

"N-n-none of us has ever d-d-done anything on this scale before."

"That's not self-doubt I'm hearing, is it, my dear Nasis?" Jenks said. He put his arm around Nasis's shoulder and took him aside, purposely leaving Tom and Margot alone at the end of the deck.

Tom's hand reached out for hers. "You've got to meet me in town."

Looking up she watched as Nasis disappeared around a corner.

"This is hell!" she said. "I don't want to be careful about us, but should we jeopardize this? Think what it would be like if we alienated him. We'd be bidding against him up at Mannar."

"I'll arrange it so he doesn't suspect a thing. Leave it to me."

When Nasis and Jenks returned, Tom said that they still didn't know what the estimated prices for the pearls would be, and Margot, with her close relationship with Bainbridge, was in the best position to find out.

"Margot," Jenks said, "you should have lunch with Bainbridge as soon as possible."

"P-p-perhaps we sh-sh-should all go."

"No," Jenks said. "Margot's done so well on her own before, we should leave her alone. What do you say, Margot?"

"I can try."

When Margot went to her stateroom to change, Tom appeared at the door.

"See what you can find out from Bainbridge, then meet me at the Galle Face Hotel at two o'clock."

A half hour later, when she appeared on deck, the only sign of her unease was hanging from her neck. She'd put on three separate strands of pearls, each a different color, as if she'd been trying to find the right one but had forgotten to discard the other two after she'd made her choice. Bedloe took her ashore.

An hour later Tom said that he was going into town to look for divers.

After he left, Nasis and Jenks remained on deck watching the tender take him ashore.

"He's going after her," Jenks said in a self-assured voice.

"Why d-d-do you say th-th-these things?" Nasis said sharply.

"I know him," Jenks said. "He's told me he would have her. He said he didn't care what it took. And it's not as if he's in love with her, dear Nasis. Nothing could compare with your love for her. Believe me, it's more venal than that. I know him."

"Wh-wh-what should we d-d-do?"

"Follow them."

"Go r-r-running after her? You t-t-told me never t-t-to do th-th-that."

"But now you've got to fight for her—or perhaps do something more difficult than that."

"Wh-wh-what's that?"

"See her as she really is."

"I know who sh-sh-she is. I won't have you s-s-say a thing against her."

"All I know is what he told me. She's a very calculating woman—and as much as I like her, as much as I'd sooner lie than say a word against her, she may have used both of us. It's just possible that all she cares about is money."

"But she has h-h-her own money."

"Or all she cares about is the pearls."

Nasis said nothing as he watched Tom get to shore and hire a carriage.

"How w-w-would we f-f-find them?"

"That's no problem. I can find them. I'm hoping against hope that I'm wrong."

"Th-th-then you'll come with m-m-me?"

"No, no, dear Nasis. You must confront them yourself."

Nasis turned to say something, but Jenks put his finger up to Nasis's lips to silence him.

"It's the only way I'll agree to help you," he said firmly.

Nasis turned away. "Th-th-thank you, Jenks. You take such good c-c-care of m-m-me."

"All I can ever hope to do is try. . . ."

Chapter Thirty-three

IT TOOK TOM quite a while to get through Fort and make his way up the Galle Road. The streets were more clotted than usual. People called to each other from their carriages or stood in groups of twos and threes in the road talking about history and fortunes to be made up in Mannar. Everyone had caught the fever; even men not ordinarily connected with the pearl trade were thinking of sponsoring teams of divers.

Ahead, at the far end of a long green, stood the Galle Face Hotel, bordered by a lagoon on one side and a beach and the Indian Ocean on the other.

The day was perfectly clear. The sun was warm, and there was a shimmering haze on the grass and the sparkling white building beyond it.

Tom felt as if all around him pressure was building. Every sound seemed to have risen a full decibel and the earth's turning must have sped up. His fortunes and his desires had never before been so inextricably tied or so unavoidably there for the taking. He wanted to leave the carriage behind and run up the green to see her waiting for him at the hotel. He looked at his watch. It was only one o'clock.

When he arrived at the hotel, he waited impatiently in the large open lobby, with its tiled tubs filled with lotus flowers. Then he moved into an open lounge, looking up at the door as each new party arrived. Then, impulsively, he walked to the front desk and reserved a suite of rooms on the third floor, facing the sea. He went upstairs to inspect it and found a large sitting room with Oriental rugs and heavy, dark furniture and a bedroom with slowly whirring fans overhead and mosquito netting draped over a burled oak bed.

Returning to the lobby, he saw her on the green, sitting in a carriage that was moving at an agonizingly slow pace. He ran outside to the green to meet her.

"I couldn't keep my mind on business," she said breathlessly as he swung her down into his arms. "I couldn't waste my time on Bainbridge today. I spent all morning walking around stores waiting for two o'clock."

"I've been here for an hour."

"What a waste of time," she said, reaching up and kissing him.

"I do love you."

They walked arm in arm toward the hotel.

"I've taken a suite of rooms for us."

A miraculous smile framed her face. "What a wonderful, illicit thing for you to have done. This is just what Madame Duntov told me would happen," she said, reaching into her purse, taking out the black pearl she'd bought from him on Manihi.

"Who's Madame Duntov?"

"Someone who once read my future—she said I'd have
no choice, I'd simply have to have you without thinking of
the consequences."

"And shall we do it?"

"Yes, let's run all the way," she said, taking off.

The strand of pearls was cool to the touch. He dangled
them lightly above her breast.

"Cream rosé," he said.

"Correct."

"Pale, pale pink from the Arabian Sea—the color of your
breasts." And leaning over, he caught one of the pearls
between his teeth, licked its gritty surface, then licked her
breast, beneath it. She moaned.

As he lowered his head to her stomach, his tongue
followed the curve of her belly down to a strand of white
pearls he had placed in the fold of her thighs. "Pure white."

"From Australia."

"From Shark's Bay, and from the very center of you," he
said, his nose nuzzling into her fold, smelling the musky
dampness there.

Her head turned this way and that on the pillow. "Ravag-
ing me," she whispered.

"Making you less mysterious."

"If I were smart, I'd hold on to my mysteries to keep
you."

"No, you'd open like an oyster shell and I'd pluck the
miraculous pearl."

Reaching up with his hands, he parted her legs, the gold
hair of her pubis spreading, and slowly he drew the strand of
white pearls through her legs into the tawny crevice. She
moaned again. He dipped inside her with his tongue to
retrieve the pearls, which were wedged into a glistening,
fiery coral fold, and again his tongue invaded it, plucking a
pearl from the very center of her, grasping it between his
teeth. And now, rising on her, heady with the smell of her, a
rich, musky, steamy smell, he pulled the pearls along her
stomach, her breasts, her shoulders.

Her hands reached for him, slid from his shoulders to his
chest, along his sinewy arms, down his smooth sides, and

across his loins to his engorged penis. She placed him inside her, daring herself to keep her eyes open and stare into his eyes.

Smiling down at her, he dropped the strand of pearls from his lips onto hers, and she felt him slide farther into her, slowly, thickly, then remain embedded without moving. She could feel his pulse beating inside her. Her arms encircled his neck. Leaning down, he kissed her through the strand of pearls.

He felt as completely entwined as he had ever been with a woman. Withdrawing himself slowly until the tip of his penis nestled in her tawny hair, he remained poised over her, avoiding the closeness of their union for one unendurable moment. Then, as her legs tightened around him and a long, low moan escaped from her lips, he slowly slid back inside her.

Afterward, they lay head to foot on the bed, he, curved around her like a shell, she, her hands wrapped around his legs, talked about everything she had ever wanted to tell him—about her childhood in the country, her parents' unfathomable marriage, her first season in London, her marriage to James Vale. It poured out of her in a torrent of impassioned monologue. He told her about his childhood, his stolid father, his fanciful, unhappy mother and her dreams of escape, which had prompted him to run off to sea.

"No unhappy love affair or unhappy marriage did that?" she asked.

He said nothing.

"You don't have to tell me anything about yourself," she said, and then added with a laugh, "Were you married?"

He did not want to think about that now.

"No mistress? No clever woman managed to snag you?"

Again, he said nothing.

"I know what you want—someone unquestioning. And perhaps I still don't want to know that much about you. I've never had a real lover before. I should be patient, suffer the agony of not knowing everything about you all at once, although I am aching to know every inch of you." She kissed his legs, her slim fingers stroking the hair that covered his shins. "You were right about me when you first met me. You said I was a woman who was used to having men automatically fall in love with her. It's true. And this time . . . you took so long." She laughed. "It was agony, but I was glad to have it be this way. It gave me time to know that I was in love, that I craved someone, really loved someone—"

"And it's me."

"Oh, yes, it's you," she said, turning onto her back. "And I crave that you make love to me again. I will die if you do not."

Just then there was a knock at the door.

"Perfect—the management has sent more champagne."

Another knock sounded.

"If whoever it is was smart or discreet, he would leave."

And another.

"Neither," he said, getting up and pulling on his trousers. Tom walked into the sitting room and opened the door.

Nasis was standing in the hall, red-faced, quivering with rage when he saw that Tom was half dressed.

Chapter Thirty-four

"YOU HAVE NO business being here," Tom said, but Nasis pushed open the door with his walking stick.

"Where is sh-sh-she?"

"I want you to leave before this goes any further. I'll meet you downstairs and we'll talk."

Margot appeared in the bedroom doorway. "I'll talk with David," she said.

Seeing her standing there with a sheet wrapped around her, Nasis was choked with rage.

"I don't want to hide the truth from you, David," Margot began.

"You d-d-don't imagine for a m-m-moment that I'd support this."

"No one's asking you to."

"Or c-c-condone it."

"That's not up to you, either."

"Wh-wh-what sort of fool do you t-t-take me for?"

"No fool at all," she said. "My greatest crime is not loving you. I'm sorry. I can't do anything about it."

"J-j-jenks was right about you af-f-fter all."

"What's Jenks got to do with this?" Tom asked.

"A b-b-better friend I've n-n-never had."

"Then I'm sorry for you, Nasis."

"He's a f-f-far sight more trustworthy a b-b-business partner than either of you."

"You're not thinking clearly right now, David."

"Y-y-yes I am. I was only in this b-b-business for your sake. But now I s-s-see how thick-skinned and c-c-conniving you are. I don't want anything to do with you. My great mistake was having ever met you," Nasis said, then turned away. "I'll have my c-c-crew bring all your th-th-things here. I s-s-suppose this is where you'll want to live."

And he left without saying another word.

"Damnit all! If we'd only had some time, he'd have grown used to the fact of us," Margot said.

"He and Jenks can do a lot of damage together."

Margot turned and walked to the windows. "We'll just have to show them how thick-skinned we are."

"We needed his backing."

"I'll finance us," she said. "We won't be able to keep all our money in pearls for long. I don't have as much as he does."

"Are you offering me a deal?" he said, walking over to her, putting his arms around her waist.

"Why not? I've got the money."

"The only deal I'd make with you is that you are reimbursed for every cent you put in from the very first sale."

"Oh, no you don't," she said, turning in his arms. "Only up to fifty percent. I don't want anything less than an equal partnership with you."

"Another English empire-builder."

"An empire built on pearls."

He kissed her. "Is that what you crave? I thought it was me."

"It is."

Her hands were in his hair, pulling his face closer. Dropping her head to his chest, she inhaled his scent. It was as if nothing had happened. She was back inside his skin again. "I want you again."

As a reply he removed the sheet from her shoulders. Her nipples were as pink as a blush. Bending, he began licking them.

"And again, and again . . ."

That afternoon Tom rowed out to the yacht to pick up Teva and Raina and another couple. He'd rented cottages for them on the hotel grounds. The rest of the Tahitians had either run off or were remaining behind with Nasis and Jenks.

When he got back to the Galle Face, he found Jenks, dressed in a new white suit, standing at the bar.

"To you and the missus," he toasted drunkenly.

Tom's right fist swung up and connected solidly with Jenks's jaw. Jenks reeled backward, then caught himself against the bar and rubbed his chin with his slender hand.

"I'll save myself, boyzo. I'm going to crush you."

Turning, Tom walked out of the bar, but Jenks followed.

"I mean to be rich," he said.

Tom pushed ahead.

"I will crush both you and that woman," Jenks hissed. A drop of blood ran down his chin, staining his immaculate white suit with a single vivid dot.

Chapter
Thirty-five

MARGOT SAT IN the bank on Chatham Street in Colombo trying to decipher the bank president's expression; would he or would he not give her the money? He was standing across the room reading a telegram.

The bank was housed in a temporary office, an open pen with clusters of wooden desks. The walls had been white-washed, and fans whirred overhead. One was just slightly out of whack and kept making a *thumpata, thumpata* sound.

The president, whose name was Fleming, finally looked up at her with an expression she was sure he must have practiced in front of mirrors. Pleasant and fixed, it gave away nothing.

"Your Ladyship," he said in a raspy voice, "I'm terribly sorry, but we don't have very good news for you. The trustees of your husband's estate will not agree to a ten-thousand-pound withdrawal unless you meet with them in person."

"I can't go to London. There isn't enough time. The fishery is only weeks away."

"Perhaps if you request less money."

"How much less?"

"We could advance you several hundred pounds if you need it."

"Thank you, but I really do need the full ten thousand. My partner and I intend to hire teams of divers and purchase pearls. Will you lend me the money?"

"With what collateral, Your Ladyship?"

"I have property."

"In England," he said. "I'm afraid it will take some time to secure a loan on your English property."

An Indian man, dressed in an English-cut business suit,

sitting at a nearby desk cleared his throat, trying to get her attention.

"Yes, of course," she continued, "and while we're waiting, why not go into partnership with us? My partner and I have developed an interesting strategy for the fishery—"

"You see, that's the problem. You want the money for the fishery, and if your trustees don't think you know anything about pearl fishing, why should *we* think you do?"

"I've done a good deal of research. My partner and I know which pars will yield the best pearls."

"Your Ladyship, no one can predict that, and we can hardly use speculation as collateral. We need something of real value."

The Indian coughed again, but Margot was too intently involved in her conversation with Fleming to hear him. As she tried thinking of a different tack, her fingers gently stroked the strand of pearls around her neck.

"Something of real value, you said? What about these?" she asked, holding up her mother's pearls.

The Indian leaned over. "My goodness yes, Your Ladyship. Exactly the point I was going to make," he said in a clipped accent. "Pardon me for interrupting, but you've got all the collateral you need hanging around your neck."

Startled, Margot turned and saw that the man had an odd face, almost like a baby's, with tiny features set in a large head. His eyes, which were close together, were little slits, and the pupils seemed to take up the entire opening.

He stood up and extended his right hand, which held his calling card. It read SHANTI JHAVERIS. "I'm a pearl merchant from Bombay. As I was saying to Lady . . . ?"

"Lady Margot Vale, Mr. Jhaveris," Margot said.

"How do you do, Lady Vale? As I was about to say, you have more than enough collateral hanging around your neck for three loans of ten thousand pounds each."

Fleming fixed his gaze on the pearls.

"Those pearls were fished from the gulf near Bahrain—I wouldn't be surprised if I had paid for the holes to be drilled in them, then sold them to the jeweler who sold them to you. They're very beautiful. May I look at them more closely?"

She slipped them off and handed them to him.

Taking out his loupe, he inspected them. "My goodness, right again. From the waters just off Bahrain. I'd say these pearls are worth at least twenty-five thousand pounds. In Paris you could fetch fifty."

"There you go, and all I'm asking for is ten. Actually, I should make that fifteen," Margot said with a canny smile to the banker.

He took the pearls from Jhaveris and inspected them himself. "Of course, I'd have to get some confirmation of their value," he said quietly.

"My goodness, yes, of course," Jhaveris said. Then, turning his head, he called out to another Indian who was standing near the door. "Chand, come here a minute, will you?"

The man, who was wearing a flowing white cotton overblouse and light cotton trousers, walked over, his slippered feet sliding across the floor like sandpaper.

"What do you think these pearls are worth, Chand?" Jhaveris asked. "Mr. Pravin Chand is one of our most discriminating Bombay merchants."

Chand held a loupe to his eye and poured over the pearls as if he were reading the small print in a legal document.

"In rupees?"

"Pounds if you would, Chand."

"Thirty thousand pounds. Very beautiful," Chand said, handing them back to Jhaveris, who handed them to Margot.

"You see, Your Ladyship, if this bank doesn't want to make the loan, I'm sure you can find someone else who will."

"It is irregular," Fleming said, "but of course we'd use Lady Vale's pearls to secure a ten-thousand-pound loan."

"Do I have to leave them here?" Margot asked.

"They'll be quite safe in our vaults."

"It's not their safety I worry about. They should be worn."

"Your vaults are in a dark and cool place?" Jhaveris asked.

"Yes, of course," Fleming said.

"Then, my gracious Lady Vale, I wouldn't worry about them, and of course you will make a killing up in Mannar

170

and redeem your lovely pearls, and that will be that," Jhaveris said, looking very pleased with himself.

It took another half hour to draw up the papers. The banker included a sentence saying the loan had to be repaid within a month after the fishery. If not, the pearls would be confiscated.

As Margot was leaving the bank, walking toward her carriage, she saw Jhaveris resting under a tree.

"Mr. Jhaveris, I can't thank you enough."

"It was a pleasure to help you, Your Ladyship, although I may have cause to regret it. We will be bidding against each other in a few weeks."

"You'll be in Mannar?"

"Oh, my gracious, yes. I wouldn't miss this fishery."

"How on earth did you know those pearls had been fished from the waters off Bahrain?"

"My gracious, I didn't. I just thought it would improve your chances with the bureaucracy if your expert sounded like one. They are from the gulf, and they have the delicate lustre that I've seen in other pearls from Bahrain. I thought it was a good guess."

"Then you are an expert."

"My people are from Surat in Gujarat, a western province that was the chief pearl trading area in all of India before it moved to Bombay. So if you mean that I know my business, I do. After Mannar, when you come to Bombay, you'll meet all the Gujarat pearl traders."

"Will I come to Bombay?"

"My goodness, of course. You can't sell everything you buy in Mannar—in fact, you shouldn't. But now I must run."

"We'll see each other in Mannar, then?"

"You seem to attract beautiful pearls. And they attract me. Our meeting again seems to be inevitable," he said. Then, bowing with a flourish, he walked off.

Chapter
Thirty-six

WITH THE MONEY, Tom hired fifteen boats and a hundred and fifty divers.

Teva, Raina, a woman named Tetuara, and her husband were not faring well. Tetuara was sick. She had a fever and sores, which began to spread and eventually covered her entire body. A week after the first sores appeared, she died. After they buried her, her husband stopped eating. Teva said that the man was *erimatua*. In a foreign culture, cut off from his family and friends, his *vahine* dead, he had lost the will to live.

Teva wanted to return to Manihi, but there was no transportation available. All ships were heading north to the fishery. Finally Tom rented a schooner and they began the voyage to Mannar.

Raina was made uneasy by the transition from grasslands to desert; she had never before seen such harsh land. For miles the shore was a barren waste of low scrubby ground and stunted trees, not a hill in sight. The sun beat down pitilessly. Further north there were no trees at all, just a haze of molten air, and the sea was like a mirror. The glare and heat were intolerable.

One morning Tetuara's husband was found dead. There was no sign of disease. They buried him at sea. As the body dropped into the water, Tom recited the Lord's Prayer. Margot, standing nearby, was scouring the shore for signs of life, but an appearance of ruin spread over everything. Teva and Raina said nothing. Their eyes, once so filled with joy, were now clouded with resignation and despair.

For weeks boats had begun arriving at Marichchukkaddi beach in Mannar from every port all over the Indian

Ocean—black Jaffna *dhoneys;* narrow, fast, brightly colored canoes from Kilakarai; clumsy-looking single-masted Tuticorin sailers; and the largest of the diving fleet, the three-masted great canoes from the Tanjore coast, which were pale blue, with curved plows. They hovered offshore like ragtag phantoms, then slowly put in and discharged their crews.

The Arab divers came first, suspicious and hawk-eyed, and with them the Tamils, who belonged to the Pawara caste, and finally the Moormen, some with "pearl eyes," the saltwater having made their eyes look like milky stones. They brought their wives and children and began constructing small, temporary houses made mostly of poles, mats, and *cajans,* the plaited fronds of coconut trees.

Then, like a faucet being slowly but persistently turned, more people began showing up. The pearl merchants —Chetties, Moormen, and Gujaratis—brought better provisions: colored tents and pole-stacked lean-tos. A confusion of tongues began to drown out the sound of the sea. Morning and evening prayers were called with a hush and the drone of devotion, and there was the tinkling sound of prayer bells and the scent of incense, sandalwood, and saffron.

And the faucet was turned full open as the rest arrived: the boat-repairers and sail-menders, food-provisioners, priests, bankers, pawnbrokers, government officials, pearl-counters, clerks, boat guards, police, coolies, domestic servants, all with wives and children. And for the entertainment of this mass of humanity came the jugglers and acrobats. One middle-aged woman from India charged ten rupees to have people watch her balance herself by her chin on top of an elevated pole. And there were gamblers, beggars, dancers, whores, and thieves as well. The riffraff of the entire Indian subcontinent seemed to have washed up on the beaches of Ceylon.

In all, fifty thousand human beings created a town that would last no more than six weeks. Time was compressed. The Ceylon fishery was the shortest in the world. Because of the weather and upcoming religious holidays, they had only thirty good days to haul in the largest catch of pearls on earth.

There were hastily laid out streets and a vast number of temporary houses. There were wells and cisterns for water, public latrines, a police court, a post and telegraph office, a bank, an auction room, a hospital, a cemetery. At a considerable distance from the settlement were the *toddis,* the enclosures for decomposing oysters and the washing of pearls.

Into this teaming mass of humanity Tom and Margot and Teva and Raina arrived, stunned by the sights and smells. Raina refused to leave the boat. Margot and Tom had to leave her behind with Teva and push their way through the crowds, which seemed to be heaviest at the shoreline. People were buying and selling everything imaginable: blankets and food, glass beads, fabric and water, and oil for lamps.

Tom finally met up with the captains of two of his boats, and they in turn rounded up five more. Eight of the other boats Tom had hired in Colombo had signed on with other outfits. Opening day was approaching, and Tom had to arrange for the inspection and registration of his existing fleet. Margot began helping in ways Tom never would have expected. Interviewing captains and crews, signing up new ones, stealing others away from merchants, she skillfully played the game; having six boats committed in the morning, losing two by noon, gaining another three by nightfall, losing another four by midnight. By the second day they were having trouble holding on to the original fleet.

"What are we doing wrong?" Tom asked her as they stood near the shoreline fending off peddlers.

"Have you seen the *kadal-kottis?"* a particularly fiesty and persistent peddler called out.

"The what?"

"The shark charmer! No one will dive for you unless you've hired a shark charmer."

"Are you a shark charmer?" Margot asked him.

"No, I'm an astrologer."

"An astrologer! What luck!"

"But I can lead you to a shark charmer."

"And do our horoscopes?"

"All for one low price."

"Lead on!"

"Margot!"

"Tom, what do we have to lose?"

"Aside from our money?"

But the peddler had grabbed her hand and was pulling her through the crowd. Reaching out, she grabbed Tom's hand and off they went.

_____ *Chapter* _____
Thirty-seven

AT FIRST TOM couldn't see anything inside the *kadal-kotti's* hut, and he hit his head on a pair of shark jaws that were tied to the roof. Gradually his eyes adjusted. A pinpoint of light came through a crack in the wall. An old man, whose face was so deeply wrinkled it looked as though someone had scarred him with a knife, was sitting on the floor with his eyes closed. He was stark naked.

In front of him was a large brass basin filled with water. Inside were two metallic fish, one larger than the other.

"I don't remember you," the man said without opening his eyes.

"No, you wouldn't. I've never been here before."

"You have teams of divers?"

"Yes, we were hoping to have one hundred and fifty of them. . . . Have you always done this work?"

"My people have been doing our work for almost six centuries."

"And what exactly is your line of work?"

His eyes blinked open. They were startlingly clear, deep, deep brown, almost as dark as Tom's.

"You know nothing of the *kadal-kotti?* The divers will not go out to the sea without us."

"That much I do know. But what sort of deal do we have to make to have you work for us?" Tom asked, but seeing the surprised look on the shark charmer's face, he rephrased

175

the question. "What I mean is . . . what donations are necessary?"

"Donations? I don't understand the word."

"How much are you people paid?"

"In ancient times we received one twentieth of the entire catch."

"But surely times have changed."

"When the Portuguese were here, we received one twelfth. A very nasty group of people, the Portuguese. Now we have the British; I prefer them. Stare down into the basin. See the silver sharks?"

As he spoke the larger fish began circling the smaller one. Tom thought it must be some trick, that the man's voice was setting up a vibration in the water.

"One male, one female. If there is to be an accident at sea, a shark biting a diver, I will know it because one of my sharks will have bitten the other. If the boat the diver has come from is protected by me, then I make sure the accident does not occur."

"I've seen sharks up close—they'll attack anything if they're hungry enough."

"Where did you see such sharks?"

"In the South Seas."

"I cannot control what goes on there. Here you have not seen such sharks. I can control those only . . ."

He placed his hand an inch above the water, moving it in a circular motion until the larger shark stopped its cruising and the smaller one began circling the larger.

"If you tried to do that, you would not be able to make the sharks move. But you don't have to worry as long as I am here. I sit in this hut, in the dark as I am now, stripped of all my clothes so that I may work with as little interference as possible, and I ask them to bolt the door so that I will be undisturbed. If I work for your divers, you are assured of getting my most complete attention. How many boats will you be using?"

"I wanted fifteen."

The man closed his eyes again. "That's asking too much. This is such taxing work, I don't want to work for more than two or three boats at a time."

"Are there many shark attacks each season?"

"Not one in more than ten years."

"Then why do I need you?"

"Why do you think there hasn't been an attack in all those years? I have been at this fishery all that time. Before I came, they were eating those divers five at a time—the water ran with blood. It was horrible for the families—those poor children left fatherless and homeless, turning to the streets. Before you knew it, mothers were maiming their babies, setting them out in the streets to beg."

"All right, I get the point. How much do you want?"

"We will take one hundred oysters per day per diver."

"Ridiculous," Tom said, getting up to leave.

"Where are you going?"

"If I want to throw my money away, I might as well toss it directly into the ocean."

"Make me an offer—it is the Eastern way."

"One shell per day per diver."

"Seventy-five."

"One."

"Fifty."

"One."

"Thirty-five."

"One."

"Twenty."

Tom merely shook his head.

"Ten? Five?"

"One!"

"Allah's will . . ." he said, and then in a clipped tone, eyes closed, he added, "Leave the registration numbers of your boats on the piece of paper outside the door. One of my brothers will collect the fee each day. And rest assured that I will be working as hard as I can for you."

Margot was waiting outside.

"Done," Tom told her.

"How does he do it?"

"Swiftly."

"Does it work? Do you think he's good at it?"

"I saw a small boy once on a train do it much faster. He'd distract you with conversation, bump into you, and before you knew it, he'd have your entire wallet."

But as soon as word passed that he had engaged the shark

charmer, he and Margot had all the divers they needed. The shark charmer was not the last person who had to be paid off, though. The government guards posted on each of the boats had to be paid just to be kept honest. And there were the *sammatti* (boat masters), who got one dive per day per diver. The *tindal* (the pilot) and the *todai* (water bailer—a very important position on these leaky vessels) also got one dive per day, and there were anywhere from ten to thirty divers per boat, so the haul was substantial. The divers also had their *manducks,* the diving attendants, who got one third of the daily catch. The Moormen from Kilakarai also contributed one dive per day to the mosque of their native town.

The night before the first dive was scheduled, Tom and Margot were sitting on the aft deck of the schooner. Teva and Raina were sleeping nearby.

"I've arranged for them to dive with a group of Tamils —they'll be coming to get them soon. Tomorrow's dives at Karativu and Madragam will be some of the richest."

"I want to watch them go. Will you wake me?"

He said he would, then she stretched out on the chair next to him and fell asleep. Tom was too excited to sleep.

Shortly before midnight he saw fires on the shore. The divers were going to morning prayer or eating their morning meal. He awakened Teva and Raina, who stood dull-eyed, shivering on the aft deck waiting for the boats to fetch them.

Shortly before dawn the Tamils came by and Teva and Raina went off with them. Tom, forgetting to wake Margot, stood on the deck and watched as their boat joined the others. Almost five thousand divers in over three hundred boats set out to sea. Sails of every shape fluttered, then filled with wind. The procession went on for over an hour, and then Tom, walking back to the deck chair, dozed off and with the first light of morning reawakened with a start.

As the opening day gun was fired, Margot opened her eyes. The sun, looking like a ripe mango, was rising slowly. The boats could be seen in the distance, their masts bobbing and twitching on the horizon.

"We should wish each other luck," Margot said, staring out at them.

"And nerves of steel," he said.

Chapter _Thirty-eight_

WORKING IN PAIRS, the divers brought up baskets loaded with oysters, and as the morning wore on, the air was thick with excitement. This year's catch would be as big or bigger than last year's. The diving continued until twelve o'clock, when another shot rang out from the guard vessel. As the divers ascended, a great cheer rose up—part song, part prayer of thanks.

Teva, who had tried to keep up with the others, struggled to the surface, his face contorted, blood trickling from his ears and nostrils. Raina had never seen him like this, and when she went to comfort him, he pushed her away angrily. Sitting silently on the deck, she watched as he counted his meager catch.

The average take on the first day ranged between fifteen and fifty oysters per diver. Better divers were averaging as many as seventy-five. Teva had only brought up twenty.

The breeze picked up, and sails were set. The vessels made for port. Now everyone was dashing about, stowing their gear or rewrapping their heads with turbans. This was the time when most of the poaching was done. Divers and masters eagerly sliced open the shells, took what they could, and discarded the meat and shells over the side.

The fleet arrived back at Marichchukkaddi at about two-thirty. Tens of thousands of merchants and camp followers lined the shore. The divers jockeyed for position to be the first ones ashore and hailed as returning heroes.

Tom and Margot were among the cheering crowd, as was Jenks. The _Distant Star_ had put in that morning. Nasis remained aloof, watching the goings-on from the aft deck.

"How did it go?" Tom called out when he spotted one of his captains.

"Good day! Our boat alone got almost two thousand. Whole fleet, maybe a half million—maybe more," he called back.

Seeing Teva and Raina, Tom waved wildly but stopped when he saw their faces. They made their way back out to the schooner without coming ashore to join in the festivities.

The oysters were unloaded by the crews and taken into the government *koddu,* a thatched-roof building with pens, each of which had a number corresponding to the number of each boat. The catch was divided among the divers, *manducks, sammatti, tindals,* and *todais.* As the divers left the *koddu* with their quota, they were deluged by offers from the native buyers, who were eager to purchase small lots for anywhere from one to twelve rupees.

Margot raced forward, twenty rupees clutched in her hand, and bought two hundred shells, which she and Tom eagerly opened. People gathered to watch. Stories circulated. A poor Tamil, someone said, five years ago had bought five oysters for half a rupee and in one found the largest pearl of the season. But Tom and Margot had no such luck that afternoon.

The remaining oysters, over three hundred and fifty thousand, were counted, then separated into lots of one thousand for the auction, which was scheduled for nine o'clock that night.

As Tom went over all the information he had accumulated on the Karativu and Madragam pars, Margot, who was pacing on the schooner's aft deck, called out, "Let's go over the procedure one more time."

"The bidding starts with an estimated price. Whoever wins the bid wins the right to take as many lots of one thousand oysters as he choses. But no one knows if he's won a fortune in pearls or a bunch of worthless shells," he said, pacing with her now. "You are making me very nervous."

"We have to be cautious."

"We can depend on Nasis not to be cautious. He may drive the prices above the world market price."

"I think our biggest problem with David will be his seeing me with you at the auction."

"That could be the key to keeping him in line—both him and Jenks, in fact. Whenever he's bidding directly, we'll unnerve him by having you bid against him. Whenever Jenks is bidding, I'll bid against him."

"It might have just the opposite effect."

"I don't think so. Nasis is still so in love with you, I don't think he could stand to hurt you in any way."

Margot looked at Tom uneasily. "That's rather cold-hearted of you."

"Basically, Jenks is frightened of me . . . We can control this."

"All this premeditation for lots of one thousand shells."

"And from one thousand shells you may get twenty-five pearls. That's a possible catch of over twelve thousand pearls just tonight—and just one of those could yield thousands of dollars."

"And we have to use every situation to our advantage."

"Isn't that what you've always done?"

"No. Now isn't a particularly fine time to be thinking about it, but I've been much more protected than that. My bankers take such care of me, they won't advance my own money to me."

He put his arms around her. "Just keep thinking about what you want more than anything else."

"Aside from you."

"You have me. What about your freedom?"

"I don't want to become hardened in order to hold on to it."

"You really are naive."

"So were you when I first met you—or maybe that was just the last vestige of it."

He held her at arm's length. "Do you love me?"

"Of course I love you."

"Then trust me."

She laughed. "On faith—just like hunting for a pearl in an oyster shell."

At nine o'clock they were standing in the auction room, which was a thatch-covered hall with rows of benches. The air was still and warm, filled with the acrid odor of rotting oysters from the nearby *koddu*.

Nasis, standing with Jenks near the podium, looked nervous.

At the other end of the hall were Indians, dressed in European suits, with walking sticks and polished shoes. One of them waved to Margot.

"That's the man I told you about. Jhaveris, the one who helped me at the bank," she said to Tom.

Jhaveris walked over to her. "My goodness, what a stir you are causing. And what a pleasure it is to see you again," he said.

Margot introduced Jhaveris to Tom.

"Is the room usually this crowded?" Tom asked.

"This promises to be a very special season. Everyone has managed to come down, and they brought their astrologers, too."

"Bidding done by the stars?" Tom asked with a smile.

"My goodness, yes. Tonight is favorable for bidding."

"My friend is not a great believer, Mr. Jhaveris," Margot said.

"Oh? What system do you use?" Jhaveris asked, his head cocked to one side.

"Numbers."

"Numerology?"

"Statistics."

"Ah, a purist, the biggest gambler in the room, I suspect."

Just then, the crowd parted and a small entourage of Arabs walked in—a group of four younger men surrounding an older one, a man in his fifties wearing a striped silk robe and white burnoose. He had heavy-lidded eyes that took in everything all at once, thick, purplish lips, and a nose that hung like a long, crooked finger. He looked impatient and nervous. He flicked his index finger and one of the boys wiped off a seat. Then the Arab sat down, scanned the room, and focused on Margot and Tom.

"His name is Ali Aziz. He's an agent for the sheiks who control most of the pearls fished from the Persian Gulf," Jhaveris whispered.

"What does he want in Ceylon?" Margot asked.

"Perhaps the sheiks want to conquer the world."

A beautiful boy with dark, curly hair and large, sad eyes crouched on the floor at Ali Aziz's feet, and Ali Aziz placed a greedy hand on the boy's head. He looked almost frantic now, like a horse at a gate panting for the opening bell.

"Ladies and gentlemen," an Englishman standing at the podium called out. "The bidding is about to commence."

Chapter
Thirty-nine

THE BIDDING BEGAN at twenty-five rupees. For one tense moment there was complete silence because it was such a high starting price, then Tom impulsively raised his hand and called out, "Twenty-six."

And instantly the bidding became heated, a contest between Tom and Jenks, Ali Aziz and Jhaveris.

At fifty-five rupees Jhaveris dropped out, but Tom, Ali Aziz, and Jenks were still in.

After a moment's pause Jenks and Nasis conferred while Ali Aziz stonily surveyed the room.

Jenks called out, "Fifty-six."

"We have fifty-six from Mr. Jenks. Do I hear fifty-seven?"

"Can we go any higher?" Margot whispered to Tom.

"Yes, and now we'll see whether or not Nasis is going to be spiteful or smart."

"What about Ali Aziz?"

Tom looked over at him. "He's looking shaky."

"Fifty-seven," Ali Aziz called out.

"Not that shaky," Margot said, reaching into her purse to grasp the black pearl. Just holding it made her feel confident.

"We'll lose him on the next round."

"Fifty-eight," Jenks called out.

"Sixty," Tom suddenly called out.

Margot looked startled.

Nasis conferred with Jenks again, then Jenks called out, "Sixty-one."

Ali Aziz turned away from the podium.

"Sixty-three," Tom countered.

Jenks wanted to counter that, but Nasis stopped him. Jenks was angry.

"Sixty-three is our last bid," the auctioneer said. "Going once, twice, sold to Mr. Street and Lady Vale."

"Done," Tom said, smiling down at Margot.

She was as pale as a cloud.

"How many lots will you be taking, sir?" the auctioneer called out.

"How many do we take?" Margot whispered.

"One hundred, at sixty-three hundred rupees," he whispered to her.

"That's more than a thousand pounds. All we've got is ten thousand and this is only the first night."

"One hundred lots," Tom called out, and the room erupted with talk.

Nasis and Jenks purchased fifty lots at the price Tom had established. Ali Aziz purchased twenty and Jhaveris ten, and then bidding reopened on another one hundred lots from the Madragam par.

The action now was not as spirited. Tom did not have as much confidence in this par, but Jenks and Nasis, who seemed to be out to prove something, were very aggressive, as were Ali Aziz and several Indians who had not participated in the last bidding. Again, toward the end, Nasis began to slow Jenks's bids, and Jenks looked increasingly angry. Finally Nasis let him go ahead, and the price to Nasis and Jenks was set at fifty-three rupees. They bought an additional fifty lots. Ali Aziz bought twenty, and the remainder went to the Indians.

The final lots were also from the Karativu par and the bidding was as frenetic as in the first round. Ali Aziz seemed to be in league with Jenks and Nasis, trying to keep Tom from winning. Jhaveris stayed in, countering Nasis, Jenks, and Ali Aziz in a friendly way until the end, but finally it was Tom and Margot who set the price at sixty-four rupees, and Tom bought all the lots. It was important, he told her, to capture the attention this first night. They had been unknown players, but not anymore.

"My goodness, we're making life very expensive for those

beautiful women in London and Paris," Jhaveris said to Margot as he was leaving the auction room. "Do you think their husbands will pay any amount to keep them in pearls?"

"I'm not sure."

"You have to know your markets very well. Of course, my goodness, there are a great many wealthy English and French in the world."

"Not to mention the Americans," Tom added.

"Or the Indians, for that matter, Mr. Street."

"Do you see a way to make life less expensive for us all?" Margot asked him.

"My goodness gracious, yes, there's strength in numbers. Mr. Street, you are a great believer in numbers, are you not?" Jhaveris said as he bid them good night.

"I'm not sure I like that man," Tom said.

"I don't know that you can afford not to."

The shells were taken from the government *koddu* and brought to a private enclosure that Tom had rented. The *toddi* was located at some distance from the camp. There the shells, exposed to the solar heat, putrefied, and the fleshy parts were eaten by swarms of bluebottle flies and maggots. The largest *toddis* were fifteen or twenty feet long and three feet deep, with smooth inner walls so that the pearls could not lodge in any crevices. The tank was covered with a matting of straw or seaweed and guarded for a week or so, to allow the flies to consume all the meat. Even that first night the odor began to penetrate the camp, and the first swarms of flies began to arrive.

Margot and Tom lay in each other's arms aboard the schooner—the odor had driven them below deck. Wine, the excitement of the auction, and their lovemaking had made them drowsy.

Nearby, huddled in the shadows, Raina waited for them to fall asleep.

Following Teva's instructions, she had crept into the room to steal money, but now she was losing her nerve and she returned to the deck.

Teva was angry with her. They had to leave this place, he said. They needed the money.

"If we wait another month, we'll have our own money," she was saying.

"A month is eternity. The water is no good. No luck for me here."

The other divers were much better than he, although he could not say this to her. He was too ashamed to stay in Mannar. It was better to be a thief and leave.

"Go back to the room, get the money for us, steal a little tonight, then more tomorrow," he said. This time she went, creeping softly down the stairs along the narrow, polished hallway, past the galley. Opening the last door on the right, she found Tom lying with his arms around Margot. Raina remembered the first night she saw him—his dark eyes and copper-colored hair.

On a table was the woman's purse. Raina decided it would be better to steal from her rather than him. Opening it, she found a comb and a pin, then a satin bag with a pull string. Inside was an envelope with pound notes, and she was about to take some of them when her eyes became fixed on a pretty lace handkerchief with the initials *MV* on one corner. It smelled of lemons and something almost as sweet as tiare flowers. The black pearl Tom had found on Manihi slipped from the handkerchief and dropped to the floor. Tom moved in his sleep.

Raina, dropping to her knees, held up the pearl and stared at it: so lustrous and warm to the touch. He had taken it from one of her fishing places and now she wanted to take it back with her to Manihi. Rewrapping it in the handkerchief, she tucked it into her sarong, took some pound notes, and crept out of the room.

Chapter
Forty

THE NEXT DAY the divers went back to the Karativu pars and brought back a huge catch.

At the camp the revolting smell of rotting oysters was pervasive, and at the auctions that night, some people looked faint from the stench.

Margot and Tom sat in their same seats. Nasis and Jenks were seated opposite them. Everyone was tense.

Jhaveris sat nearby, wishing Westerners weren't so unpredictable. Ali Aziz arrived with his entourage of boys. He looked as intent as he had the first night, as though he relished the tension.

The bidding began.

Nasis took the lead.

Tom whispered to Margot, "Are you feeling up to going against him?"

"If you think it will do any good, I am."

He nodded and she instinctively reached into her purse to clutch the black pearl for good luck, but it was gone.

"The black pearl I bought from you—it's not here," she whispered.

"Probably back on the boat."

Ali Aziz and Nasis were bidding against each other, and everyone was looking over at Tom and Margot to see if they would counter.

"No, I always keep it with me."

"What difference could it make? Are you up to doing this or not?"

Ali Aziz had just pushed the price to fifty-eight.

Nasis countered with sixty-one.

Tom went to raise his hand, but Margot stood and called out, "Sixty-two."

There was a burst of wild talk; a woman had never before bid at an auction. Nasis was startled, as if she had just slapped him. He began to counter the bid, but could not.

Jenks rose beside him, calling out, "Sixty-three."

"Sixty-four," Margot said.

"Sixty-five," Ali Aziz responded.

"Six," Margot countered.

Nasis, staring at her with a stricken look on his face, told Jenks to sit down.

"You'll hand it to her," Jenks said, sitting with his arms folded angrily across his chest.

"S-s-seventy," Nasis called out.

"Seventy-three," Margot said.

"Calm down," Tom whispered to her.

"M-m-margot, you d-d-don't know w-w-what you're doing," Nasis impulsively called out.

"Your bid, Mr. Nasis?" the auctioneer asked.

"Margot, s-s-stop this nonsense before you wreck us all."

"Your bid?"

"S-s-seventy-five."

"Seventy-six," she said in a strong voice.

There was a hush in the room. No one moved a muscle as they waited for either Ali Aziz or Nasis to counter her bid. Then Ali Aziz took his seat. Now everyone turned to Nasis, who was standing there red-faced, his upper lip quivering. Finally he sat down.

"What incompetence," Jenks fumed.

The man at the podium banged his gavel and awarded the bid to Lady Vale.

"I want all the lots," Margot said, as startled by her resolve as Nasis had been.

Later that night Raina crept into Margot and Tom's cabin and stole ten of Margot's pound notes. Then she and Teva swam to shore.

The moon was not visible.

As they made their way south away from the camp, the odor became stronger and stronger. Raina kept Margot's sweet-smelling handkerchief pressed to her nose, and Teva fought back the urge to vomit.

The guards dozing near the water opposite the large *toddis* wore masks that were saturated with fresh lemon juice. Beyond the *toddis,* tucked into a cove, was a small *dhoney* that Teva had stolen. They spent the night there.

At dawn Teva awoke. There was a terrible buzzing. His eyes opened a crack. He and Raina were covered with flies. She screamed. He put his hand over her mouth, but she couldn't stop screaming. Fanning her frantically, he tried to shoo them away, but they clung to his hands and her arms and neck. Raina was twitching violently and finally Teva pulled her into the water and submerged with her. When they came up to the surface the flies were gone, but Raina was still trembling and she sat in the boat clutching the pearl as he pushed off.

One of the guards awoke and saw them set the sail and head south. He called out to them and waved, but they were too far off shore to hear.

The wind was constant all morning, then it began to die, and at noon they lay in the boat, tired and hungry, dazed by the heat. A breeze picked up in the early afternoon and carried them farther south until they reached the grasslands.

Pulling the boat ashore, they explored a small cove that was as green as home and just as peaceful. The air was tepid and restful. Using a jagged, thick shell, Teva sharpened a point on a stick for spearing fish. When he went off, Raina spread out their *tapaku* and stared up at the sky, which was streaked with salmon and gold, darkening slowly until the salmon turned to rose and the gold to pale lavender. Taking out the black pearl, she saw the colors of her home—the deep blackness of the sea at night, the gray dawn streaked with pink, the green water, and, closing her eyes, she saw the lagoon, the *hoa,* the white line of surf crashing on the outer reef.

A rustling in the grass interrupted her reverie. It sounded like something was being pulled through the underbrush. Clutching the pearl, Raina walked to the edge of the grassy field and peered in. She saw nothing, then heard a snap, a tug, and a low satisfied growl. She started when she heard a moan. Someone in trouble, she thought, walking into the tall grass, clutching the pearl in her hand. She pushed aside the sticky, soft grass with her free hand. There was a slithering sound, and looking down, she saw a trail of blood. She'd stepped into it before she'd seen it and now it covered her foot. In the dense silence she shivered; a chill penetrated the air. The sun had gone, and she felt alone. Then, hearing another snap and parting the grass, she looked down and saw a fallen antelope. Silent, lifeless, its glazed eyes stared at her. Its neck was broken and there was a seeping, bloody wound. Excited and scared, she went to touch it, but suddenly it jerked backward. She gasped and, looking out, saw the thing that had killed it—a leopard, its tense black eyes fixed on hers, its mouth covered with blood.

Raina backed away and the leopard lunged forward. She turned, screaming Teva's name, and started to run out of the grass, her hands clutched tightly to her chest. The leopard sprang up as if it were mounting her, its claws grasping her shoulders, its mouth agape, and sank its teeth into her neck, straight to the bone. Dazed, all she could think of was how warm it was—the leopard's fevered breath and her own blood, which was pouring forth—so warm, and finally the warmth enveloped her and she could no longer even hear the sound of her own screams.

At the very last moment she felt for the pearl, still embedded in her palm, and it, too, felt warm. She saw its blackness spreading out, covering everything, warm and comforting, like the sea at night at home.

Chapter
Forty-one

WORD SPREAD THAT Teva and Raina were missing and everyone was questioned except the guards up at the *toddis,* because no one wanted to go near the source of that foul smell. No one except Jenks, that is, who had tied a rag drenched in lemon juice over his nose and was creeping through the *toddis* Nasis had rented. Prying open a wooden frame, he took out a dozen shells, and sure enough, inside one were two small, speckled white pearls, which he pocketed.

Just as he was about to reach in for more, a gloved hand grabbed him around the neck. Turning, Jenks threw all his weight at his attacker's legs, knocking him backward, then he scrambled onto the man's chest and held him pinned, his fists poised above the man's face. It was a Sinhalese guard, also wearing a lemon-drenched rag around his face.

"It's you, Mr. Jenks, sir, I didn't know. Thought it was a thief. Please let me up, Mr. Jenks, sir."

Jenks crouched above the man's chest, pulling his head up with the rag.

"You surprised me, Mr. Jenks, sir. No one comes out here."

"I'm impatient."

The guard laughed nervously as Jenks stood.

"No way to speed things up, Mr. Jenks, sir. You shouldn't be out here. The smell is bad for you."

"And not bad for you?"

"After years of it I smell lotus blossoms and they smell too sweet, make me feel sick."

"Can you tell the difference from year to year? Will this be a rich pearl harvest?"

"This smell is pungent, but it could be stronger yet. Last year it was like sitting in a large vat of dead animals. This year it smells more like dead fish. It's a good sign."

Jenks shuddered and the guard laughed.

"People are cowards when it comes to smell, Mr. Jenks, sir, because odors blot out memory. You'll see it start soon. People will run away, scared they may lose their wits, even with the promise of money to be made. Already started —two days ago I saw two light-skinned natives, a man and a woman, sailing away."

"Which natives?"

"Not from here and not Arabs, Mr. Jenks, sir."

"You saw the Tahitians?"

"Sailed off at dawn. Couldn't take the smell," he said, laughing. His lips and teeth were stained red from chewing betel.

"Which direction were they heading?"

"South," he said, spitting out some red juice.

"You know Mr. Street and Lady Vale?" Jenks suddenly asked, seeing a way to get Tom and Margot out of the auction.

"Yes, Mr. Jenks, sir. They have all the *toddis* in the west part of the field."

"Those natives worked for them. They'd pay you good money to know their whereabouts."

The guard spit out some more juice and looked toward the encampment.

"You should tell them about it, but wait until tomorrow," Jenks said. "On second thought, tell them late afternoon tomorrow," he said, handing the guard a couple of shillings. "You say that the natives looked scared and crazy when they ran off. And make it sound like you don't think they could have gone very far . . ."

"Not very far," the guard parroted.

"How many days ago did you see them?"

"Two days."

"You tell them you think they only left a couple of hours ago."

"Couple of hours ago, Mr. Jenks, sir. How much money do I ask for?"

"Whatever you think they'll pay."

"And how much more will you pay me not to tell them I spoke to you?"

Jenks glared. "I'd call you a stinking bastard, but you'd take that as a compliment," he said, reaching into his pocket.

Tom and Margot lifted anchor as soon as the guard finished telling his story. But there was no sign of Teva and Raina on shore or out on the water. The schooner put in for the night inside a cove at a tip of some barren land.

By the next morning the heat was intense and the deadened land sizzled with the dry sound of crickets. They lifted anchor, set sail, and headed south, reaching the grasslands by noon, and in another hour, the captain, a good-natured Englishman named Fell, sighted the small beached *dhoney,* its bare mast pitched to one side on a stretch of sand.

"There's no camp, no fire," Tom said, looking out uneasily.

He and Fell put the tender over the side and helped Margot in.

They landed just to the left of the *dhoney.* Inside it was Margot's satin pouch and a roll of pound notes.

Fell said he was going to walk around the cove to see if there was any sign of them on the other side. As Margot and Tom walked toward the tall grass, Margot suddenly stopped and pointed at a stick that was embedded in what looked like a mound of speckled sand. On closer inspection, they saw it was a leopard lying on its side, a spear in its chest, its left legs curving protectively around its middle. Its eyes were open, and its left front paw was tensed, ready to attack. Tom, kneeling behind it, touched it. It had been dead for at least a day. Its mouth and paws were covered with dried blood.

Tom pulled the stick out of the leopard's side.

"It's an *oka paru,* a fishing spear. Teva taught me how to make one. They must have been surprised, but he fought it off."

A piece of white fabric caught Margot's eye, and inching forward into the grass, parting it slowly, first she saw a trail of dark blood, then her own handkerchief—the pearl was

193

gone. Turning, she was startled by the sight of a fallen antelope, only its head intact. Then her foot hit something brittle, and there at her feet lay Raina, turned on her side, her eyes wide open.

Margot gasped and Tom, racing into the grass, saw the corpse. He dropped to his knees and touched Raina, but immediately withdrew his hand. She wasn't human anymore; all the warmth had gone out of her.

Tom stood up and began yelling, "Teva! Teva!" Thrashing farther into the bush, he followed the trail of blood into another clearing, but Teva was nowhere to be seen and the trail of blood ended.

"Mr. Street!" Fell called out from the shore. "Mr. Street! Down here—I found him!"

Together, Tom and Margot ran down to the shore. Fell was standing at one end of the cove over a bloated body.

"Drowned," Fell called out. "Don't come much closer, Your Ladyship."

Margot stopped when she saw Tom drop to his knees and begin to weep.

Tom could not stand to look at Fell or Margot; he hated them and himself for being alive. He could not even talk, and remained on the beach near the bodies. He felt unhinged, unsafe.

Hours later Fell built a bonfire to keep the vultures and jackals away. The bodies were lying near the shore. Tom was still sitting beside them, guarding them, when Margot came back from the schooner with some sheets.

"We have to bury them," she said. "I've made shrouds."

"I wish I were in a place I thought of as home, surrounded by a horde of people I'd known for a very long time. . . . I was safe with them out on the atoll, but I couldn't stay, and I could blame that on finding the pearls or being with Jenks or meeting you, but I had to leave. I wanted my own fortune. . . . I should have protected them from my ambition."

Margot, saddened by what he was saying, was as much in love with him at that moment as she had ever been with anyone in her life.

Tom turned away, looking uncomfortable, as if he wanted

to cry and was frightened of showing her. "We'll return them to the sea. It's where they found me," he said quietly.

Working by the blazing light of the bonfire, they cleaned the bodies. Tom placed night-blooming flowers on both their heads. Margot, trying to place a bouquet in Raina's hands before wrapping the shroud around her, saw the black pearl held tightly in Raina's left hand.

"She had my pearl with her at the end."

Tom looked up with a curious, reviving expression, and putting aside any thoughts of her having stolen the pearl, he said, "She must have been thinking about home."

Chapter
Forty-two

WITH TOM AND Margot gone, Nasis, Ali Aziz, and Jhaveris battled to control the fishery. Nasis was driving up prices, paying over ninety rupees for some lots.

Aziz asked for a meeting with Nasis.

It took place aboard the *Distant Star*.

Something was very wrong, Jenks thought as Ali Aziz came aboard. Aziz looked nervous, almost desperate. Was the middleman caught in a squeeze?

"We cannot allow the price of pearls to rise unchecked. No one will make money," Aziz said.

"Are you h-h-here to d-d-deliver a w-w-warning?" Nasis asked.

"No, Mr. Nasis. I'm here to talk sense."

"The w-w-world market has n-n-never been as hungry for pearls as it is now."

"That's very true, but it's changeable, and we can either continue to make life expensive for each other or we can talk about an alliance."

"What sort of alliance?" Jenks asked, pushing his way into the conversation.

"We hold the price at last night's level—ninety-two rupees," Aziz said cautiously, looking at Nasis. "We split lots from certain pars."

"We b-b-become partners."

"There are a number of ways a partnership would benefit us. The people I represent purchase large quantities of pearls."

"Who are they?" Jenks asked.

"Their names are not important," Aziz said quickly.

"The sheiks of the Persian Gulf?" Jenks asked.

Aziz looked annoyed. He didn't want to answer Jenks's questions—he wasn't sure what Jenks's position was. All he knew was that Nasis had the money and Nasis was controlling the prices.

"Do you work for the sheiks?" Jenks persisted.

Aziz nodded curtly, dismissing Jenks, and focused on Nasis again.

"Mr. Nasis, are you planning to sell into the European market?"

"C-c-certainly into London."

"You have family there," Aziz said. "The Arabian market is almost as large as the European, and you cannot sell to it without me. I can help you there."

"Why do we need you? If we have the pearls, anyone will buy from us," Jenks said, but Nasis cut him off.

"Mr. Jenks does n-n-not s-s-speak for me, Aziz. I'm very interested in the Arabian m-m-market."

"You and he are not partners," Aziz said, not looking at Jenks.

Nasis said nothing, and Jenks sat there, quietly seething.

"Perhaps we can come to some agreement, then," Aziz continued, "before Mr. Street and Lady Vale return. I have not approached them."

Hearing their names, Nasis shifted uncomfortably in his wicker chair, then rose. "I will n-n-not be p-p-part of any deal involving them."

"We must keep them in line," Aziz said.

"I'm b-b-being as clear and definite as I c-c-can be. Do you understand m-m-me?"

"Perfectly."

"Th-th-thank you for your offer. I'll g-g-give you my answer tonight. Jenks, s-s-see Ali Aziz to his boat," Nasis said, then left.

Jenks, relegated to servant status, was momentarily speechless. Recovering, he turned to Aziz. "Nasis and I *are* partners."

Aziz, walking to the gangway, said nothing.

"I don't want you to think any different. I own half the pearls in our *toddis,*" Jenks persisted.

"Mr. Nasis's money bought those pearls and pays the rent for the *toddis.*"

"Half are mine. What you were saying before about access to the Arab market . . . that interests me. We should talk about that. I can deliver half our catch from this fishery. Would you give me access to the Arabian market?"

Aziz, who now stood at the base of the gangway, looked up warily. "For a price, Mr. Jenks, anything is possible."

"Don't underestimate me, Aziz."

"When I see your half of Mr. Nasis's catch, I won't," Aziz said, stepping aboard his boat, then disappearing beneath a striped canopy.

Jenks ran from the port rail to Nasis's stateroom.

Nasis was sitting at a satinwood escritoire, writing a letter to his uncle, Lord Alfred Nasis, who had financed his expedition.

"What do you mean, treating me like a servant, telling him I don't speak for you? We're equal partners. That was our deal."

"What d-d-deal are you referring to, Jenks?"

Jenks threw aside a chair. "You forget who brought you here."

"I'm sure if I d-d-do, you'll be the f-f-first to remind me. D-d-don't worry, you'll be nicely paid for y-y-your work."

"Paid? We're partners!"

A servant appeared in the doorway.

"F-f-fix Mr. Jenks a d-d-drink. He n-n-needs one," Nasis said, then went back to his letter.

Jenks pushed his way past the servant and stormed out of the room.

Chapter
Forty-three

THAT NIGHT TOM and Margot were back at the auction. The lots were evenly split between Nasis and Ali Aziz. The price held at ninety rupees.

The next day people began showing up at the *toddis,* outfitted in lemon juice-drenched masks. The pearl-extraction process was now moving into a crucial stage.

The tanks were filled with seawater to float out the maggots and other debris. Nude coolies squatted along the sides of each tank to wash and remove the shells. The valves of each were separated, the interiors examined for attached or encysted pearls. Guards with rifles were posted every ten yards to watch the coolies. Every once in a while a shot rang out over the coolies' heads. The guards wouldn't allow them to put their hands in their mouths or put them anywhere else a pearl could be hidden.

The most conspicuous pearls were picked out and trans-ferred to tightly woven baskets, which were brought, under armed guard, to the owners of the different *toddis.* Tom and Margot's were delivered to the schooner, where Captain Fell kept careful watch.

Nasis put Bedloe in charge of his, leaving Jenks with no access to the pearls, which were kept in strongboxes in Nasis's study onboard the yacht.

The rest of the material in the *toddis* was examined, sifted, resifted through ever-decreasing-sized sieves, and afterward, when it seemed as if every scrap of valuable material had been taken out, the remainder was turned over to women and children, who picked out the *masi-thul,* or dust-pearls.

Onboard the schooner that afternoon Tom and Margot

finally got to see what the diving and bidding had been all about. There were baskets filled with pearls. They were small, but many were perfectly round, the very best of the Ceylon catch, and although they had not as yet been treated in hydrogen and ether or put out in the sun to bring up their high lustre and subtle colors, they were a soft white, a good starting color.

Several were the size of beetles, and perhaps ten more were larger than that. Two were extraordinarily large, the size of walnuts, but these were badly mottled and their colors were cloudy and dim.

Then it seemed as if all the businessmen on the Marichchukaddi beach began to show up at the schooner, selling all sorts of services or wanting to buy early.

Several workers were hired to help size the pearls. They worked with sizing baskets, about six to eight inches in diameter and two or three inches high, each with holes in the bottom. Pearls that didn't pass through the holes of baskets one, two, three, and four were called *chevo*. The larger ones, those that didn't pass through baskets five, six, or seven were called *vadiu*. The ones that didn't pass through numbers eight, nine, and ten were *thul*, and the very smallest, the *masi-thul*.

Tom and Margot sold some of their *masi-thul* to the local dealers, which raised enough money for the rest of the auctions. The money Margot had borrowed was almost gone.

The pearl sizers were a gossipy lot. Tom and Margot heard that they and Nasis were coming away with the best of the catch. Jhaveris was also doing well. Ali Aziz was not having as much luck.

All this gossip was perfectly timed to spur on the divers, who, after weeks of work, had become tired. Now they saw not only an end to their work, but also to the riches buried inside the shells they were bringing up. The nightly auctions became even more lively. Bidding became wilder, more based on intuition. Alliances were breaking apart as people paid exorbitant prices. The price broke new records each night, and now hovered near a hundred rupees per lot. Both Tom and Margot were nervous, on the brink of getting in over their heads. Margot suggested that they take what they had and leave the fishery, but Jhaveris intervened with another solution.

"We should band together. Whenever possible, we keep the price from soaring, and we split the cost of all the lots we purchase from now on."

Margot and Tom exchanged quick looks.

"I am not trying to manipulate. I happen to know this business better than you," Jhaveris said, tapping his small hands together. "The pearls have to be treated. Bombay is the only place to have that done. I have been living and working in Bombay all my life. And I have access to certain members of the princely families who might be interested in buying huge lots of pearls immediately—I'm thinking of one in particular who buys more pearls than anyone in India. Have you come up with any large pearls thus far?"

"Only two very large ones, but they're mottled."

"Oh, my gracious, that's no good. We need at least one spectacular, large pearl to get to the prince I'm thinking of—a calling card, if you will. Everyone will be after him, but if we can give him an extraordinary pearl, he'll buy from us."

"I hate to be the voice of doom in all this," Tom said, "but we can't control the price unless Nasis and Ali Aziz and the others throw in with us, and I don't expect that to happen."

"And my pearls are still in Colombo. I have less than a month to retrieve them," Margot said.

"That's where my prince comes into it. He'll buy quantity, but he'll need a treasure to get him to move quickly."

"A bribe—"

"No, no, my dear Tom, we don't call it that when we're dealing with a prince. We call it a gift," Jhaveris said.

The next day's catch was extremely large and from a very rich par. That night the tension in the auction room was at its peak.

Nasis, looking overconfident from his bidding earlier in the week, led, with Ali Aziz and Tom and Margot and Jhaveris lagging behind. Then Jhaveris went after him. Tom and Margot dropped out, as did Ali Aziz, and Nasis finally won the bid, establishing the price at a hundred and three rupees. The next lots were as equally heated and Nasis drove up the price to a hundred and ten.

The next day word spread that cholera had broken out in the camp. People began moving to other sections of the beach. They said the smell was causing the disease. A week later, the last week of the fishery, Margot began to feel sick. She was tired and nauseated. Tom wanted to bring in a doctor, but Margot said she would wait until they got back to Colombo.

That night the prices continued to soar. Jhaveris and Tom could not hold them, and finally Nasis took the largest lots for a hundred and fifteen rupees. Additional lots were put up for auction, but before the bidding could begin, there was a clamor in the street just outside the auction room, and suddenly the word *fire!* rang out, and bells were clanging.

Tom ran from the room. Smoke was billowing up from the northwestern end of the encampment, rolling across the flat, dry land like fog. Above the smoke a lick of flame appeared. A strong wind was blowing toward the most populated part of the beach, and to the *koddus* that held the day's catch.

Margot was running up from the shore with Captain Fell.

"We saw the flames from the deck," she called. "We've got to save the *toddis*. The pearls are flammable; they'll burn!"

Tom began running toward the *toddis*. "Find shovels, anything you can use to dig," he called out.

The sea smells mixed with the smell of smoke, of human flesh burning. Everything could be lost. More people began running to the *toddis* as the fire moved closer.

When Tom reached it, it was untouched, and the crowd was staring out helplessly at the encroaching flames.

"Start digging!" he yelled. Dropping to his knees, he began tunneling a trench, running east to west.

No one moved.

"Dig!" he screamed, and one or two joined him, then several more.

Margot and Fell made their way up the beach carrying shovels.

Margot began digging beside him.

"You're not well—" he started to say.

"Everything will be lost—"

A line of people spread out, some with shovels, most on their hands and knees, scooping out sand like dogs trying to bury bones.

When the trench was deep enough, Tom turned on the seawater pumps that were used to clean debris from the shells and flooded the trenches. The wind was blowing from the north now, heading toward the *toddis*.

Margot began to feel the heat of the flames on her face.

"The pearls melt," she said to Tom, "or just burst into flame."

Standing behind the trenches, Tom and Margot kept the pumps trained on the long, wide vats of putrefying shells. The fire rolled over the beach, and when it arrived, it sizzled into the trenches and was held as more smoke billowed up, engulfing swarms of bluebottle flies.

Then suddenly the wind changed and headed west.

The crowd began running to the auction room. Tom handled the pumps and wet down the *koddus*. But he was forced back by the heat, which was so intense that some of the surrounding buildings had burst into flame. Shells inside the vats began to crackle, popping open, and the meat inside them was sizzling. Tom and Margot watched helplessly as the pearls began to melt.

By midnight, more than half the camp lay in smoldering ruin. But the *toddis* were safe—the trenches had held.

Late the next morning Margot was worse, unable to get out of bed. Tom tried to find a doctor, but only two remained, and they were busy treating burn and cholera victims.

Chapter
Forty-four

EACH BLOW OF the crowbar against the strongbox released a little more of Jenks's venom. It wasn't even a strongbox anymore, it was their heads. God, how he hated them.

Stupid, stuttering Nasis—

"Made me his servant!"

And Street, with his frigging fairness, his impulses, his passions.

And Margot's unapproachable beauty.

"Wouldn't let me near her! Wouldn't let me near her! Wouldn't let me near her!"

The words were spit out in cadence with the blows as his mind reeled through a catalog of their injustices:

Their money. Their background. Their faultless, guiltless looks. His whole life he'd had to toady to the likes of them.

The ship was dark and deserted. He was alone in Nasis's study. The pearls were so close he could almost feel them. And again the crowbar slammed down and the box's hinges rattled and shook, and loosened.

Both hands wrapped around the crowbar, he pounded the box again and again. The hinges loosened further. Now on his knees, he pried them open. One snapped. The other remained fastened. With a deep breath, he attacked it, kept seeing the pearls inside—his fortune, an orgy of spending.

As the hinge snapped, he pried open the box.

The pearls were in glass containers. Hundreds and hundreds of them. Opening one, he poured its contents into his hand. Dazzling, like moon dust, like stars, milky white. His fortune. His very own fortune.

"Just wh-wh-what do you think you're d-d-doing?" Nasis said.

Jenks, his mouth as dry as dust, rose. Nasis stood at the door, holding a small pistol in his hand. Jenks threw the handful of pearls at his feet.

Nasis scrambled forward to stop the onrush, and Jenks whacked the pistol out of Nasis's hand with the crowbar, then made a dive for it. Nasis tumbled after him, but Jenks had the gun in one hand, the crowbar in the other.

"You think you can beat me?" Jenks hissed.

Nasis cowered on the floor.

"That what you thought? Beat me? Come on, then, beat me!"

His fist, coiled around the crowbar, came slashing up into Nasis's face. Nasis reeled backward, stunned.

And again Jenks's fist coiled up and slammed into Nasis's face. Bones were splintered. Nasis was hurled against a wall.

"On your feet, then, on your feet."

Jenks was over him now, swinging his fist from left to right. Nasis's head slammed into the wall, splattering it with blood.

There was the sound of footsteps in the hall.

Jenks dropped the crowbar, crouched, and held his bloodied hand over Nasis's slack mouth.

The footsteps passed by the study, then went out on deck.

Nasis had passed out, and now Jenks was dragging him to his feet, then pitching him over his shoulder.

He carried Nasis to his stateroom, propped him up in a chair, then lashed him to it and gagged his mouth.

Taking the flowers out of a vase, Jenks threw water in Nasis's face.

Nasis moaned. His eyes fluttered open.

Jenks was eye to eye with him.

"Want the key to the other box. You understand?"

Nasis nodded limply.

"Where is it?"

The dazed eyes looked up toward a satinwood bureau.

Jenks rummaged through the top drawers and found an envelope with two skeleton keys.

"These?"

Nasis nodded again, then his head rolled forward onto his chest.

Jenks took another pitcher of water and threw it in Nasis's face.

As Nasis's bruised head rolled up, Jenks brought the pistol to the center of his forehead.

"Did you really think I would let you keep all of the pearls? Just how stupid did you think I was? It's you who's stupid, not me. It's you who's led around by the nose, you dumb, spoiled prick."

Reaching down, Jenks wrapped the pistol in a pillow, then brought it up to Nasis's head and held it there for one excruciating moment. Nasis began to scream under his gag. Then, lowering the pistol, holding it next to Nasis's calf muscle, Jenks calmly pulled the trigger. Singed feathers flew out everywhere. Nasis slumped forward, unconscious. Blood began to seep slowly from his leg.

"Can't follow me now," Jenks said.

He ran to the study and, working quickly, unshackled the second strongbox, then loaded the contents of both into a duffel bag. Then he went on deck and lowered a skiff.

As he was about to push off, Bedloe came on deck and shouted down at him.

"Was that a shot, Mr. Jenks? Something wrong?"

"Thieves have stolen our pearls. I'm going after them," he said, lowering his oars into the water.

"Where's Mr. Nasis?"

"In the engine room," Jenks said, doubling his strokes.

When he got to shore he began running through the burned-out part of town, searching for Ali Aziz. But his tent was gone.

In the distance Jenks saw that Bedloe and some of the other crewmen of the *Distant Star* were lowering the tender. Jenks rushed through what remained of the burned-out town, stopping when he saw a drunken woman.

"Kiss me bloody red rectum, you missable sea fart," she was saying, shaking her husband's inert, sodden body.

"You there!" Jenks called out.

She turned, all mottled and red-veined, and looked him up and down.

"I need your help."

The woman's arms went round his neck in a greedy embrace. "A'ways good for a li'tle help."

The tender was coming closer.

"Need to find the Arab that was camped here, Ali Aziz. You know him?"

"The one what wears all the bafrobes? He left."

"I need someone to take me to him."

"That was mo'e an a hour ago. We seen 'im take off, Cappin and me, a course that was before the friggin' Cappin fell inna the friggin' bo'tle," she said, planting a kick in the drunken man's midsection.

Bedloe and the others landed.

"You have a boat?"

"Does a mother have nipples?"

"I'll pay you."

"Wif what?"

"Got pearls—*chevos.*"

"Where'd you get 'em?"

Bedloe and his men had now begun to fan out on the beach, searching for Jenks.

"Never mind how I got 'em. I'll give you three of my best if you'll take me to Ali Aziz."

Catching sight of Bedloe and his men, the woman said, "Kiss me red rectum. I ain't gettin' invovved wif any low-down scheme. Piss off!"

Jenks backed away from her and ducked behind the charred remains of a hut. "How much?"

"Piss off, I tell ya."

"Five *chevos.*"

"My ass."

"Five of my best—pink-white ones. You can get five hundred or more apiece for them."

"Let me see 'em."

"Not now. Get a boat, meet me in the cove on the other side of the *toddis.*"

"What if I don'?"

"Don't be a fool."

"Don't be callin' me names—"

"I see him—here he is!" one of the crewmen called out. He was standing behind a hut, staring straight at Jenks.

Jenks, shifting the duffel to his left shoulder, took off, careening through what remained of the hut, its walls collapsing in a flat puff of dust.

The crew, with Bedloe behind them, began running up the beach, but the loose sand slowed them down.

Running, turning his head this way and that, Jenks made his way south through a maze of huts and market stalls, stopping now and then as one or more of the crewmen passed by on other side streets. Finally Jenks, seeing Bedloe quite near, pushed open the door to a hut and crouched inside. There was a frightened couple, a diver and his very pregnant wife, huddled against the opposite wall. Jenks put his finger up to his lips, and they sat silently for a moment.

"He's around here somewhere," a crewman called out, passing directly in front of the door.

Then the morning call to prayer rang out and the diver's wife slowly got to her feet. She grabbed her broom and began hitting Jenks with it. The diver grabbed it from her and began poking Jenks with the pointed end. Reaching inside his coat, Jenks took out the pistol. The woman began to scream, turning frantically in a circle like a dog who'd had its tail set on fire.

Bedloe began banging on the hut door—Jenks held it closed with his shoulder—and the crew outside began a count. On three they pounded against the hut. Dust shook out of every crevice. Then another count began. On three Jenks stepped aside and the men came tumbling in with such force that the far wall began to wobble and Jenks charged past Bedloe and ran out into the street.

Heading south, he saw the trench that Tom had built. The smell was overwhelming. Keeping his hand clamped over his nose, panting as he ran, he made his way into the *toddis*.

Bedloe and his men approached the trench, but the smell stopped them.

Dropping to his belly, Jenks crawled up a narrow aisle. The bluebottle flies were buzzing overhead. He tried breathing only through his mouth, but the flies flew inside and felt like a living, furry soup, adhering to his gums, expanding, the buzzing inside resonating round his brain. Jerking himself up to his knees; he tried spitting them out, but they were embedded in his teeth, biting his tongue. He gagged and tried sweeping them from his face, but they kept coming. Crawling now, the rot sizzling up his nostrils, he vomited and dead flies dripped from his lips.

Slowly he made it through the long aisle and came out on the other side of the *toddis,* the flies still covering him, the duffel clutched to his chest. The water was in sight, but the woman and her drunken husband were nowhere to be seen.

Bedloe and his men, avoiding the odor and the flies, were taking a longer route around the *toddis,* heading east. Jenks made a run for the water, diving in head first, cleansing himself of flies and filth. He lay facedown for a long moment, then scrambled back to the shore, picked up the duffel and, heading through a clump of flat scrubby trees, made his way to the cove.

The woman was not there, either, and huddling with the duffel close to his chest, he watched Bedloe's progress.

The sun was rising steeply now, the heat fanning out in rippling intensity.

Bedloe was inching closer when suddenly Jenks saw the woman rowing into the cove.

Standing, running into the water with the duffel on his head, he began to laugh uproariously.

Never underestimate the power of greed, he thought. *Never!*

Chapter Forty-five

THE NEXT DAY the divers went out for the last time. The bottom looked as though it had been swept clean. A record had been set; over seventy-five million oysters had been brought up.

With sails furled, the diving boats drifted aimlessly back to the beach. The divers straggled to shore and delivered their hauls to the government *koddus.* There were no cheering crowds—many of the hangers-on had left after the village burned—and the divers worked as if by rote, waiting for their take with solemn expressions and weary eyes.

The last auction was tame. With Ali Aziz out of the picture and Nasis mysteriously absent, Tom and Jhaveris controlled the final bids.

The next day Jhaveris left for Bombay, saying he'd find suitable housing for Tom and Margot, and also to set up an audience with the Rana of Dholpur, the Indian prince capable of buying all the pearls at once.

The last of the catch was brought to the *toddis*. In a week all the pearls and pearllike material would be gone, and the rotting shells, all the debris and rubble from the fishery, would be left to the shorebirds, the flies, and the jackals.

Margot remained onboard the schooner, feeling ill for some part of each day. A packet of letters from Baron Clausen had been forwarded to her from Colombo. Felix's tone was gossipy and endearing.

As she sat on the aft deck, writing to him, she felt homesick.

Dearest Felix:

The trouble with adventure, or its chief reward, is that it is habituating and you never know where it will take you. We are still in Ceylon at the fishery, and will be leaving for Bombay to sell what we have bought here.

Earlier, David's yacht pulled up anchor and headed out into the Indian Ocean. There were rumors circulating for days. Some say he's sick or that this man Jenks wounded him in a fight. I went out to the *Distant Star* to see if there was anything I could do, but his man, Bedloe, turned me away.

I feel badly about how things turned out between David and myself. I've fallen in love with Tom Street, and that has destroyed any chance for a friendship with David. He can't forgive me for this.

Cholera spread through the camp. At first I was worried because I haven't been feeling well. I'm queasy in the morning and tired all the time. But I'm not ill. I know these symptoms—I felt them twice before when I was married to James. My other two pregnancies. I'm being offered a third chance, Felix. I'm ecstatic and scared and determined to bring this infant into the world. I haven't told Tom as yet. I see him on shore now, about to push off in a little skiff. The day is ending here, my dearest friend. I don't know what you would make of the way I've been living. But I trust you wish me well. I see your kind face smiling at me.

Your loving friend,
Margot

Tom rose from the skiff after tying it to the schooner, then walked over and kissed her full lips.

"You look lovely—you must be getting better."

She laughed.

"What's so funny?"

"I used to think that you'd been married and had a family, but now I'm not so sure that you've ever been through this before."

He frowned.

"I think I'm about to frighten you," she said.

"Well, go on, don't leave me waiting for it."

"It's not that awful, although I'm scared to death. I've lost two, but I won't lose this one, I'm sure of that—it wasn't right before this."

"What are you—"

"I'm going to have our baby," she said.

He froze.

"Are you happy?"

He was too confused to talk.

"Haven't you ever wanted children?"

His own were somewhere in the world.

"What's wrong?"

Tell her you love her, he said to himself, but he could not open his mouth.

His silence startled her, and she wondered if she'd misjudged him.

"I love you," he finally said.

"I hope so. I'm not sure I know what we should do."

"It's too soon to think clearly . . ."

"But you're happy?"

"You should see a doctor in Bombay. Make sure that it's true."

"I know it is."

"But a doctor will certainly know."

"Tom, I don't understand. Don't you want this child at all?"

Images of Antony and Susan and Jelly kept whirring through his mind. Margot was staring at him with a frightened look, and he knew that just then, he was incapable of allaying her fears or answering any of her questions.

IV

Like a Pearl, Transformed

Chapter
Forty-six

DUFF ST. JOHN had seen Jelly Bridge Aspinall only twice between the time that Tom Aspinall had deserted her and the winter of 1892. Both times were in public because no one invited Mrs. Aspinall into their homes anymore.

Sometime between Thanksgiving and Christmas he saw her at the skating rink in Central Park accompanied by a manservant, a nanny, and her children. She was wearing a red velvet skating outfit trimmed in ermine, a large ermine and velvet hat with an egret feather that swept up one side and shivered in the breeze blowing across the frozen pond. Adversity had strengthened her, Duff decided, watching her from a safe distance. Her face looked leaner, her fine bones more pronounced, her eyes larger, more defiant. What a pity it was to have her be so miserably excluded, there being such a paucity of beauty in New York that season.

As he was leaving the pond, their eyes met for the briefest of moments, and he smiled and lifted his hand in the limpest of waves. She smiled back very quickly, like a contaminated patient resigned to her quarantine.

He saw her again just after the New Year, on a sunny, crisp day. She was following some moving men out of her house on Gramercy Park. He had heard that her father had rented it and that she was now living with her children and servants in his mansion on Fifth Avenue. Duff was walking in the park with his cousin Borden Chamblis, an attractive distant relation who had come to the city and made quite a name for himself trading stocks and bonds on Wall Street. It was he who first spotted Jelly.

"Who on earth is that?"

Duff shook his head sadly. "One of the saddest episodes of my life, I'm afraid."

215

"You lost her."

"No, no, she was married to a friend of mine. She was about to leave him, and he left her. Caused quite a stir up at the Claremont Inn last year."

Borden took a few steps in her direction, a broad grin spreading out on his face. It was an angular face, with ruddy cheeks, dark eyes, and a thick brown moustache, which partially concealed a cynical and determined mouth.

"Anjelica Aspinall," he said. "They say she took a whip to old Colonel Jay and his party when they arrived at the Claremont that day. She's Preston Bridge's daughter, isn't she?"

"Yes. The scandal happened the week before the ball that was going to launch her, but as soon as word spread—it was too awful, no one showed up."

"Did you?"

"No."

"I would have."

Just then Jelly got into her brougham and, fixing herself in her seat, turned sharply and saw Duff and his cousin standing in the park. She looked away, embarrassed to have been seen, then looked back and stared defiantly at them.

"My God! Look at those eyes. She is angry, isn't she?" Borden said. "She looks like a caged cat—doesn't like her confinement one bit. We should help her."

"But how?"

"We should talk to her."

"I think that would only make things worse. We couldn't invite her anywhere."

And as if Jelly already understood the limitations that her situation placed upon the two men, she ordered her driver to drive off.

Borden stepped into the street to stare after her.

"I'm going to talk to Maisie Searington-Furst about this."

"She won't go near Jelly Aspinall—no one will."

"That might appeal to Maisie. She'd do anything to rattle Caroline Astor and the rest of the guard. Maisie's last party is in a week."

"What makes you suddenly so interested in Jelly Aspinall?"

"Good God, man, did you see her? She's ravishing."

"For all I know, she's still legally married to Tom Aspinall."

"Where is he?"

Duff shook his head sadly. "No one knows. Some say he's dead. I think the police now even list him as dead."

"You must find out—I want to know everything there is to know about her—and we'll get her into Maisie's party one way or the other. I want to see her up close. I want to see if she shimmers in the candlelight. I'll wager she does."

"Indeed she does," Duff said, now cursing himself for not having gone after Jelly himself.

When she arrived at her father's house, one of the footmen told her that Marcus Puddy was waiting for her in the study.

"Is my father with him?"

"No, ma'am, he's alone."

She groaned silently, then stared at herself in the hall mirror. She hated the stifled expression that had lately crept into her eyes and around her mouth—it made her look humorless. Exhaling a full, weary breath, she walked into the purple and gold light of the main hall, head erect, hands clenched at her sides.

When she walked into the study, Marcus Puddy rose from one of the large tasseled sofas.

"My dear, so good of you to see me without any notice."

Walking toward him, she brought up both her hands, which he eagerly grasped and held for a moment longer than she would have wished.

"Don't be silly, Marcus. You know I always have time for you."

Perhaps that was the wrong thing to say, because he stepped closer to her and she smelled the acrid odor of stale pipe tobacco trapped in his breath. She moved away.

"Any news?"

"Finally, yes, my dear, some very good news," he said, reaching into his briefcase to remove her file. "The court agreed to hear our petition, and they have ruled in our favor."

"They've granted me the divorce?"

"That is now only a formality—they've agreed to accept the grounds. The trouble all along was their unwillingness to accept the case for desertion. Tom had left all his belongings behind, which to their eyes indicated his intent to return, and, of course, we have never been able to find conclusive proof that he has indeed died."

She turned away from him.

Walking up to her, Marcus placed his pudgy hands on her shoulders. "It's almost over, my dear—be brave for just a little while longer. Your divorce should be granted within weeks."

"And there have been no further reports from any of the detectives."

"Only the one witness who said he saw Tom boarding a ship at South Street, and, of course, as we know, the ship was lost at sea."

Jelly brought her hand up to silence him.

Puddy shook his head sadly. "First his parents, then poor, deluded Tom. Sad, very sad . . . although he only had himself to blame."

"And now the custody question is settled. The children are mine—" she said.

Puddy coughed into his hand uncomfortably.

"What problem could there be? I'm their mother, and if the divorce is granted—"

"Your father is still pressing this point," Puddy said quietly.

"But it's unnatural for the court to award custody of my children to him."

"He makes a very strong point. He's in the best financial position to raise them, and the court knows that you will be close by to offer maternal care."

"It's his way of getting back at me for having ruined his European plans."

"My dear, you know it wouldn't be prudent of me to interfere."

"No, of course, Marcus, you wouldn't want to risk losing your richest client."

"That has nothing to do with it," Puddy said, moving

close to her again. "He makes the best point, because if you only had a man in your life, a provider and father for your children, the court might be disposed in your favor. You know that I would like to help you. I'd do anything in my power to help you," he said, taking her hand again, holding it so tightly she thought she would scream. "If I said more—well, my dear, I'm a proud man."

Unfortunately, his cloaked proposal was not something she could afford to overlook. There were few who would even speak to her, let alone marry her, and as much as she would have liked to poke out his eyes, she simply smiled at him, indicating how much the idea might appeal to her once the divorce decree was granted.

Dropping her hand, Puddy went back to retrieve his briefcase, then, taking her hand again at the study door, he kissed it and said good-bye.

Closing the door behind him, she wiped her hand on her skirt, then turned to the fire.

"It's all too horrible," she called out to the empty room, tears streaming down her cheeks.

But just two days later it seemed as if her luck might change. An invitation to Mrs. Searington-Furst's final party of the winter season was delivered by liveried messenger, and although Jelly knew she had only been invited as an afterthought, she wept with joy when she read it.

Chapter
Forty-seven

JELLY WAS THE last guest to arrive at the six-story Venetian mansion.

A liveried footman announced, "Mrs. Thomas Aspinall," and everyone who heard him turned. Word quickly spread to other parts of the house, and those people who had heard of her exploits up at the Claremont but had never met her assembled in the front hall.

She was wearing a spectacular Worth gown of scarlet patterned silk, opera-length white gloves, and a simple gold bracelet studded with rubies. Her unremarkable strand of pearls was roped around her slim neck. Her hair was upswept in a towering, smooth, dark pompadour and her pale eyes flashed, taking in everything all at once—the doge colors of Mrs. Searington-Furst's reception hall—gold, crimson, and deep brown—and the formidable, handsome-faced woman herself, who was advancing toward her.

As Mrs. Searington-Furst stretched her right hand toward Jelly, she thought to herself that Borden Chamblis was right—Jelly Aspinall was the find of the season. "My dear, it's so good to see you again."

"It's very good to be seen at all," Jelly said so pointedly that Mrs. Searington-Furst laughed, sending out ripples of laughter among the assembled guests, and quite suddenly Jelly relaxed.

In the ballroom, people were, for the most part, more curious than courteous, and Jelly quickly perceived that what she had done, her great scandal, was part of her cachet. She also felt an acute sense of disappointment in them for having so readily accepted her into the fold.

Seeing Duff St. John standing across the room, she walked over to him. "Something tells me that I have you to thank for this. You saw how miserable I was this winter, and you intervened on my behalf with your friend," she said, indicating Mrs. Searington-Furst.

Duff looked up meekly and exchanged quick looks with his cousin, with whom he was standing.

"It's not true, Jelly. Although I am very glad this messy business might finally be coming to an end, I didn't have anything to do with it."

"I did, Mrs. Aspinall," Borden Chamblis said.

Jelly looked at him intently and, pleased with what she saw, offered him a generous smile.

"Anjelica Aspinall, my cousin Mr. Borden Chamblis."

"How do you do?"

"Very well now that you're here, Mrs. Aspinall," he said, taking her hand and kissing it lightly.

Jelly blushed. "And why have you intervened on my behalf, Mr. Chamblis?"

"For purely selfish reasons, ma'am. It has been a long and dreary season and all of us are in need of you. You are the most beautiful woman in New York."

She blushed again, and seeing how quickly his shameless flattery worked with her, he stepped closer, offering her his arm. "May I take you round the room?"

"Will you join us, Duff?" she asked. But Chamblis spoke before Duff could open his mouth. "We'll catch up with him later," and Duff was left behind, to finish his champagne alone.

Borden Chamblis seemed to know a great many people. He introduced her to his friends or made pointed comments about those people he didn't know. He was charming in a slightly superficial way, though not unintelligent—he pointed out several paintings in Mrs. Searington-Furst's gallery and made interesting comments about the painters and the styles they'd used.

During dinner they were seated next to each other, and afterward they danced. He was romancing her the entire time, which surprised and flattered her since he was one of the most handsome men in the room, and certainly one of the most eligible.

He took her on a tour of the house. They climbed a broad stairway and talked about the size of someone's jewels and another's yacht. Taking her hand, he pulled her along a broad hallway like a child pulling a beautiful balloon, and then, looking around as if he were planning a prank, he opened a door and they were inside an enormous bedroom done in a heavy Gothic style. It was dominated by a monstrous three-hundred-year-old bed that sat on a dais.

"This is Maisie's room."

"I won't ask how you know that."

"Maisie and I are good friends. The bed was made for a cardinal."

"It could certainly accommodate God. I'd be very lonely in a bed like that."

"She is, too. She sleeps in a little one in her dressing room."

"All this information you have at your disposal."

As she walked over to the fireplace to warm her hands, he stood next to her, took her hands, and warmed them. The room was very still. Jelly was trembling.

"I wouldn't want to be the center of another scandal tonight. We should go downstairs," she said, but he brought her hands up to his lips and kissed them, then placed them on his shoulders and, holding her around the waist, kissed her lips.

She held on to him for a moment, then backed away.

"Perhaps the hope of a scandal is now my greatest appeal," she said, walking to the door. "Men don't seem to be as damaged by it as women. As a matter of fact, I think a man could have his reputation made with one."

"You take my attentions too lightly, Mrs. Aspinall."

"And they seem so premeditated."

"No, they're sincere."

"How could they be? We don't know each other."

"I've met no one to compare with you—you're worthy of me."

"What a shameless thing to say," she said as she left the room.

He followed. "I feel shameless when it comes to you—I mean to pursue you."

There was something familiar about his determination. It reminded her of Tom.

"I arranged for you to be here tonight. Duff said it would be impossible, but I did it, and I will continue to pursue you."

"To what end?"

"I'm going to marry you."

She could not decide whether to bristle at him or smile, which only spurred him on because he loved a challenge.

"I'll pretend I did not hear you say that."

They descended the broad staircase to the main hall. A Hobby Horse Quadrille was being called in the ballroom, and there were people standing in the hall, some looking up at her with arched eyebrows.

"Now see what you've done," she was whispering to him. "They think that I lured you upstairs."

"What do you care what they think?"

"You have obviously never been confined to a dungeon."

She turned sharply away from him, and saw something that startled her. Nearby was a pale-skinned, light-haired woman wearing the black pearls Jelly had always wanted, the three strands that had once belonged to Catherine the Great. Seeing them made her remember her unhappy bargain with her father, her loss of Tom, and all the other things she had ever wanted that had fallen beyond her reach.

"Would you like to meet her? I can arrange it," Chamblis said, noticing her interest. "She's the Countess Montebano di Campana."

"I know who she is," Jelly said slowly, staring at the pearls, drops of liquid rose beetle-colored darkness, seeing how they caught the light.

The woman looked up and caught Jelly's eye.

"Would you do anything to have me?" Jelly asked him.

"Anything in the world."

"Get me those pearls," she said with a half smile, and was stunned when he walked up to the woman and said,

"Madame, I would like to purchase your pearls."

The countess reflexively touched them with her dainty hand. "They are not for sale, young man," she said crisply, then turned away.

Jelly, her breath caught in her throat, was startled and thrilled. When Borden Chamblis turned to walk back to her, she decided that he was either mad or more taken with her than anyone had ever been.

Chamblis had always wanted to get a glimpse inside Preston Bridge's looming mansion, and when he took Jelly home, he found that it lived up to his expectations. As he stood in the center of the glass-roofed main hall, his eyes quickly took in the Gobelin tapestries, and he decided that he could easily be happy living here.

"Would you like some brandy or cognac before you leave, Mr. Chamblis?"

She led him into her father's dark study. She was surprised to see a fire lighted in the fireplace this late, and then she heard a curious wheezing noise. Walking around one of the large couches, she was startled to see her father on the floor, his hands clutching the tight collar of his shirt. His eyes were frightened, wide open. Beside him was an over-turned snifter.

When he saw Jelly, he wheezed, "Need air—open my collar—"

She knelt down beside him, undid his collar, and fanned him. Chamblis refilled the overturned snifter with brandy from the table and handed it to Jelly, who held it to her father's lips.

Bridge's color returned, but he was stunned, and he sat with his eyes closed, his back against the couch, trying to catch his breath.

"Don't know what came over me. So sudden, couldn't catch my breath," he said. Then he opened his eyes, sipped his drink, and finally looked at her, taking in her gown and jewels.

"Where have you been?" he snapped.

"At a party."

"They're inviting you places again?" And then he saw Borden Chamblis. "Who the hell is that?"

"Father, I think you should relax—"

"Don't *Father* me," Bridge said, rising with some difficulty, then flopping onto the couch. "Who in hell are you?"

"Father, this is Mr. Borden Chamblis. Mr. Chamblis, my father."

"How do you do, sir?"

Bridge rolled his eyes, ignoring Chamblis's outstretched hand. "Never heard of you. Do you work at anything?"

"Bonds, sir, at Bartleby and Tucker."

"They were of no help to me when I needed them. Conspired against me, in league with that pirate Morgan and his International Mercantile Marine. Wouldn't let me into their steamship club. I lost ten million dollars. Have you ever made ten million dollars to lose?"

"Not as yet, sir."

"What are you, a smart young Wall Street man? We've had our fill of smart young Wall Street men around here. We will not require your services."

"Stop it!" Jelly said.

"My daughter has this knack for falling in love with men who can do nothing for her."

A chilling silence spread into the room, and finally Chamblis, appraising the situation carefully, decided that his best course was to side with Jelly.

"Sir, I think you discredit your daughter when all evening she had only the nicest of things to say about you. I think it might be better for me to come back and have that brandy some other time," Chamblis said. "I look forward to meeting you again under more pleasant circumstances."

"I doubt that will happen."

"But I mean for it to happen, sir. I will be coming here quite regularly."

"You will not be welcome."

"We'll leave that to your daughter to decide. I mean to court and marry her."

"You what?"

"Mr. Chamblis!" Jelly exclaimed.

"You will do no such thing," Bridge said, but Chamblis, leaning over, grasped Bridge's unwilling hand and shook it firmly.

"But I mean to, sir."

_____ Chapter _____
Forty-eight

"IT'S A RISK. I know that, Duff, but it's a calculated risk and I like those," Chamblis said as he read the ticker tape in the basement bar of the Café Savarin at One Twenty Broadway.

Although it was early, Duff was drinking champagne. What he liked most about the bar at the Savarin was that there were no windows, no possible way of knowing what time it really was.

"But Jelly's a capricious character, and if you've already alienated Preston Bridge . . ."

"No, I haven't alienated him, Duff, merely piqued his

interest. I like these warrior princes. He was testing me, that's all."

"Jelly's not about to be swept off her feet just because you tell her you love her—she wants to be out in the world."

"Access to which I offer."

"And money?"

"An unlimited supply of which, unhappily, I cannot offer her at the moment."

"And what about love? She can afford to marry for love."

"She may already love me. I stood up to her father," Chamblis said, cutting off a scrap of ticker tape, letting the rest fall into the carved mahogany bucket at the base of the machine. "Mr. Bridge's stock is recovering from his steamship debacle. He needs young blood to look out for his interests. I'm going to make a very good son-in-law."

Poor Jelly, Duff thought. First the monstrous father, now the monstrous lover.

During the next few weeks Borden became not only a fact of Jelly's life but its chief fact; he was everywhere she went.

"Borden, you don't understand the position you're putting me in with my father," Jelly said one day, the second time that week that they had run into each other at the skating pond in Central Park.

Nearby, Miss Aberdeen glared at them.

"That woman is in my father's employ. She reports everything to him."

"How can you still care about that when I tell you I love you and want to marry you?"

"My father is threatening daily to close his house and take us back to Colorado."

"He's bluffing."

"You don't know my father."

"Meet me later, alone," he said.

"It's too difficult for me just now."

"Maisie Furst is having a small dinner party tonight. She specifically requested that I invite you—there'll be so many people you'll enjoy meeting."

"Why is life so complicated?"

"Don't you want to come with me?"

"Of course I do, Borden. It's all I want to do. You don't know what it's like to be cooped up in that house with no friends." She began to cry softly. "And to have you inviting me out again, to have Maisie Furst wanting me to have dinner with her . . ." Jelly was close to sobbing now. "My father won't let me have any of it now. He'll lock me away—he'll take my children."

"He can't do that."

"After my divorce is granted, he's going to have custody of my children."

"But that's horrible," Borden said, finally seeing a way of breaking through her resistance.

Antony, who had been skating nearby, looked over, saw his mother crying, and came over to see what was the matter.

"Maman, what's wrong?"

"Nothing is wrong, Antony. Say hello to Mr. Chamblis."

"Hello, Tony."

"My name is Antony, sir."

"I see you as more of a Tony than an Antony. It's the jaunty way you skate. Do you like to skate, Tony?"

"Very much, sir."

"And may I join you on the ice?"

"If you like."

"I would like very much."

"What does jaunty mean, sir?"

"Sprightly, airy—have you taken skating lessons?"

"My father taught me," Antony said, then looked away sadly.

Borden knelt down in front of the boy. "Do you miss your father very much?"

Antony looked at him cautiously, surprised by the question. "Yes, I do."

"May I coach you? I'm very good."

Antony looked at his mother, who was now smiling through her tears, then back at Chamblis. "Yes, I would like that very much."

"And I may call you Tony?"

"If you like, sir, thank you, sir," he said, then went back to the ice.

"Children need a father," Chamblis said to Jelly, then went off to put on his skates and join Antony on the ice.

Later that afternoon Chamblis met Duff for a drink at Duff's club on Fifth Avenue.

"There's something I'd like you to find out for me about Mrs. Aspinall's divorce decree," he said.

"What about it?"

"The custody of the children."

"Preston Bridge is planning to go to court to get custody."

Borden tapped his fingers nervously on the slick surface of a mahogany table. "How could he possibly be able to take those children away from their mother?"

"From their unmarried, deserted mother is the point to be made."

"But what if she were married?"

"That would certainly be a start."

"And what if her husband adopted her children, gave them his name?"

Duff stared at his cousin with more interest. What a worthy monster he really was! "I imagine it would start a custody battle, and in my opinion, Mr. Bridge would not stand a chance."

Chamblis stared at Duff with a self-satisfied grin.

That night Jelly, making up some excuse, got out of the house and went to dinner with Chamblis at Maisie Searington-Furst's house.

Afterward, alone with her in his carriage, Chamblis told her he loved her and had to marry her. Again she said that it was impossible, and he told her about his plan to adopt her children.

"No court on earth would rule against us. Your father would have to accept us."

How very clever he was, she was thinking. How very much like her father.

"You're not saying anything, Jelly. Do you agree? Will you marry me?"

"Yes," she said slowly, finally seeing a way out of all her troubles.

Chapter
Forty-nine

HER DIVORCE BECAME final the next week, and Chamblis began pressuring her to announce their marriage plans. She was waiting for the right moment to approach her father. His company's stock, which had been steadily rising, had taken a sharp decline, and he was always too busy to talk with her.

Finally one night she went to his study and found him alone. He told her to leave.

"No," she said calmly. "The time has come for us to have a talk. My divorce has come through."

"I will not throw you a celebration ball, missy. Now leave."

"No," she said firmly. "I've come to tell you that I will be married."

"That Chamblis fellow? You could have done worse. But when he finds out that you are not coming to the marriage with any money, he may not be as eager to marry you as you think."

"Why do you hate me so?"

"That's like asking me if I hate a mine that doesn't pay off. I don't hate you. I have just had to close you down. Where do you plan to live?"

"In New York."

"It's a pity you won't be seeing more of your children. I'm taking them out west with me."

"No, you won't."

"I'll have custody of them before the month is out."

"Mr. Chamblis is beginning proceedings to adopt them. He wants to be their father."

Bridge looked up at her. "Those children are mine," he said slowly.

"Oh, no—they are most definitely mine—mine and Mr. Chamblis's. The pity is that you will not be able to see them more often."

"I'll fight you."

"You won't win. Ask Marcus Puddy, he'll tell you. So if I were you, I would reconcile myself to this fact and begin to think about settling some money on me to help support my children. That is, if you want anything to do with them."

"Don't you dare talk to me this way."

"It will cost you a good deal of money—I'd say at least five million per child."

Preston Bridge rose from his chair, breathing hard, color rising in his face, but she undercut his rage with her own.

"That will be a minimum of ten million dollars to see them again. Do I make myself perfectly clear?"

Not waiting for his reply, she turned and left the room.

Later that night her father's valet pounded on her door.

"Mrs. Aspinall! Mrs. Aspinall! Come quickly. It's your father."

She pulled on her robe and followed the valet down to the study.

Preston Bridge was lying on a couch, his eyes wide open, his mouth twisted in a lopsided grin.

"Is he dead?"

"Not dead, no, ma'am, but near dead."

"Has anyone called a doctor?"

"Yes'm."

Finally, moving closer, Jelly heard her father's labored breath gurgling up from his chest. His eyes were focused on a spot on the ceiling.

"Father," she said, bending over the couch. "Can you hear me?"

He said nothing. His eyes blinked once, then remained rigidly fixed.

"Apoplexy, do you know the word? A loss of voluntary motion due to a rupture of a blood vessel in the brain," the doctor was saying.

"Can you do something for him?"

"There isn't much we can do."

"I don't understand. He'll be hospitalized, won't he?"

"If you want, but it won't make that much difference."

"What are you saying? Is he dying?"

"He's paralyzed. We'd better send for Marcus Puddy. We don't want the papers to hear about this."

Jelly was stunned. Approaching the couch again, she knelt beside it and waved her hands in front of her father's unmoving eyes. The servants had come back into the room and stood waiting for her to do something. The doctor was also waiting.

"Jelly, do you want me to send for Marcus?" the doctor asked.

He's asking me, Jelly thought. How odd to be asked anything in this house.

"Yes, send for him," she said.

How quickly everything changes, she was thinking. How quickly and completely.

Puddy arrived within an hour with a group of young lawyers in tow and went to work in the study.

The servants moved Preston Bridge up to his bedroom.

In the late morning Puddy asked to see Jelly.

"Of course we'll be bringing in another group of specialists to confirm the diagnosis, but plans have to be made now. I'm afraid there will be a great deal of responsibility on your shoulders, my dear."

Jelly looked up, trying to temper her reactions, which were running frantically between grief and joy.

"What do we do, Marcus? Is there a provision in his will for this?"

"Everything is left to you and the children on his death."

She was stunned. "Everything?"

"Of course, but in answer to your question, there was no specific provision for anything like this."

"I don't understand, Marcus. Is there no one person in control?"

"My dear, you've got to be very brave. There will be a great many people for you to turn to—"

"Is it me, Marcus? Has everything been left in my control?" she asked. She just wanted to hear him say it again. "And I thought he had such little regard for me."

"He saw a great deal of himself in you," Puddy said as he took her hand. "And as you know, as I've tried so many times to tell you, you'll always have me nearby in whatever capacity you wish . . ." The stale smell of his tobacco was as thick as cement.

"Please, Marcus," she said sharply, "you'll have to excuse me—this is so much to think about." She left the room.

The next week she announced her marriage plans, and two days later she told Marcus Puddy that his services would no longer be required. She was taking her business to Cadwallader, her husband-to-be's firm.

Borden Chamblis proceeded with his plans to adopt Antony, who was now almost exclusively called Tony, and Susan, who did not like Chamblis. She stubbornly guarded the memory of her father and thought he would return. Chamblis maintained the adoption would be insurance against whatever might come up in the future.

Their wedding was a simple affair with a few close friends, Maisie Searington-Furst and Duff St. John among them. After a honeymoon night at a hotel, where Jelly discovered what a strong and competent lover Borden was, they returned to the mansion on Fifth Avenue, where Jelly began reorganizing things. First among these was the relocation of her father.

"A smaller room will be better for him," she said, addressing her full staff, which she had gathered in Preston Bridge's cavernous bedroom. "I think he's overwhelmed with the scale of this room. We'll move him down the hall. My husband will move in here after I've taken out all this furniture."

She walked to the bed, and bending over, speaking loudly enough for every servant to hear, she said, "Can you hear me, Father? I have gathered together all the servants because they will be moving you to a smaller room, where I think you'll be much happier. We'll be emptying this room of all your possessions. My husband will be taking this room. Can you hear me, Father? My husband will be taking your room," she said in a triumphant, vengeful tone of voice.

Preston Bridge's expression remained unchanged, caught perpetually between a gasp and a silly smile.

Chapter Fifty

BOMBAY WAS MADE up of seven islands connected by marshes and bridges. A city of smoke and heat, it housed incredible poverty and riches. Millions of people clogged the streets, jostling for position among carriages, hacks, free-roaming oxen, and two-wheeled carts piled high with bolts of cotton or baskets and sacks of spices.

There was the sound of bells ringing in the Parsi fire temples announcing the arrival of worshipers to the presence of God. There were drums and sudden thudding silences and kiss-kiss sounds made by men clearing a path through the crowded streets.

The odor of human excrement and sandalwood incense filled the hot, dry air as Tom, sitting beside Jhaveris in an open carriage, was taken into the Jhaveri bazaar to sell some of his pearls. Tom, with no money left, had paid Captain Fell in pearls for the use of the schooner, and now he needed money to pay for the suites he had taken at Watson's Hotel for himself and Margot. And other expenses loomed—a gift for the Rana of Dholpur, the man known in India as the Prince of Pearls.

They left the carriage and proceeded on foot into the throbbing center of the bazaar, the canopied, sprawling jewelry stalls that circled the Mumba Devi Temple. Tom, so eager to make his first sale, was running ahead carrying a muslin sack with ten of his best pearls and a dozen lesser ones, and Jhaveris was running after him, trying to keep up.

"My goodness, Tom, slow down, everything takes its own time. You won't make your fortune today."

"But I have to."

"These people have been here for decades, and no one is going anywhere. You'll lose money if you rush. You should let me do your trading for you."

"No, you've been a wonderful teacher, but I'll do the trading myself."

Jhaveris clucked to himself. "But I'll stay with you, if you don't mind. Consider me one of the gods who has come down to perch on your shoulder and offer guidance."

Tom dashed ahead to the center of a street opposite the Mumba Devi Temple, then up a road past a lovely blue-tiled fountain. He rushed from Sheikh Memon Street to Dhandi Street, where the pearl merchants, in white cotton coats and trousers, gathered on corners with bags of pearls in their hands. In open stall offices they sat opposite one another, their hands covered by black cloth, trading back and forth.

"You'll see some familiar faces from Ceylon," Jhaveris said, his eyes scanning the merchants' faces. "These are the buyers and sellers. But we're looking for one man in particular. There he is—he's Pravin, the broker. Let him come over to you—and my gracious, once he sees what you have to sell, he won't leave your side," Jhaveris said as he went off to speak with a short man in a white cotton suit. He had a pleasant but somewhat pushed-in face, a long flat nose with wide, flaring nostrils, and a crafty smile.

Pravin nodded from a distance, his eyes focusing on the bag of pearls in Tom's hand. As the smile became hungrier, his eyes crinkled.

"Mr. Street, Mr. Street, Mr. Street," Pravin said as he approached. "Any friend of my friend Jhaveris is a friend of mine."

"Thank you, Pravin. I'm interested in selling some pearls."

"And there are many buyers, but I represent only the best in all of the Jhaveri bazaar. May I see what you would like to sell?"

Tom opened his muslin bag, brought out one of his best pearls, and when Pravin saw its high quality, he almost wept.

"The gods bless me today. And I offer up a simple prayer that pearls as lustrous as these find the right buyer and then the right neck to adorn. And you must be blessed, Tom Street, and I beseech the gods to bless you for being so wise to have bought these pearls at Mannar, to have come here to sell them, for having made you wear such a beautiful linen suit and fine trousers and such soft leather shoes. The gods should bless you for all this and more—"

"Please, Pravin. I'd like to do business."

"And that voice of yours, Mr. Street. It should also be blessed. It is like the sound of the *bulbul,* the nightingale. And which does my most worthy and dignified friend Mr. Tom Street—and dare I even humble myself to ask him such a question—but which does he wish—and he knows his every wish is there for my bidding, he is such a noble, clever man—which of his incomparable pearls is he willing to sell?"

Tom chose five of the pearls.

Pravin dropped his head into his hands and looked as if he would weep again. He railed against the gods, against Jhaveris, against Tom for offering so few, although he was quick to add that Tom was a prince among men. He wept, he laughed like a madman, he dickered for other pearls to be included, looked at the pearls again, wept again, then led Tom and Jhaveris up another street crowded with merchants. Overhead were thick-striped cotton canopies, some white and red, some aqua and blue. Pravin stopped at a stall that was set up on stilts and had cushions on the floor.

"Wait here," Pravin said, then went off to another room and came back leading a man in a turban and a white beard, who took a seat opposite Tom and inspected the five pearls without a trace of emotion. He spoke to Pravin in Hindi, then Pravin spoke to Tom.

"Please, my princely friend with such an incomparable voice and such beautiful shoes and trousers, are there no others?"

"No—just these for now."

"That is your wish and I must grant it because you are a prince among all men. And I may only offer up a simple prayer to the gods to ensure a good sale, and may they ensure your health and the health of your children born and unborn."

A crowd was beginning to form around the stall. Everyone was interested to know what price would be established for pearls of high quality from the Ceylon fishery.

Pravin told Tom to commence bidding.

Tom removed a thick black piece of cloth from his pocket and draped the cloth over his right hand, then reached out and grasped the bearded merchant's right hand. According to custom, the bid had to be secret yet conducted in full view of other merchants. The amount bid, counterbids, and the final amount paid were arrived at by hand signals under the black cloth, which Tom had practiced all morning with Jhaveris.

Covering the man's entire right hand with his own, which indicated a bid of one thousand, Tom pressed the man's hand fifteen times, indicating that he wanted fifteen thousand rupees for the five pearls.

Then the bearded man grasped Tom's entire right hand, pressing it ten times, then grabbed Tom's five fingers, pressing those, indicating that his counterbid was ten thousand five hundred.

The growing crowd began to murmur excitedly, watching the action under the black cloth. Sprinkled throughout the crowd were men who claimed to be experts at reading blind hand signals, and when they called out their guesses, other merchants took off to report their findings, which was how a market price was established.

Tom countered with fourteen thousand five hundred, and the bidding speeded up. Tom's heart was racing because the bearded man was expert with his hand signals. As the bidding became more intricate—each finger was one hundred; half a finger up to the middle digit was fifty; the fingertip was ten—Tom thought he was losing count. As far as he could tell, the last bid had been thirteen thousand six hundred and sixty.

Tom stopped for a moment.

The bearded man was staring at him quizzically. Jhaveris looked down, waiting for Tom's next move, and Pravin was beside himself, his eyes rolling toward the heavens, his lips muttering small prayers.

Tom grabbed the man's hand, pressed it thirteen times, then grasped four of his fingers and five of the tips—thirteen thousand, four hundred, fifty. The bearded man stared intently at the black cloth, then finally nodded, indicating his acceptance of the price. A cheer went through the crowd.

Pravin dropped to his knees and offered a prayer of thanks.

Tom removed the black cloth. His palm was slick with sweat.

As he and Jhaveris left the stall, Jhaveris shook Tom's hand.

"You are an exceptional man."

"In the United States you would say that I am one lucky son of a bitch."

Pravin would not leave their side now. He steered Tom into several other stalls, and within several hours Tom had sold all the best pearls, collecting almost fifteen thousand dollars, enough to retrieve Margot's pearls from the bank in Ceylon, and pay for some expenses, but not enough to purchase a single large pearl of good enough quality for the Rana of Dholpur.

As Jhaveris had warned, the prices in Mannar had been so high that it was becoming difficult to make back any money on the original investment.

"But the Rana of Dholpur is capricious," Jhaveris said toward the end of the day. "He will pay any amount for pearls that appeal to him. We must find him an exceptional one to whet his appetite."

Pravin, changing roles as quickly as he offered prayers, now became a seller's agent and took them on a hunt for a large pearl of the finest quality. But they could not find anything that was suitable for a price they could afford.

Finally they returned to the fountain at the base of the Mumba Devi Road. Nearby, worshipers were walking in and out of the temple, ringing bells as they entered. The air was redolent with the smell of burning incense and flowers. Tom, his mind numbed by everything he had seen and done, slipped his hand into the sack of pearls and brought out the two large, mottled ones.

"If only these were worth something," he said.

Pravin, asking to see them, began babbling away in Hindi with Jhaveris.

"What's going on?"

"Pravin knows a man—we all know him, Shah is his name. He's a pearl doctor who works miracles."

"What on earth is a pearl doctor?"

"He can literally heal pearls by using different oils, and he can peel others," Jhaveris said, holding up the larger of the two.

"Let's find him," Tom said.

"It's getting dark. He's Gujarat like me, a Jain, very religious. He won't work after sundown."

Tom grabbed the pearl. "Then we don't have a moment to lose."

They found Shah on Dhandi Street standing on a corner inspecting some brownish pearls that a merchant wanted Shah to peel and render white. But Pravin pushed his way in front of the merchant and began beseeching and imploring, and finally Shah broke away to inspect the two large mottled ones.

"The size is in your favor," he said after a cursory glance. "You can afford to lose at least half the weight and still have a good one."

Shah looked up at the sky. The sun had dropped behind the Mumba Devi Temple.

"This takes a great deal of time. Come to my stall tomorrow."

"We don't have time. Can you start one today?" Tom asked.

"You can't rush these things."

"My goodness, no, you can't, Tom."

"How much money do you want, Shah? I'll pay you a good price, the best price in Bombay, if you can give me an exceptional one."

Pravin began another battery of prayers and beseeching. Shah finally said that they would discuss price if he was able to come up with anything, and then he led them to the top stall of a rickety building made of timber and brick, where he inspected the pearls more carefully.

Tom was pacing. Jhaveris kept clearing his throat, squinting to see what was happening. Pravin was offering prayers to every deity in the pantheon, dropping to his knees, leaning out the window, throwing his fists up to heaven, then clutching them to his chest, moaning and crying.

"Doesn't anything shut him up?" Tom asked.

"This is what you pay him for," Jhaveris said wryly.

Shah first weighed the larger of the two pearls, then, fitting it into a clamp on a small file board, took out several goldsmith's files, which were flat and triangular with smooth and coarse sides. He also used two knife blades that had been ground and sharpened, some ruby powder, and grinding paper. Then he went to work, scraping with one of the sharp blades uniformly over the entire surface of the pearl. Because pearls consist of many concentric layers, the whole, rather than just a part, of one layer had to be removed. Several layers dropped away, revealing a less mottled texture. But a deep black spot appeared.

"Not a good sign," Shah said. "It usually means that the pearl is cracked. Cracked pearls are harder to heal. It takes much longer and requires certain oils, which are hard to get."

"And the other?" Tom asked.

"I don't know."

"Then try to peel it."

Shah looked out at the darkening sky.

"There's time enough for you to start," Tom urged. "Please, just start."

Shah heaved a sigh, then turned his attention to the other pearl.

Tom stood close by as Shah began to work, again scraping the first layers with a file. One layer, then another, began to drop away and lay on the table like a heap of fine chalky powder. Then a deep crack developed in the surface, and Tom's face deflated.

Pravin looked away, near tears, and Jhaveris stood stone silent.

Shah stared down intently, slowly placing the file he'd been using on the table. Then he carefully selected one of the sharpened knives, tracing the line of the crack with the blade. Cautiously inserting the blade into the crack, Shah jiggled the blade slightly, then waited. Sweat was now dripping down Tom's forehead. Jiggling the blade again,

Shah saw that the crack was widening and widening still, and suddenly a solid piece of thick skin dropped away, showing a brilliant rose-tinted skin beneath.

Pravin gasped.

Tom moved in closer, hovering over the board.

Shah began to look tremendously excited, and suddenly another entire skin split in half, like the shell of a walnut, and out fell the most exquisite, perfectly formed pearl—a drop-shape, without blemish or flaw, luminous as the moon.

Tom let out an exultant cry.

Pravin began wailing.

And Jhaveris, stepping closer now, picked up the pearl and inspected it.

"Fit for a prince," he said.

Chapter Fifty-one

"A SHAWL, *MEMSAHIB*? If it please you, look at my shawl. Would *memsahib* like cotton or silk or Kashmiri wool? Look at this one, *memsahib*, a wool shawl so fine it can fit through a ring." The vendors had gathered on the veranda of Watson's Hotel all morning to hawk their wares: embroidered shawls, silk rugs, and papier-mâché, exquisite miniatures painted, the vendors said, with a single eyelash.

Margot was not indifferent, just distracted. She was becoming the sort of woman she had always hated. Her eyes could not stay fixed on any one object for any length of time because they were so intent upon seeing Tom again. They were trained on doorways, on windows, on roads and carriages, waiting for a glimpse of him. But where was he, she wondered as she stared out at the *maidan*, the green in front of the hotel, which was not green at all but balding, scorched brown by the heat and coated yellow with dust.

"If not a shawl, a rug, *memsahib,* a Kashmiri rug woven of finest silk."

"No, not now."

"What price, *memsahib?"*

"Nothing, thank you."

"What price?"

"No."

She stood and began pacing up and down the veranda of the hotel, which looked like a huge bird-cage with its cast-iron pillars and tiers of wrought-iron galleries. At both ends were *punkah-wallahs,* men whose sole job was to pull a rope connected to a fan suspended from the ceiling, which provided the only breeze.

Margot reached one end of the veranda and turned on her heel and headed for the other. She was feeling enslaved by her pregnancy, which had so suddenly changed all the rules of her life. It made her fragile and vulnerable, moody and tired.

Just then another vendor spread out another rug at her feet.

"No!" she yelled.

Everyone on the veranda turned to look up at her; the dandified *box-wallahs,* European businessmen, the *memsahibs,* looking fussy and aristocratic. Margot froze. Her "no" had been meant not only for the vendor but for herself. "I'm sorry," she said to him, and rushing into the hotel, she arranged for a carriage and a guide.

At first her driver would only take her through the streets of the British section, as far as the Bombay Gymkhana, a British open-air club, which was at one end of the *maidan.* But staring at all the proper Englishmen sipping drinks in their wicker chairs, she could not forget herself or her problems, and she told the guide to go on.

They crossed a very definite line and suddenly Margot found herself in another Bombay altogether—a world of bazaars, small workshops and stalls, temples and mosques. Taking Abdul Rehman Street, they passed the Great Mosque in the heart of the cloth market, the Moslem stronghold of town, where all the signs were written in delicately etched Urdu, and then into the Hindu strongholds of Girgaum and Khetwadi with their mixture of sagging houses and galleried tenements. Looking behind, noticing that a black closed carriage had been behind her for the longest time, she told her driver to go farther into the labyrinthian *Chorrbazaar*, the thieves' market at Mutton Street. Once there, again seeing the black carriage, she thought that perhaps she was being followed, although she did not know why or by whom.

Getting down from her carriage, Margot made her way from one stall to the next, picking through piles of iron tools, copper trays, brass buckets, cane furniture, glass lamps, jeweled boxes, safes, spoon-backed chairs, and teapots. She looked behind her every once in a while, still seeing the closed carriage waiting near her own, and now, a native servant walking behind her, dogged her every step.

She left the market.

In the western part of the city, with the closed carriage still close behind, Margot was driven up the Malabar Hill and stopped halfway at the cloaked Tower of Silence, a round stone tower where the Parsis placed their dead. Vultures were clustered around the rim, jostling each other like a hungry family at mealtime, waiting to consume the bodies.

Looking up, seeing the vultures winging around the tower, she told the driver to continue. Suddenly the closed black carriage came up beside her own, and a man ducked behind a leather post. She sat up and tried to see who it was, but she couldn't. The closed carriage sped up and passed hers. She told her driver to follow it.

With the crack of a whip they took off. The other carriage climbed steadily, then finally turned into what looked like a small street but was actually a large set of gates in front of a white stone mansion that sat on a rocky ledge.

"Do you know who lives in this house?" she asked her driver.

He didn't know, and after a short while she told him to drive on.

When she arrived back at the hotel, Tom was there. He was tense because Jhaveris had gone off to arrange an appointment with the Rana of Dholpur, and there had been no word for a week.

Tension filled the air between them at dinner. Either unwilling or unable to acknowledge the pregnancy, Tom had become moody in her company. Margot excused herself and went to her room rather than continue eating in silence.

Fifteen minutes later there was a knock at the door. A servant stood there holding a note, which he dropped into her hand, then disappeared.

> *Dearest Margot—Please forgive my cruelty. I misunderstood so much of what happened between us. A carriage will be waiting to take you to my house tomorrow morning, where, if you are generous enough to accept this offer, I would like nothing more in the world than to apologize to you in person. If you can find it in your heart, please come to see me. Yours, David Nasis.*

Waiting for her the next morning was the black carriage that had followed her through the markets the day before.

Margot was driven to the white stone mansion on the Malabar Hill.

The house was large and pristine, almost like a museum, with long airless corridors leading into wide rooms filled with blackwood armchairs, French clocks, and Venetian glass. It was a neatly arranged storehouse of booty collected by David's grandfather, Solomon Nasis, a life-size marble statue of whom dominated the front hall.

The statue could have easily been a child's idea of what God looked like. The eyes were daunting, deep set like David's, but impassive. His word must have been law. His nose was long, bony, and Semitic. His expression was muscular and stern, but his mouth, like David's, was sensual, almost womanly. He was dressed in a turban and flowing robes, entirely exotic, and try as David might to deny it, beneath his meticulous British-cut suits lurked all this color. David, she finally realized, was still in rebellion.

"You l-l-look as though you s-s-see something familiar in this statue," David said, his eyes darting between it and Margot. He was very nervous to be in her presence.

"The patriarch," she said hesitantly.

"Surely your f-f-father did not dress th-th-this way."

"It's the expression in the eyes and the mouth. What I remember most clearly about my father was the very fine line I had to walk, careful to appeal to his compassionate side, fearful of provoking the stern side." Saying that, she realized she had been walking that same line with Tom for the past couple of weeks. "My father drank. One moment there would be the thundering, disapproving voice, the next, he'd be on his knees, my size, playing with me on the nursery floor . . ." Her eyes drifted away from the statue and fell on David, who was eagerly awaiting her every word.

When David took her arm and led her into a sitting room, she saw that he was limping.

"What's happened to your leg?"

David, turning beet-red, sat opposite her on a deep yellow couch, his leg sticking straight out like a pole. Looking away, he said in an unfaltering tone, "It's a price I've paid for having treated you so miserably."

"Please, David, don't talk nonsense. I never wished you any harm or ill. You were very hurt by me, but it was never my intention to do that."

"It was Jenks," he said, turning now to look at her. "It w-w-was all his fault. He t-t-turned me against you wh-wh-when we should have b-b-been the dearest of friends. He was j-j-jealous and s-s-spiteful, a madman. He shot me and stole my pearls. He's thrown in with Ali Aziz." David shrugged as if tossing off the very thought of Jenks, and then his eyes softened. Sitting up, he reached out and took both her hands in his. "I've missed you."

"You're right when you say we should be the dearest of friends—I need your friendship now more than ever," she said, her eyes filling with tears.

David moved closer to her. "Tom can't give you what I c-c-can. I adore you, Margot. I'd do anything in the w-w-world for you."

"But I need him."

"That's what I feel for you, Margot. I adore you."

"It's your friendship I need now, David. I'm in terrible trouble."

"If it's money—"

"No," she said softly.

"Anything he's done to you, I can make it right—"

"David, I'm going to have his child."

David froze. "I s-s-see."

"I'm frightened. I've already lost two infants. I want this child, but he won't even talk about it with me. He's letting me go through this alone. I'm frightened to be so alone."

"I'll m-m-marry you."

Looking up at him now through her tears, Margot was unable to respond.

"Friendship is a wonderful p-p-place to start a marriage. You are my dearest f-f-friend."

"But I want him, David."

"I know all th-th-there is to know about him. I have wires back and forth from New York and London c-c-confirming it. I know his real name and where he c-c-came from and wh-wh-where he worked, and this I do know—he will never marry you."

"Why do you say such a thing?"

"Because h-h-he is already m-m-married. He has t-t-two children."

She was too stunned to speak, and she stared at him clear-eyed.

<hr />

Chapter
Fifty-two

TOM SPENT THE day waiting for Margot and for word from Jhaveris. Between breakfast and tiffin he paced, between tiffin and tea he worried, and after the sun set, he drank alone in his dark room.

At six o'clock Margot came up to the room. She looked serene.

"Where on earth have you been?"

She walked to a table and raised the wick in the oil lamp. "You've been drinking."

"I have," he said defiantly.

"I like it when you drink," she said, sitting down across from him. "Drink makes you patient."

"Patience is something I've been trying to come to grips with all day. I'm not a patient person."

"Luckily for us, I am," she said in such a calm voice that he thought he'd scream. "I've had the patience to get through all this unpleasantness we've been experiencing lately—"

"Your use of the word *we* indicates a true democratic spirit, Margot."

"—and finally I've arrived at the truth, or a semblance of it, which seems to satisfy me. The truth, Tom. You know what I mean by that, don't you?"

"Are you angry with me?"

She stopped and took a deep breath before continuing. "I was, but that was before I understood what the truth was."

"You're tossing that word around like an anarchist does a bomb."

"I can unlock the truth with just two words."

"And the words are?"

"Tom Aspinall," she said quietly, staring intently at him.

He had not heard the name, had not even thought it, for so long that he repeated it to himself, then turned away from her.

"Tom Aspinall died on a ship called *Medusa*," he said slowly. "How did you find out about Tom Aspinall?"

"David Nasis remembered that you worked at a law firm in New York. He asked questions."

"Has he told anyone I'm alive?"

"I've asked him not to. Don't you want your wife and children to know that you're alive?"

"No."

"What sort of man are you?"

"Are you just asking yourself that question?"

"The man I fell in love with could not have deserted his wife and children."

"But I did."

"And that's all? No explanation, nothing?"

"Don't push me, Margot. I just might walk out of your life the way I walked out of theirs."

"You owe me an explanation!"

"What would satisfy you?"

She leaped to her feet. "Don't you dare be callous with me!"

"It was my life, Margot. It has nothing to do with you."

"I'm carrying your child. Are you getting ready to leave me as well?"

"No. I couldn't leave you," he said, burying his head in his hands.

"But you did leave your wife."

"My wife and her father conspired against me. She was willing to sell my children to him."

"What does that mean? Couldn't you prevent it?"

"My father-in-law is very rich and powerful. He would have destroyed my children to get them."

"But you were their father. Why didn't you protect them?"

His eyes were stern and fierce. "Don't you think I've asked myself that? Was it my pride or his will I didn't want to do battle with? I didn't want to drag my children through the courts!"

"Did your wife want you to?"

"She wanted me to stay and fight him. But he owned me. He would have cut us off without a cent. She's better off now, and so are my children. They have his money."

"But if she wanted you to stay . . . did she want you to stay?"

"Yes! Don't ask me any more questions."

"But I have to. It's as if you've already abandoned me. You can't talk about this. You can't even look at me. Tom, please, look at me!"

"She wanted another life. I'm sure she's gotten it," he said bitterly. "Let her be damned to it."

"You still love her . . ."

"I love you, Margot, I love you . . . I despise the choice my wife made. She wanted to throw parties for the rest of her life and to toady to self-important people. But her choice uncovered what my life had been all about. Her father controlled me—owned our house, paid for our servants. I couldn't have lived with myself and stayed with her.

And as for my children . . . it's better for them to think I'm dead. That's what *Medusa* did for them. Washed all traces of me away for good."

"But you've also lost them for good."

"Don't you think I know that?" He wiped his tears away, then looked at her. "This child you're carrying is my second chance." Leaning forward, he took her hand.

"You are my second chance. I did love Jelly when I married her. But she changed, or I did. I wasn't in love with what she became. You are what I wanted. We've given each other the lives we dreamed about. That's the only truth I believe in now." He stood up, and leaning over her, kissed her cheek, then her hands, then brought his hands down to her stomach. "This child seals our truth. I love you."

"I've been so afraid. I've lost two—"

He put his finger up to her lips. "Don't say it. I'm with you. I'll never leave. This child is as alive as our love for each other is."

"I keep wanting to run off with you somewhere, draw a curtain around us to protect us—but we have run off, we're at the ends of the earth."

"Margot, I do love you."

"I know you do." She stood up and put her arms around him. "Tom Street—it's our name. I want to take it."

"To marry me as Tom Street?"

"Right here and now—take my hands in yours," she said, and he clasped her hands again. "I give myself to you."

"I give you myself."

"Wait, a ring," she said, reaching into her pocket, bringing out the black pearl. "This pearl, which you brought to me from the bottom of the sea, I take as a token of your love."

Enfolding her hands again in his own, he smiled. "And we will be for each other," he said.

"Yes, for each other."

Leaning forward, they kissed.

Later, when they made love, she held the black pearl very close to her heart.

Chapter
Fifty-three

A WEEK LATER a wire arrived from Jhaveris, saying, "Very difficult situation. Need your help. Come to Dholpur immediately."

Traveling for the first time as man and wife, Tom and Margot spent days cooped up in stiflingly hot railway carriages.

Smoke and bloated puffs of yellow dust covered the great brown plains and khaki rivers they passed, and there were endless hordes of people, speaking either Hindi or Tamil or Telegu: women with blunt, stoic faces and bodies wrapped in colorful saris; men, dressed in *dhotis,* who ran beside the cars, hawking water or sweetmeats or bread. *"Hindi pani, Musselman pani!"* was the cry of the water carriers, who sold water separately to Hindus and Moslems. And everywhere there was the sweet and acrid smell of curry and saffron.

Traveling north-northeast, they finally reached Dholpur, which stood between Gwalior and Agra on a finger of Rahasthan that separated Madhya Pradesh and Uttar Pradesh.

Jhaveris was waiting for them on the platform, mopping his oversize head with a limp handkerchief and squinting, for the glare was intense.

"My goodness, what a time I've been having. I'm so glad to have you here. Was the trip hard, Your Ladyship?"

"I'm Mrs. Street now, so you must call me either that or Margot, and I'd prefer Margot."

"My gracious, I could never do that, Your Ladyship, but congratulations, I'm sure. This is wonderful news," he said, smiling, patting Tom on the back.

"Thank you," Tom said, ecstatic to hear Margot describe herself as Mrs. Street.

Jhaveris mopped his forehead. "We should be celebrating, but my goodness gracious, this man will drive us all mad."

"I can live with madness a lot easier than poverty," Margot said.

"Will he buy the pearls?" Tom asked.

"You've become the key to that. I told the Maharaj Rana about your diving in the South Seas and the admirable way you handled yourself in Ceylon and in Bombay. The more he heard, the more interested he was to meet you, and finally it became apparent that he would not discuss business without your being here."

"Well, then, let's go meet him."

"My gracious, if it were only as simple as that. He won't see you today. He has his horoscope done almost hourly, and today, this morning at any rate, was not a propitious time."

"What do we do?"

"We'll go to the palace and wait. Regrettably, I can offer no other suggestion or solution."

"Didn't he like the pearl from Ceylon we gave him?"

"My goodness, yes, that's the only reason we're here at all. But he likes to be . . . indulged."

"Jhaveris, my friend, I'm willing to be as indulgent as the next man, but our money is running out."

"Yes, I know. I know. Just a little while longer," he said, then took both their arms and led them to one of the Maharaj Rana's gold carriages.

Waiting beside it were two dwarfs, the state dwarfs of Dholpur, dressed in gold braid, epaulets, maroon tunics, matching turbans, gold belts, and swords. One had a beard and a fearsome expression, as though his height was a genetic misunderstanding. The other was beardless, round-faced, and frightened.

After their casks of pearls and luggage were loaded, they took off.

Dholpur was twelve hundred square miles, one of the nineteen states that formed the Rajputana Agency. The Maharaj Ranas of Dholpur were Hindu, descended from

Jats, members of the thirty-six "royal races," who claimed to have been descended from the moon. The British, when they divided the states, created three main classes—at the top were the First Division States, also known as the Salute States, their rank being measured by the firing of gun salutes that descended by odd numbers from twenty-one to nine. Dholpur was accorded fifteen—rulers with thirteen guns and more to their name were regarded as *maharajas,* or "great kings."

The current Maharaj Rana was thirty-eight and had married a second cousin, who had produced six children —four girls and two boys. The eldest, at fifteen, would be the next ruler. A spirited hunter, the Maharaj Rana was something of a mystery. He had designed and built the palace in which he lived, and his collection of pearls was considered to be the best in the world.

In two hours they reached an embattlement, which, Jhaveris told them, was the beginning of the prince's palace grounds. They did not reach the palace itself for another two hours.

Made entirely of pink stone, the palace had a cluster of domed towers and minarets and rows of arched windows fringed with gold that caught the light and made everything seem to glow as if it had been fired from within. Guarding the entrances were huge stone elephants, twenty feet tall, their front legs raised in salute, their trunks upturned, trumpeting.

The reception hall, also of pink stone, was starkly empty, with a sweeping staircase. Off it were period rooms; a drawing room was done in the Louis Quatorze style, with copies of the original period furniture done in solid silver. On the walls were Flemish tapestries, and in front of those were cases of silver objects. Another drawing room was done in the Japanese style, and there was a smoking room with furniture and hangings from Morocco. But most startling of all was what was called the *darbar,* a two hundred-foot-long pillared hall capable of accommodating thousands of people. Its parquet floor had been laid on huge stone beams, which had been tested by elephants. And elephants had also been hoisted to the roof to test the strength of the ceiling, which supported the hall's most

spectacular feature—three two-ton crystal chandeliers. In
the center of the *darbar* was a vast woven rug that had a
two-foot border of pearls.

Everywhere they went there were guards watching every
move, and in some rooms there was rustling behind screens
and tapestries and the sound of fleeing footsteps before they
approached. It was as if the palace were a vast and glamorous prison.

Margot and Tom were given a room with matching
four-poster beds made of cut crystal with blood-red velvet
covers. Margot, tired after the journey, slept. But Tom
toured the palace on his own, studying the rugs woven with
pearls. Everywhere he went, he felt the presence of eyes
behind the frescoes and screens, eyes behind the mosaics
that depicted hunting scenes of men chasing boar with
spears—until he too felt as if he were being hunted.

That night Margot, Tom, and Jhaveris were escorted to a
dining room that was decorated in an entirely Indian style,
with a low copper table, silk cushions, and carved and
brightly painted walls.

They were served skewered kabobs called Kabob-E-
Goscht Barra, black and yellow Dal, and Murg Ke Tikke,
chicken cooked in clay. This was washed down with a cool
drink of cuminseeds, tamarind juice, and mint, called Jal
Jeera.

Two musicians played *jal tarang,* music made by tapping
on the edge of bowls filled with water, accompanied by a
tabla drum.

While Tom and Jhaveris discussed the price of pearls and
various ways of dealing with the Maharaj Rana, Margot saw
a pair of eyes staring at them from behind a screen.

"I wouldn't discuss anything at this particular moment,"
Margot said quickly.

The eyes disappeared.

Suddenly a singer and a beautiful dancer with a long dark
braid appeared.

"What is his point?" Tom asked in a whisper, looking up
and seeing a pair of eyes behind the screen.

"To keep us amused," Jhaveris offered.

"Or to keep us from selling the pearls to anyone else,"
Margot said.

The dancer's feet slapped the marble floor. Her arms and hands undulated softly and evocatively.

"It's as if he's softening us up for the kill," Tom said.

But no prince arrived, to do either harm or business.

The next day a servant said that the Maharaj Rana wanted to inspect the Ceylon pearls, and the casks were taken away. That night the pearls were returned without comment.

Two more days passed. The hidden eyes seemed to rule the palace, and although it seemed that Tom and Margot had complete freedom of movement, servants guarded certain doorways and courtyards and the restrictions became more and more unsettling.

Tom was offered a sleek Arabian horse for morning rides, and Margot saw people standing at windows with their eyes trained on him as he rode out. At mealtimes more eyes behind the screens appeared, disappeared.

"What a damned nuisance," Margot said at the end of dinner on their fourth night.

"Patience," Jhaveris said. "I had to wait three days before he granted me an audience."

On the fifth day Tom decided that he had had quite enough.

"Margot and I are leaving this afternoon."

"My goodness, I don't think we can do that."

"You mean we're prisoners here?"

"I don't know. He's never behaved this way."

"We'll do business elsewhere. He isn't the only *maharaja* in India."

"Tom, my goodness, I wouldn't be so impulsive."

"We have the finest pearls from this year's fishery. I'm not worried about finding buyers."

But when they went back to their rooms to pack, they found their belongings had been placed under armed guard.

Tom stormed into the ornate *darbar* hall.

"I demand to see the Maharaj Rana," he called out. His voice echoed around the vaulted ceilings. The crystal chandeliers tinkled gently, and finally a servant appeared to say that the Maharaj Rana would like Tom to join him on a *shikar* at dawn the next morning—a pig stick, considered the most dangerous sport in India.

Chapter
Fifty-four

AT DAWN TOM, Margot, and Jhaveris were driven from the palace to a flat grassy plain. Midway on the plain, at the edge of a coconut plantation, stood an enormous open-sided tent, which Jhaveris called a *shamiana.*

"It's the prince's tent."

"Which one is he?"

"You can't see him from here—oh, my goodness, yes, now you can. He's sitting in the center, on the *gadi.*"

"The what?"

"The royal couch."

Flanked by a group of servants and guards wearing bright green tunics and red turbans, the Maharaj Rana was of medium height, somewhat stout, but not overfed. He looked square and tough sitting crosslegged on the *gadi,* which was of heavily embroidered satin and velvet. His skin was badly pitted, and his eyes were stern and dark.

As their carriage drove up, he remained sitting. It was not enough that he had imprisoned them, now he wanted them to pay homage. Jhaveris, making a slight bow, was the first down, and he introduced Tom and Margot.

The Maharaj Rana nodded but said nothing to them, spoke only in Hindi to his servants. His tone said everything; he was a man who was used to being listened to.

He was wearing a small evenly folded scarlet turban and a khaki riding outfit. On the lapel of his coat was an enormous baroque pearl stick pin. His eyes took in everything. He saw that Margot was nervous and lovely, that Jhaveris was fawning, and that Tom, while polite and respectful, did not seem cowed. He was studying the prince as intently as he was being studied.

254

As they were served morning tea, Jhaveris made polite conversation. The Maharaj Rana said nothing.

When the sun began to rise, large and molten, directly across from them, the prince gave a quick signal to one of his guards, and the beaters were sent out into the coconut plantation. Then the tension rose. Margot smiled, but was twisting the handkerchief that contained her black pearl in her hand. Tom could hear the beaters spreading out behind the *shamiana*.

Horses were brought out from their makeshift stables. The Maharaj Rana's mount was a black Arabian with a small head and a long, elegant neck. Tom's was the same horse he'd used on his morning rides. Two servants appeared with spears and sharpening stones.

"You'll follow my lead," the prince said. His English was impeccable. "Remember that you're depending on the pig to charge to drive your spear through his shoulder into his heart. If you don't get the pig on the point of your spear and it grazes off, the pig will continue the charge and try to cut you or your horse."

A servant offered the Maharaj Rana a leg up.

Tom turned to Margot, who kissed his cheek and whispered, "Please be careful."

Jhaveris offered a nervous little wave, and then Tom got up on his horse.

As the two men rode off, Jhaveris said to Margot, "My goodness, what have we gotten him into?"

"It's a fine time to be asking that," she said, taking a seat inside the *shamiana*, clutching her pearl.

The Maharaj Rana was silent again as they rode over to a thicket to wait for the pigs to break out. A servant followed close behind, also on horseback, carrying fresh spears.

The sun was now at eye level across the great plain. It would be hot very soon. Tom was already sweating. The horses were nervous, blowing and snorting as if they were communicating their fear to each other. In the background Tom could still hear the beaters, some of whom were making harsh shrieking sounds. There was a good deal of thrashing about, but no pigs broke from the thicket.

The Maharaj Rana had his eyes fixed on the plain.

"My love of pearls is not based purely on greed, although I don't discount it as a motive," he said suddenly, as if he were picking up an interrupted conversation. "Within ten years pearls will become the most precious commodity on earth." He turned abruptly, annoyed at the beaters for not having already driven a pig out into the plain.

"I'm also a philosophical man, and pearls, with their quality of transformation, appeal to me on that level. Are you as philosophical about them?"

"Quite honestly, I've been too busy."

"You've dived for them?"

"Yes, in the South Seas."

"And traded them with the merchants in the Jhaveri bazaar?"

"Yes, pearls from the very lots we've brought to the palace for you to look at."

"If I had your freedom to move about, I would control the harvest and sale of every pearl in the world."

Holding this conversation now, like two merchants discussing their products, gave an air of unreality to the event about to happen, Tom thought. But as the heat intensified and the plain began to sizzle, reality shifted once again. There was a sudden burst of movement behind them. Pigeons and wild turkeys took flight, spiraling in the air.

"Here they come," the Maharaj Rana said, sitting up in his saddle.

The horses began rearing. Tom held his reins tightly.

As many as five boars broke from the thicket. They were thick, grizzled animals, tough and fearsome.

The Maharaj Rana could not hold his horse back any longer. As he let go, the horse charged forward.

Tom's horse also bolted ahead, running neck and neck with the Maharaj Rana's.

The boars fanned out in wide circles, some getting lost in the high grass, others stopping with ferocious suddenness.

Tom tucked his spear under his arm and clutched it so tightly his knuckles drained of color. The feeling was familiar: not fear—you had to be expecting something terrible in order to feel fear—but more an amazing sense of exhilaration, like the first time he'd climbed into the rigging on *Medusa* or the first time he'd dived for pearls.

The Maharaj Rana, wanting the first kill of the morning, bolted ahead.

One of the boars began cutting across to the right directly in front of the Maharaj Rana's horse, then it cut away, ran in another wide arc, turned, and charged the Maharaj Rana's horse. The Maharaj Rana's eyes narrowed. He hunched down, his spear poised, and the boar lowered its head, gnashing its tusks, the bristles on its back shooting up like porcupine quills. The prince lunged forward, spearing the boar just at the shoulder, and the boar, completing its charge, ran up the stick, then took off with the spear embedded in its heart, blood spurting from the wound. Fifty feet ahead it fell.

Turning, Tom spotted another boar, zigzagging across the plain. Taking off after it, he saw that this one was huge, with large tusks on either side. Its eyes were frenzied, darting ahead, then over at the horse, now running beside it. Suddenly it cut over to the left and Tom followed, his spear poised in the crook of his arm.

Looking up, Tom saw the Maharaj Rana, with a new spear tucked under his arm, charging through the high grass toward him. He wanted this kill too, but Tom was determined to take it. Urging his horse on, he ran ahead of the boar. It suddenly stopped, and lifting its grizzled head, trumpeted a fierce grunt and pawed at the dry earth. Then, with its head lowered, tusks slick with saliva, it charged.

Tom faced it head-on across a small patch of bare plain. Its hide glistened with sweat. Tom held the spear pointed down. He could hear the grunting grow louder and louder, punctuated by the sound of his own pounding heart. The dust was rising between them, a puffball of smoke and heat, and suddenly he was directly above it. Now, he said to himself, do it now! He drove the spear down, not above the shoulder, but directly into the boar's head. As he passed it, he was swept out of his saddle and ended up on the ground, still holding the butt end of the spear. The boar lay only a few feet away, stone dead.

The Maharaj Rana, having seen the kill, was heading out into the plain after two other large ones that were heading back to the safety of the coconut plantation. A servant tried goading them either to the left or the right, but quite suddenly one of them turned and charged, hitting the servant's horse squarely in its flanks and sending the servant flying. The boar then fled toward the *shamiana.*

Margot stood up when she saw it. Jhaveris took her arm to pull her back, but she stayed where she was for a moment, watching the Maharaj Rana charge headlong after the boar.

The animal charged blindly ahead, then stopped fifty yards in front of the tent. The Maharaj Rana jerked his reins fiercely to the right. His horse's right front leg buckled and sent the prince flying out of his saddle. He stood in the center of the deserted plain with his spear poised. As the boar charged, he hurled the spear, but it only grazed the boar's side and the animal, carrying off the spear, ran in a wide arc, bucking and kicking, then charged once again.

The Maharaj Rana turned, heading for the safety of the *shamiana.* His turban was uncoiling, fluttering on the ground behind him like a giant, scarlet snake.

All of them were in danger now. Jhaveris had crawled to the back of the tent and was calling out for Margot to join him, but she was glued to her spot. She could see the panic in the Maharaj Rana's eyes—the game had suddenly become so dreadfully real.

Servants ran for their horses, but the dust cloud, rising above the boar, was coming closer and closer.

The boar lowered its head and charged, knocking the Maharaj Rana down and cutting him across the back. The boar lowered his head again and began a second charge, clipping the prince's foot, then he turned back for the kill.

Tom, galloping up from behind, his spear held straight up in his clenched fist, reached out and stabbed the boar in its haunches. The animal screeched and, turning, just inches away from the Maharaj Rana, charged Tom, who jerked his reins to the left and bolted ahead, leading the boar on a heated chase onto the plain.

Tom was panting. Sweat poured down from his forehead, clouding his vision. He could hear the sound of the horse's hooves pounding on the dry earth and the gnashing grunts of the boar pursuing him. Enveloped in dust, his mouth dry and gritty, Tom turned. The animal was closing in under him, trying to cut his horse's right rear leg. Tom brought up the spear and, twisting to the right, held it poised above the boar's shoulder. With all his remaining strength, he drove the spear down. Bones and muscle would not give way, but then there was a crunch, and the blade slivered through just as Tom lost his balance. The boar ran off to the right, the spear embedded in its heart. Tom fell from the saddle, landing with a terrific thud squarely on his bottom and thighs. Nearby, the boar reared, then dropped. The spear quivered.

There was a terrific ringing in Tom's ears. Stars exploded before his eyes—bursts of heat, light, a glowing twilight, spread out then dissolved. He lost sight of where he was. His head dropped to his chest and bobbed as he breathed. Then, looking up, seeing the *shamiana* rising in the distance like a mirage, it all came back. Pearls, he said to himself—he was there on that dusty, bloodied plain to sell pearls. Rising, shaking the dust from his trousers and coat, he began hobbling toward the tent, trailing wings of dust after him. He began walking more steadily and determined. He'd saved the prince's life, now he'd make the man pay.

Chapter
Fifty-five

"YOU'LL SEE, LADY Vale, word of what happened this morning will find its way to Bombay, then everywhere. Tom's a hero," Jhaveris said that afternoon at tiffin, which was being served in the Maharaj Rana's private dining room, a pillared hall with vaulted ceilings and pale walls decorated with gold and enamel.

Tom and the Maharaj Rana were sitting at one end of a low, long table talking quietly. The Maharaj Rana was on a velvet *gadi* that was framed by two enormous gilt mirrors. He looked less stern, as if Tom had passed some test and was now to be respected. Margot, who was sitting with Jhaveris at the other end of the table, could see Tom's face in one of the mirrors. For a while he listened patiently, then Margot thought she saw the expression on his face begin to change. Gradually, he was becoming wary, his gestures more deliberate. He was transforming himself into a businessman.

"Just look at the two of them," she said to Jhaveris, "conspiring to take over the world."

The Maharaj Rana was now offering Tom instruction. He had brought out a small part of his collection of pearls and was holding up the most spectacular ones, talking about their lustre and size. He was wearing the famous Dholpur pearls, seven strands of the most magnificent white pearls Margot had ever seen. Each was the size of a child's marble, as luminous as pale satin.

Turning, winking confidently at her, Tom called out, his words echoing through the hall, "Margot, may we use your shawl?"

She took the Kashmiri ring shawl off her shoulders and gave it to a servant, who passed it to Tom.

"We've agreed to trade under the shawl for the entire lot of Ceylon pearls."

"Another story! You see how it happens," Jhaveris whispered. "They'll be talking for years to come about how Tom Street traded his catch from the Ceylon fishery to the prince using the hand gestures from the market."

"We need witnesses," Tom called out.

"I'll be a witness," Margot said. She stood and walked to the other end of the table, Jhaveris following close behind.

"We're making a small change in the rules," Tom explained. "Grasping the entire hand will equal one hundred thousand rupees, each finger becomes ten thousand, half the finger, one thousand, the tips, hundreds. Shall we begin?"

The Maharaj Rana nodded.

Tom covered his hand with the shawl, reached out and, grasping the Maharaj Rana's hand, squeezed it seven times, then grasped all five fingers. Seven hundred and fifty thousand rupees was the opening bid.

The Maharaj Rana returned a much lower bid, which Tom automatically countered. When the Maharaj Rana countered it, the bidding sped up. Tom kept his wits. The Maharaj Rana was a capable trader. Back and forth, squeeze for squeeze, hands, fingers, tips—the final price Tom proposed for the lot was five hundred and fifteen thousand rupees. There was a moment's pause while the Maharaj Rana made a quick mental calculation, then, withdrawing his damp hand from under the shawl, he nodded in agreement.

Tom and Margot had each come away with just over a hundred thousand dollars and Jhaveris had cleared fifty thousand, the largest single sale he had ever made.

When Tom and Margot returned to Bombay, they decided to settle there. The city had brought them good fortune and it was a pearl trading center. They rented a large house near Nasis's mansion on the Malabar Hill and commissioned the building of another, which would be their permanent residence.

Tom and Nasis were now each other's chief competitors in Bombay, and although they could hardly stand to be in the same room with each other, Margot staunchly maintained her friendship with Nasis. He was her only link to the past.

Tom's ambition became the dominant force in their lives. Now merchants came to him with pearls they either wanted to sell or have him sell. While Jhaveris became his liaison with the day-to-day trading life in the Jhaveri bazaar, Tom became the chief purchasing agent for the Maharaj Rana of Dholpur, as well as the Gaikwar of Baroda and several other *maharajas*. The British, more comfortable dealing with a Westerner, asked Tom's advice about the management of their pearl fisheries in India and Ceylon, as well as Australia and Burma, which gave him access to pivotal information.

Famous gems came into his possession. Two pear-shaped pearls reputed to have once belonged to the unfortunate Mary Stuart and which had been sold to Queen Elizabeth in 1568, found their way to Bombay, and for several weeks Tom owned them. Then, hearing a visiting baronet express interest in them, Tom sold them for a hundred thousand dollars, realizing a profit of fifty thousand dollars in just under ten days.

Then the pear-shaped Gogibus pearl, reputed to have been the largest in Europe at one time, weighing one hundred and twenty-six carats, five hundred and four grains, was brought to Tom by the son of a valet, who had inherited it from his father. Originally brought from the West Indies to Europe in 1620 by a man named Gogibus, the pearl had been sold to Philip IV of Spain, then resold, stolen, and sold again.

Tom brought it to Dholpur, where the Maharaj Rana confirmed its authenticity. Tom purchased it but could not find a buyer in India. The Maharaj Rana was having trouble with his British resident at the time, who thought that the prince of pearls was spending entirely too much on gems. The Maharaj Rana told Tom that he would find his best price in Paris, but Margot was in the last weeks of her pregnancy and Tom didn't want to leave her.

It was as if he was going to be a father for the very first time. Margot wanted him to know everything that was going on, every move and tug and pinch and queasy breath.

"I'm a terrible, bloated bother," she said one morning as they sat in their garden, which was bordered by a craggy ridge. She was wearing a white cotton coat—her *shamiana,* she called it. "I'm so short of breath and swollen, and yet all I want to do is make love to you."

"I don't know about the logistics," he said, smiling.

"My God, but I'm fat! Just roll me down the Malabar Hill—I'll eventually land in the ocean and float!" She laughed, then opened her hand and stared at her black pearl, which she now always carried. "I'm like a sow or cow, my body simply does its job. I have nothing to say about it. When I was younger, I never liked losing control. Do you suppose that's what went wrong the last times? The babies and I were in a tug of war for control, and I wouldn't let them live because I couldn't give mine up."

"Don't think about it."

"I'm not that delicate. I think about it all the time. Both babies were born dead, I carried them inside me for nine months—I felt them move and kick, and yet they died. You won't be angry with me if this one dies?"

"Please don't talk nonsense. This is our baby—he'll live."

"A 'he'—you think it will be a he? I want you to have a daughter," she said, staring down again at the black pearl. "The woman who predicted our meeting and your finding this pearl for me told me that it would accumulate all the love that was felt by each of its owners and that would be passed on to the final owner. I was so selfish at the time, I wanted all the love for myself, but if we have a daughter I want to give this to her—and if I don't live, you must have it for a time and then give it to her."

"You will live. The baby will live. When you give birth and everything is all right, I'll take the pearl to Paris and have it set in a pendant for you."

"Or a ring."

"Or a ring that you'll wear for years and then pass on to your daughter."

"You'll be very happy with a daughter. You'll have someone to dote on you in your later years. I want to name her for your mother."

"Jessica—I like that name."

"Yes, Jessica Street—it was your mother who brought us together."

"How so?"

"Her dreams got you on that ship and the ship got you to that island."

"Atoll."

"Atoll or island—you're here with me, and it was all Jessica's doing."

Tom thought about his mother for a moment, saw her standing on the bridge of the *Albion*. If she lived at all now, it was through the life that he and Margot shared.

"I like this idea of a daughter more and more," he said.

Margot kissed him gently, then said, "Repeat what you said to me before."

"What's that?"

"You will live, the baby will live—"

"Yes, the baby will live, a daughter, and after I see that everything is all right after the birth, I'll take your black pearl to Paris and have it set in a pendant."

"No, a ring."

"A ring that you will wear for many years, and when you're ready, you'll pass it on to your daughter."

Margot flinched suddenly as she felt her legs and white coat become drenched with water.

"It's time," she said.

"I'll send someone for the doctor."

"No, don't leave," she said, grasping his hands. "Put your hands on my stomach. Is she still moving—is she alive?"

Leaning over her, Tom pressed his ear to her stomach and heard a heartbeat, Margot's or his own, a stirring.

"She's alive."

"Then, quickly, get the doctor," Margot said, shutting her eyes against the brilliant sun. She repeated over and over again, "She is alive, she is alive . . ."

For eight hours he paced outside, first on the lawn in the garden, then downstairs in the hall. Margot's cries rang out, punctuating the heavy silence, and Tom suffered along with her—first sitting, then pacing.

It was after midnight when Tom heard the wailing cry of a baby. Running up the stairs, he called out.

"A girl or a boy?"

"A girl," the doctor said.

He ran into her room. Margot was pale. The baby was being held by an Indian woman, an *ayah,* who unfurled a little blanket. The baby was tiny and fresh, and her mouth was like Margot's, puckered up in a wince. She was about to have another good cry.

Margot, looking up drowsily, saw him and smiled.

"Done," she said triumphantly.

Chapter Fifty-six

TWO MONTHS LATER they moved into a new house, a grand *pukkah* bungalow, as the mansions in Bombay were called. Situated on a craggy point on the Malabar Hill, it had large rooms and a great many windows, some with painted glass, which filtered the harsh sunlight and showered the marble floors with gemlike colors.

Nasis paid a call to see Jessica. Tom was barely courteous

to him. Nasis was still so devoted to Margot, so trapped by his devotion, that he could not see an alternative to his love of her.

After the visit, when Tom showed him to the door, Nasis, feeling the bitterness of his situation so acutely, stopped and turned to Tom.

"She is a very b-b-beautiful little girl, but I cannot help feeling s-s-sorry for her. What do you plan to tell her about yourself?"

"Are you really feeling sorry for her, or are you jealous of me?"

"What you've d-d-done is very selfish. I w-w-would have married Margot, g-g-given your child a real name."

"But Margot didn't want to marry you, Nasis, and whatever trouble comes to my daughter may well come from you, because you began meddling in my life."

"I'm m-m-more honorable than you th-th-think."

"Oh, I'm sure of it. Now, good night," Tom said, opening the glass doors that led to the front courtyard.

"I won't do anything to h-h-hurt Margot, and I w-w-won't hurt her child."

"The child is also mine, Nasis. That is the saddest fact of your life. Jessica is mine."

"Will you h-h-have her baptized? W-w-will you make the sh-sh-sham complete?"

"Good night!" Tom said, closing the door firmly behind him.

The very next week another famous pearl came up for sale on the Bombay market. Called the Oviedo, it had once belonged to Rudolph II, emperor of the Holy Roman Empire, brought to him from Panama sometime during the sixteenth century. Weighing over thirty carats, it attracted a great deal of attention, and both Tom and Nasis were interested in obtaining it. Tom's anger outweighed his judgment and he bought it for much more than he had expected to spend just so Nasis would not have it. Almost all his money was now tied up in the two extraordinary pearls, the Oviedo and the Gogibus, for which he could not find buyers.

In November there was more bad news. The colonial office gave him the first findings of the Ceylon fishery. The

1891 and '92 fisheries had been so successful, the beds had not had a chance to replenish—the '93 yield would be very low.

Tom had no choice now but to leave Margot and Jessica and go to Paris to sell his pearls.

"Of course you will be extraordinarily strong when you're faced with all the temptations Paris has to offer," Margot said as they lay in bed the night before his departure.

"Why do you assume that?" he asked, leaning over, kissing her breasts, tracing their fullness with his lips.

"Because I have spoiled you so and you know how very small the world can be. And because if I hear of your having been unfaithful, I will hire an assassin."

Parting her legs, he inserted himself inside her.

She moaned.

She turned her head away, but he held her face with his hands and forced her to look at him. Her arms slipped around his neck and pulled his lips to hers.

"I love you," she whispered.

"You say it so softly—don't you want anyone else to know?"

"No, it's our love—no one else's. I love you so," she whispered again.

The next morning he was in the garden with Jessica when Margot gave him her black pearl.

"I'll have it set," he said.

"Or just carry it, then I'll always be with you."

Reaching down, she took the baby from her *ayah*.

"Now, please walk to the end of the garden and look back at us."

He did as she asked. Margot and Jessica were framed beneath a towering banyan tree. The sky behind them was cobalt blue, and above, several kites were circling lazily.

"Is it a very pretty picture?" she called out.

"Very."

"Incomplete without you. Come back to us soon," she said, and smiled. "Very soon."

Paris in 1893 was a city of courtesans and dandies, scandals and gossip, passion, art, jewels, and fashion. But for Tom it was the city of Heliotrope, that year's most fashionable fragrance. It was everywhere he went—wafting on the cool breezes that blew down the Champs-Élysées or in the Bois de Boulogne or the Parc Monceau; floating echoes of ladies turning here and there, chatting, fingering their pearls, twirling parasols, nodding stiff-necked swathed in ermine or sable. Ladies with enchanting, dark eyes peered down from their carriages through veils, smiling secretively, self-possessed, caught in beautiful webs, in a thrall: to be living in the center of Paris at the very center of the world.

To buy and sell the best pearls in all the world, Tom went to the ninth arrondissement, behind L'Opéra, on the rue Lafayette, where all the players in the pearl trade were assembled. It was much like Jhaveri bazaar in Bombay, although in Paris the trade, like everything else, had become an art.

Day after day the brokers, who looked sleekly courteous, joked with the haggard, worried-looking dealers. The dealers barely tolerated the brokers, the way sharks tolerated pilot fish. A mixed lot, the Paris pearl merchants were Armenians, Syrians, Arabs, Parsis, Jews, Frenchmen, Catalans, and Neapolitans. At first Tom merely watched the trade, eavesdropped, and picked up the jargon.

Parcels of pearls were handed back and forth from trader to trader and trader to brokers in an elaborate chain. Handshakes and initials signed on flimsy envelopes ensured deals. Dealers, once they put their seal upon a bid, had to abide by their prices. And prices were calculated either per grain or per base—the base price being the square of a pearl's weight in francs. At lunch in the early afternoon, at tea, or after work, they gathered in cafés, which functioned as their offices—the Brasserie Universelle, famous for its hors d'oeuvres, and the Café Scossa, at the intersection of the rue Lafayette and rue Drouot, not far from the Salle Drouot, where the crown jewels of France, including the famous Regente pearl, had been auctioned in 1887.

Tom sat in the Café Scossa appraising each broker and dealer, waiting to choose one to begin conducting business with—and one emerged, the largest of them in fact. He was a rotund man with a goatee, a pale face, long, pallid brown hair that curled, in thick ringlets, over his coat collar. His name was Hubert Blisky. Tom chose him because he seemed to be in the center of each large deal, and rather than splitting his time between pearls and other gems, he specialized in pearls. He was calm and yet greedy; his weight gave that away. His instincts were finely tuned. He rejected as many deals as he accepted, and for the most part he was well liked by his fellow traders. He usually sat waiting for business to come his way, his shoulders hanging lank in a tight-fitting coat, his dainty hands clasped over his tremendous stomach. Blisky looked as if he had just eaten the entire world whole in one bite.

After a week of being scrutinized, he pulled up a chair beside Tom and introduced himself. "You are not a Frenchman, monsieur, nor do I think you are English."

"I'm an American, a pearl merchant like yourself."

"There is no one quite like myself, monsieur. Are you a buyer or seller?"

"At the moment a seller."

Blisky's eyes, which had been trained on a passing tray of tarts, suddenly turned toward Tom with more interest.

"My name is Hubert Blisky, monsieur, and yours?"

"Tom Street."

Upon hearing the name, Blisky tapped his small index finger to his brow. "Mr. Street of Bombay?"

"Lately of Bombay."

"The one who saved the prince from being eaten alive by lions?"

Tom laughed. "It was a boar hunt."

"But we've all heard of you, monsieur. You've been a diver, and you cornered the Ceylon fishery. It's only natural that you've come to Paris, everyone must. But what have you come to sell?"

"Two very large, famous pearls."

"Why not put them up for auction?"

"My nature is somewhat more discreet than my reputation."

"And discretion is my middle name, monsieur," Blisky said, dropping his voice to a conspiratorial hush.

"I'm interested in selling these pearls privately."

"Do you have them with you?"

"No, they're in a safe at my hotel, but I think their

names will suffice for the moment. The Oviedo and the Gogibus."

Blisky smiled like a cat who had just fallen into a bucket of milk. He knew the pearls, or had heard of them, and was already calculating his commission.

"Have you had dinner, monsieur?"

"I was planning to eat at the hotel."

"But I insist that you eat with me. We have a great deal to discuss, not the least of which is my trustworthiness. Come," he said, rising, taking Tom's arm. "You'll be my guest. My wife will cook you the best meal of your life."

Blisky and family lived nearby in a pleasantly crowded apartment off the Place Adrien Oudin on the Boulevard Haussman. The center of his cramped little world, Blisky was fussed over by a small, square wife with a pointed chin and oversized nose and two small but fat children, a boy and a girl. His nemesis was his mother-in-law, a red-haired harridan called Madame Moulin, for whom enough could not be done and from whom no one ever received a word of gratitude.

After dinner Blisky and Tom were left alone. They talked about the world market and about the fisheries coming up that spring. Tom said that Ceylon would be disappointing.

Blisky took the news in stride. "This year and last, all the rage has been for Venezuelan pearls," he said, showing Tom several, which were lovely. Some were golden tinted, others, pinkish gray.

Blisky said he had always wanted to go to Venezuela; he had a keen eye for these pearls. Tom filed away that bit of information, then asked Blisky to tell him something more about his life.

"The short version or the long?"

"The short will do."

"I came to Paris and began my career"—whenever he used this word, he waved his hand back and forth in an expansive way—"by hanging around the auction houses. I had only forty francs in my pocket and began by buying a Normandy cupboard, splitting my take with the craftsman who repaired it. Then I went into everyday objects—umbrellas, cod liver oil, herring—marinated them to get a higher price. It was a career.

"Then someone sold me my first pearl and I resold it, then acquired another. Soon I was becoming prosperous and opened a store, but lean times came and the store was not for me. I am more a man for the street. Offices are stuffy—I'd rather spend my time beneath God's blue sky, breathing freely. I am, in short, the consummate middleman."

Tom knew he had found his man.

Blisky escorted Tom to his hotel, the Ritz, where Blisky inspected the pearls. His reaction was shrewd, temperate. He did not carry on the way Pravin had in Bombay. He had a plan, he said. He knew of a man who might be persuaded to buy both pearls at once—a rich banker who was keeping a demimondaine, a famous actress named Jolie, in grand style on the rue Fortuny.

"Her love of jewels and your good looks are the key to selling your pearls, monsieur."

"But I'm a married man, Monsieur Blisky."

"So is the banker. Trust me, the pearls are as good as sold."

Chapter Fifty-seven

JOLIE, WHOSE REAL name was Lizette Wolff, began her acting career in her mother's brothel at the age of thirteen, where her well-timed sighs and moans were among the best performances she ever gave.

With a pouting smile, gray, mysterious eyes, and a will and nerves of steel, she was one of the most beautiful girls in all of Paris. At fifteen she ran away and was admitted to the Conservatoire to study acting. In two years she was asked to join the Comédie Française, but chose instead to become a star in the boulevard theaters, where she specialized in comedy and light melodrama. What set her apart from other actresses of the day was her unique style, which some referred to as modern. She spoke rapidly, her hands always moving, her gorgeous face thrown back, her eyebrows arched superciliously. Her gestures were imitated by thousands of women all over Paris.

But her special allure was her reputation. Were her lovers men or women? It was said that the lovers she chose possessed a similar quality—each was ugly or deformed in some way. Dubbed Beauty and Her Beasts by the gossips, she confirmed all the stories by taking up with the immensely wealthy banker, crippled since birth, Lucien Chary, who had married into the Bonaparte aristocracy and was a father of four and fearful of encroaching age.

Jolie lived in a small garish palace on the rue Fortuny, filled with seventeenth-century tapestries, Venetian chandeliers, and footmen and butlers in gold braid and wigs. It was a little girl's idea of how a fairy princess should live.

When Tom arrived, he was shown into a monstrous sitting room, which looked as if someone had drooled gilding down the walls. He waited . . . and waited. She never arrived, never sent anyone to fetch him or to convey her apologies. After a half hour, as he was about to leave, he noticed a small door behind a screen that had been left ajar. Pushing it open, he found himself inside a boudoir, as pink and smooth as a bowl of strawberries and cream.

Jolie was on a chaise longue having her hair combed by a midget, a dark-haired mannish woman.

Jolie stared at him, heavy-lidded. She could have been drunk or drugged—the room was filled with sweet-smelling smoke. Her titian-red hair fell about her shoulders in loose waves. She was ravishing, and she seemed imminently dangerous.

The midget left them alone.

"In just another minute or two I was coming to see you," Jolie said to Tom.

Holding her bottom lip curled between her teeth, she continued studying him.

"I was expecting an old badger, but you are quite beautiful and one should never keep beauty waiting. Monsieur Blisky always sends me the most beautiful things."

"A thing is what you think I am?"

"Being a thing embarrasses you—and I don't want to insult you. Never insult beauty, you only confuse it. It doesn't know what to do when it isn't appreciated."

"Like the pearls I've brought—they've been lying in vaults, unappreciated."

"Very clever—what a deadly combination beauty and wit can be. Now you'll sell me anything you want. May I see what you've brought?"

Walking toward her, he slipped his hand into his left coat pocket and brought out the velvet boxes that contained the two pearls. He was conscious, the entire time it took to cross the room, of her heavy stare, which was like a net she had thrown out and was now using to pull him closer.

Standing beside the chaise, he handed her the boxes. The first one she opened contained the Gogibus. Taking it out, she rubbed it on her teeth.

"Gritty from the sea," she said.

After taking out the Oviedo, she held each in one of her palms as if she were weighing them.

"Monsieur Blisky told me they were famous."

Tom gave her a brief history of each.

"I'm famous. I've a pearl named for me," she said, then raising her leg and propping up a foot on the chaise, she opened her frilly lace robe to show him a garter into which had been sewn a forty-grain white pearl. Her finger grazed it lightly, then rested on her pale thigh midway between the garter and the few stray reddish gold hairs that curled tautly between her thighs.

"You can see it better if you kneel," she said.

"I can see from here how very beautiful it is," he said broadly.

As she laughed, her left hand floated up from her thigh toward his lips. Bending, he kissed it and in an instant she reached her right hand into his right coat pocket and pulled out another velvet box.

"A trick I learned in my mother's house," she said, opening the box, seeing Margot's luminous black pearl now mounted in a ring, which Tom had had set in platinum and diamonds.

"That one is not for sale."

"And of course it is the one I must have."

"Impossible, madame. It belongs to my wife."

Closing the box with a pout, she handed it back to him.

"Wit and beauty and honor—perfection is sometimes very boring," she said, shrugging. Her foot dropped to the floor, and her hands greedily held the two other pearls. "I want them both."

"The price is steep."

She stood up, imperious and distant.

"Where is your office?" she asked.

"I'm staying at the Ritz."

"Monsieur Chary and I will be there this evening. You must show me both of the pearls, but have one priced lower than the other. He will buy the cheaper one, and when he refuses to buy the more expensive one, you must offer it to me as a gift."

"A very lavish gift . . ."

"You will simply have to trust me," she said, then left the room.

That night Jolie and Lucien Chary arrived at Tom's suite. Chary had a palsied hand that was twisted up like a shriveled leaf. As thin as death, he walked with a limp, his foot slapping the floor flatly.

Jolie was more animated than she had been that afternoon, as if she were showing Chary off and his ugliness was his chief virtue.

Tom showed Chary the pearls, gave him their history, then the price, making the Oviedo ten thousand francs more expensive than the Gogibus. As Jolie had predicted, Chary wanted only the Gogibus. He took out his checkbook and wrote a check for it.

Jolie was adamant; she wanted both.

Tom told her that if she really wanted the other, he would give it to her. He added a little flourish of his own invention here—he mooned over her as if he were wildly in love with her. And she, playing her part deftly, plucked the Oviedo from his hand and held on to it tightly.

Chary said nothing. Tom's heart stopped. Jolie said it was time to leave, they were joining friends at Voisin. Chary stood. Tom escorted them to the door and held it open, all the color draining from his face as Jolie walked out with both pearls in her possession. When Chary reached the door, he stopped and reached into his coat pocket with his withered hand. He brought out his checkbook and purchased the Oviedo for the price Tom had quoted.

As they were leaving, Jolie turned and blew Tom a kiss.

Tom recounted the entire story to Blisky the next day at the Café Scossa. Blisky acted as if business was always conducted in this manner in Paris.

Tom had made a small fortune, for which he gave Blisky a sizable commission, the largest one Blisky had received that year.

After the exchange of money, Tom proposed backing Blisky at the Venezuelan fishery. At first Blisky protested that he couldn't be away from his wife and children for that long. But Tom made a pointed reference to Blisky's mother-in-law, and by the end of the afternoon an agreement was reached. Papers would be drawn up and letters of credit issued at a nearby bank.

The two toasted each other well into the evening at the Café Scossa with bottles of champagne, and a crowd of traders and brokers gathered around them, offering their toasts. Finally a harried-looking man came up next to Tom and asked what all the commotion was about.

"A partnership is born."

"Between you and Blisky? What's your name, monsieur?"

"Street—Tom Street."

"The American?"

The man suddenly looked frightened. Tom thought he was familiar, but he couldn't place him.

"Your partnership, monsieur, is to buy pearls?"

"Yes, Blisky will go to Venezuela."

"And you?"

"To Australia."

The man seemed relieved. "That's good."

"Why?"

"You should stay away from the Persian Gulf."

Blisky, who overheard this comment, interrupted. "But why? The best pearls are there."

"You don't want to go there, monsieur," the man said to Tom. "You've been warned."

The man suddenly ran out of the café.

Tom dashed out after him. "Monsieur," he called out, but the man wouldn't stop.

Finally catching up to him Tom grabbed him and spun him around. "Who warns me, monsieur?"

"I didn't tell you—you didn't see me. He was in Paris not two weeks ago. He was saying horrible things about you, monsieur. They say he killed a man."

It was the phrase that triggered Tom's memory. The man resembled Stringy Peele from the *Medusa*. He had that same frantic quality in his voice and terrified look in his eyes.

"Who killed a man?"

"The Englishman—Jenks."

"Jenks! What's he got to do with anything?"

"Please, monsieur. I've got to stay on his good side. He controls all the best pearls coming from Arabia now, Sheikh Akhbar's supply. I was talking to him not more than a week ago."

"Jenks was in Paris?"

"He knew you were here, monsieur. He told a group of us to spread the word—a warning to you. I believe him, monsieur."

"What was the warning?"

"Don't follow him into the Persian Gulf."

"I'm not afraid of him."

"He killed Ali Aziz. They say he slit his throat."

"Don't you believe it."

The man shuddered. "Slit his throat, and while he was dying, Jenks threw the body to the jackals—they ate him alive."

"Don't you believe it!" Tom called out as the man ran off.

"Believe him, monsieur!" the man yelled back. "Don't follow him into the gulf! He's warned you."

Chapter
Fifty-eight

IT WAS AN ugly kingdom, dry despite the presence of so much water, hot and salty, but still, it was his kingdom. Jenks had a palace in Hormuz and another in Muscat, from where he oversaw his empire, the traffic in pearls that flowed from the beds of Al Bahrain, Al-Katr, Kateef, Shargh, and Halliol.

He had come to Sheikh Akhbar with pearls from Ceylon in a year when the pearl beds the sheikh controlled were dry. He came with riches. That was what the sheikh respected most.

Aziz was an obstacle, but assassins were plentiful. It was they who slit the nervous middleman's throat.

Within a year any merchant wishing to purchase pearls from the richest beds in the gulf had to pay a visit to Jenks's white palace in Hormuz. He carefully selected clients, didn't give too much of the best quality to any one of them, and kept them hungry, fighting among themselves. He scrupulously avoided any dealings with brokers or traders who dealt with Tom or Nasis. Or if he could not avoid them, he charged them inflated prices for inferior gems.

"You tell Mr. Street in his big house on the Malabar Hill that he cannot have the pick of my catch," Jenks railed at Jhaveris after one of the fisheries. It was October, two years after Jenks's arrival in Hormuz. "You tell the same to Mr. Nasis."

"My goodness, Mr. Jenks, you can't keep us out indefinitely. We're becoming too rich."

Jenks whirled around, shaking his fist in Jhaveris's face. "Tom Street doesn't have enough money, he never will. Doesn't he understand it? I control the sheikhs. Mr. Street will take what I offer, and what I offer this year is nothing. Now, get out!"

Guards were called and Jhaveris dispatched.

Jenks perched in an archway that overlooked the harbor. He was rocking back and forth nervously. His face was drawn, filled with tension. He was rich, but it wasn't half as satisfying as he thought it would be.

He leaped up and ran down a cavernous empty hall. He'd brought back girls from Paris; a harem of whores had taken over a wing of his house. He kept them in clothes and jewels and drugs. Approaching their door, he heard them squabbling. He turned away in disgust and returned to his perch above the harbor. His eyes were trained on the sea. He thought about Margot, and he cursed her beauty.

"I'll have her," he whispered, rocking back and forth.

Another fishery was called—June through September. Jenks oversaw his business, could trust no one but himself, and this particular fishery was immensely successful. At the end there was more money than he had ever dreamed possible. The merchants came and went, trailing in and out of his white, airless palace. Bribes were offered—cash, jewels, houses, donkeys, date palms, gold, horses, women.

When the trading was over, winter set in. Hardly winter at all. At dusk the sun, like a glowing pumpkin, dropped into the sea and during the day the hills and the shore were all a single color, grain yellow, broiling in the heat. He was trapped, with no one to trust, no one to talk to—

From the very depths of his isolation an answer came.

His son, Paul, was waiting to be freed from the mission school in Tahiti. Paul could be the perfect cohort.

Jenks sent a trustworthy servant to the South Seas to fetch the boy—"Bring him back under gunpoint if necessary!"

In two months Jenks received word that Paul would arrive in Muscat that very spring.

Jenks had the house scrubbed. First he installed the whores, then he moved them back to Hormuz, then he sent word to Hormuz that he wanted only the youngest one, Flobelle, brought back.

When the boat arrived, Jenks spotted Paul before the boy

saw him. He was tall and dark-haired, with high cheekbones and penetrating, dark, almond-shaped eyes.

Jenks approached Paul warily. The boy was silent, staring at the dry hills in the distance.

"You said you were going to take me to England," he finally said in an odd accent, part Cockney, part French.

"This is as good as England."

"No it's not," Paul said, then pushed ahead and climbed into a waiting carriage.

That first week in Muscat, Jenks offered Paul the run of the house, but Paul seemed uninterested. He acted dull-witted and brooding. Then the trouble began. Small sums of cash began disappearing from Jenks's strongbox, and the servants said there was food missing, and finally Flobelle reported that a brooch Jenks had given her was missing. Snooping around Paul's room, Jenks found the brooch and a cache of stolen money and trinkets.

He began to follow the boy.

Paul crept out of the house every night. Like a renegade tourist, he covered the city in the dead of night. Jenks liked that. Paul watched the shadows, was adept at dodging the thieves, and could pass almost unnoticed through bazaars and ports.

One night Jenks was waiting in the dark on the boy's bed when he returned.

"You're very good," Jenks said, rubbing his chin. "But I was better at your age."

"Good at what? What do you want?"

"At your age I had three disguises, three separate accents, and three entirely different ways of walking. You are always who you are, night after night. Anyone could spot you."

"You been following me."

"I've been doing more than that, boyzo. I've been study-ing you. Come over here."

"Don't order me about. I'm not your slave."

"I like that," Jenks said, smiling. "You don't even look like you're shitting in your pants. That's very good. Get over here!"

Paul took a step or two but would not give his father the satisfaction of standing near the bed.

Jenks, sitting up, quickly grabbed one of Paul's hands and

bent it backward, forcing the fingernails down toward the forearm until the palm drained of color and Paul sank to his knees, screaming. Jenks released the hand and the boy stared up, gloomy and hateful.

"Come over here," Jenks said again, sitting back, patting a space on the bed beside himself.

The boy sat down.

"You run through this town at night as though you were plotting a crime."

"I'm not plotting no crime," Paul spat out.

"What are you thinking when you sneak around?"

"Not thinking anything."

Jenks laughed again. "Why go to the bother is what I keep thinking."

"Who asked you?"

Jenks's hand flew up and he hit the boy's head brutally, sending him hurtling to the floor.

"Don't want you on the floor, boyzo, want you sitting beside me here on the bed, father and son-like. We're going to be very close, you and me, very, very close."

Paul got up and sat on the bed. A thin line of blood trickled down from his nose, which he wiped on his sleeve.

"There's a lot you're going to learn from me, boyzo. And the first thing I'm going to teach you is that if you're going to sneak around a place looking like you're stealing something, then you might as well steal something."

"I don't steal nothing."

Jenks hit him so hard that Paul once again landed on the floor. Then Jenks reached under the bed and pulled out the trinkets and money.

"See, boyzo, I don't care that you steal—just not from me or anyone else in my house. You'll only steal *for* me." He reached down and pulled the boy up by his hair and threw him onto the bed again. "And I want you to start stealing for me tonight."

"You're crazy."

"There's a prayer rug the old men keep in a mosque near the market. It's made of silk and it's got pearls sewn into it. I want you to get me that rug." Jenks pulled out a watch. "You've got an hour."

"That's a crazy thing to do."

279

"If you don't, I'll keep you locked up with no food and no water and twice a day I'll personally come and beat you to a pulp."

Paul said nothing.

Jenks held out his watch.

"You don't want less than an hour to do it. They keep an armed guard at that mosque."

Paul stood up.

"An hour," Jenks said, "no more, no less. Starting . . . now."

Paul ran out of the room.

When Paul returned to the room with the rug, Jenks hugged him warmly, fed him, then put him to bed.

The next night Jenks asked Paul to steal a silver water jug he had admired in the market, and Paul left the house and returned with the jug.

This went on night after night for weeks, until one night, Paul, anticipating Jenks's next request, stole a bolt of silk from the market. Jenks beat him brutally until the boy understood that he was not to do anything that had not been requested of him.

After several months Jenks requested that Paul return each of the objects he had stolen. The boy was dumbstruck, but he did exactly what he was told. Within a week he had returned everything.

By summer the boy's will had been completely broken. Jenks was actually disappointed that he had been so skillful so quickly, but he had better uses for Paul. Instead of having him steal, he sent Paul into the market to overhear things, to bring back reports on the comings and goings of the pearl merchants. A new fishery was under way, and information of this sort was at a premium.

Jenks began to reward Paul with payments, sometimes money, sometimes pearls, while keeping the threat of the beatings palpably real by having Paul witness beatings of servants and whores.

Slowly the lessons began sinking in. Paul was not a stupid boy; he did not even hate his father—he began to admire him. And seeing how the other merchants fawned over Jenks, Paul began flattering his father, seeking his advice, dressing like him, and Jenks rewarded him by teaching him more about the pearl business, about money, and the management of people—friends and enemies.

By the time the fishery ended and the long, dull, hot winter came, Paul had become an ally. Jenks sent him on trips to gather information in other parts of the gulf. Paul never disappointed—but that in itself was a kind of disappointment.

"Without adversity, there's no joy," Jenks said drunkenly one night, and when the boy nodded too eagerly in agreement, Jenks dismissed him.

Jenks was alone again in his arid empire with no adversary left, no great joy.

Then a merchant came to the house to pay his respects and brought a token of his friendship, a Cockney whore named Rachael.

When Jenks first saw her, he was startled. She had no delicacy and her hair was lighter, but she looked remarkably like Margot.

"Those the only clothes she comes with?" he asked, walking around her.

"Stop tawkin' laike I'm not 'ere," the girl said. She had a shrill voice.

Jenks slapped her across the face and just as quickly she slapped him back.

The merchant was beside himself, apologizing, but Jenks just rubbed his face and smiled.

"I want her dressed in a white linen suit with a long jacket and a broad-brimmed straw hat and ropes of pearls—I want her hair darker, if that's possible, and worn in a pompadour."

"I ain' havin' me 'air any darkah—I laikes bein' blondy-'aired," she said, her ears still ringing from Jenks's blow.

"Bring her back when you've gotten her done up like that," Jenks said.

A day went by, then another.

When Rachael returned, Jenks ordered everyone else to leave the house.

With the darker hair, the white linen suit, and the pearls, she could have been Margot.

"I reminds you a someone, don' I?"

"Don't open your mouth," he said, walking around her again.

"I reminds you a someone who wou'lnt gi' you the time a day."

"Shut up!"

Jenks's pulse was racing as he stepped closer to her.

"You be naice ta me, I'll let ya kiss me." She pulled away, took off her hat, and tossed it on a couch. Then she removed her jacket, turning her back to him with a swish of her skirts. "You really shou' be naice ta me," she said, sitting down on the couch, crossing her legs. "And wha' I wou' find particularly nice is if you wou' kiss the 'em o' me dress."

"I could kill you for talking that way to me, arrange it so that no one would ever know."

"But then you woul'n't have me—and you wan' me. I know you do. I'm not a dumb girl. I'll be 'appy to be whoevah she was."

Jenks sank to his knees, touching her dress with his index finger. She was smiling down at him just like Margot, with that same secret look in her eyes.

Leaning over, he took the hem of her dress in his hands and brought it up to his lips.

"Wha' was 'er name?"

"Margot," he said, touching the hem to his lips.

"You can cawl me Margot if you wan'. Wha' wou' you like Margot to do for you?"

But he couldn't speak.

She slowly began lifting her skirt—from her ankles to her calves, to her knees, to her thighs. Her legs parted. He placed his hands on her thighs and pushed the skirt higher.

"Very slowly, Jenks," she said. "Margot likes it to be done very slowly. You shou' cawl my name out."

"Margot," he whispered.

She pushed herself down on the couch until she was squatting over him, and reaching down, she undid his trousers. "Say my name again."

"Margot."

Reaching out, she grabbed his hair, pulling it until he screamed. Then she sank onto his penis, pushing him backward. His eyes closed—she was riding him—and when he opened his eyes, he saw her smiling down at him. It was

Margot, but coarser than she. Just as he was about to ejaculate, she stood up. His penis flopped out of her and landed on his belly with a thud.

She walked away.

"You can't have me jus' yet. You ain' good enough," she said with a laugh, and he lay there, throbbing, enraged, his hand reaching out for her.

Chapter Fifty-nine

IN A FEW years Tom gained control of the Ceylon, Australian, and Venezuelan fisheries and developed a brisk and powerful trade in Paris. But no matter how fickle his Parisian customers were—one year they craved Venezuelan pearls; the next, Australian—the Persian Gulf pearls remained the most prized, and Tom was locked out of the gulf by Jenks. Gaining a foothold there became an obsession; he was no closer to it now than he had been when he first arrived in India.

In Bombay Margot embraced convention as eagerly as she had once flaunted it. As far as anyone knew, she was a happily married wife and the mother of a daughter as keen-spirited and beautiful as herself. And although she was an astute and gracious hostess, for the most part she kept to herself. She had her friendship with Nasis and her voluminous correspondence with Felix Clausen. Their letters contained feelings that she kept hidden from the rest of the world, even from Tom, because they sometimes expressed fears about where Tom's ambition would lead. Felix had a knowing, tender heart; he did not judge her—he admired her. His letters gave her strength.

And then she began receiving letters from her sister, Kate Carneelian. Kate's letters were chatty and, like Kate herself, prying and scolding. She began pressing for an invitation to

Bombay almost as soon as she learned Margot was living there. Receiving none after many years, she finally announced, in a letter that Margot received in August, that she was planning to visit that autumn.

On the tenth of October Margot received a ship's cable saying that Kate would arrive in five days. She was traveling onboard a steamer that was known as the *P and O Traveling Hotel,* one of a line of steamships that regularly made the trip from Southampton to Bombay.

The ship was crowded with young people returning to India from home leave. Kate could have been swept up in a whirl of parties and flirtations, but her chief reason for being on that particular ship was to be the chaperon of the daughter of an acquaintance, a member of what was known as the "Fishing Fleet." These were the highly eligible daughters of wealthy people who were coming out to meet eligible men and marry. Kate took her duties very seriously and remained, throughout the voyage, brittle and unyielding.

Now in her mid-thirties, Kate looked flat and stale. Her eyes, which had always been her best feature, had become narrow and crinkly, and her mouth, her next best feature, had tightened into a thin line that separated her straight nose from her firm chin.

When they landed at the Apollo Bunder, the main dock in Bombay, Kate saw that Margot hadn't changed a bit in the five years since they had seen each other.

Margot was as fresh as the day was hot and sticky—and ravishingly beautiful and happy—much too happy for a conventional married woman, Kate was thinking.

"But where's your mystery husband, my dear?" Kate asked as she kissed her sister's cheek.

Margot explained that Tom was in Paris and was due back in Bombay in a week.

"I haven't come all this way to miss him. And the little girl?"

"I don't like to bring her into town."

"Lord only knows what we're contracting just standing here breathing," Kate said in disgust, having made up her mind about Bombay. "What I can't understand is your having married any man who would keep you locked up in this dreadful place."

"But he doesn't keep me locked up. He wants me to move to Paris. I haven't wanted to leave."

Kate looked at Margot with a pitying frown. "Brave Margot. Darling, I'm here now. You can spill your heart out to me," she said with a sisterly pat on the hand, then turning, she screamed at some Indians who were carrying her bags.

In the carriage Kate could not take her eyes off Margot's black pearl ring.

"It's very beautiful," she said, her eyes narrowing to little slits. "Large for daytime, don't you think?"

When she arrived at the house on Malabar Hill, she was flabbergasted. It was three times the size of her own.

"I suppose there have to be some compensations for putting up with life in this dreadful place," she said as she was being shown around.

When Jessica was brought in by her *ayah* to say hello to her aunt, Kate, so startled by the little girl's beauty, which reminded her so acutely of Margot's as a child, burst into tears and clutched the little girl so fiercely that Jessica began screaming for her mother.

"Nonsense," Kate said, fluffing Jessica's golden hair, "Auntie Kitty Kat has children just like you, loveliness. Four boys who love your Auntie Kitty Kat. Now, you must calm down, precious. You must stop those tears and kiss your Auntie Kitty Kat's tears away."

This only made Jessica scream more loudly.

Margot went to pick Jessica up, but Kate held the little girl back.

"No, Margot, it's very bad to give them too much lead. Stringency is my motto! Raised each of my boys that way. You should see my boys, Margot. Honorable, decent young men."

Jessica wailed.

"No, Margot. She should kiss me. I'm her one and only maternal relative. She must kiss me hello. Now, kiss your Auntie Kitty Kat's cheek, precious." As Kate leaned forward, Jessica bit the cheek energetically.

Kate screamed. Margot pulled Jessica free and handed her to the *ayah* who led her out of the room.

That night Nasis came to dinner. Kate thought he was wildly attractive and couldn't help but notice how he doted on Margot.

"Mr. Nasis, are you any relation to the merchant banker Lord Alfred Nasis?"

"He's m-m-my uncle, Mrs. Carneelian."

"Is he," Kate said smoothly. "Why is it that you Hebrews manage money better than anyone else?"

Nasis swallowed hard but offered Kate a pleasant smile. "I th-th-think it was one of the few trades left open to us during the M-m-middle Ages. We're basically t-t-trading peoples."

"The chosen people, my husband always says—chosen for finance. You are in the pearl trade?"

"Yes."

"Then you must be a friend of Margot's husband."

Nasis and Margot exchanged quick glances. "We're c-c-competitors."

Margot changed the subject.

After dinner when Nasis had left, Kate, sitting with Margot in the library, was all aflutter.

"Now, Margot, you must tell me the truth. That wonderful-looking stuttering Jew is your lover, isn't he! My darling, it's too exotic for words."

"You are a very rude woman, Kate."

"You're just angry with me because I've caught on to your little secret. He's very handsome, my dear."

"You are rude and loathsome."

Kate burst into tears. "What a horrible thing to say to me when I've come all this way to see you—"

"I certainly didn't ask you to."

"Did you ever stop to think that was exactly why I came? Someone had to vouchsafe our family honor."

Margot stood up and counted to ten.

"Do you know the stories that have been circulating about you? Do you have any idea how embarrassed I am every time your name is mentioned?"

"Look at my life, Kate. Do you see anything out of the ordinary?"

"It's all extravagant to me," Kate said, picking up a paisley silk pillow, then tossing it aside.

"I don't give a damn about what people say."

"Well enough for you, but what was I to say to people who've asked me about this man you've supposedly married? Where'd he come from? Where'd you meet him? Why on earth did you leave England as abruptly as you did?"

"It's all too complex, and most of it happened too long ago for me to go into now."

"If Mother and Father were only alive. What do you think they would say about your having thrown over everyone who had ever meant anything to you? For years the only information I could gather about you I had to get from that damned old goat Baron Clausen."

"Please don't start running down Felix, Kate. He is my dearest friend."

"Was, you mean," Kate said quickly.

Margot froze. "What are you saying?"

"He's dead, my dear. Died over a month ago. Heart, I think. Everyone's heard it," she said, as if delivering an old morsel of gossip.

Margot, the color having drained from her face, turned away. "I didn't know. I heard from him a little while ago. He didn't say anything about not feeling well."

"It happened in St. James Park, someone told me. He just fell over."

"Felix," Margot whispered, suddenly seeing him lying on a path alone.

"It's not as if he were family," Kate said.

Margot slowly began walking out of the room. "You know where your room is, Kate. If you don't, one of the servants will help you. I'm going up to bed," she said over her shoulder.

When she got to her bedroom, she took out Felix's letters and wept.

With Tom traveling somewhere in Europe and Felix gone from the world, Margot suddenly felt very much alone.

The next morning before breakfast she stared at herself in the mirror as she combed her hair. She had tried so very hard to be so very normal, as complacent and unobtrusive as a burgher's wife, and for what? To please the Kate Carneelians of the world?

"To hell with them!" she heard Felix Clausen say, and she called out, "To hell with each and every one of them!"

And that morning, as if something inside her had inextricably changed, she began to embrace her eccentricities as eagerly as she had her conventionality. She showed up at breakfast wearing a sari that the Maharaj Rana had given her. Her eyes were lined with kohl, and she had rubbed saffron oil on her skin.

Kate, sitting at one end of a glass-topped table on the veranda eating poached eggs, was startled when Margot walked in, although she refused to give Margot the satisfaction of appearing startled. Halfway through the meal, she began fanning herself with her handkerchief.

"There is the most sickeningly sweet odor in the air."

"It's saffron."

"Your cook uses it?"

"I'm wearing it."

"Good for pests and bugs, I suppose."

"Not all varieties," Margot said coolly, looking down the table at her sister.

After breakfast Margot took Kate on a tour of the city—the streets were teaming with snake charmers and sword swallowers, holy men and beggars with missing limbs. Kate was frightened and disgusted and would not leave the house for the rest of her stay. She was appalled that anyone in his right mind would choose to live in Bombay.

By the time Tom returned from Paris, Margot had transformed herself. She wore nothing but saris or tight pants with voluminous silk overblouses. Her hair was tied in a tight braid that dangled down her back. Her eyes were rimmed with kohl, and her temper was fierce and passionate.

"Your sister has quite an effect on you," he said as they kissed in the front hall.

"Thank God you're back. Now at least she'll leave."

"Where is this witch?"

"Oh, I've missed having a friend around the house," Margot said, drawing his arms around her waist, kissing him. "Have you been a loyal and faithful subject?"

"Yes, Your Ladyship."

"You have not succumbed to French actresses?"

"No, Your Ladyship." He kissed her again.

Kate Carneelian, who had been standing in a corner watching this little display, coughed.

Tom turned and almost laughed when he saw the sour facsimile of Margot standing there. Kate managed to smile and offer him her hand, although her anger at his being so very attractive almost overcame her good manners.

They had drinks on the veranda, then dinner inside. The tension between the two women was thick, and Tom quickly discovered what was disagreeable about Kate Carneelian —most especially her prying, unrelenting questions. She wanted to know everything about his past—his family, his seafaring days—and the pearl business. Would he get her some pearls at a reasonable price? Just a short strand—she was particularly fond of pearls from Bahrain.

"That will be difficult," he said, sipping some wine.

"Why? All my friends have necklaces made of pearls from Bahrain."

Tom told Kate an abbreviated history of his rivalry with Jenks.

"Well, go around this Mr. Jenks. Go directly to Sheikh Akhbar."

"But that has been the problem all along, Mrs. Carneelian —everyone has the money to bribe him, but no one can get close enough to do it. He won't listen to anyone but Jenks."

Kate thought about this for a moment and decided it was all very simple. "You remember *A Thousand and One Nights?* You should do the same," she said. "Create some sort of illusion, tell a good story, have him come to you." And, her eyes darting from Tom to Margot, she added, "Both of you are adept at creating illusions, aren't you?"

Tom looked at her with more interest now.

After dinner Tom eagerly went to work in the library —Kate's idea was actually more interesting than she could have guessed.

The two women were left alone in the dining room.

Kate was seething.

"God only knows how many commandments you've broken," she said. "That man is no more married to you than I am. No husband of five years is as affectionate as that. He treats you like a mistress because that is exactly what you are. Aren't you ashamed? My God, to have brought a child into it."

"You've accomplished your mission, Kate. Now I want you out of my house."

"Then you won't even deny it."

"I won't dignify what you're saying with a denial. And I won't have you spreading malicious stories about me or my daughter."

Margot rose from the table, but Kate reached out and grabbed her hand.

"They aren't stories. It's true. I'm sure of it." And looking at the pearls Margot was wearing, their mother's pearls, she felt a sharp twinge of resentment as she did every time she saw them. She held them up. "Swear that it isn't true, Margot, on Mother's memory, on her pearls. Swear that you're married to this man and your daughter is his legitimate daughter."

Margot stared down at her, angry and silent.

"You can't do it, can you?" Kate taunted.

Holding the strand of pearls, Margot remembered a look of delight on her mother's face as her father fastened the clasp on the necklace—they were going off to a ball on a warm summer night. An image of beautiful women and proud, handsome men whirred round Margot's brain. It was a world of people and things she had turned her back on. It suddenly seemed as if these pearls were the last vestige of it. She removed them and left them dangling in Kate's hand, then left the room.

Kate began to cry. Of course she had always wanted them, but not this way, not given in anger. Damn Margot, Kate thought, she was always ruining everything.

Margot did not leave her room for the next two days. Tom arranged Kate's passage back to England, and the day of her departure Margot stood at a window watching her go. Kate looked up at the window with a tight, judgmental stare before getting into the carriage. Margot felt cast adrift.

In the following weeks she became moody and avoided people. Nasis was just another reminder of her transgressions and the England she had left behind. She went off alone into the city during the day, submerging herself in everything that was wildly exotic. She dressed as a boy and dashed through the bazaars. She stole things, and drank, then at night she lustily played the part of the wife/mistress. She dressed in exotic costumes that the nautch-girls in the prince's harems wore. If she was going to be labeled a whore, she wanted to be a royal courtesan.

A month went by, then two. She became pregnant again. It was something she wanted to flaunt. But like her other pregnancy something about it was frightening too. Tom was busy, embroiled in a scheme to test Jenks's supremacy in the gulf. He was leaving soon to put his plan into action.

"Why don't you just leave Jenks alone in his precious gulf?" she said to him the morning of his departure.

"It's not in my nature. I see a way of taking everything from him."

"He's such a snake. You'll never know where or when he'll strike."

"Without access to the sheikhs, I have to pay a fortune to buy their pearls. It's either Jenks or us, and I'm going to have the gulf."

"What if I asked you to stay? Would you still go?"

"But you're not asking me to do that. There's nothing to worry about. In a month or two I'll be back."

"Don't go after him, Tom. He's warned you. Stay here with us."

"Oh, I should have let him die when I had the chance."

"Maybe he's already won," she said bitterly, circling the large leather-topped desk in his study. "You've become as angry and bloodthirsty as he . . ."

Chapter
Sixty

TOM TRAVELED FROM Bombay to Muscat at night in an Arab boat, a bughla, with a high square stern and enough cargo room for the fifty strongboxes he had brought along. Each was filled with silver coins, but as soon as he boarded the ship, he let the word spread that the cases were filled with gold. A cordon of tall Sikh soldiers had been hired and stood guard around the boxes with loaded rifles poised and ready to fire.

The next morning Paul Jenks was at the docks as Tom's bughla put in. Paul counted the boxes and saw that the Arab stevedores were struggling with them.

"What's inside?" he asked a merchant who was standing nearby.

"Gold coins."

"From where?"

"Bombay."

"Whose are they?"

"Man named Street."

"Tom Street?"

"Traveling north with it into the desert."

The Sikh guards closed in now, pushing Paul aside, but not before he caught sight of Tom, who was watching coolly as the boxes were unloaded from the hold.

At that particular moment his father's enemy looked entirely too proud and confident, and Paul took off, running up the hill that led to his father's house.

Jenks lay in bed with a fever. A doctor was examining him. He had lesions in his mouth and dry reddish bumps and blotches on his genitals and between his toes. His throat was sore, and his eyes hurt and were red-rimmed.

"I could be gentle with you, but I already know what's wrong. It's syphilis," the doctor said.

Jenks shuddered and called a servant into the room. "I want all the women in both houses examined."

"It's too late now," the doctor said.

"I want them thrown out into the street. Don't give them any money, just what they're wearing on their backs," he said to the servant. Then he turned back to the doctor. "You'll have to give me something."

"There isn't anything."

"Don't tell me that."

"I can treat the symptoms, and they'll go away soon enough. You're highly infectious now, but you'll be fine once the symptoms disappear."

Jenks jumped up from the bed, grabbed the man, and threw him against a wall.

"What? For five years? Ten? I want you to find something for me to take," he said, and threw the man out of his room.

When Paul got to the house, Jenks was sitting downstairs, naked, on a windowsill.

"What are you doing here? I told you to stay in the market," Jenks, said.

"I had some news."

"What news?"

"Tom Street is here. He's just arrived at the harbor. He's putting together a caravan and going into the desert."

Jenks stared down at the water. "Why's he doing that?"

"He's carrying fifty cases of gold coin."

Jenks stood up. "Who told you that?"

"It's all over the marketplace."

"What's he doing with it?"

"No one knows."

Jenks grabbed Paul by the collar. "A man arrives with fifty cases of gold and no one knows why? Get me some clothes. Quickly! I'll find out for myself."

Jenks's head was throbbing as he made his way down to the docks. He was sweating and short of breath.

Twenty or more pack camels, called *jamal bosh*, were standing beside the docks, each laden down with supplies and locked strongboxes.

Tom was climbing onto a female, a *hega,* which roared and gurgled as it unbent from its crouching position.

When Tom saw Jenks standing at the edge of a small crowd, he called down, "Come to see me off?"

Jenks squinted into the blinding light.

"It won't work. Whatever you're planning—I'll see to it."

"I don't think we'll have you to worry about much longer."

The Sikh guards were now positioned around the caravan, and the camels began their lumbering walk toward the desert.

"Don't do anything you'll regret," Jenks called out, but Tom had turned away. "You become too much of a bother, boyzo, and I'll destroy you—destroy everything that means anything to you."

Jenks began running with the caravan.

"You hear me good. I'll twist you and your life around, put you in a bloody hell if you dare come up against me. I've warned you!"

But the caravan was moving slowly toward the west, and Jenks, his breath labored, his head throbbing, slowed down, then stumbling over his own feet, he fell by the side of the road.

The Bedouins guided Tom inland to Buraimi, then north. Tom had no exact destination, he simply wanted to make a large circle up to Al Kuwait, then back along the coast to Muscat. All he cared about was having the word spread that he was traveling through Sheikh Akhbar's territory carrying fifty boxes of gold coin. And all he could do was wait to see if the sheikh had either heard or believed the rumor.

Tom's chief guide and translator was a hawk-nosed and steely-eyed man called Abdullah Mohammed. His people were called the Beni Yas, part Beduoin and part Hadhr. He had been raised outside a town called Dubai on the Pirate Coast and had once met Sheikh Akhbar and knew all about the sheikh's family. They had been pirates not more than a century ago. The sheikh was a fearsome character who was trying to live up to his ancestors' reputation.

The days were long and hot. Wind storms made large

dark clouds of sand in the distance, but the caravan managed to avoid them.

Tom's mount was comfortable enough; it was like a ride at sea. He sat behind the hump, which Abdullah Mohammed said was the riding style for people from Oman; in Yemen, they sat in front of it. The saddle was called a *sheddard* that had been made in a place called Wezwa. The camel provided the caravan not only with transportation, but its hair was used for weaving tents and its milk was used for food. The Deroo, Al-Waheebeh, and Awamir were the best camel breeders, Abdullah Mohammed said, and the camel was like the Arab who bred her, resentful of injustice, revengeful, but durable and reliable.

Each morning the call to prayer rang out: "God is most great! Come to prayer. Come to salvation. Prayer is better than sleep. God is most great and there is no god but God!"

Each evening the call would ring out again.

As the Sikh guards kept their watch, the caravan moved steadily north, and still there was no word from Sheikh Akhbar.

That did not mean he was unaware of their progress, Abdullah Mohammed said. He pointed out several of the sheikh's men posted on dunes, who were following every move the caravan made. As they reached an outpost called Hofuf, a cordon of men riding horses came down from the hillside. The Sikhs, their rifles poised, took up their positions around the stalled caravan, but in a fight they would be outnumbered. Tom counted almost a hundred riders.

"Have you ever seen one animal sniffing another? Prepare to be sniffed," Abdullah Mohammed said.

The riders surrounding the caravan were armed, but their rifles were slung across their backs. One of them came closer, riding a black stallion, his burnoose wrapped around his face so that only his eyes were visible. He made one complete tour of the caravan, then stopped ten feet away from Tom and Abdullah Mohammed, calling out questions in an Arabic dialect.

"This is Akhbar, isn't it?" Tom asked Abdullah Mohammed.

"Yes, but he doesn't want us to know that."

"What's he want with us?" Tom asked.

"Sniffing, as I said."

"Tell him my name and say that I have been eager to meet Sheikh Akhbar. If he could arrange a meeting, I would be most grateful."

Akhbar listened with interest, then asked a question.

"He wants to know why you are traveling north."

"To prove a point," Tom began, and as he spoke, Abdullah Mohammed translated. "For years I have been prevented from buying the best pearls from the Persian Gulf because it is said that I do not have enough money. I have come now with my entire fortune to purchase pearls."

After Abdullah Mohammed finished his translation, there was a dead silence, then Akhbar began laughing.

"Who has prevented you from purchasing pearls?" he asked.

"The Englishman Jenks has prevented me and other rich merchants from participating in the fisheries. He has become rich, and Sheikh Akhbar and the other sheikhs of the Persian Gulf suffer because of it."

"They have never been as richly paid as they are now," Akhbar said.

"It's not a tenth of what is possible. The Ceylon fishery, which is smaller than the Persian Gulf and lasts a much shorter time, is capable of earning a half million pounds from its pearls. The Persian Gulf can realize more than that if trade is loosened up and more people are allowed to buy."

Akhbar listened attentively, then asked, "Why has Jenks singled you out?"

"Not only me, any other merchants more powerful than himself."

"But why you?"

"Because he's frightened that I will seize control and get rid of him."

"Won't you?"

"Yes."

Abdullah Mohammed whispered to Tom, "A little moderation—Jenks is this man's friend."

"But this is business. You tell him that I can make him more money than Jenks."

Abdullah Mohammed translated, then waited for Akhbar to pose another question.

Akhbar began to ride off, then turned and spoke over his shoulder.

"He says that you should meet Sheikh Akhbar in Hormuz —he will arrange it. He will leave some of his men with you to help guard your fortune. It would be a pity, he says, to lose it all in the desert before you have a chance to spend it on pearls in Hormuz."

When they got to Hormuz, a trading center at the mouth of the gulf referred to as the Pearl of the Orient, Tom was treated well, but Akhbar wasn't there.

He and Abdullah Mohammed were given the use of a house that belonged to Akhbar, which was filled with a jumble of inexpensive French furniture and resembled a warehouse. It had no windows, only wooden shutters covering the arched doors that overlooked the harbor.

A group of sheikhs, armed to the teeth, arrived. Many carried bags of their best pearls, which led Tom to believe they had come to do business. But business was not discussed. They were waiting for Akhbar. Everyone seemed to defer to him.

Word finally arrived that Akhbar would meet with Tom, but not in Hormuz. The meeting would take place in the port town of Lingan, which was several hours away. Dry and desolate, containing a labyrinth of some one hundred houses, Lingan was a small pearl trading center, a jumping-off point between the riches of Dubai and Hormuz. A guide was necessary because the streets seemed to lead nowhere, and the town's inhabitants looked as though they would rather not spare the lives of those they robbed. The Koran permitted them to rob from the dead, not the living.

Akhbar was waiting in a small, undistinguished house. He was taller than the other sheikhs, and scarred, as if he'd survived dozens of hand-to-hand battles. There was a wide gash up his right cheek, and half of one of his ears was missing. A retinue of servants followed him everywhere. Two carried hooded falcons poised on their arms.

Akhbar asked Tom if he wanted to visit one of the oyster beds, and Tom was enthusiastic.

The entire group went back to the waterfront, where divers brought up several hundred shells, but none produced a pearl. The divers, Tom was told, earned roughly three hundred rupees for a season, but they were not paid in cash. Food, water, and shelter were supplied for a price, plus enough money for the divers to pay back the merchants for these services. The divers were virtual slaves.

The divers held a rope and kept one foot in a stirrup, on which a stone weight was hung. Each pressed down on the stone and descended into the water with a basket around their neck. The stone and rope were then pulled up to the surface, leaving the diver free to collect the shells with both hands. The divers used noseclips, glovelike finger protectors, and ear wax when they were diving in great depths. They stayed down for a minute or so, then signaled a "puller," who yanked them up to the surface.

Akhbar seemed very proud of the efficiency of this system, and Tom showered him with compliments. Akhbar was pleased, but still no business was discussed. Instead Tom was invited to lunch, at which he drank a great quantity of ginger syrup that covered the taste of the food, which was dry and hot.

After lunch, as a slave served coffee and rosewater, Akhbar began asking Tom about the world price of pearls. The conversation moved slowly. Tom's English was translated into Hindi, then Arabic—an exchange of twenty words seemed to take a half hour. Tom made the point that the world price was soaring, and he wondered if Akhbar and the other sheikhs were participating in the profits that were being made.

Subtly but firmly, he hammered away at Jenks, guessing that Jenks was taking an unfair percentage.

"To take more than fifteen percent commission on the sale of your pearls is criminal, except in certain circumstances."

He explained that if the sheikhs had an agent to sell their pearls directly into the Paris market, they could make more money more quickly. He said he was such an agent—his contacts in Paris were unsurpassed.

Akhbar was unyielding at first, then Tom told him the

story of Jenks's partnership with Nasis and how it had ended.

"I didn't come here to discredit your friend, but his actions have already discredited him. Nasis was Jenks's partner, Sheikh Akhbar, and Jenks maimed him, stole from him."

As Akhbar leaned back to stare at Tom, there was a quick change in his expression. His eyes became almost imperceptibly softer.

Tom leaned closer. "My reputation is as strong as the camels that have carried my fortune into the desert. I have come all this way and gone to great expense to show Sheikh Akhbar that I am worthy of representing his interests. My reputation is worth more to me than all the gold in my strongboxes. My reputation is my fortune."

Akhbar smiled quickly, and in that instant Tom knew he had won.

The meeting moved back to Hormuz and lasted three more days. Jenks, who was in Hormuz trying to get an audience with Akhbar, was barred from it.

His spies reported that the sheikhs were particularly impressed with Tom Street's idea of selling directly into the European markets and giving them all a healthier cut of the proceeds. Then the spies stopped reporting altogether. Alliances were changing quickly. Jenks was feverish, and his eyes were bad. His head rang with defeat. He had no desire to be done away with like Ali Aziz.

Heading back to Muscat, he and Paul gathered up all that remained of the empire—sacks of the best pearls from the gulf—then they booked night passage on a bughla heading to Bombay.

"Is Bombay where we'll live?" Paul asked.

"We'll turn some of these pearls into cash, then move on," Jenks said, his fierce eyes fixed on the dark horizon. He was shivering with fever, his sores were throbbing, and his shins hurt. "And there's unfinished business in Bombay," he said, his mind spewing forth images of Tom and Margot —Margot in particular, because she was what Tom Street loved most in the world. Jenks was determined to make good his threat to destroy that.

Chapter
Sixty-one

JENKS FOLLOWED MARGOT for two days as she came and went from the house on the Malabar Hill.

She looked odd, he thought, seeing her in saris, wearing her hair braided, like a wog. Taking no notice of him, she disappeared into the depths of the *Chorrbazaar*.

Dogging her every step, he stood in doorways, planning how he would strike out against her. Shivering with fever in the heat of the midday, he thought of a way.

That night after dinner, sitting with Jessica, Margot took out all her jewels and lay them on the bed. She told Jessica stories about each—the *Medusa* pendant that had brought her to Tom, and the story about his ship and his rescue. But the story that Jessica loved best was the one about the black pearl.

"The pearl accumulates all the love that each of its owners possess. It's love that gives the pearl its lustre and you'll own it someday," Margot said, rocking Jessica back and forth, allowing her to hold the ring up to the light.

An unseasonable breeze blew across the room through the open window, and Margot heard something that sounded like glass breaking. Going to the window, she called out to one of the servants, asking if anything had broken downstairs. The servant said no, nothing.

Jessica's *ayah* came to take her to bed. Margot allowed Jessica to take the black pearl into her room, but later, after Jessica had fallen asleep, Margot took back the ring, slipping it on her fourth finger.

She went down to the library and poured herself a brandy. She was lonely without Tom. Sitting, staring at the lazy whir of the overhead fans, she read for a while, then went up to her bedroom, undressed, and quickly fell asleep.

Jenks, who had come into the garden at dusk, waited until nightfall to begin prowling around the house. He climbed up to the second-story terrace and walked around, staring into each room. He saw Margot holding the little girl in her lap. He waited for the little girl to fall asleep, and waited until Margot read and drank her brandy. After she'd come upstairs and undressed, he waited at her open window until he heard the sound of regular breathing before entering her room. He locked her door and stood near the bed watching her sleep under a cover of netting—so peaceful and a touch sad. He reached out his hand toward her—there were sores now between his fingers. He felt as if his entire presence soiled the room.

The black pearl ring was on a velvet cushion on a table beside the bed. He took it, dropped it into his pocket, then knelt down beside her. From so close, he could smell how fresh and sweet she was. His mottled hand, holding a silk scarf, crept under the netting, moving slowly across her cotton blanket. When she felt his hand, she turned.

"Tom," she whispered.

When Jenks grabbed her head roughly, she started and her eyes opened. He wound the silk scarf around her mouth, pulling it tightly. Unable to scream, she flailed her arms up at him. He pushed her down, then took a rope from his pocket and tied her hands first above her head, then to the bedpost.

She lay panting, her hands twisting in the ropes as he stood above her, staring down, dazed by the sight of her. Taking out a long thin knife, he traced a light blue vein that ran down the side of one of her breasts. The knife tip caught on the material of her gown, which he slit. One full breast, a pale nipple, rising and falling, was exposed. His hand looked bruised and raw next to her skin. Stepping back, he began undressing. His chest was covered with sores and dry, scaly blotches. He raised his arms to show her the sores in his armpits, then, dropping his trousers, he stepped onto the bed and knelt above her. There was a festering chancre on the tip of his penis and red boillike sores beneath his black pubic hair. He touched himself, and his penis lengthened and thickened, mottled and crusty. He tore open her gown and forced her legs apart. Then, rubbing his penis with his spit, he entered her.

Tears were running down her cheeks. He brought his head close to hers and whispered harshly in her ear.

"It's syphilis," he said, parroting his doctor's voice. Then he moaned, sliding in, then out to the tip, then in to the hilt, then in again harder, his testicles bouncing on her. "It's syphilis," he said again, and laughed. "Greek word—means hog-loving," and laughed again, eyes closed, moving against her more harshly, quickly now, reaching under and pulling her legs around his back and pounding into her. Her sobs became weaker, her voice hoarse and raw. His eyes opened and he smiled because she was so close and he was inside her. The inevitable pressure built up inside his scrotum, sending shoots of grainy pleasure up through his penis.

"Mine," he panted. "All mine—as dirty as me," he hissed, exploding inside her, moaning, then collapsed on her chest. He wheezed and bit her, panted, then rolled to one side.

Turning away from her, not wanting to see her so defiled, he crawled from the bed, dressed, and stood above her, unable to look at her.

He untied her hands, and they fell limply to the bed. He saw her chafed skin and some of his body hair twisted in her folds. Her legs hung loosely apart, and a drop of him was seeping from her. His mouth dropped open, and he groaned. In a flash, her fingers, twisted into a forklike fist, drove sharply into his left eye. He screamed and, holding his hands over his eye, ran from the room.

At first, all her actions were frenzied. She ripped the bedding from the bed and ordered the servants to burn it.

"Mattress, sheets, pillows! Everything! Now!"

They built a bonfire in the garden.

Then she had them fill her bathtub with scalding water, and she submerged in it and scrubbed herself.

The next morning, she was queasy with morning sickness. She vomited and thought she was ridding her body of anything Jenks could have spewed into it.

In the early afternoon, when the *ayah* brought Jessica into the room, Margot wouldn't allow herself to touch the child.

She ordered a carriage to take her into town to the doctors, but halfway there, she had the driver stop.

She fled into the *Chorrbazaar,* where she wandered aimlessly, trying to get lost, but she kept returning to familiar stalls.

That night she dreamed of a baby covered with scabs. She awoke in a sweat. Is this it? she wondered. A fever?

But by morning it had passed.

Perhaps it wouldn't happen to her. She'd once heard there were people who were immune to it. She pushed it from her mind, thinking that negativity would contaminate her. But the words he had whispered in her ear, the image of the scabs and the reddened skin, insinuated themselves into her thoughts.

She could tell no one. If she kept it to herself, she would control it. Whenever it entered her mind, she automatically replaced it with a positive thought—Jessica, dancing in the garden, Jessica laughing. It would work, Margot thought. She'd escape.

A week had passed and there were no signs of the disease. Her mood brightened. She played with Jessica and told her stories. In another week there were still no signs. She knew she'd escaped. She relaxed, almost welcomed her morning sickness—it was normal sickness.

A wire from Tom arrived. He'd be in Bombay within the week.

She had the servants remove every piece of furniture from her bedroom and replace it with furniture from the guest wing.

Two days before he returned, she awoke with a fever, and later that day she developed a headache that would not go away. She would not leave her room, sat huddled on the bed, rocking back and forth, whispering positive thoughts over and over. By night she began feeling twinges of pain in her bones.

"Go away, go away, go away," she cried.

She wanted to escape into the bazaars again, but she could not move.

By morning, a chancre appeared on the inner lip of her vagina.

* * *

Tom returned triumphant. When Margot walked into the library, he was loading bags of pearls into a huge iron safe.

"Did you win?" she screamed at him. "Did you send him off and packing? What did you win? These?" she said, picking up a handful of pearls and throwing them at him.

"What's wrong? What's happened to you?"

"Don't come near me. Don't touch me! These are your life—not me. Your ambition ruined everything," she said, and she ran from the house, calling to the servants to fetch her a carriage.

He ran after her and tried to reason with her, but she wouldn't look at him and stood on the other side of the gates in the road, waiting for the carriage.

"Whatever's happened we can fix. I left you alone. I'm sorry. I wasn't thinking of anything but what I needed for myself. You were frightened again. I understand now. I didn't help you. Please, Margot, talk to me."

But the carriage had pulled up and she climbed inside.

As it moved away, he ran into the road, grabbing the horses.

"Where are you going?"

She was sobbing now, screaming at the driver to whip the horses, to trample Tom.

"Let me go!" she screamed at him. "Let me go!"

Finally he stood aside. The horses bolted down the Malabar Hill.

Running back to the stable behind the house, he saddled a horse and rode out after her, but she'd disappeared. There was no sign of her in the bazaars.

He returned at dusk expecting to find her, but she wasn't there. One of Nasis's servants appeared at the door and began screaming for Tom to follow him. And when Tom reached Nasis's house, he saw the doctor's carriage outside.

Nasis was in the main hall, looking pale and stricken.

"What's happened? Where is she?" Tom cried.

"We couldn't s-s-stop her. She'd found a l-l-long needle —she t-t-tried to abort the ch-ch-child."

"Are you mad? She'd never do that!" Tom yelled out, running past Nasis up the stairs.

Two nurses were carrying large steaming buckets, and Tom heard the doctor calling out orders.

"More towels."

"She's still bleeding."

"Towels."

"We're losing her."

Running into a bedroom, he saw her on the bed. She was covered with blood. Blood everywhere—on the sheets, the floor, on the walls. Margot was white, like death itself. He called out to her. Her eyes closed.

"No! Please, wait," he screamed out, then kept calling her name.

They were working on her, but it seemed useless.

Margot knew she was dying. She lay limp and penitent, exhausted. Dear God, what have I done? Then she saw Tom in a fading light, and she tried holding on to the sight of him, kneeling now beside her, holding her hand, weeping like a child being ripped from his mother.

"Please, Margot, wait for me. Don't leave me. Please don't leave me."

She remembered the first time she had seen him on the beach, then at the dinner table on the *Distant Star*. It had happened just a moment ago. Now he was covered with her blood. She could not bear to see him that way. Behind her tightly closed eyelids, there was light as warm and lustrous as her black pearl. She closed her fist reflexively, thinking that she still held it. She felt herself falling. It was like a dream unwinding within a dream—all the light, all the sounds, all the frantic energy, all her thoughts were fading . . . fading, like the world itself.

Chapter
Sixty-two

WHEN THE SOUND of Tom's bitter cries subsided, silence spread through the house. There was only the muffled sound of voices upstairs as the nurses cleaned up the room.

Nasis, his eyes swollen with tears, sat alone in the hall beneath the statue of his grandfather.

When he heard Tom's footsteps on the stairway, he cringed. He didn't want to share his grief with Tom. But when he saw Tom's crumpled face, his clothes covered with her blood, he felt compassion, not jealousy. She was gone —neither of them had her anymore.

"It happened so q-q-quickly. She c-c-came in and told me that I h-h-had to help her find a doctor who would d-d-do away with the child. She'd c-c-contracted syphilis."

"I don't understand any of it."

"I t-t-told her that I couldn't help her d-d-do that. She said she had to h-h-hide here. I had the maid put her to b-b-bed. I went up to see h-h-her. She told me the story. Jenks infected her—"

"Jenks," Tom whispered in disbelief.

"She said Jenks had raped her. When I l-l-left the room, she did this to herself. She m-m-must have brought that needle with her." His voice choked, and he began sobbing. "I loved her. She was all I ever really loved in the world."

Tom was speechless.

"We'll t-t-track Jenks d-d-down. We'll f-f-find him and k-k-kill him."

"Not us, Nasis," Tom said coldly. "He's mine. Jenks is mine."

The word was passed through the network of merchants and dealers in the Persian Gulf, in Paris, and throughout

India. Any sale of Bahrain pearls, or any sighting of Margot's black pearl ring, was to be reported to Tom immediately. Jenks would need money to live and all he had were the pearls. Eventually he would show himself.

Exactly four weeks after the day of Margot's death, Jhaveris came up to the house on the Malabar Hill.

He would not have recognized Tom had he not known him so well. Tom looked bitter. He was unshaven and had been drinking.

"This isn't fair to yourself."

"What does the word *fair* mean?"

"You look as though you're blaming yourself, and you did not cause any of this to happen."

"She thought so. She told me so in this very room, so please don't tell me what you think I should do for myself. I'm doing what I must do."

"But your daughter!"

"The *ayah* is very good with her."

"It isn't fair to have her see you this way."

Tom turned away. "You talk too much about fairness. I've got no use for it. Vengeance is another story. I'll have that if it's the last thing I ever do."

"My gracious, I don't know that I want to be part of that."

Tom turned around to look at him. "You've found out something."

"I'm a religious man, Tom, a Jain. The holy men in my temple are so careful about harming creatures that they wear masks on their mouths so they won't even eat an insect while they're saying their prayers. Your idea of vengeance is wrong, Tom."

"You do know something. You're my friend, Jhaveris. You were her friend."

"This matter should be brought to the police or the resident commissioner."

"It's far too complex for that. Please help me, Jhaveris. Help her."

"There was something . . . At the end of the day, yesterday, an old merchant, a pearl driller I know, came to me and said a young man had shown him the most beautiful

Bahrain pearls. He hadn't seen any like it since the gulf fishery two years ago."

"They're Jenks's pearls! Where's the old man?"

"He doesn't want to become involved in any unpleasant business."

"Tell me where he is."

"In the bazaar, in a little stall opposite the Mumba Devi Temple. His name is Mahendra."

It must have been a holy day because the Mumba Devi Temple was filled with people. Tom pushed through the crowd, asking people he recognized to direct him to Mahendra's stall. It was located on a tiny street and seemed to be deserted.

Behind it was part of a small building that must have been smashed by a storm. Worn steps, bowed in the middle from years of use, were all that remained, and they led to an enclosed room, where three women were sorting seed pearls.

"Mahendra?" Tom asked. The women pointed to another room.

A pearl driller was sitting in front of a raised piece of petrified wood holding a stylus that had been strung like a bow for drilling. He dipped a pearl in water, then placed it in a small indentation on the board. He rotated the stylus until a hole was formed, then he dropped it into a solution and took another.

"Mahendra?" Tom asked.

The pearl driller looked up slowly and nodded.

"Do you speak English?"

He nodded again.

"I'm looking for a man who came to see you yesterday. He had pearls from Bahrain."

The man looked away quickly. "I didn't buy his pearls. I don't have that much money."

"How old was the man?"

"Not a man at all. It was a boy, seventeen, eighteen."

"Were they his pearls or was he selling them for someone else?"

"I don't know," Mahendra said. He looked nervous.

"I'm trying to find the man who owns the pearls."

"Wouldn't buy them even if I could. Didn't like that boy." Mahendra picked up the stylus.

Tom covered the pearl with his hand. "I have to know this. The man who owns these pearls killed my wife. You have to tell me everything you know."

"The man wasn't here. This was his boy."

"His son?"

"I don't know. Not English, but not Indian, either, English-sounding."

"Where was the man?"

"Somewhere outside the city. The boy wanted me to take a small sample of the Bahrain pearls to other merchants, but I didn't like the boy. I said no."

"Where outside the city?"

"I don't want to say. The boy will come back."

"No, I'll see to it. Where outside the city?"

"On the island."

"Which island?"

"Gharapuri."

"I don't know it."

"The caves, the Hindu caves."

"Elephanta," Tom whispered, throwing some rupees down on the board.

The local name was Gharapuri, but the island and the caves had been known as the Elephant Caves ever since the Portuguese had found them hundreds of years ago. At one time there had been a huge statue of an elephant, which the Portuguese had seen from their ships, but over the years the statue had disintegrated and had been removed. The island was an hour's boat ride from the Apollo Bunder, roughly seven miles to the northeast of Bombay.

Tom chartered a small boat and stood at the bow as it cut slowly through the water. The sun was low. It would be dark soon. In the distance he could see the island, two wooded hills separated by a narrow valley ringed with mud and sand, and a fringe of mangroves and palms.

When they pulled ashore, the boat owner pointed out the path that led up the rocks to the caves and gave Tom a lantern.

The foliage was tropical, sweet-smelling. Monkeys darted

across the path, then disappeared up trees that shivered with activity. Tom climbed the rocks that had been worn down by religious pilgrims and tourists.

A native woman darted out of the woods.

"Do you know the Englishman?" Tom called out.

She stood at the edge of the forest, staring at him intently. She was the color of wood bark. She pointed in the direction of the caves, then ran off.

The path rose steeply, then flattened out abruptly. In the distance Tom saw the caves carved out of rock—towering dark gray pillars, a raised altar, a doorway, and inside, a flickering fire. He blew out his lantern, then, crouching, approached the first entrance.

On either side were huge carvings of Shiva. Tom huddled under the one depicting Shiva dancing.

Behind a series of pillars was another huge carved figure, an enormous three-headed sculpture—the creator, the preserver, the destroyer. Beneath this was a small campfire and beside that, Jenks was stretched out with his back to the cave opening.

As he crept into the cave, Tom heard water trickling somewhere. Inside, it was damp, and the air was full of smoke. The crackling sound of the fire bounced off the carvings and ricocheted around the walls—from Shiva dancing to Parvati preening.

Jenks turned slowly.

"Is that you?" he called out.

Tom said nothing. He crept closer.

Jenks's sharp nose and rigid chin, framed by the unkempt black hair, were visible now.

"Bring food?" he asked, turning. Pale eyes drained of life looked up, startled to see Tom. "It's you," he said, inching back toward the fire. "Looking at me the same way you did the first time we met." Leaping up into a crouch, he bobbed on his haunches like a deranged monkey, his arms dangling between his legs. "You stole what was mine. I defiled what was yours. Even trade, boyzo."

"She's dead," Tom said, moving steadily toward him.

Jenks hopped back behind the fire, directly beneath the three-headed sculpture of Shiva.

"I didn't kill her," he said, his mouth slack.

"I'm going to kill you."

Tom crouched. As his hands came up, he remembered the first fight on the pier at South Street, then the fight onboard *Medusa*. He knew all of Jenks's tricks—surprise and stun. Lunging through the flames, Tom flew at him, hands poised in a tightening vise, and, grabbing Jenks, pressed his Adam's apple. Jenks's pale eyes popped open, his voice was lost in a gasp. He dropped to his knees, bringing Tom down on top of him. Above Tom's shoulders the face of Shiva, the destroyer, loomed, laughing wickedly.

Jenks stretched back flat against the earth. His right hand slithered toward the fire until it grasped a log. With a sudden surge, he swung the log, its red tip flaming, into Tom's right eye. Tom screamed and toppled backward. Jenks held the flaming tip on Tom's face, then, grabbing Tom from behind, pulled him toward the fire and pushed his face into the flames.

"Stop!" Paul screamed out from the cave entrance.

Jenks looked up, startled and confused. Tom rolled away and lay at Jenks's feet, screaming.

"Quickly!" Paul grabbed Jenks.

"Let me finish him," Jenks panted, but Paul pulled him away and they fled into the darkness.

Tom lay huddled in a ball beside the fire. Half his face was disfigured, charred beyond recognition.

Chapter
Sixty-three

THE HOUSE RANG with Tom's screams. He lay shivering on his bed, calling out Margot's name. Sleep was no escape. He was tortured by dreams—she was drowning in blood and he reached out to save her, but she was gone. Awake again, the

LUSTRE

pain was intense. The doctor gave him morphine and
dressed the wounds as best he could. Jessica heard him
screaming from her room at the top of the house and hid
under her covers.

Weeks later, when he could walk, he shuffled through the
marble halls like an old man. He ordered some rooms
closed. He could not bear to look at Margot's things.

One day he was sitting in the garden and the *ayah* brought
Jessica out to play with him. When she saw his bandaged
head, she wouldn't walk over to him—she kept calling for
her mother.

"Jessie, don't be scared," Tom called out, but she
wouldn't come, and afterward she would never look at him
directly. He began to feel deeply ashamed of what he looked
like, and of what he had done.

One evening, he lay shivering with fever, his mind dazed
by the morphine. Jhaveris was sitting at his bedside.

"I told Margot I wouldn't desert her," Tom said. "But I
left her here, and Jenks has won, just as she said he would.
Evil always wins out." He tried to sit up. "Must leave this
place. Can't bear to stay here."

"Shhh, Tom. Rest. Time is all you need. Lay back. Sleep."

Scabs began forming beneath the bandages. His face may
have been healing, but his soul was in torment.

The doctor came every day to check on Tom's progress,
and finally he decided to remove the bandages.

Tom sat beside a window and a servant held a mirror. The
doctor worked slowly, unwinding the layers of gauze.

"Try to remain calm. Your face, of course, will be
changed. But we don't know how bad the scarring will be,"
the doctor said. But Tom couldn't focus on the words. His
eyes were riveted on his own incomplete reflection.

When the last layer of gauze was unwound, the servant
lowered the mirror. Tom grabbed it and held it up.

His face was like a half-burned candle—intact on one side
and melted, swollen, with purplish-red scars on the other.
His hands were trembling and the image in the mirror
blurred. His right eye was half closed by a thick envelope of
mottled skin. His right ear had been completely burned off,

312

and the skin on his cheek, neck, and jaw had the texture of oatmeal.

Tom dropped the mirror, and it shattered on the floor.

Punishment fits the crime, he was thinking. The crime was that he had lived and Margot had died, that Jenks had lived and Margot had died.

It was night. He sat in the shadows of the garden. No one was allowed to come near him. He watched as the lights were turned on in Jessica's room. She was brought to the window to say good night to him. She cupped her hands around her eyes and searched for him, but he moved farther back into the darkness. He couldn't bear to have her see him.

"Don't be scared, Jessie. I'm here. I love you, Jessie. Love you."

He could not touch the only thing left on earth that he loved.

Fit punishment, he whispered, and turned away.

Jhaveris was scribbling in a small notebook. Tom sat behind a screen in the dark, dictating a letter to Blisky —Blisky and Jhaveris were now running the day-to-day operations. Tom stopped suddenly.

"Do you know of anyone who works with leather?" he asked.

"There is a man in the *Chorrbazaar*."

"Bring him up to the house. Tell him I want a mask made."

"What sort of mask?"

"One that covers half my face. Do you think he could make me one like that?"

"Yes, yes, it's a wonderful idea," Jhaveris said excitedly. "You could go out into the world again."

"I don't care about that. I want something that won't scare my daughter."

"But it's a start. Very good, dear Tom."

The next day the man arrived with samples of material, and as he began taking measurements and saw Tom's face, he gasped.

"You may well be the last person to ever see this side of my face. Can you help me?"

The man nodded, but couldn't move.

"Don't be scared. The scars won't eat you," Tom said bitterly.

The next day the man returned with the mask. Made of soft black leather, it resembled an oversized eyepatch. Fastened at the hairline, it slanted diagonally down, covering the right eye, cheek, ear, and jaw and was held in place by a thin strap worn around the neck.

Tom, stepping into the light for the first time in weeks, inspected it in the mirror.

It wasn't frightening; it was just odd. Because one half of the face had been untouched, it was like looking at a half-finished painting. The damaged side was permanently consigned to the shadows.

Tom had the *ayah* bring Jessica into the garden. He was dressed in a gray linen suit and kept the masked side of his face turned away and the undamaged side toward her.

When she saw him looking so well, she began running to him, her golden curls shimmering in the sunlight. He suddenly thought about Susan running to greet him at the end of a day in New York, then he turned and Jessica stopped, but she didn't look scared, just amazed. She brought one of her fingers up to her mouth and studied him.

"It's all right, Jessie," he said, kneeling.

She waited another moment, then ran to him. She reached out for the mask tentatively, and feeling its softness, smiled and hugged him.

"Daddy!" She said the word gleefully, as if she'd invented it.

"It's better now," he said, hugging her to him, and he wept. No one had touched him in such a long time. Her love washed over him. "My dearest, dearest girl," he said, rocking her slowly back and forth.

Standing up, still holding her in his arms, he walked toward the house. Margot's presence was everywhere—in the gardens she'd planted, in the rooms she'd furnished.

He carried Jessica up the stairs to her room.

The door to Margot's room was closed, but Tom could

not lock out the memory. The image of Jenks gaining access to the room merged with the image of Margot covered in blood. He held Jessica more tightly and continued to climb the stairs.

"We shall go away," he said.

He'd protect her. He'd hide her away from all the evil in the world.

Chapter Sixty-four

HE BOUGHT A chateau at Chaumontel, fifteen miles outside Paris, around which he built high walls. Jessica was not permitted to leave the grounds.

The walls signified his isolation, and his shame. Having failed Margot, he could not live comfortably with himself. Late at night a servant ferried in prostitutes, who ritualized the shame with rites of denial.

Tom favored a pretty young girl with golden-red hair. She would enter a darkened room at the top of the house. He'd be hidden behind a screen in a corner. She'd take off her clothes very slowly near a candle that cast a light bright enough so that he could just barely make out her pale, smooth skin. She posed for him, not knowing in which corner of the room he was. Then she saw the strands of pearls that he'd left on a table. She draped herself with them, passing them through the tawny hair of her pubis, rubbing them over her stomach, and twining them around her nipples. She'd begin searching the corners for him. Excited, he'd stare wildly at her. She'd dance—the clicking of the pearls would merge with the sound of his own heartbeat.

The clicking came closer and closer until she found him. Then, sinking to the floor, she sat, splay-legged, running the pearls up and down between her legs, faster and faster. Her breath came in short, fierce bursts as the friction of the pearls became more intense. He saw the folds of her vagina contracting. The pearls were slick with her juice. Inching forward, pressing the pearls into herself, she would moan, calling out to him to help her.

But he sat hidden in the shadows, unwilling to touch her or satisfy himself.

Slowly and deliberately, using Blisky and Jhaveris and Sheikh Akhbar, Tom created an empire built on pearls.

As one century ended and the new began, his power became unquestioned. He controlled more than half the world's supply and the purchase of some of the most famous pearl jewels in history. Anyone interested in buying pearls of the highest quality had to make the trip to Chaumontel and sit in a dark room.

"I would like you to assemble a necklace of perfect pearls for my wife," an American named Astor said one day as he tried to peer through the dark screen to get a good look at Tom Street. Blisky, who was standing nearby, discouraged the man with a curt nod.

"Perfect pearls are hard to come by," Tom said.

"I won't discuss price with you," Astor said coolly, adjusting his monocle.

"I happen to have seven perfect pearls in my possession."

"That's a start."

"What length necklace would you like?"

The man placed a hand over the center of his chest. "To here."

"Monsieur Blisky, show Mr. Astor the seven pearls."

Blisky brought out a black velvet case on which were placed seven perfectly round pearls of such exquisite lustre that they glowed even in the dark room.

Mr. Astor nodded. "Yes, these will do nicely."

"I'd be happy to assemble the necklace for you. It will take a minimum of seven years," Tom said.

"Seven years? We could all be dead in seven years."

"I said a *minimum* of seven, sir. It could take as long as ten. And taking the fluctuating world price into account, you'll have to plan on spending at least half a million dollars."

Even to an Astor, the sum was staggering. "I've recently purchased two Rembrandts for under half a million."

"But half a million dollars for a strand of these pearls will be worth twice the price by the time the strand is completed," Tom said in a tone that indicated the meeting had come to an end.

Mr. Astor went away feeling as though he'd actually gotten more for his money, and Tom alerted his purchasing agents all over the world to begin searching for pearls for Mrs. Astor's necklace.

Tom was now considered one of the wealthiest men in all of France. There was no jewel he could not afford, although one eluded him—the black pearl he'd given Margot, which he now referred to as the Margot. It had vanished with Jenks.

The years did not dim Tom's obsession with Jenks. And although Paul Jenks, who had surfaced in Hong Kong in the pearl trade, contended that his father had died of natural causes onboard a ship somewhere between India and China, Tom didn't believe it. He knew Jenks was alive the way some people knew rainstorms were coming. Jenks's evil gnawed at him.

Some Asian merchants claimed to have bought more of the Bahrain pearls directly from Jenks in Singapore, and then an Englishman named Spears surfaced in Paris with three pearls he'd supposedly bought from Jenks in China.

Blisky brought Spears to the chateau.

Tom, keeping his face away from him, sat at a distance enveloped in shadows. Spears was drinking champagne as if it were Vichy. Tom had already agreed to purchase all the man's pearls in exchange for information.

"Where did you say you got these pearls, Spears?"

"In China, 'at's where. I awready tol' your frog gennelman that. I was with Jenks in China. It was jus' las' year—September 1901, ta be exact, guv'na. I was in China when the trouble broke out, the Boxer trouble. I was there. He was, too."

"Who was? Paul Jenks or his father?"

"The father, guv'na, the father hisself. When all the shootin' started in Peking—them Chinks were as mad as bats, firin' at every European bugger they could take aim at. Jenks was in the middle of it. You see," Spears said conspiratorially, leaning over a desk now, "soldiers was makin' deals. They'd looted the summer palace, called Yuen-Min-Yuen. See, these soldiers stold the royal pearls, and it was Jenks who bought 'em."

"And he sold them to you?"

"No, I made my own deals with them Chinks. I din' have as much money as he did. An' he knew how to sell 'em. Set his son up in business in Hong Kong to do the sellin'. They're gettin' a thousand pounds per pearl out there. I can let you have 'em cheaper. Wha'd you say to two thousand for the whole lot?"

Any price was worth it, although the pearls were only of middling quality. It was the confirmation Tom was after. Jenks was alive.

Tom hired agents to track him down in Hong Kong, but they kept coming up with the same information. It was what Paul Jenks had maintained all along—that Jenks had vanished from the face of the earth.

V

Of Love and
Undoing

Chapter
Sixty-five

As more English and American industrialists came to Paris to buy pearls, Tom was pressed to open offices in either London or New York. London was temporarily out of the question because he and Nasis had reached an understanding not to compete directly in each other's major markets. While New York was open territory, it was a place Tom wanted to avoid. At first he sent Blisky to New York, but in the autumn of 1905, the reason and the means for Tom to make a move in that direction were brought to him by a woman named Madame Mirijana Osbenski de Costa.

She'd been born in St. Petersburg but raised in Paris. Her family had been soldiers and jurists since the Middle Ages, but her father and grandfather were artists. Through them, she developed a love for music and art, but unfortunately, she lacked talent. Her father, who doted on her and gave her the nickname Mia, by which she was known all her life, told her that lacking talent, the next best thing she could do was support it in others.

Mia was a very shrewd girl.

Although she studied piano at a conservatory and learned to play reasonably well, her greatest joy was lavishing praise and attention on a fellow student, Gustave Laurent, who went on to become world-famous and who remained her lover until well after her marriage to Valerian de Costa, an industrialist who had made a fortune in the steel business.

Mia did not love Valerian de Costa, but she respected him and treated him well. With his money she supported artists. Paris celebrated its famous patrons, and Mia de Costa became part of an emerging fashionable world of aristocrats, painters, bankers, and ballet dancers. While still in her twenties, she was fawned over and courted, written about and painted. And then, when Mia was in her early thirties, Valerian de Costa discovered her love affair with Gustave Laurent and, after setting her up in a grand style, divorced her and went on to marry his mistress, a prima ballerina with a tawdry reputation.

Mia wasted no time crying, even though Gustave Laurent married someone who forbade him to ever see Mia again.

Mia threw lavish parties, attended the opera, and became what one waspish writer called "the complete and professional best friend."

It was in this capacity that she left her house on the rue de Constantine early on the morning of October 20, 1905, to visit the reclusive pearl merchant Tom Street. A friend of Mia's had fallen on hard times and needed to make a discreet sale of a pearl necklace, one of the most valuable in the world.

It was a particularly beautiful autumn that year. Mia was driven from the city in an open automobile. She sat with one hand holding down a large hat that partially covered her flame-red hair. Her face was round, her skin and eyes remarkably clear. She had the look of a woman who knew she was beautiful, but she treated her beauty in an offhand way. What she chose to cultivate was her wit and it was evident in her eyes, which were bright blue and incisive, and her voice, which was alternately assertive and soft, as lilting as a whisper, as resonant as a French horn.

At Chaumontel, a town Mia knew well because she had cousins in nearby Chantilly who often invited her to their chateau, the driver turned right and headed into a narrow country road. Clouds of dust rose on either side of the auto like the wake of a yacht. They reached an iron gate. When the gatekeeper opened it, Mia entered the grounds alone.

As soon as she saw it, she fell in love with the place. There were fields bordered by chestnut trees and meandering streams, and a moat in which the house was reflected. The chateau was beautiful; it had three round towers topped by pointed turrets, which were covered with russet-colored vines that looked like shaggy hair. The house had a gray slate roof, gray shutters, and rows of square windows. At one end of the moat was an island with a single wooden bench beneath a huge maple tree. Beyond it were meadows and fields flushed with gold light where black and white cows grazed languidly under willows, red maples, poplars, and pines. Here and there were flowerbeds filled with yellow, purple, and white pansies. There were statues of poets, of beautiful girls dancing, of fawns with ears poised. All the beauty a man could will into being had been lavished on the house, and Mia was so moved by it that tears welled up in her eyes.

When she walked into the garden, she saw a beautiful golden-haired girl reading a book at the base of one of the statues.

The girl looked up, then stared at Mia clinically, as if she had never before seen another adult.

"Hello," Mia called out to her. "I didn't mean to disturb you. I've come here on business, but I thought your garden was so beautiful that I stopped for a moment to admire it. It is your garden, isn't it?"

The girl nodded, then, tossing her pale curls behind her, stood up. "It is," she said in a proprietary tone.

"The most beautiful garden I've ever seen. Whoever designed it was very smart and must have been thinking about this very time of year. The way the light filters down, layers and layers of light."

"In the morning there are mists," the girl said, pointing at a mowed field as if it were all a part of her very own kingdom, "that cover the lawn with a silver shroud that lingers until midmorning. It's my favorite time because it's filled with mystery."

"Do you like mysteries?"

"I like uncovering them—the mist lifts, you get to see what it's been covering. And it's not the same every day. The mist always leaves behind something new—a dandelion or a bluebell or a shimmering coat of dew."

Mia extended her hand. "My name is Madame de Costa."

"How do you do? I am Jessica Street."

"Tom Street's daughter?"

"Yes. Do you know my father?"

"I've never met him, but I've come here to do business with him."

Jessica looked over at the house warily. "Does he know you're coming?"

"Monsieur Blisky arranged it."

"Monsieur Blisky is in America. My father is an American."

"Yes, I've heard that."

"My mother was English."

"Was she?"

"She died a long time ago, when I was very young."

"Are you alone here—no brothers or sisters?"

Jessica shook her head, then asked, "Do you have children?"

"No, I don't."

"But you're married."

"I'm divorced."

Jessica looked at Mia as if she were thinking, Here is someone as exotic as myself. "Do you live in Paris?" she asked.

"Yes."

"I've never been there."

"I would think you'd go all the time. How long have you lived here?"

"Five, almost six years."

"You've never gone to the museums or the gardens or the ballet?"

"No, I'm not allowed to leave," she said rather matter-of-factly.

"Where do you go to school?"

"Here. I have my own tutor, Monsieur Berger. He can speak five languages. He's teaching me English, Italian, and German."

"Where are your friends?"

Jessica looked ashamed not to have any, then she stared up intently at Mia. "Tell me, Madame, does everyone who knows you call you Madame de Costa?"

"No, I'm also called Mirijana."

"I like that."

"Also Mia."

"Mia—I like that best of all."

"Jessica!" a man called out from the house.

Mia turned and tried to see who it was or from where the voice had come, but she couldn't see anyone.

"Yes, Papa."

"Who's with you?"

"Madame de Costa."

Mia took a step forward. "Mr. Street, is that you?"

"What do you want?"

Again, Mia scanned the rows of windows, searching for him, but she couldn't see him.

"Mr. Street, I'm Mirijana de Costa. I spoke with Monsieur Blisky."

"Monsieur Blisky is not here."

"Yes, I know that. He told me to come out and see you."

"He's in America. He won't be back for another month."

"It isn't Monsieur Blisky I wish to see," Mia said, taking another step forward, squinting.

"You're not supposed to look at him," Jessica said.

"You can see Monsieur Blisky in Paris when he returns," Tom Street called out.

"He's in the second-floor study, third window from the left," Jessica whispered.

Mia saw the tops of his trousers and what looked like the tail of a brocade smoking jacket.

"I've brought a very valuable necklace for you to look at."

"Your necklace?"

"No, it belongs to a friend, Contessa di Compana. The necklace belonged to her grandmother. It's very famous—it was given to her grandmother by Catherine the Great."

There was a long pause, then Tom said, "Black pearls?"

"Triple strand—the most beautiful black pearls I've ever seen, Mr. Street."

Tom was silent. "Like flies buzzing on a sultry day," he finally said.

"What's that?"

"Jelly's black pearls," he said as if he were talking to himself.

"No, Mr. Street. I assure you they belong to my friend, the contessa."

"I'd like to finally see them," he said in a low voice.

"What's he saying?" Mia asked Jessica.

"You're very lucky," Jessica said, walking toward the moat bridge.

Mia followed closely behind Jessica, and when they crossed the bridge, she looked up at the second-story window. But Tom Street had vanished.

Chapter
Sixty-six

THE GIRL LED Mia into a lovely oval-shaped vestibule, at one end of which were tall glass doors that opened onto a stone terrace. A large grandfather clock ticked loudly. The tapestries covering the windows had been pulled aside to let in the light. On either side of the vestibule were nicely proportioned rooms; one, a sitting room, had a fireplace and high-beamed ceilings, and the other was a dining room with a cherry-wood table, another fireplace, and glass doors that also led to the terrace and a garden beyond it.

Jessica, who had stopped in the center of the vestibule to allow Mia the time to look around at everything, now proceeded to a small staircase. Then, looking behind, making sure Mia was following, she climbed the stairs and began talking as if she were conducting a tour.

"When I bring you into his study, you mustn't say anything about the room. He likes it to be dark. He'll be sitting at one end of the room behind a screen. Don't try to look through it or around it. He won't like that."

"There are a lot of rules, aren't there?"

"Yes, and you're a woman. He never sees women. You must have something he wants very much."

"What else must I do or not do?"

"I don't think you should ask him many questions. He doesn't like that. He'll talk first, probably ask you to push the necklace you want him to see through a slot in the screen. Then he'll take the necklace to a small room that's filled with light, where he'll inspect the pearls. Leave as soon as you've finished conducting your business with him."

They reached the second landing, which was much darker than the first. There was another sitting room with low ceilings and overflowing bookcases. It was a man's room, with worn leather couches, a few paintings, but none of any value. Following Jessica, Mia walked down a narrow hall that was long and crooked. On one side were small windows that looked into the garden, on the other were oak doors.

Jessica stopped and whispered, "This is where he'll see you. It will be dark inside, so wait at the door for a moment for your eyes to adjust—it's what I always do."

"Do you ever see him directly?" Mia asked lightly, but Jessica answered in a serious tone.

"Oh, yes, every day. It wasn't always that way, and when I was very young, I was once frightened by him."

"What's wrong with him?"

Jessica lowered her voice even more, her eyes gleaming with excitement, as if she had never before discussed this with anyone.

"It's his face," she said. "He was burned in a fire. That's why he uses the screen," Jessica said. "It's not to be mean—it's just to spare you the unpleasantness of having to look at him. Now, you must go in. He'll be waiting for you. He can probably hear us talking. You don't want to make him angry."

"No, no, of course not."

Jessica walked down the hall in the direction of the library.

Mia straightened a fold of her light wool suit, then, removing her gloves, slowly opened the door.

The room, almost empty, was dark and much larger than she had thought it would be. At one end there was a long Napoleonic campaign desk on which stood a single lighted candle in a bronze holder. Behind it was a gilt-framed screen through which she could see the figure of a man sitting at what looked like an identical campaign desk. A chair had been pulled in front of the desk closest to her.

"Your name again?" Tom asked as she took her seat.

"Madame de Costa."

"Any relation to Valerian de Costa?"

"He was my husband."

"He once bought something for you from me," Tom said.

"Yes, a very beautiful necklace," she said.

How bizarre, Mia was thinking. His voice was calm, less businesslike than she had thought, and he was speaking slowly, as if he were taking his time to study her. She felt naked.

"Do you always conduct business this way?"

"Yes, always."

"It's rather like going to confession."

"No one has ever said so before. May I see the pearls? Just pass them through the screen. I'll take them into another room for a moment to look at them, then I'll come back and we'll talk."

Mia brought out a slim velvet bag. Opening it, she took out the necklace, which glimmered even in the faint candle-light. Seeing a slot in the screen, she passed it through, and he took it, then rose and walked to a door. The room was momentarily flooded with light—she could see that he was tall and trim—then he quickly disappeared.

She walked over to a window and pulled aside the heavy curtain. She saw him standing in a tower room, framed in a tall, narrow window. He was inspecting the necklace in the daylight. He had his left side to her: he was perfect-looking. His features were handsome, his skin so pale and clear and his hair such a beautiful color that she stared, transfixed. He lowered the necklace slowly and stared out at the window with a distant look.

Turning suddenly, he saw her standing at the window. She quickly pulled the curtain into place and began walking to her side of the screen.

When the door opened, she was still standing, and she caught a quick glimpse of him. He was immaculately dressed in a gray business suit, half his face covered in black. Their eyes met for a brief but harrowing moment.

Closing the door, he remained standing until she sat. The room was dark again, the air between them filled with tension.

"I'm terribly sorry. I'm as curious as a child sometimes. I didn't mean to see anything I shouldn't have seen."

"How much do you want for them?" he asked in a grave tone.

She quoted a ridiculously high price, thinking he would want to bargain with her, but he merely said, fine, would she take a bank draft or did she want cash?

She was speechless for a moment, then she said she would take cash.

"That will take me at least a day. I'll have it for you tomorrow."

"I'll give you my address in town—" she began to say, but he interrupted.

"I don't go into town. You'll have to come here to pick it up."

"But, monsieur, that's half a day, back and forth. I've already done it once."

"Monsieur Blisky usually runs my errands in the city, but he isn't here. It's impossible. Either you come back tomorrow or we have no business to discuss, madame."

"If that is your only condition . . . you're certainly being generous in every other regard. Will you keep them here for me? I'd rather not travel with them." She picked up her purse, then leaning forward, added, "Do you put everyone you do business with at this disadvantage?"

"I'm sorry you choose to see it that way. Perhaps the disadvantage is mine."

"You needn't protect me. I've seen many things other people have considered unpleasant—they've never struck me as such. It's just more of life, isn't it?"

"Madame, you have never been ugly," he said sharply.

"What's ugliness got to do with it? Is that what you think you are? The worst is over. I've already seen you at the window and you don't look ugly to me, monsieur. On the contrary, you look very handsome."

He shuddered or sighed, she couldn't tell which, and suddenly she regretted having used such a strident tone of voice.

"Monsieur, are you all right?"

"Yes," he said sadly.

"I wish I were," she said, finding that her eyes were suddenly filled with tears. "You've gotten me quite upset."

Unexpectedly, he laughed.

"At least you can laugh, even if it is at my expense," she said, wiping her eyes with a handkerchief. "Your child is very beautiful."

"Yes, she is."

"Do you plan to keep her locked away forever?"

"If I choose to."

"I only ask because she seems so eager for friendship and she's such a charming girl—she should see something of the world."

"If I thought all this advice came with the purchase of the pearls, I would have thought twice about it."

"Oh, I know you haven't asked my advice, but I thought I would give it to you anyway. It equalizes us—you and your screen, me and my opinions. If you keep that girl locked away like this, she will grow to hate you in time, and I think the time is growing near. I know this because I would hate you for taking the trouble to educate me and have me read books and then deny me the world."

"Is that all?" he asked, standing.

"No, perhaps you're forcing her to hate you the way you hate yourself. Whatever you've done, Monsieur Street, is not as ugly or as hateful as what you are doing to your daughter."

"The gatekeeper will have your money tomorrow by noon. He won't let you inside the grounds again. I thank you for having brought these pearls to me. Good day, madame."

"To hell with you, Monsieur Street."

Jessica was waiting downstairs for her, sitting on the steps. "How did your meeting go?"

"I accomplished what I set out to do," Mia said, but the girl saw how upset she was.

"He's made you cry—he doesn't mean to."

Mia touched the girl's shoulder warmly. "You mustn't be such an adult all the time. You must be what you are—a wonderful girl."

"But he's made you so angry."

"That's all right. I can take care of myself. Would you like to visit Paris?"

"Did he tell you I could do that?"

"I'm asking you."

"Yes, I would."

"Then we shall. Come, walk me to the gate."

Mia opened the large glass front door, but Jessica stayed behind.

"Are you teasing me? Will you really take me to Paris? He won't let me go."

"We'll persuade him."

"No, he won't let me. You'll make him angry."

"I'll take care of it. Now, please walk me to the gate."

Jessica looked around nervously. "No, I'll have a servant take you."

And then Tom's voice came booming down from the second landing.

"Jessica! Come up here at once!"

"You have made him angry," the little girl said.

"I didn't mean to—I'll see you tomorrow and we'll talk more about this."

"Jessica!"

"No, I can't," Jessica said, backing away from the door. "Don't come back here. You've made him angry and sad. Please don't come back here."

"Jessica!"

Jessica ran off without saying another word.

Chapter
Sixty-seven

"I DIDN'T ENCOURAGE Madame de Costa," Jessica said to Tom later that day as they sat upstairs in his library.

"I didn't say you did, Jess. I'm not angry with you." He looked up at her from his books and papers.

"She loved the garden. That's why she stopped to talk with me."

"We won't have her bothering us anymore."

"She wasn't bothering me."

He smiled softly at her. "You disapprove of what I've done, Jess. I can always tell. You sound very sure of yourself—just like your mother. Come sit with me." He moved over to give her room in his large leather chair. She sat primly at first, then leaned against him. "Do you like living here in the country?"

"I suppose I do," she said.

"You didn't say that with much conviction."

"I'd like to see Paris—a zoo or a dress shop or the ballet."

"I can arrange to have the ballet come here."

"It wouldn't be the same."

"Madame de Costa has put ideas in your head. She's meddlesome. There are people like that in the world."

"Are we hiding from them?"

"Hiding? Why do you use that word?"

"There was a man in a book I once read, a hermit, who hid from people because he was scared of them. He lived in a cave deep in the woods."

"We're not hermits."

"Then we should have more people visit us."

"We have everything we want here. We have each other."

She got up from the chair. "The hermit in the story was finally persuaded to leave his cave by falling in love with a beautiful woman."

"Is that what you'd like me to do?"

"Did you notice Madame de Costa's eyes? They're very beautiful."

"You want me to fall in love with Madame de Costa?"

"I want . . ." her voice trailed off as she turned away from him.

"What do you want, Jess? I'll try to give you anything you want."

"I want you to be happy again, the way you were with Mother."

"But I am happy here with you."

She smiled at him, and her smile seemed to see right through him.

The prostitute was a new girl, but she had the same reddish-gold hair as all the others. Through the years, the ritual had become more elaborate. Although he participated and was not hidden behind a screen, he still sat at a distance while she undressed and lay on the floor stroking herself. Whenever he wanted to move toward her, he found he couldn't. Now, slipping his hand into his coat pocket, he withdrew the black pearl necklace.

"Take it," he ordered.

As she reached out, she grazed his hand.

"Don't touch me," he snapped.

She recoiled, then rubbed the necklace over herself, twining it around her breasts, on her nipples, down across her stomach. When she sat, the pearls coiled like liquid darkness in the fold of her thighs. Her legs opened.

"What do you want me to do?" the girl asked.

"Don't talk."

Rubbing herself, she moaned.

"Stop doing that."

He was confused and suddenly frightened.

It was the woman's fault—Mia de Costa—he should have sent her away immediately. She had a familiar quality he'd banished from his life. He couldn't name it.

Reaching down, he grabbed the necklace. "Get out!" he shouted at the girl.

Rolling away from him, she began to gather her clothes.

He held the cool necklace against his face and cursed Jelly and Mia de Costa and all women like them—even Margot.

The girl stood at the door.

"Wait," he called out, again wanting to get lost in his nightly ritual. "Don't go . . . come back . . ."

His voice was filled with resignation and regret.

Mia had written Tom a letter of apology and included in it her request for his permission to take Jessica into the city to see the ballet.

When she arrived at the chateau the next day, the gate was closed. The gatekeeper had a large envelope filled with franc notes and a receipt for the sale of the pearls. Mia gave him the letter for Tom and asked him to fetch Jessica, but he said he had strict instructions not to.

She gave the man ten francs.

"It's all my fault. What if I come back at the end of the

week, at about this time? Would you fetch her then and bring her here?" Mia asked, handing him another ten francs. "Please, monsieur, for her sake."

"Are you a relative of hers?"

"No."

"Then why are you doing this?"

"I don't think it's fair, that's all," she said, staring up at the wall. "Is he very cruel to her?"

"No, madame, he loves her very much."

"What sort of love is it that keeps her locked up?" Mia asked. Receiving only a shrug, she said *au revoir*, and left.

A week later she returned. Jessica was called from the house by the gatekeeper.

"If he sees you, he'll be very angry," Jessica said when she saw Mia. "Why do you keep coming to see me?"

"Because I've arranged for you to have a tour of the ballet."

"He says you're meddlesome, poking your nose where you don't belong."

"Perhaps that's true. It sounds like me. But this has more to do with you. You're exceptional. I knew it the first time I saw you."

"I wasn't doing anything exceptional. I was reading a book."

"With being exceptional comes the responsibility of knowing it and reveling in it."

"Are you exceptional?"

"No, not in the least—only I am able to see it in others."

Jessica laughed quite suddenly, sounding like her father. Looking back at the house, she undid the latch and opened the gate. Mia slipped in and the two walked into the garden, staying hidden behind the chestnut trees.

"What exceptional things do you see me doing?" Jessica asked.

"Do you dance?"

"No, but I've always thought I could."

"You paint."

"Yes, but not exceptionally well."

Mia stepped back, studying Jessica more carefully. "A writer!"

"How did you know?"

"The way you described the mist in the morning the first time we talked."

"I've written a description of you . . . 'Madame de Costa has the brightest blue eyes, signposts to her very soul, cunning and warm at the very same time.'"

Mia hugged her. "I knew I was right about you."

"Madame de Costa! I told you not to come back to this house!" Tom Street was standing nearby, half-hidden behind a tree.

Jessica jumped away at the sound of her father's voice.

Mia's hands dropped to her sides, and she was speechless.

"Papa, you're being very rude."

"I want you to go into the house, Jessica."

"But Papa, Madame de Costa has asked me to accompany her to Paris to see the ballet."

"I don't care what Madame de Costa has asked you to do. I want you to go back to the house."

"But Papa, this isn't fair."

"And life's unfairness will be your lesson for the day. Go back to the house."

"Such cynicism is not worthy of you, Monsieur Street," Mia said. "Please don't blame the child for my mistake. I'll leave."

Jessica's eyes welled up with tears as Mia began walking back to the gate.

"Papa, may I walk Madame de Costa to the gate? Then I'll go back to the house. Please, Papa."

He said nothing, and Jessica followed Mia, whispering, "Madame, please don't be angry with him—he's terribly sad, that's all. Just terribly sad."

At the gate Mia stopped and looked back at Street. He had turned away and was walking, his head bowed, back into the garden. Jessica was right not to be angry—he seemed to be enveloped by a sadness over which he had no control.

Opening her purse Mia took out a piece of paper and a tiny gold pen and wrote down her address.

"If we can't see each other, then you must write to me—at least once a week. Will you do that? In time we'll prove to him that I'm not a bad influence. He'll let you come to Paris with me," she said, bending down, kissing the girl lightly on the forehead.

During the next couple of months Jessica wrote to Mia every week, and Mia dutifully responded. Jessica's letters were filled with richly detailed descriptions of everyday life at the chateau. Mia took them to a publisher friend, who thought enough of them to include an excerpt of two of them in a magazine, and when it appeared, Mia had a dozen copies sent out to the chateau.

A week later a letter arrived from Jessica saying that her father had agreed to allow Mia to take her to Paris for a day.

The trip was a great success—they had front-row seats during a rehearsal of the corps de ballet, luncheon at Chateau d'Eau, a walk in the Tuileries, and a tour of the Louvre.

When they arrived back at Chaumontel, it was nightfall and Jessica was sleepy. An old servant, Père Daudet, came running out to say that M. Street wanted to see Mia.

"Does he want me to sit in a darkened room behind a screen?" she asked the old man.

"Oh, no, madame. He's waiting for you downstairs in the sitting room."

Chapter
Sixty-eight

INDICATING A CHAIR for her near the fire, Tom kept the masked side of his face turned away from her. But he could not stay still. Her presence agitated him.

His face looked so perfect on the one side—the mask could have been a shadow. But when he talked, Mia realized that his mouth was pulled back as if something were holding it, and he seemed to be in pain.

"Some things are not as pleasant up close," he said quickly.

"I'm not frightened."

"Or easily deterred." He turned back to the fire as if he were too uncomfortable to speak to her directly. "Thank you for what you've done for Jessica."

"I should thank you for allowing me to show her off. She's a wonderful girl." Mia dropped her gaze, then added: "And I apologize, monsieur. I realize now that I was asking too much when I first came here. You had no idea who I was or what I could have wanted from you or your daughter."

"But I knew you."

"You did?" she said, taken aback.

"Women like yourself, so brave and determined—you're a breed apart. I've always had a weakness for you." He turned toward her now, as if his candor had equalized something between them, and she was confronted for the first time with the blankness of the mask and her own fears about what lay behind it. "You were the first person in years to talk to me the way you did. It provoked me to think . . ."

"And I thought it was just the pearls I brought you," she said, changing the subject because he looked so intensely sad.

"They were reminders of another life." He took a seat opposite her. "Tell me something. Do you love pearls?"

"They're beautiful, but I would not sell my body or soul for them."

"I've spent almost fifteen years of my life searching for them, buying and selling them, and I'm still trying to understand them. An Indian prince once told me that their fascination had to do with a quality of transformation. But it's more than that." He took a large pearl from his pocket and held it out to her. The pearl was luminous and pale, a contrast to his hand, which was heavily scarred. As if aware of her scrutiny of it, he retracted his hand self-consciously.

"I think the fascination with pearls has to do with a drama of innocence and beauty," he continued. "The worm innocently entered the shell, then, to protect itself, the shell entrapped the worm. When innocence is sacrificed, beauty is the byproduct."

"Is that your drama, monsieur?"

"I've lived my life so quickly there was no time to think about it."

"And now you've had the time to do too much thinking."

He turned away from her, lost in a thought he could not express.

"How brave are you, monsieur?"

"Haven't you heard anything of my reputation? I'm supposed to be very brave."

"And yet you've hidden yourself away."

"You may choose to see it as that."

"They say that you lost someone you loved very much."

He said nothing, and her heart went out to him. "You must miss her—you must be very lonely."

He stood up abruptly. "I won't keep you any longer, madame."

"I'm sorry—it's my nature to be so dreadfully honest."

"I just wanted to thank you for what you did for Jessica."

Mia picked up her purse and, standing up, stepped close to him. "You can't always hide. It's really why I'm here. You wanted to talk to someone."

"People visit me all the time," he said curtly.

"You need to talk to a woman, monsieur. And I am eager to talk with you."

"Are you fond of novelties or freaks?"

"Just simple conversation."

"Tears and pity, madame?"

"What's wrong with either if it is what I have to give?"

"Neither is easy to accept."

"You're still keeping me hidden behind a screen. Why do you wear that mask?"

"You wouldn't want to see what's behind it."

"How can you be so sure? I might want to see your face."

"I can't do that."

"Are you protecting me or yourself?"

"I think you should go."

"Perhaps I should. Only I thought we might become friends."

"Why do you want to be my friend?"

"I thought I could help you."

"Don't make the mistake of thinking you're in love with

me, madame. It's wrong to fall in love with someone you feel so sorry for."

"You've become so brittle, locked away by yourself," she said, turning away.

"It's acceptance you offer, but I don't want that, either. I hide away here because it makes the world more bearable."

"The world is neither as deformed nor as beautiful as you. It's your equal. You should confront it. You owe it to yourself and your daughter."

"We have everything we need here."

"Jessica doesn't know the world. She won't be able to survive in it if all this is taken away from her."

"I'll make sure it never is."

"You cannot be so sure, monsieur. Now I must go."

"You're angry."

"Of course I am. It's the walls you've built around yourself as well as your house. You're rigid, and though I admit it's a failing of mine, I cannot stand rigidity. Good evening, monsieur."

She left the room and stood for a moment in the vestibule, pulling on her gloves.

He appeared in the hallway behind her. "What has the world to offer that I can't provide for myself?"

"Diversion—if nothing else—wisdom and silliness. Good food."

"The opera," he said, smiling cynically.

"Yes, and the ballet and the theater and all the pompous asses and true believers who attend such events. In short, life, Monsieur Street, banal and ecstatic."

"You're a very passionate woman, Madame de Costa."

"I'd have it no other way."

"Not an easy way to live."

"I could contradict you once again and say that nothing good is easy, but I will keep my tongue—which, I assure you, is about the most difficult thing I do."

He smiled again, more generously this time, but said nothing.

"Let's see how brave you are," she said. "Would you join me at the opera next Monday night? Don't say a word now. I'd prefer the uncertainty. Good night, monsieur. It was a pleasure seeing you."

Chapter
Sixty-nine

WHEN TOM STEPPED into Mia de Costa's loge at the opera, she smiled delightedly, and seeing how nervous he was, she took his arm and offered him champagne.

"This is your chance to see how your pearls are being worn," she whispered. "Simply stare at them with as much interest as they have in you. You'll put them in their place soon enough."

The red velvet loge was perched on a balcony directly over the left side of the stage. When Tom took his seat, a steady buzz of voices rose up. Looking down, he was dazzled by what he saw. Drenched in diamonds and pearls, the women wore feathered, bejeweled aigrettes in their hair—luxuriant plumes that shivered on invisible breezes. A woman in an adjoining box was wearing a pearl choker and strands of forty-grain pearls that Tom recognized. He'd sold them to her husband.

During the intermissions Mia's friends poured into the mirrored salon through which one entered the box, to sip champagne and gossip and gawk. Tom felt overwhelmed and was kept at arm's length from them by Mia.

By the time the evening ended he'd been given a nickname, "le masqué," by which he was to become known in the popular press.

Invitations began to arrive and despite himself, Tom was flattered by the attention. These people wanted adventures with none of the dangers, and he was an adventurer —romantic and mysterious. It was like the world he'd left behind years ago in New York, but now he was not dependent on his rich father-in-law to secure his position; he had his own power and money.

Like a child released after a long confinement, Tom was interested in everything—fashion and art and jewelry design. He became a familiar presence in the offices of the Cartier brothers, in the design workshops of Paul Poiret, who was revolutionizing the way women dressed, and Raoul Dufy, who designed fabrics for Poiret.

In time Tom took over some of Blisky's duties and reestablished relationships with his chief Parisian competitors, Jacques Bienenfeld—with whom he maintained a flotilla of ships off the coast of Venezuela during the fisheries—and Baron Lopez, Bernard Citroen, Victor and Adolphe Rosenthal and their brother, Leonard, who, with Tom, was known as the "king of pearls."

Although Blisky argued against it, Tom opened an office on rue Lafayette, where he set up a design studio and began to see more clients. It had three main rooms—a waiting alcove, a workroom that had ten designers working at two tables under a large wall of windows, and a private office—a large airy room with a huge gilt mirror above a fireplace, and a large desk at which Tom worked.

It was here that Tom commissioned and designed his own jewels: the aigrettes he'd seen at the opera had sparked his imagination. Shimmering and opulent, his jewels soon became popular and he found himself in the middle of yet another business—the importation of feathers—the most popular being the white Egyptian egret, from which the jewel had gotten its name.

It was a hectic time, and Tom was glad of it. He found and furnished a grand apartment on the rue de Rivoli. Slowly, with Mia's help, his emotions were beginning to re-emerge. But although she encouraged it, they were not lovers. He was just beginning to see a way out of his long mourning for Margot when, in mid-winter, someone showed up at the office who brought back all the old memories.

It was one of those dank, gray Parisian days when the sky threatens snow but only a chilling rain falls. A cold wind was blowing up the rue Lafayette. People were struggling with umbrellas, seeking temporary shelter in doorways and alcoves before moving on.

It was mid-afternoon, and most of the designers had gone home early. Blisky was in the front room reading a newspaper, eating a tart. The front door opened and a youngish man with dark hair and chiseled cheekbones appeared and asked Blisky if he could speak with Tom Street. He had some pearls he thought Mr. Street might find interesting. His accent was difficult to place—he spoke a rough French that Blisky had heard only sailors use. Blisky said he often handled these purchases for Mr. Street, but the young man was adamant and handed Blisky his card.

Tom was sitting at his desk going over the designs of some pearl necklaces that one of Cartier's designers, Charles Jacqueau, had executed for him.

When Blisky walked in, Tom didn't look up because he was too interested in the intricacies of Jacqueau's work.

"Buyer or seller?"

"Seller."

"You handle it, Blisky."

"He'll only see you."

Blisky put the card on Tom's desk. It read, PAUL JENKS, DEALER OF FINEST QUALITY PEARLS, HONG KONG.

Tom froze for a moment, then his head snapped up angrily. "What the hell is he doing here?"

"He's got pearls to sell."

"The black pearl? The Margot?"

"He didn't say."

"It would be like them to sell it back to me. Show him in. And, Blisky . . . I want you to stay."

Tom sat back in his chair, his hand covering the masked side of his face, which had begun to throb as it always did when he was tired or nervous. When Paul Jenks walked in, Tom leaned forward—he'd only caught a quick glimpse of the young man in the entrance to the cave all those years ago, but he would have known him anywhere. He had his father's face, not feature for feature, but the arrogant expression was the same. And the cocky way he walked toward the desk as if anything he did would be excused or, if not excused, then tolerated.

Paul was surprised, but not startled, to see Tom's masked face. Smiling, he approached the desk, but he could not conceal his nature, which was brooding and covetous of everything he saw.

Blisky showed him to a seat, then remained standing near the windows.

Tom spoke in a mean-spirited tone that Blisky had never before heard. "Why have you come to see me?"

"We're both in the business of buying and selling pearls," Paul said calmly. "I thought enough time had passed."

"Why do you think that?"

"This is business, only business."

"Are you naive enough to believe that? Why has he sent you here? What does he want?"

"Who?"

"Your father. What does he want?"

"My father is dead and has been dead for almost six years."

"I don't believe you. He's been seen in China and in Vienna. Only a month ago someone told me they saw him in America—not looking well, either. Is he very sick from it? Is he almost dead?"

"He is dead, Mr. Street. There are always stories—there are even those who say you killed him."

"You know better. You were there."

"I saved your life, Mr. Street."

"Have you come back to have me repay your kindness?"

"No—I've come to sell you pearls."

"Tell your father that I will treat him and you the way he treated me in Arabia. I won't sell to you or buy from you."

"Those times are over."

"Are they? I have given strict instructions to my men in the Persian Gulf and in Bombay to sell to neither you nor your father. Nothing has changed. And the only pearl I want to see from you is the black pearl he stole from Margot. Do you know the one?"

"No. It wasn't among his things when he died."

"I want that pearl! You can tell him that for me."

Paul rose, looking so arrogant and calm that Tom thought it was Jenks himself standing there.

"You can dismiss me now, but you'll have to deal with me sometime soon," Paul said, reaching into his pocket and taking out a small package.

"He's still alive. He's feeding you these threats—probably raised you on them."

Paul opened the package, then emptied its contents onto Tom's desk—three perfectly round, lustrous pearls. "Pearls from Japan."

"I already have a Japanese supplier."

"Look at them—pink-white, perfectly round."

"Get out!"

"Man-made," Paul said.

Blisky picked one up, then rubbed it on his teeth. It was gritty and the color was superb.

"Tatsuhei Mise made them and holds the patents for them. We're partners. This is the future, Mr. Street."

"Beads, glass beads like Majorca pearls. Get out!"

"It will be like the time when we controlled the Persian Gulf, Mr. Street, but this time it will be Japan."

"Blisky, see Mr. Jenks out," Tom snapped.

Blisky pulled the young man from the office and when he came back, Tom was standing at the windows, holding the Japanese pearls up to the fading light. "They say you can see the bead inside if there's enough light."

"These look perfect."

"Telegraph our people in Tokyo. I want to know more about this."

After Blisky left, Tom found that his anger was turning slowly to curiosity and nervous speculation. It would be like Jenks, forced out of the world's supply of pearls, to create his own. And they looked so real, Tom was thinking, holding them in his hands—so incredibly real.

Chapter Seventy

THE FIRST EXPERIMENTS to culture pearls began in China in the thirteenth century. By inserting foreign substances, in this case images of the Buddha, between the mantle and shell of mussels, a thin coating of nacre developed over the

LUSTRE

images, creating "pearlized" Buddhas. Then, in the 1890s, Kokichi Mikimoto, the son of a noodle seller, began producing half pearls, or "blister" pearls, in a laboratory, and now Tatsuhei Mise was producing perfectly round ones.

Tom's immediate concern was about prices. The pearl market was built on scarcity. If pearls could be produced the way steel was, in a controlled environment, prices for natural pearls would tumble.

That spring, although Paul Jenks managed to sell the small supply of Japanese pearls he had brought to Paris below current market values, the price of natural pearls continued to rise. In London, Lady Henry Gordon-Lennox's necklace of two hundred and eighty-seven graduated pearls brought over twenty-five thousand pounds sterling at auction. In Paris, Madame Polovtov's pearls, four strands weighing almost four thousand grains, were sold for more than a million francs.

But if Tom Street was relieved by these figures, he did not show it. He was as obsessed with the idea of destroying the market for Japanese pearls as he had been with ousting Jenks from the Persian Gulf. He became adept at spotting the differences between his pearls and the Japanese variety. The color and skin texture of Japanese pearls were inconsistent. He initiated an international lawsuit to have the Japanese pearls called cultured pearls. It was hotly contested, but Tom kept the suit going.

He became unpredictable, alternately bleak and discontent, then overexcitable, chasing after diversion, of which Mia seemed to provide an unending supply—costume balls and parties at Maxim's and earthier evenings at Rodolphe Salis' Chat Noir, the club that had, a decade earlier, "created" Montmartre, where Le Petomane, "the world's most accomplished farter," played familiar tunes by breaking wind.

High and low, it was a world of innocent excess over which Mia de Costa ruled, and beside her, sometimes straining in his role as black prince consort, Tom sat, brooding and frustrated, unable to allow himself to return Mia's love.

Mia certainly appeared to be Tom's mistress. They went

everywhere together, and he lavished jewels on her—she wore an exquisite pearl-and-diamond necklace with an eighty-five-grain pink pearl pendant that he'd given her. But she lacked the confidence of actually having him. They'd never made love, although she certainly tried to seduce him. But he was unable to express that side of himself with her. She began hearing stories about his escapades with prostitutes, and things between them became increasingly tense. And then one night Jolie re-entered Tom's life.

Tom and Mia were at the Moulin Rouge when Tom spotted her.

She was no longer kept by the crippled banker Chary. She was parading around Paris with a rather severe-looking black-haired woman, the Marquise de Nucingen, and she was not taking the trouble to disguise the nature of their relationship. The marquise, whose nickname was "la bosse," regularly wore men's clothing. The two women were often seen caressing each other while watching a show. That night at the Moulin Rouge, they took their sideshow center stage and enacted a parody of a witless romance in which Jolie was currently starring. Jolie, obviously drugged, was just barely dressed in a flimsy chemise, and "la bosse" was storming around the stage in a tuxedo, puffing a long cigar.

"This looks like trouble," Mia whispered to Tom. "I think we should leave."

But Tom, who was drunk, insisted on staying.

At a pivotal moment "la bosse" threw Jolie on a chaise longue and kissed her passionately, taking great pains to show the now cheering audience how far her tongue could reach into the beautiful actress's mouth.

All hell broke loose when gendarmes, who had been called, began blowing whistles. The marquise fled the stage, but Jolie remained behind, laughing uproariously.

Mia grabbed Tom's arm and began moving toward the nearest exit, but Tom broke free of Mia, rushed to the stage, and grabbed Jolie, wrapping his opera cape around her shoulders.

She looked bewildered to see him, and caressed his mask with one of her long fingers.

Scooping her up, he carried her outside.

Mia was waiting in Tom's Duesenburg. The chauffeur had the motor cranked and running.

"Where are you taking her?" Mia called out.

"We've got to get her out of here."

Jolie, still laughing, stared at Mia, who looked lovely in a peacock-blue satin gown. She reached out and stroked Mia's cheek.

"Oh, yes," she said. "Let's all take me home."

She kissed Tom passionately, then Tom deposited her between Mia and himself.

"Quickly, before the gendarmes surround us," he said.

The driver took off.

"Take me home first," Mia said to him.

"But why?" Jolie asked in a little girl's voice, wrapping a languorous arm around Mia's shoulder. "Stop her from leaving. You will come home with us, won't you? We'll spend a delicious night together."

When the driver pulled up in front of Mia's house, she ran from the car.

Tom followed. "I told you not to fall in love with me."

Mia was trying to conceal her tears.

"I warned you!" Tom repeated.

"It was not something I could prevent. It's the same as your compulsion to run after that woman."

"What do you know about her?"

"It's what you think you deserve. Fine, if you want it."

"It's not fine—you're enraged."

"Yes! And you'd like me to stop you. I love you. Is that what you want me to say?"

He was stunned by her words. In the distance he heard Jolie's rude laughter.

"Send her away," Mia said. "I love you, Tom."

But he deserved the cackling whore. He didn't know how to respond to Mia.

"Please, Tom, send her away."

As he reached out to touch Mia, he saw his scarred hand. He retracted it and ran back to the car.

Jolie stretched out on the velvet couch in the library of the rue de Rivoli apartment. She was staring intently at Tom's mask.

"It's very exciting to wonder what's behind it," she said, her finger lightly touching the forehead strap.

He flinched and, getting up, walked to the fireplace.

"You haven't been touched by anyone in a long time. I can always tell," she said.

She stood up and pulled her chemise over her head, then stood there naked before him.

She was perfection, with full breasts and tiny pink nipples that stood out stiffly. She had a long waist and full hips, and the tangle of hair at the center of her was soft and thick.

"Don't you want to touch me? I haven't been touched by a man in a long time."

"It isn't what I want anymore."

"How do you know?" she said, walking over to him and touching the mask again. This time he allowed her to. "It would only excite me more to see you."

"You like repulsive things."

"Beauty and the beast all in one. Let me see—please let me see," she panted.

Slowly her fingers undid his tie and shirt collar—she could see some scarring on his neck—then she loosened the neck strap. The mask hung loose but revealed nothing. When she began to undo the small buckle behind his head that held the forehead strap, he heard her breath quicken again. And then she peeled the mask down as if it were a layer of skin.

Her breath caught in her throat. The hidden side of his face was flaccid and discolored—it seemed to contain no muscle or bone, just crumpled skin that hung loosely, as if something were weighing it down.

Reaching up, she touched it. Then, as she kissed the scars, she began to moan.

"You are perverse," he said.

"I want you inside me."

"You want to see all of my scars?"

He began pulling off his shirt. His shoulders and chest were streaked with scars.

"Nothing shocks you or scares you."

"Nothing," she whispered. "Do whatever you want —anything."

He moved her toward the couch and pushed her onto it. Undoing his trousers, he stood above her, his penis arched, full and thick.

Reaching up, she pulled him on top of her. He slid inside her and as he bent over to kiss her, she pushed him back and said fiercely, "Let me look at you—let me look . . ."

She stayed the next day and the day after.

Her sensuality complemented his despair, and when he thought he'd grown tired of her and wanted to discard her the way he'd discarded countless prostitutes before her, she refused to go. She was a tireless and somewhat indifferent lover—it could have been his penis or the bootblack's inside her—but he craved her now. Even her chilly disregard kept him tied to her.

Jessica hid whenever Jolie was in the apartment, for Jolie was jealous of Jessica. She threw tantrums and made Tom choose between them. Tom, thoroughly ensnared by Jolie, drove Jessica away.

And two months later, when Jessica saw Mia de Costa on the street, she confronted her angrily. "Why did you give us up?"

"It wasn't my choice," Mia said.

"But he loved you all along."

"Please, you don't understand."

"If you had loved him you would have fought for him, and me. You've left me alone—and I'm the only one who's fighting for him. His whore has won."

"It will be over soon—it will burn itself out."

Jessica was so beautiful, but her eyes had lost their innocence.

"Try to remember that," Mia said. "It will be over soon and you'll have him back."

"And what will you do?"

"Try to forget—" Mia began, but Jessica interrupted.

"I won't let you. I've written down all your secrets. I want everyone to know how you and he and that witch have lived your lives."

"What are you saying?"

"Everyone will know," Jessica called out over her shoulder as she walked away.

"Jessica!" Mia cried.

But the girl had run ahead and disappeared around a corner.

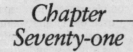

_____ *Chapter* _____
Seventy-one

FOR THE NEXT two years the affair with Jolie disrupted Tom's life. Jessica became estranged from him and watched his deterioration in a detached, clinical way, writing down each evidence of it in a notebook she kept hidden in her room.

"You look after Mr. Rockefeller," Tom said to Blisky one day at lunch at Maxim's. The glittering restaurant seemed garish and was filled that day with many of Jolie's friends, who were talking about him behind their hands.

"But Monsieur Rockefeller wants us to assemble a necklace."

"No, I can't see him. You handle it. Tell him that I'm choosing the pearls but I'm not seeing anyone."

As Tom drank a glass of champagne, he was staring across the room at a young Spaniard, whom Tom had heard was having a secret affair with Jolie. Then all talking stopped for a moment as the Marquise de Nucingen walked in, her cool eyes sweeping past Tom as if he didn't exist.

"They're fools, aren't they?" he said to Blisky, but did not wait for Blisky's reply. "So self-important—they could only exist in this city. . . ."

The young Spaniard, who had just finished paying his check, put on his gloves and looked pointedly at Tom before getting up.

"He looked over to see how many courses we have left—he's going to see her. Oh, she's faithless. I know that about her. Have you ever seen her, Blisky? On a stage she's a complete fabrication, but in life, standing next to her—you think she's my ruin?—I am ruined."

"Do you want me to answer your questions or to sit here like an overfed ear?"

The Spaniard had stopped two tables away to say hello to a friend.

"No, Blisky, talk to me, tell me what the good bourgeoisie thinks."

"I have seen this woman. She's beautiful, as you say, and you're obsessed with her. It's impossible to reason with obsession. But this I do know: It vanishes as quickly as it comes. All at once the mind clears and you get to see who you've been in love with—and you never recover from that blast of clarity."

Tom watched the Spaniard leave. "He's going to see her."

"How do you know that?"

"Everyone's talking about it."

"They have nothing else to talk about."

"I can't keep her and they know that."

"Why?"

"Look at me, Blisky—who would stay with me? It's perfect punishment."

"For which crime?"

"She's having a fitting at Patou. They meet in her fitting room."

"Have you caught her there before?"

"It's like an addiction."

"No, it *is* an addiction," Blisky said.

Tom rose abruptly. "I have to see her."

"You haven't finished lunch."

He handed Blisky some franc notes to pay the bill, then left the restaurant.

On the street he looked around for the Spaniard but couldn't find him. Then Tom began running toward Patou. Finally, flagging a cab, he had the driver race there.

At Patou he momentarily regained his composure. He politely asked for Madame Jolie and the help were equally polite—he paid all of Jolie's bills—but they were also evasive. He suddenly found he could not control himself and ran into the main salon, then into the fitting rooms, which were swathed in pale silk. Seeing Jolie standing on a platform being fitted for a sable coat, he rushed toward her, flinging open the door of the cubicle nearest her.

"What are you doing?" she shrieked.

Not finding the Spaniard in the first booth, he began opening others. Half-dressed women screamed—and Jolie became enraged.

"Have you lost your mind as well as half your face? Get out of here!"

Tom was seething. "I saw him at lunch—he was watching me—he's meeting you here, isn't he?" Tom shouted.

Jolie grabbed a pair of scissors. "Where is he?" she screamed. "Where is my secret lover?" Then she ripped the sable coat off her shoulders and began hacking away at it with the scissors. "Here he is! The only one I've spent the afternoon with. Here he is!" She threw the ruined coat at him and ordered him out of the salon.

The story spread quickly.

Mia de Costa heard about it, but pushed it out of her thoughts—she had thrown herself into a new project, raising money for the Ballet Russe, which had just had a successful first performance at the Théâtre du Chatelet. Diaghilev himself had appealed to her to join with him and his artists—they were about to transform the world, he said. Mia gratefully accepted, and for the moment Tom and his lover and even Jessica were forgotten.

Mia became the center of a new society built around the patronage of the Ballet Russe. Success followed success —*Les Sylphides, Carnaval,* and finally the triumphant sensation of *Scheherazade,* with all its explosive exoticism. It revolutionized fashion and design. All the chic Parisiennes began dressing like potentates—Poiret had them swathed in beads and pressed silk, in tassel fringes, in turbans and ropes of pearls.

Jolie, jealous of Mia's notoriety and the success of the Ballet Russe, wanted her own theater, and she began badgering Tom to build it for her. Théâtre Jolie, it would be called. She had the decorator Hector Guimard prepare sketch after sketch for it, but nothing was quite opulent enough. Nothing anyone could do quite satisfied her. She increased her intake of morphine and cocaine. She taunted Tom when he would not join her.

One spring morning Jolie, who'd been injecting cocaine all the night before and could not sleep, was prowling around Tom's apartment. She happened into Jessica's room and began rifling through her desk. She found the manuscript of a novella that Jessica had been working on; Jolie was a central character. As Jolie read the book, she became enraged. Jessica had described her as a whore's daughter, a witless, tyrannical actress.

When Jessica returned from school that afternoon, Jolie flew at her and began beating her. Jessica called out for her father, but at first he didn't hear and Jolie, grabbing the manuscript, raced down to the library and tossed it into the fire.

Jessica reached into the fire to retrieve it, and Tom came into the room just as Jolie was raising a poker above the girl's head.

Grabbing her roughly, he threw Jolie back.

"See what she's trying to save," Jolie screamed out. "It's all about you."

Jessica pulled from the fire what remained of the manuscript and stamped on it. Sparks flew over the floor.

"Burn it *and* the little monster. She's betrayed you with each word!" Again, she flew at Jessica.

Tom reached out, pulled her away, and held her.

"What is this?" he asked Jessica.

"Whatever it is, it's mine!"

"It's a book about you and me and that cow de Costa!" Jolie screamed.

"Yes," Jessica said, backing out of the room, holding the ruined manuscript to her chest. "All of you and your sad, stupid lives."

She ran out of the room.

Jolie tried to run after her, but Tom held her.

"You'll side with her, won't you? It's just like you to side with anyone against me."

Tom stared at her and saw a glimpse of what she would look like in another ten years. Her anger would eat away at her. She'd become shriveled and pathetic.

"Stop her and burn what she's written!" Jolie commanded, arrogant now, confident that he would do whatever she ordered.

But he held her at arm's length. "Don't ever touch my daughter!"

In reply Jolie spat in his face.

He brought his hand up to hit her, but quite suddenly he understood that it was exactly what she wanted.

"Hatred's the only thing between us," he said, shaking his head. "Your hatred of me, my hatred of myself."

He began pushing her toward the door.

"Let me go," she said in a frenzied voice.

Turning, he grabbed her arm and began pulling her.

"What are you doing? Stop this! Stop it!" she screamed.

It's just as Blisky said, he was thinking. It comes as a startling revelation, then it's over.

He opened the front door of the apartment and tossed her out. Then, slamming the door shut, he stood with his back against it as she pounded and cursed him.

It's over, he kept saying to himself. The nightmare that started with Margot's death had ended. It was finally over.

Jessica was in her room smoothing the rumpled pages of her manuscript. She heard her father calling out from downstairs.

"It's over! Jessica! It's over!"

As she began to write, she shook her head.

"Oh, no it's not," she said. Then, placing her pen on the page, she wrote the title of her novel—*Family Secrets*.

Chapter
Seventy-two

By THAT FALL Tom was back at the office on rue Lafayette dealing with clients, preparing for the Persian Gulf fishery. The affair with Jolie had almost been forgotten, but then Jolie was found dead of an overdose of morphine. The Marquise de Nucingen accused Tom of having driven the beautiful actress to suicide. As a final, macabre note, two nights after the burial, her grave was robbed and the Gogibus pearl she was buried with was stolen. It reappeared on the London market several months later, where it was bought by David Nasis.

In October Jessica Street kept an appointment with a publisher to have him look at her completed manuscript of *Family Secrets.* The publisher realized that it was a thinly veiled account of Tom's, Jolie's, and Mia de Costa's lives and how very easy it would be to publicize the authoress, who at only seventeen seemed to have a commanding insight into the workings of the human heart. He bought the book but did his friend Mia de Costa the great favor of sending her an advance copy.

Mia was appalled. Names were changed, but even the smallest details of her relationship with Tom were kept intact. Jessica had even been so specific to say that Mia had shown up at the chateau to sell Tom a triple strand of black pearls that had once belonged to Catherine the Great.

Mia threatened to sue but was encouraged to withdraw her threat by her attorneys, who said that the action would simply draw more attention to the book.

The novel was published in spring to enormous success. A favorite game in Paris became matching up the fictional characters with their real-life counterparts.

Tom and Mia were hounded by journalists, which affected Mia's life more than Tom's because he had withdrawn once again and rarely went out.

Jessica was swept up by a world she was too young to distrust and just young enough to overvalue. She was courted by the same journalists who hounded her father, taken up by a garish crowd of artists and psuedo-artists. She often saw Mia de Costa and she knew Mia well enough to see just how deeply she had been wounded.

Jessica pretended not to care about any of this, but she was feeling increasingly adrift and began running through an unlikely assortment of unworthy men, as if she were searching for someone to help stabilize her life. Her relationship with her father was now strained almost to breaking.

That summer privately printed English versions of the novel began appearing in London and then finally in New York. One of these copies was given to Jelly Bridge Aspinall Chamblis, who read it, taking particular note of the mention of the black pearl necklace that had once belonged to Catherine the Great.

Jelly dealt with the New York branch of the Jacques Bienenfeld firm, and she called to ask if it was true that Tom Street was now the owner of the necklace. After exchanging telegrams with its Paris office, the firm confirmed that the necklace was indeed in Mr. Street's possession.

In July, rather than going up to their summer retreat in Lenox, Massachusetts, Jelly and Borden Chamblis booked passage for France. At the last minute Tony, who had just finished his final year at the Harvard Law School, decided to join them.

They arrived in Paris the first week in July and took a suite at the Ritz. The day after their arrival, Jelly had Borden call the rue Lafayette office to say that they wished to look at pearls in their hotel suite. They were informed by Blisky that Monsieur Street no longer visited clients in their hotel rooms. If they were interested in seeing pearls, they would have to come to the office.

Jelly was furious. "Who do they think they are?"

"The best pearl dealers in the world," Borden said.

He had, through the years, lost some of his rakish good looks. His dark hair was thinning, his face was puffy, and he had a solid paunch—perhaps because he did too much of what he was doing at that very moment, pouring himself a stiff shot of whiskey.

"He obviously doesn't know who we are," Jelly said, tapping her fingernails on a marble tabletop. "I know what you can do. Drop by the office, leave your card, and have them call us."

"What will that prove?"

"Don't be so modest. If he knows anything at all about American banking, he'll have heard of you. He is an American."

"How do you know that?"

"The book his daughter wrote—I told you to read it. He came to Paris years ago and made a fortune in pearls. He sees almost no one. Maisie Furst told me that when she wanted to have him assemble a necklace for her, he wouldn't even talk directly with her. He sat behind a screen in a little dark room. Maisie says it's because he's terribly scarred from an accident."

"If he saw Maisie, he should see us."

"Exactly . . . maybe I should have her wire him. At any rate, he'll see the Fifth Avenue address on your card and know there's enough money here to take seriously."

"Perhaps we should use your father's name," Borden said, meaning it wryly, but she took him seriously.

"That wouldn't be a bad idea—you go along, drop off the card. I'll wire Maisie."

After Chamblis left, Jelly dictated a wire to the concierge, then dressed to go shopping on the rue de la Paix. As she was leaving the hotel, she ran into Tony, who was with a French boy he had known at Harvard.

Jelly was sometimes startled when she saw Tony unexpectedly because he looked so remarkably like his father. But Tony was more sensitive than Tom had ever been; he cared too much about what other people thought of him.

"Maman, you remember Charles Leblanc," Tony said.

"Yes, of course. You're the actress's son," Jelly said quickly. She did not entirely mean it as a slight, but she did wish Tony would meet some more suitable European friends—the streets were simply littered with young counts and dukes. "Where are you off to?"

"We're having lunch with the infamous Jessica Street. She and Charles are friends."

Jelly looked at Charles with more interest. "How did you meet her?"

"Through friends of friends."

"Why don't you bring her round after lunch? I'd like to meet her."

"Have you read the book?"

"Of course. Hasn't everyone?"

"I haven't," Tony said. "I hadn't even heard of her until this morning. What sort of a girl writes a novel about her father and his mistresses, anyway? What if I were to write a book about you?"

"You'd have very little to say, my dear boy. You run along and have a good time. Do you need money?"

Tony's face reddened in embarrassment. "No, thank you."

"Have a good lunch, and be sure to bring Miss Street round afterward. Good-bye, Charles. Remember me to your mother."

"She means well enough," Tony said somewhat sadly after she'd left.

"You're very good with her."

"Do you think so? Whatever I do never seems enough for her. It's a very bad thing when women have as much money as my mother—they're never quite satisfied with anyone or anything. You remember that when you find yourself trying to marry one like her."

"Listen to yourself. Who else are you going to marry except a woman with some money?"

"I want an independent woman."

"And we have an engagement to keep with the most ravishing one in Paris," Charles said, taking his friend's arm and steering him into a taxicab.

Borden Chamblis tried to get an appointment with M. Street, but M. Street was too busy to see him. As Jelly had requested, Chamblis left his card. When he returned to the hotel, there was a message saying that Street had called, but Chamblis put off returning the call and went to the bar.

When Jelly returned for lunch and read the message, she had Chamblis paged.

"What did Street say?"

"I haven't called him as yet."

"You what?"

"I was put off by the man. I took the trouble to go round to his office, and he wouldn't even see me."

"You've got to return the call."

"Jelly, you'd better calm down or we'll wind up paying a fortune for that necklace."

"I'll pay the fortune, not you, and I don't care. I want it. Call him back!"

Borden did as he was told.

Blisky answered the phone, then passed it to Tom, who was staring down at the address on Chamblis's card as he began talking.

"Mr. Chamblis? This is Mr. Street."

"Oh, yes. Thanks for calling us so quickly."

"I'm sorry I couldn't see you today."

"That's quite all right. I had other things to take care of."

"You were interested in assembling a necklace."

"For my wife, yes."

"What sort of necklace?"

"Well, actually, we were thinking of buying a necklace that you own."

"Which one?"

"Triple strand of black pearls."

Tom looked at the card with more interest. "The Catherine the Great necklace," he said.

"Yes, that's the one."

Jelly pulled the receiver toward her ear so that she could hear.

"It isn't for sale," Tom said.

"My wife has always been fond of it. She has her heart set on seeing it."

"I see. Mr. Chamblis . . . your house on Fifth Avenue."

"Yes, Fifth Avenue at Fifty-sixth Street."

"Was that the house that Mr. Preston Bridge built?"

Jelly covered the mouthpiece. "You see, I told you he'd know who we are," she whispered to Borden.

Chamblis pulled back the receiver. "Yes, that's right."

"Has Mr. Bridge died?"

"No, no. He's not well, hasn't been for quite some time, but he's still alive."

"He had a daughter."

"Yes, my wife. I'm married to Mr. Bridge's daughter."

There was dead silence on the line. Tom's pulse was racing—he felt like a child who was doing something terrifically bad and terrifically pleasurable.

"Hello, Mr. Street? Are you still there?"

"It's your wife who's interested in seeing the necklace?"

"Yes, she has her heart set on it. Do you think we could arrange it? Our dear friend Maisie Furst suggested we call you. We know you don't often deal directly with people —she mentioned the screen and all."

Jelly grabbed the mouthpiece from him and whispered, "No, don't say that. You'll embarrass him."

"It will take a couple of days," Tom said.

Jelly covered the mouthpiece again. "Fine, fine—tell him we'll be here for a week."

Chamblis took back the receiver. "A few days will be all right. We'll be in Paris for another week."

"I see. Well, why don't we say in two days, then, on Thursday. Thursday morning. At my office."

"Yes, that's fine."

"I'll show it to you then. Good-bye."

"Good-bye," Chamblis said, hanging up the receiver.

Jelly whirled around with delight. "I'm finally going to own it!"

Chamblis was staring at her skeptically. "Don't get all your hopes up—that's one peculiar man."

"Oh, you. He's just eccentric, that's all. Parisians love eccentrics. Maisie's told me all about him."

"It was almost as if he knew you."

She looked at him coolly. "Of course he knows who I am. I'm Preston Bridge's daughter," she said pointedly.

Chapter
Seventy-three

CHARLES LEBLANC TAPPED Tony Chamblis's shoulder for the second time in five minutes. "You're staring again."

"I can't help it. Every time I look up, she's staring at me, and with the strangest expression on her face. Look at her now."

"Have you ever seen eyes that color?"

"No, they're extraordinary. And she's so young. I can't believe I'm hearing half the things that are coming out of her mouth. How does she know so much about life?"

"She was brought up in Paris."

"I feel like an adolescent next to her."

"But it's obvious she wants to talk with you."

"Look, there! She's doing it again."

"Shall I make another introduction?"

"No. I can talk with her if I want."

"Well?"

Tony straightened his tie and brushed back his hair with his hand. Then, looking up, he met Jessica's deep blue-green eyes and smiled back at her.

"Good boy," Charles whispered. "Now, I'll distract that greasy little poet next to her."

"She makes me feel so self-conscious."

"Here I go."

"No, wait, Charles. Please."

But Leblanc had walked over to the poet and pulled him away from the table.

Jessica was left alone.

Tony walked over and sat down beside her.

"Do you know my father?" she asked.

"Your father? No, who is he?"

"Tom Street."

"No."

"I'm sorry to have been staring at you all through lunch, but you look so much like him—not as he is now, but what I remember him looking like when he was younger, before the accident."

"What accident?"

"Haven't you read my book?"

"No, I'm sorry. I haven't."

Jessica smiled less confidently than she had before, which Tony liked enormously—she was much more accessible that way.

"Charles said you had read it and were a great fan."

"No, I'm afraid I was brought here under false pretenses."

"You're an American—it hasn't been published there."

"There are some copies. My mother read one."

"I'm not making any money on those. It's a terrible crime if you ask me. They were smuggled out of France and translated in London."

"I see."

"It's amazing how much you look like him. I wonder if he'd be interested in seeing a facsimile of his younger self. I don't imagine he would. I think it would make him feel much worse than he already feels."

"Is he a sad character?"

"I've made him even sadder by writing my book. Would you do me a favor?"

"Of course."

"Would you take me out of here? I don't think I can stand another minute of being the center of attention or talking about that book."

They left the restaurant, then walked down to the Seine and stared out at the Eiffel Tower. It was a glorious day—billowing clouds were scudding across the sky, and below, the bateaux were gliding up the river.

Suddenly Jessica began to cry.

"I'm sorry," she said, regaining her composure. "It's something about you—you're so serious and you look so . . . noble, you make me feel quite ashamed of myself."

"I feel terrible—I should have read your book."

"No, it's not that. I've been fooling everyone, running around this city having a gay old time. You know, I'm only seventeen."

"When I was seventeen I could hardly talk to anyone, I was so shy, and here you are having published a book—"

"I've betrayed everyone I ever loved in that book—my father and a woman who was once very kind to me."

"I'm sure it's not as bad as that."

"It is. I've tampered with people's lives."

"But that's what a writer is supposed to do," Tony said, handing her his handkerchief.

She wiped her eyes. "I don't think my father can forgive me."

"Has he read your book?"

"He knows I've betrayed him. He won't talk to me about it—won't talk to me about anything anymore."

"He'll get over it. Parents always do with their children." He looked down at the river and saw a fisherman sitting in the bow of his boat dangling a line lazily into the water.

"What's your name? I'm afraid I've forgotten it."

"Antony Chamblis, but everyone calls me Tony."

"Tony Chamblis—I like the Tony part."

"Chamblis isn't my real name. My father died and my stepfather adopted my sister and myself. My name originally was Antony Aspinall."

"I like that even better."

"I've thought about changing it back again—my sister wants to change hers, but I don't know. It's been such a long time. So many people know me as Chamblis, and I'm about to begin my career. If I'm going to do it, I have to do it soon."

"What sort of career?"

"I'm a lawyer."

"Why on earth would you want to be a lawyer?"

"My father was a lawyer, and so was his father."

"That's no reason."

"Well, it's too late now."

"How awfully resigned to life you are, Antony Aspinall."

Hearing her say the name, he smiled and impulsively reached out to smooth back her golden hair.

"And you . . . are almost too beautiful."

"How old are you?"

"Twenty-four."

"You seem younger."

"You'd do well to seem a little younger," he said.

"I'm glad you haven't read my book."

"Speaking of that, my mother wanted me to invite you to her hotel to meet her. She's a great fan of yours."

Jessica scowled. "I'm sick of great fans. I'd rather spend the afternoon with you."

"My mother will be disappointed."

"You always do everything your mother wants you to do?"

"No."

"Prove it."

"Let's not go back to her hotel."

"You always do everything I want you to do?" Jessica asked with a smile.

"Oh, you—" he went to grab her, but she ran off.

And he followed.

Chapter
Seventy-four

"BUT, TOM, I don't understand. Why the screen again? I thought we were over that," Blisky said as Tom moved fitfully around the office rearranging furniture.

"Don't ask questions, Blisky."

"You know how impossible that is to ask of me. Who are these people? Chamblis—sounds French."

"I'll find out about him soon enough."

Tom positioned the screen in front of his desk, which he had put in front of a door that led to a rear entrance.

"Now sit behind the screen," he said to Blisky, who

shrugged his shoulders and sat. Tom could not make out his features. "Yes, perfect, perfect."

Blisky walked over to the mantel and picked up the velvet box that contained the black pearl necklace.

"Very beautiful. I never thought you'd part with it."

"Who says I will?"

"You're acting very strangely—even for someone as strange as you. What's gotten into you?"

A girl walked into the office and said, "Monsieur and Madame Chamblis are here."

Tom suddenly looked as if he didn't want to go through with it, then, taking the box from Blisky, he stared at the three rows of perfectly round black pearls. How Jelly must be panting to have them. He wanted to see her face when she looked at them.

"Blisky, you tell them the procedure—just like the old days at the chateau. You knock on the back door after they've been seated. I'll pass the necklace through the slot. I want to be alone with them. Do you understand?"

"Yes, yes, like the old days—*meshuga.*"

"I know what that means."

"It's good to know what you are," Blisky said, then left the room.

Hearing the unmistakable sound of Jelly's nervous laughter, Tom opened the door behind the screen and waited on the landing, holding the velvet box. He was trembling as he strained to hear their voices. Blisky was talking. Sounding apologetic, he said he realized that these were odd conditions, but Jelly interrupted, saying that she knew all about it. Her friend had been through the same procedure.

Then Blisky knocked on the door. Tom waited a moment or two to give Blisky enough time to leave before he opened the door and took his seat behind the screen.

Jelly's head was tilted quizzically, and her eyes were riveted on the screen. She was still incredibly beautiful, though perhaps more willful than proud now. And her features had become severe. He supposed she'd become more difficult to live with. Chamblis reminded Tom of Preston Bridge, although without Bridge's strength. He seemed soft, a schemer, with a petty expression in his eyes.

Chamblis and Jelly exchanged quick, uncomfortable looks, then Jelly sat up in her chair.

"Monsieur Street?" she asked. "Are you there?"

Tom cleared his throat. "Yes, I'm here. Sorry to keep you waiting," he said.

Jelly gasped.

"Is something wrong, Mrs. Chamblis?"

"No. It was your accent. I don't know why—I knew you were an American, it just startled me to hear . . . your accent," she said.

"You were interested in seeing the black pearl necklace."

"The triple strand," Chamblis added.

Jelly looked as though she was caught between wanting to see the necklace and wanting to see through the screen, to place the voice that had so startled her.

"Monsieur Blisky has told you the procedure. I'll pass it through the slot in the screen and you may try it on. If you have any questions, please feel free to ask them," Tom said, pushing the velvet box through the screen.

She reached out eagerly. But it had been such a long quest and now that she had them, she found she couldn't touch them.

Chamblis, who had leaned over, stared at them and urged her to put them on.

"I just want to look at them for a moment," she said.

"Take as long as you wish," Tom said.

And looking at them, even the sound of his voice faded —she couldn't believe her good fortune. She removed her gloves so that she could touch the pearls with her bare fingers.

"So cool," she said. "I can't believe I'm actually touching them."

"There are ninety black pearls, weighing two thousand eight hundred grains. The largest is seventy-three grains."

"They were commissioned by Catherine the Great."

"Madame Chamblis knows something about their history. Catherine the Great had three children by her liaison with Prince Potemkin, one of whom married Count Branicki. The necklace was passed down through his family."

Jelly was transfixed.

"Well, put them on," Chamblis said impatiently. "It's why we're here."

"You'll have to excuse my husband for not appreciating them."

"I appreciate them, all right. They're very pretty."

Jelly lifted the necklace, then placed it around her neck. Chamblis helped her with the clasp.

"There's a mirror on the opposite wall—you should step into the daylight if you want to see them at their best," Tom said.

Jelly rose, her back stick straight, her head held high. Tom smiled, watching her glide over to the mirror, and heard the intake of her breath as she stared at them.

"They're so beautiful—I can't quite believe they're real. They feel warm on my neck, not cool at all—as if they were made for me."

She brought her hands up and arranged them, pulling them back, lenghtening them. She was wearing a pale silver dress with a scooped décolletage, and her dark hair, which was still worn upswept, and her pale skin were enhanced by the luminous pearls.

"Notice the color," Tom said. "What does it remind you of?"

"Like nothing I've ever seen," she said breathlessly.

"A fly buzzing . . . in a room on a warm, sultry day," Tom said tentatively, and Jelly turned sharply toward the screen again. Noticing a mirror behind it, she narrowed her eyes and caught a quick glimpse of his back and the back of his chair.

Looking up, seeing her reflection in the mirror, realizing that she could see him, Tom removed his mask. All she could see was the scarred side of his face. Turning away, she brought her trembling hands up to her eyes.

"Are you all right?" Chamblis said, standing, seeing how ghostly white she'd become.

"Yes, yes, I'm fine. It was just the excitement of finally having them around my neck. I've wanted to own them for a long, long time." She took her seat.

"Don't go on like that, Anjelica, or Mr. Street will leave us no room to negotiate," Chamblis said.

"There is no room for negotiation," Tom said in a grave

tone. Having seen her reaction to his face, he wanted them to leave. "Would you put them back in the box please, Madame Chamblis, and pass them through the screen."

Jelly's hands were poised protectively over the necklace.

"I don't understand, Monsieur Street," Jelly snapped. "We were told you were interested in selling it."

"You were misinformed. Your husband only said that you wanted to see it, and I've shown it to you."

"But I want to buy it."

"It's not for sale." Tom rose. His body was shaking, and his gut was knotted.

"But everything has its price," Jelly said quickly, sounding so much like her father.

"Not this necklace. Please take it off."

"See here, Street, we came to do business with you," Chamblis began, but Jelly interrupted.

"I'll handle this. Monsieur Street, I want this necklace."

"Do you get everything you want?" Tom said.

"See here, to whom do you think you're talking, Street," Chamblis blustered.

"Shut up, Borden!"

To have been left alone with her would have been the ultimate perversity. Tom sat down again and tried to calm himself. "I know you came here to do business. It's just that the necklace is very rare—"

Jelly interrupted.

"Do you think price disturbs me? I'm a very rich woman. You know who my father is."

"Will your father pay my bill, Madame Chamblis?"

"I will pay it, sir. My father suffered a stroke a number of years ago. He's paralyzed. I administer his estate."

She looked so fierce and demanding—she'd gotten everything she ever wanted. But he still had the necklace.

"You operate your father's mines?"

"Gold, silver, and copper," she said pointedly. "Did you ever meet my father?"

"Once, in his house."

"You sold him some pearls?"

"No."

"He treated you poorly. That's why you won't do business

with me. He treated a great many people poorly. I can only hope that you won't be prejudiced against me because of anything my father may have done."

"Still and all, Madame Chamblis, my price may be too high for you."

"Name it."

She wanted to complete the picture of herself at a fancy dress ball—Catherine the Great descending the huge stone staircase under the scrupulous eye of the haughty creatures in the Gobelins.

"Monsieur Street?" she asked eagerly.

But she had to give up something to get what she wanted, Tom was thinking.

"Your price, Monsieur Street—"

"The house," Tom suddenly said.

"I beg your pardon?" Chamblis said, sitting up. "The house? Which house?"

"Your father's house on Fifth Avenue."

"It's not his house any longer. I own it."

"It's what I want for the necklace."

"But that's ridiculous."

"Perhaps, but it's the price I want. What's your profession, Mr. Chamblis?"

"Banker."

"Then you know something about value. This necklace is worth several million, and its value is rising steadily with each year. Your house is worth about that."

"But we'll pay you cash," Jelly said.

"Hold on, Anjelica. Let the man talk."

"It's the house I want. I'll be opening a New York office. I need a place to live and work. I think your house will do nicely."

Jelly looked down at the necklace again.

"You seem very attached to those pearls," Tom said. "You'll want to hold on to them for a long time, then pass them down to your children. Do you have children?"

"Yes," Jelly said distractedly.

"See here, Street, I think your proposal is an interesting one, but you aren't leaving us much room to negotiate," Chamblis puffed.

Jelly took off the necklace and placed it in the velvet box.

"I have to think about this, Monsieur Street," Jelly said. "How soon would you like an answer?"

"Pass the box through the slot, please," Tom said.

Jelly begrudgingly closed the lid and pushed the velvet box back through the screen.

"You may take your time, Madame Chamblis."

"Is anyone else interested in the necklace?"

"Everyone is interested in pearls these days, madame. Good-bye. Call me or wire me when you've made up your mind."

Tom left the room.

"Damnedest thing I ever saw," Chamblis said.

Jelly stood up and walked around to the other side of the screen.

"He could see us perfectly well," she said. "I looked up at this mirror at one point and caught a glimpse of his face. It's been destroyed—totally destroyed."

"We should leave."

She stood staring at the back door, then collected her gloves and purse and they left.

When they were on the street, she looked back at the windows and said, "I want that necklace."

"Well, you're closer to having it than you were before you walked in."

"What I want to know is what on earth my father did to him."

"You won't find out from your father."

"But someone's sure to know. I'm going to find out."

Chapter
Seventy-five

IT WAS THEIR last day together in Paris, and Jessica and Tony decided they'd walk until their feet gave out.

They began at the Trocadero, then followed the Seine to Notre Dame. From there, they went up to the Luxembourg Gardens, then back to the river, crossing it on the Pont Neuf. Finally, at the sandy entrance to the Tuileries, they sat down, their feet throbbing.

While Jessica talked about the history of the place, Tony sat captivated. He was memorizing the contours of her face.

"This isn't fair, Tony. I tell you every thought I have and you simply stare at me."

"It's your youth that's trapped me."

"I did not lay a trap. Anyway, old man, how old are you? Ninety-four?"

"You'd like that, wouldn't you? A new scandal for all your yawning friends; notorious Jessica Street runs off with ninety-year-old."

Taking his hand, she brought it up to her lips, then kissed it quickly. "There, our first kiss. Now you don't have to be so nervous with me."

Leaning over, he kissed her cheek. Just the smell of her—her freshness—made him feel so thoroughly trapped by her that his insides churned.

"Not on the cheek, silly. Don't you have any passion at all? Don't you crave me?"

"I do. I love you, Jessica."

"Don't spoil it, please. Just kiss me."

Leaning over again, he kissed her soft lips, tentatively at first, then she reached around his neck and pulled him to her.

"Do you love me at all?" he asked.

"I don't know," she said, staring at him as if she was quite surprised by her power over him. "I don't like to think of that."

"You'll break my heart without thinking about it."

"Yes, I mean to be very cruel with you."

Getting up, she walked into the garden. He followed close behind.

"My mother was angry that you wouldn't have tea with her."

"Your mother sounds as if she's always angry at everything and everyone."

"Especially since your father won't sell her that necklace. She says he's the most mysterious person she's ever met. He wouldn't talk to her without using a screen between them."

Jessica turned abruptly. "He's using that again?" Her expression deflated.

"What's wrong?" he asked.

"I brought back all his unhappy memories . . ."

"It seems to me your book was necessary to have him see what he'd done to you. He locked you up as if you were a prisoner, then went from one love affair to the other. If anyone's to apologize, it's your father," Tony said.

"Why do you always sound so sure of everything?"

"It's old business, isn't it? Why dwell on it? Let's not spoil a perfectly wonderful last day together."

She knelt down in front of a bed of poppies, and her face was brightened by the vivid reds and oranges.

"Don't you love me just a little, Jessica?"

"Just a little," she said with a smile. "It's my prerogative as a child to be capricious."

Kneeling beside her, he put his arms around her and held her. "I love you."

"I know you do."

"Now you'll torture me—and I've gone to the trouble of memorizing your face just so that I'll see it whenever I close my eyes."

She kissed him again. "No one has ever said anything that beautiful to me before."

"Then you do love me—and you'll come to New York to see me."

"I don't know."

"You're old enough to write a book, you're old enough to travel. Haven't you a friend to take you?"

Mia would have taken her, Jessica was thinking. She got up and began walking away.

"I have to go."

"No, please, stay just a little while longer."

"But I've got to go."

"Will you write to me?"

"Yes, I write to everyone."

"Please be serious with me."

"You're serious enough for both of us. Good-bye, Antony Aspinall."

"You remembered my name."

"It's my favorite of all your names," she said, then kissed her fingertip and, walking back to him, pressed it to his lips.

When she got home to the rue de Rivoli, she found Tom sitting in the library sipping cognac and staring sadly into the fire.

"May I sit here with you?" she asked as she walked quietly into the room.

"I didn't think you'd want to talk with me," he said.

"Why?"

"The book and everything that's happened."

"Then you've read it?"

He looked up, surprised, then looked back at the fire.

"Of course I've read it. I loved what you wrote about your mother—it was like seeing her again. Her superstitions, and how much she had to struggle with who she'd been and where she'd come from. Neither of us thought about those things. We just lived our lives—she was my dearest friend. Sometimes I think I've gotten over it, but it comes back. I hate the past. There's nothing you can do with it, nothing you can change."

"I'm sorry I brought it all back. I was only thinking of myself. I wanted to see, step by step, what had happened to all of us. It was the only way I could make sense of it. I'm sorry if that hurt you," she said, reaching out for his hand.

"It's I who should apologize, Jessica. You showed me what I'd made of my life."

Listening to him, she realized that Tony was really leaving and that she'd miss him and that perhaps she did love him.

As Tom took her hand in his, a butler walked in saying there was an urgent telephone call.

Tom took it in his office. It was Chamblis.

"You are quite a salesman, Street," he was saying. "My wife cannot leave Paris without that necklace."

There's still time, Tom was thinking. *Take the necklace off the market. Let her go, and let the past dissolve.*

"She's agreed to it. She'll give you the house for it."

Tom almost laughed as he saw himself evicting them, turning that monstrous and pretentious art-filled mausoleum into an office or a shop.

"Street? Did you hear me?"

"Yes, I heard you."

"And do you agree to it?"

He wondered if the very idea of throwing them out of the house was what had pushed him all along. Then he had an urge to end the game, to retreat back into his world, leaving Jelly and his children, unaware, in theirs.

"Well, do you agree or not?"

To be in New York again—he thought of Antony and Susan. He could reclaim what he'd left behind and take Jessica along. Start fresh.

"Yes," he said. "Tell her the necklace is hers."

"She'll be very happy."

"I'm sure she will. It's what she's always wanted. Blisky will call you tomorrow and make all the arrangements."

When he returned to the library, Jessica was surprised to see him so filled with energy.

"I've just had some wonderful news. I've traded that necklace Mia brought me for a house in New York."

"New York?" She'd spent the entire time he was out of the room thinking of a way to ask him if he'd let her go there to see Tony—

"I've bought us a mansion."

—but she didn't want to mention Tony to him just then. He seemed so happy to be sharing this with her.

"Will you come with me?" he asked.

"I've always wanted to go to New York."

"And this house is a chateau in the middle of Fifth Avenue."

"I'll have a season in New York."

"Yes," he said, taking her hands. "We'll leave everything behind here—we'll start fresh."

"What a wonderful notion," she said, laughing, as if she believed that both of them could really escape the past.

Chapter
Seventy-six

IN THE LATE spring of 1912 the house on Fifth Avenue was signed over to Tom, and he and Jessica, with two servants, arrived in New York. As soon as word spread that he was in town, he was besieged by matrons and industrialists wanting to buy pearls. Because New York was now the preeminent pearl market, he'd brought along a collection of some of his finest older pieces and samples of the best of the Bahrain and Ceylon fisheries. Among these was the necklace that had taken more than ten years to assemble for Mr. Astor, who had, by this time, died.

Consisting of seventy-seven pearls weighing well over two thousand grains, it was delivered to Mrs. Astor, who wore the necklace that Monday to the opera, where she was entertaining her youngest son's prospective in-laws, people named Worsham. Seeing the necklace, Mrs. Worsham became fretful and began badgering Mr. Worsham to get an appointment with the infamous Tom Street.

"Could we meet at the Metropolitan Club, Mr. Street?" Worsham asked over the telephone Tuesday morning. "I have an urgent problem I think only you can solve." Worsham had a flat, nasal midwestern voice.

Tom agreed to meet Worsham at three, and a little after two in the afternoon he began walking up Fifth Avenue to the Metropolitan Club at Sixty-first Street. He kept getting sidetracked, wandering up and down streets he had not been on in over twenty years.

He was as much a source of curiosity that day, with half his face covered by the black leather mask, as he had been when he'd commandeered Duff St. John's coach and raced up to the Claremont to confront Jelly. But the passersby were rushing ahead more quickly now, not stopping to stare, merely shooting quick, quizzical glances, then walking on, and there were no coaches at all on the streets. The odor of manure had been replaced by the smell of fuel as dozens of automobiles, and automobile buses and trucks, with rigid rubber and wooden wheels, jockeyed for position on the newly paved streets.

There were several hotels where there had been mansions, and on the cross streets, apparel and food stores and restaurants had taken the place of residential brownstones. The city looked flush and hurried, and Tom felt alternately like a fugitive and the hometown boy who had made good.

By the time he got to the Metropolitan Club, he was over a half hour late. The entrance hall, with its white marble walls, had a Renaissance chandelier suspended from a barrel-vaulted ceiling. A servant, who avoided looking at Tom's half-covered face, took Tom's hat and cloak and led him through a Palladian archway into the Great Marble Hall. It was an enormous reception room, two stories high, lighted on one wall by stained glass windows. Worsham was waiting at the base of two flights of stairs. He was tall and had white hair and bushy eyebrows that almost obscured his bright blue eyes. His expression was eager and a little overimpressed with himself and his surroundings.

"Thanks for meeting me on such short notice," he said, leading the way up the staircase.

When Tom and Worsham reached the second-floor gallery, Tom saw Borden Chamblis talking with Duff St. John. Duff looked overfed and lank. His head was partially hidden behind Chamblis's shoulder. But suddenly Duff turned, and seeing the strange sight of a half-masked person standing on the other side of the gallery, he stepped away from Chamblis to get a better look. At that moment

Worsham grabbed Tom's arm and steered him into the sitting room.

Worsham pulled up a tufted leather chair and indicated one for Tom.

"The nature of my problem, Mr. Street, is a ticklish one," Worsham was saying, "and I think you are both the cause and the solution . . ."

As Worsham continued, Tom kept watching the door nervously. There would simply be too much to explain to Duff St. John if he walked through that door. Too much time had passed—and anyway, could Duff be trusted to keep secrets? Tom began wondering how he could get out of the club undetected.

". . . the trouble is Mrs. Worsham . . . Mr. Street?"

"You were saying there was some trouble, Mr. Worsham."

"Well, the real trouble is that Mother is a little put off by Mrs. Astor, and she doesn't think she has the right pearls —like the ones you just brought over for Mrs. Astor. Well, I needn't tell you that Mother is rightfully upset. In the church, people are bound to notice these things, and I want Mother to have a strand of pearls as nice as Mrs. Astor's strand."

"I see," Tom said, opening a black leather case that contained several strands of excellent pearls.

"Of course, you have to understand, Mr. Worsham, that it took over ten years to assemble the Astor pearls."

"We don't have ten years—we've got less than ten days," Worsham said, putting on his glasses and looking at each of the strands.

"No, this isn't right, Mr. Street. I want something bigger than this for Mother, something as large as Mrs. Astor's strand. Don't you have anything like it?"

"There is one very rare strand that belonged to Empress Eugénie—"

"Who?"

"Empress Eugénie of France."

"Never heard of her—I'm not one for history. How big are they?"

Tom took out an exquisite strand of pearls. Each pearl the size of a robin's egg.

"They rival Mrs. Astor's and perhaps even outdo them because they're famous."

"Yes, this is more like it," Worsham said eagerly, grasping them. "How much?"

"One and a half million dollars," Tom said slowly.

"Fair enough," Worsham said, putting the pearls aside, then reaching inside his coat pocket for a check. "That's Street with two E's," he said, writing out a check for the entire amount.

Tom was almost speechless, but managed to say, yes, two E's. He had bought the Empress's necklace at auction less than five years before for less than a quarter of the selling price.

"You have a box for them?" Worsham asked, handing Tom the check as casually as if it were for five dollars.

"Not on me."

"Hmm—well, we should have a box. Will you have one sent over to the club?"

"Of course."

"Pleasure doing business with you," Worsham said, rising, putting the pearls into his pocket.

After saying good-bye, they walked out to the gallery. To his relief, Duff and Chamblis had disappeared. Tom quickly walked down the stairway. In the great hall he picked up his hat and cloak, then fled to the street, where Duff and Chamblis were just about to enter a limousine.

Turning abruptly, Tom walked, half ran, down Fifth Avenue, back to the safety of the mansion.

With Worsham's one and a half million in the bank, Tom spent the remainder of June interviewing art and antique dealers to begin the elaborate job of furnishing the house.

Henry Duveen, known as Uncle Henry, the antique dealer, was eventually given the run of the house. More servants were hired, and by late summer five of the thirty bedrooms had been furnished, as had the library and the upstairs and downstairs sitting rooms. The cavernous main hall stood vacant, although Uncle Henry's plan was to fill it with enormous Rubens canvases, which he had his nephew, Joseph, eagerly snatching up in Europe.

378

Jessica was stunned by the size and scale of the house and spent the first month of her stay assisting Uncle Henry and writing in another journal that contained her New York experiences. She waited until August to contact Tony Chamblis, but he was out of town and would not return until the fall.

As Tom was about to begin the delicate task of tracking down Susan and Antony, world events suddenly took a disastrous turn, and he was completely swept up by them.

Europe had been an armed camp since 1907. Rivalries and tensions having to do with sea power existed between Germany and England. Anti-German sentiment had been running high in England, and new alliances were forming. All sides began increasing the size of their fleets and armies, and world empires, which had been expanding throughout the last century, became issues of political friction. In the summer of 1911 the world had been brought to the brink of war because of a crisis in Morocco, a French colony, in which the Germans intervened. In the summer of 1912 war broke out in the Balkans that involved the Turks, Italians, and eventually the Austrians, the Russians, and the rest of the "old men" of Europe, who were called in to mediate.

The earlier skirmishes had not had too drastic an effect on the pearl market because they were limited to specific areas. But the Balkan conflict raised the specter of a wider European and, possibly, a world war, and the pearl trade, which depended on a stable European economy—one carefree enough to purchase jewels rather than rifles—began to soften. Finally, it collapsed.

The first signs of this were in Bombay, where, by early fall 1912, trading had all but stopped.

Jhaveris wired Tom in New York to say that merchants were going broke. Tom remained calm, patiently reviewing the situation, until word began to spread that the banks that financed much of the pearl trade were becoming shaky. Then Tom left for Bombay, by way of London, on the first boat he could book passage on. At her request, Jessica stayed behind.

Tom put together a consortium of investors in London and Paris and then went out to Bombay. He intended to shore up the weakest of the banks and pearl merchants and to buy up all the pearls he could get his hands on—to stabilize the world price until events returned to normal.

Jessica spent the early fall attending classes at Barnard College for Women. In mid-September her French publisher came to New York to discuss the publication of an American version of *Family Secrets*, but things between Jessica and her father had been going so well, she put the publisher off.

She had few invitations and finally, assuming that Tony must have returned to town, she dropped Mrs. Chamblis a note saying that she was sorry to have missed having tea with her in Paris, but she would be happy to make up for it now.

Jelly was as interested as ever in finding out more information about Street and his daughter. She accepted Jessica's invitation but could not bear the idea of having tea in the old house on Fifth Avenue. Instead, she invited Jessica to join her and her daughter, Susan—there was no mention at all of Tony—in her "temporary dwelling," the house on Gramercy Park.

The house had changed considerably in the intervening years. Although Jelly was only planning to spend a year or two there at the most, until her new Fifth Avenue palazzo, designed by McKim, Mead, and White, was completed, she had brought in a decorator who transformed the dark, overcrowded house into white and gold rococo rooms in the Louis XV style. Gilded moldings adorned almost every wall and door, above many of which were paintings of bare-bottomed cupids, in the Boucher manner, of which Jelly was inordinately fond.

When Jessica arrived, Jelly thought she was like no other girl she had ever seen. It was the combination of her carelessly beautiful looks and keen, observant mind.

"I've read and reread your book," Jelly said as they sat in a downstairs drawing room.

"I'm very flattered," Jessica said, taking a cup of tea.

"Of course I had a motive for reading it. I wanted to find out more about your father. He's the most interesting man I've ever met, or not met—I never saw him."

"Tony told me. It surprised me because my father hasn't used the screen in a long time."

"You know, I had the strangest feeling that he had known us. Did he mention anything about it to you?"

"No."

"Borden said it was just my imagination, but there was something familiar about his voice. And I was surprised, because if he had known us, I wondered why he wouldn't come out and say so. He told me he'd known my father. Did he mention that to you? My father's name is Preston Bridge."

"No, but that's not unusual. We never talk about his business."

"Where's your father now?"

"In India."

"He left you all alone in New York?"

"There are two servants with me who have been working for us since I was a child."

"Still and all, alone in New York . . . you're very independent." Jelly smiled as she sipped her tea. "I don't think I'd like to go to India."

"It's very beautiful."

"That's where he was scarred. Burns, wasn't it?"

"Yes, a fire."

"What a life he's having."

"Even more than I've written about. He's dived for pearls in Tahiti, survived a shipwreck, hunted with maharajas—"

Jessica stopped her recitation when Susan opened the door and entered the room. She was tall, in her early twenties, dark and thin like her mother, but less severe. She had a smile that made her look at once vulnerable and accepting, and rather than accentuating her attractiveness, the way her mother did, she dressed plainly and wore her hair in a tight chignon.

"I've seen you up at school," Susan said, walking toward Jessica with a direct and determined stride, her hand extended. "A friend and I saw you pass by on the way to Classics. My friend said, 'There goes the most insightful girl in the world.' She'd read your book." Susan grasped Jessica's hand warmly.

Then she explained she was helping teach a course in

Shakespeare at Barnard that semester, but added that she wasn't sure she was cut out to be a teacher.

"It's a thankless life," Jelly interjected. "Being a writer must be much more rewarding."

"If you have the talent for it," Susan added, the tensions between mother and daughter already evident. Susan sat down and took a cup of tea. "Maman thinks women should be more decorative than instructive."

"Now, Susan, I've never said any such thing—it's a generational problem. In my day the only women teachers I knew were spinsters."

Susan's eyes rolled, and Jelly smiled tensely.

"I haven't had much formal education," Jessica began, but Jelly interrupted.

"You're self-taught. Exceptional people don't need formal education."

"Maman thinks all of us should be exceptional."

"That's not true, my dear. I've always said it's better to know your limitations than to drive yourself mad trying to be something you're not."

Susan said wryly, "Let me rephrase that—she would have liked us to be exceptional."

Jelly smiled again. Jessica couldn't decide which was more important to Jelly—to have made her point or to put up a good front. As she was about to pour a second cup of tea, a servant came in and said there was a problem.

"What sort of problem?" Jelly asked.

The servant motioned toward the upstairs floor. "It's Mr. Bridge, ma'am."

Jelly sighed exasperatedly, then excused herself.

"It's my grandfather," Susan said. "He's misbehaving again. He won't calm down until she comes into the room. Tony and I think he does it just to remind her that he does have some control over her life even if it's nothing more than to disrupt it."

"Where is Tony? I was hoping he'd be here."

"Probably waiting on some street corner wondering if he's up to seeing you. You've gotten him more scared than I've ever seen him."

"Scared?"

"He's wild about you, but he thinks you're too young and you'll break his heart. Tony is the cautious type. He doesn't like to even enter a room until he knows who's inside and what the conversation is going to be. I can see him now, pacing up and back in Gramercy Park, memorizing his opening lines, and trying to adjust his face to look natural and unconcerned when he sees you." Susan looked intently at Jessica, appraising her. Unlike Jelly, Susan wasn't comparing Jessica to herself. "I can see what he sees in you. You're lovely."

"Thank you . . . I see a lot of him in you."

"I'm complimented. I love my brother."

"And you're both very much your mother's children."

Susan smiled. "And here I was thinking how much I was going to like you."

"You're fighting her off too hard because you're frightened of being like her."

"Mama's right—you are exceptional. You have no idea how I have utterly disappointed her."

"I think she's more disappointed in herself than you."

Susan put her cup of tea down. "Mama's really quite tragic. With all her money, she's never gotten what she wants. When it comes, it's never what she thought it would be . . . she lost the only thing that ever mattered to her."

"Your father."

Susan looked up, surprised. "How'd you know that?"

"Tony may think I'm a child and I know I act like one when I'm with him, but I understand him. He seems so wounded by having lost your father. It's made him very rigid. He knows the way the world should be—what's right and wrong."

"Tony hates my father." Susan paused for a moment. "My father left us when we were children, but I don't think it was as simple as that. Who knows what went on between them. I don't hate him. I'm the only one who keeps his memory alive. I don't think Tony even remembers what he looks like, and the funniest thing is that Tony looks just like him. Staring at him, I see my father."

Jessica flinched—she didn't know why—and just then the sitting room door opened and Tony was standing there, looking—just as Susan had said—as though he were an actor who had memorized all his lines.

And once again, Jessica was momentarily startled because he looked so much like what she remembered of her father before his accident.

_____ *Chapter* _____
Seventy-seven

TOM REMAINED IN Bombay. He and Jessica sent telegrams back and forth. He sounded cheerful, but he said he was overworked, that the situation was worsening and demanded all his attention. Jessica's messages were oblique because she was feeling so unsure of herself. . . .

Tony was pursuing her everywhere she went—at school, on the street, in the park. He asked her to lunch, which they lingered over for hours, or to join him at the theater, where they held hands in the dark, oblivious of what was going on around them.

After the opera one night he took her home and, standing in his grandfather's huge vacant main hall, kissed her.

He was so much more brave than he had been in Paris. She couldn't control him as easily, and that excited her.

"You love me, too—I can feel it."

"Yes. But I'm scared," she said.

"Of what?"

"I've never had these feelings for anyone."

He pulled her into a darkened alcove and held her tightly, then kissed her again. She felt raw and exposed—she seemed to know everything there was to know about him without having ever asked a question.

His hands came up to her breasts, then stroked her neck.

"Marie-Louise will be down in a minute."

"Who's that?"

"My maid. She's like a mother hen—she still thinks I'm her little girl."

"She doesn't know that you're my little girl," Tony said, kissing her again. "Let's lock ourselves away in a room where she can't find us." He took her hand and pulled her into the library. Behind it was a little anteroom with a couch and a small fireplace. He locked the door. "I used to hide in here when I was a boy." He turned, staring at her as she knelt in front of the fireplace, lighting it. She'd taken off her coat and was wearing a satin dress with a scooped neck and a pearl necklace roped around her slim throat.

Kneeling beside her, he held her.

"I've never had a real love affair," she said.

"You'll have one with me," he said, kissing her lips, then her neck.

She shivered. The room was cool, and yet she was flushed. His lips were moving slowly down her neck, his breath was like a feather. He began to slip her dress from her shoulders. Pulling away, she unbuttoned the dress, which fell to the floor and lay at her feet like a shimmering pool. Underneath it she wore only a silk slip. He could see the dark outline of her nipples and the slight flaring of her hips.

Reaching out for her, he pulled her to himself and lifted the slip over her head and kissed her.

"Have you ever made love to a woman?"

"No."

"It's perfect, then. We'll discover it with each other." Now, she felt just as brave as he and began undoing his tie and collar.

"It is perfect, isn't it?"

"Yes."

Her breath caught in her throat when she saw how ruggedly handsome he looked without his shirt—he had a shaggy, burnished chest and corded arms . . .

"Are you still scared of me?" he asked her.

She couldn't answer—perhaps that was fear. But she kissed him eagerly. He pulled her onto the couch. She liked the feeling of tumbling down on top of him—no resistance, no fear, lost with him, moving against him, then with him, in the darkness.

* * *

Their love affair became their great secret. Hidden from everyone but Susan, it was special and set them apart, made them the only lovers on earth.

Susan was their confidante. Not in love herself, their affair became part hers and she cherished it, protected it from her mother's prying eyes.

Of course, Antony began to have difficulty keeping it secret. He wanted to marry her now and pursued her as vigorously to accept him as he had pursued her to fall in love with him.

Jessica refused to give him an answer, and for the time being said that her father's absence kept her from doing anything about it.

But in early December a wire arrived from Bombay saying that Tom would be home within a month.

Chapter
Seventy-eight

JESSICA WENT TO the dock to meet Tom when he arrived from London. It was early morning. There were foreign dignitaries onboard, so the place was swarming with photographers and newspapermen. Tom appeared on the gangplank, trying to hide his face behind his hands, and made his way as quickly as possible through the crowd. He looked haggard, but he brightened when he picked her face out of the crowd.

"You didn't have to come down to meet me."

"I thought all this hoopla was for you."

He looked back at the reporters. "No, it's this European situation—we had the American ambassador to France onboard."

"What's it like in Europe?" she asked as they battled their way through the crowds.

"Very tense."

"Will there be war?"

"I don't think so. The Triple Alliance has been renewed —Germany and England are cooperating. Russia and France seem to have been appeased. But Italy and Austria are tense. It's good to be in New York," he said, hugging her. "It's good that we're both here. Are you well? You look wonderful."

"There's a lot to talk about, but it will keep."

"Yes, let me get home and get settled."

But once Tom got home, there was work to attend to. He had brought back all the pearls he had managed to buy in Bombay—he'd invested a fortune. There was a shortage in New York, and as soon as he got on the phone, dealers and store owners began snapping the pearls up.

Jessica waited outside Tom's office for over an hour, then at mid-morning Tony showed up and wanted to meet him, but Jessica said, no, she would handle it herself, and he left.

At midday she had the cook prepare a tray, which she took into the office. She demanded that he put down the phone and eat.

He was starved, he said. And while he was eating, she began telling him what she had been up to.

"I was writing."

"Oh, not again," he said dryly.

"Keeping a journal—from which you are conspicuously absent. I've been taking courses at Barnard College."

"Commendable," Tom said, reviewing a letter on his desk as he ate.

"I've been seeing a lot of the Chamblises."

He froze. "You what?"

"Mrs. Chamblis invited me to tea, to introduce me to her daughter."

Tom's face drained of color. "To Susan?"

"Yes, how did you know her name? Anyway, I met Tony Chamblis in Paris."

He stood up abruptly, knocking a teacup from the desk. "You never told me that."

"What's wrong with you?" she asked. "Tony was quite taken with me in Paris, and I've been seeing a great deal of him."

Tom stumbled forward and grabbed her by the shoulders. "I don't want you seeing them again."

"What are you talking about? Tony and I are in love."

"What have you done?" he said, shaking her. "What have you done?"

"I've fallen in love! He wants to marry me."

"Stop it!"

"What's wrong with you?" she said, horrified. "Take your hands off me! Father! What's wrong?"

"You can't see him again."

"Why not?" She was crying now. "Why can't I see him?"

Turning, he walked past her and grabbed the telephone. "I'm sending you back to Paris."

"No! You can't do that to me. What's this about? What do you have against Tony?"

Throwing the phone aside, he ran from the room and began calling out for Marie-Louise.

Jessica grabbed hold of him, but he pulled his arm away. "What's Tony done to you? I won't leave without your telling me what's happened!"

The maid appeared on the staircase above the great hall.

"Pack Jessica's things and book passage for her and yourself on the first boat to Le Havre."

"No! You can't order me around like this! You can't do that anymore!" Jessica screamed. "Is it something Tony's done to you, something his family's done? His mother thinks you know her. Is that it? Talk to me, please. Please!"

Burying his face in his hands, Tom said, "It's nothing to do with Tony—it's something to do with me and his mother."

Jessica ran from the hall and left the house.

A taxi picked her up at Fifth Avenue and Forty-eighth Street and took her to Gramercy Park.

"Wait for me," she said as she ran out. She knocked on the front door of Jelly's house. The butler opened the door, and Jessica pushed past him, asking where Mrs. Chamblis was.

"Upstairs, miss."

"Tell her I must see her—it's urgent. Tell her to meet me in the downstairs drawing room. Is Tony here?"

"He's also upstairs."

"He mustn't know I'm here. Please, get her—it's urgent."

As the butler went upstairs, Jessica walked into the drawing room and paced until Jelly arrived.

"My dear, you look awful. What's happened?"

"Close the door, please."

Jelly flushed and, closing the door, walked closer to Jessica.

"When you met my father in Paris, you said there was something familiar about him. What was it about him? You couldn't see him—it must have been something he said."

"It was his voice, and a phrase he used."

"What phrase?"

"He was describing the color of the pearls in the necklace I bought from him. I don't know why I even gave it a second thought, but it was the exact phrase I had once used to describe that very necklace."

"To him?"

"No, it was years ago—to someone else."

"Who?"

"My first husband."

"Where is he?"

"He's dead."

"How did he die?"

"He was lost at sea."

Jessica was trembling. "How do you know that?"

"He disappeared, and I wanted a divorce. We hired detectives. There were lots of leads, but only one seemed convincing—they said he'd boarded a ship, which later was lost at sea."

"Where?"

"I don't know where. Why are you asking me all these questions?"

"Tony looks just like his father, doesn't he?"

"Yes, he does . . . what are you saying?"

"My father was presumed lost at sea on a ship called the *Medusa*. It exploded off the coast of Tahiti. My mother once told me the entire story. He survived—your husband survived."

"How can you say such a thing!"

"My father and your husband . . . Tony and I—" Jessica stopped abruptly.

"No! He died! Tom died!"

Hearing the name, Jessica ran from the room.

Tony appeared on the stairs as she reached the front door. "Jessica!"

She turned, startled.

"Don't ever see me again. Do you understand? Never again!" she screamed, then left the house.

He ran outside, but her taxicab had pulled away.

Jelly came running out of the house, her coat thrown round her shoulders.

"What's she said to you?" Tony asked her.

"Have them get me the car."

"What's she done?"

"Get the car!" Jelly yelled, and he ran back into the house.

The chauffeur drove Jelly to the house on Fifth Avenue. She pounded on the door, but no one answered. She looked up at the caged windows above the door and began screaming, "Mr. Street! Mr. Street!"

Still there was no answer.

This cannot be, she kept thinking, the girl is mad. Tom is dead!

Then, turning her back to the door, she began thinking of ways to prove that he was dead. Who would know? Someone had seen him board a ship. The ship had been lost at sea. Puddy had told her that. She ran back to her car and had the driver take her downtown to Wall Street, to the offices of Puddy, Cuddahay.

A male receptionist stopped her. "May I help you?"

She turned, frantic and nervous, searching for Puddy's face.

"May I help you, ma'am?"

"Mr. Puddy—I must see him."

"Do you have an appointment?"

"No—tell him Anjelica Chamblis must see him immediately."

"Please wait here. I'll see if he's in."

"Tell him it's urgent."

He walked toward the door in the pilastered screen of colored-glass windows.

Jelly's eyes darted around the open office and found that every eye was on her. Young men and old, pale and detached, sat at desks, penned in behind low railings—no wonder Tom had fled. She began to cry.

Two of the men stood up to help her, but she moved away from them and then ran toward the door in the pilastered screen.

"Madame, you can't go in there," someone called out, but she ran into the stiflingly hot inner hallway. The receptionist was walking toward her.

"Mrs. Chamblis, you'll have to wait outside."

"I have to see him."

"He can't see you now."

"When?"

"He wants you to call ahead and arrange an appointment. Perhaps next week."

"My father's money built this firm!" she screamed, pushing past him, running down the hall, throwing open doors looking for Puddy. Finally she found him in his corner office, sitting behind his oak desk, bent over a book that was propped up on several others.

He looked hoary with age, but his eyes were intent. He stared at her with contempt. "What do you want?"

"I have to ask you a question."

The receptionist came running in behind her. "Mrs. Chamblis, you'll have to leave. I'm sorry, Mr. Puddy, she just ran in without waiting."

"There's a question you want answered, Anjelica?"

"Yes, about Tom."

"About Tom, is it?"

"The boat he put out to sea on, the boat that was lost—what was the name of it?"

"Questions about Tom and boats lost at sea. Is this very important to you, Anjelica?"

"Yes, Marcus, important to me and my children. Please, Marcus, if you know, tell me. Was the name of the boat *Medusa?*" Do you remember that, Marcus?"

Puddy looked away. "Escort Mrs. Chamblis to the door," he told the receptionist.

"Marcus, please help me. If you don't remember, then maybe the detective agency you used will. Which one did you use?"

Puddy raised his hand and shook it as if it were a whisk broom cleaning off a table.

"I told you to escort her to the door," he said, then returned to his book.

The receptionist took Jelly's arm and steered her into the hall.

She began crying again, "Marcus, please help me. Please."

Other partners and associates were standing in the hall watching her now.

"Which detectives did you use? I have to know. Please, help me."

She broke away from the receptionist, and stood there sobbing for a moment. When she regained her composure and saw all those men staring at her, she raced down the hall and fled the office.

In the street her driver held open the door to the car, but someone was calling out to her from the lobby.

She turned and saw a young associate running toward her.

"It's the Markham Agency, Mrs. Chamblis, on Broadway," he said. "I don't know the exact address, but it's the agency Mr. Puddy always uses."

"Thank you," she said grasping his hand.

"Of course I remember the case, Mrs. . . ."

"Chamblis," Jelly said to Peter Markham in his dusty, cramped office.

"It was Preston Bridge's daughter—a case of desertion." He was rifling through his files as he talked.

"I'm Mr. Bridge's daughter."

Markham stopped suddenly and looked over at her with more interest.

"You know, Mrs. Chamblis, I'm a very busy man. I can't afford to spend the afternoon going through all my files. We had a lot of files on that case."

"How much do you want?"

"It's not a matter of money, Mrs. Chamblis—"

"A thousand should cover it, I think."

"—I've got lots of clients I've got to attend to."

"Five thousand—just for a name, Mr. Markham. The name of a boat."

Markham grinned. "Five thousand should cover it nicely," he said, going back to his files, then pulling one. "Thomas Aspinall."

"That's it."

"Born eighteen sixty-one."

"The name of the boat, Mr. Markham."

"Disappeared May one, eighteen ninety-one. He was spotted in a bar, O'Leary's, on Fourteenth Street. Someone reported seeing him board a train to Buffalo. You sure it wasn't a train, Mrs. Chamblis?"

"No, it was a boat."

"Here it is."

"The name—" Jelly held her breath.

"Medusa."

"Lost at sea?" she whispered.

"Burned off Tahiti—no known survivors."

She stood up and turned away.

"Mrs. Chamblis—my money."

As she walked out of the office, a phrase Jessica had used was running around her brain—"he survived, your husband survived."

_____ *Chapter* _____
Seventy-nine

JELLY WAITED IN her car opposite the house on Fifth Avenue for over an hour. No one came in or out. When Tony showed up, Jelly had the chauffeur drive a block away, but she could still see Tony banging on the door. No one answered, and finally Tony left.

It was late afternoon when another car drove up to the house and she saw a man, wearing a large dark fur coat, get out. His collar was pulled up to cover his face, but Jelly could see the mask. Leaving her car, she ran up Fifth Avenue, and as the man reached the front door, she grabbed hold of his sleeve and spun him around.

It was Tom.

"Get away from me!" he called out.

As he turned to walk inside his house, she ran in behind him.

"Get out!"

But she stood there looking at his face in the half light of the hall. She reached up to stroke his cheek . . . her mouth had fallen open in amazement.

"It *is* you," she said, her lips trembling.

"What do you want? To remind me of everything I've lost? Why have you come here?"

"Not in anger. Please don't be angry with me."

"Angry? Jelly, you're such a child."

Standing in the middle of the main hall, staring up at the stained-glass ceiling through which the setting sun was now casting sad, pale shadows on the floor, he said, "I've never fit here. Even now, owning it, I don't feel at home."

"Why did you come back?"

"You wanted your black pearl necklace."

"That's so cruel."

"I can't imagine what you've made of me over the last twenty years. But whether you made me a villain or you've glorified me, the truth is I'm not that much different from anyone else—I am as petty as the next man." He walked toward her shaking his head. "The day you left me for that anemic count and took my children, I stood outside this house banging on that door. When I got in, you weren't here. My children weren't here—" His voice was booming in rage, but he stopped suddenly and shook his head again, his hand sweeping out in front of his face as if he could dispell the memory with it. "Time erases nothing. It's useless to try. I have the house and feel no sense of revenge. I've lost everything!"

Jelly reached for him, but he backed away.

"No, don't. It doesn't do any good to be comforted by you. Our life together ended over twenty years ago. I don't want your apology, your sadness, your judgment, or your comfort—I want nothing from you! Our lives are tainted —whatever mistakes we made, however small, however petty, have now brought the world down around our heads!" He turned away from her and ran his hand through his hair.

"I chose to live an extraordinary life and I've paid an *extraordinary* price for having made that choice," he said quietly. "Someone I loved dearly once said that to me. It's the only thing that makes sense to me. It's not your fault. Not mine. We were free. We made choices."

Someone was banging on the front door.

"Mr. Street!"

Jelly turned, startled. "It's Tony," she said.

Tom shook his head sadly.

"Mother! Are you in there? Jessica!"

One of the servants appeared in the hall and asked Tom if he should open the door.

Tom said nothing.

"Jessica! Mr. Street! Let me in!"

"Do you want to leave him out there the way you were left out there?" Jessica said from a darkened alcove above the hall. She'd been sitting in the shadows, listening to everything.

Looking up, Tom saw her. "Where'd you go? I went looking for you. I wanted to explain," he said.

Tony continued banging on the door.

"Don't worry about me, Father. I'm much more . . . flexible than Tony. He needs your explanation."

"How can I explain what I don't understand?"

"It's what you just said—you made choices."

"Do you understand it, Jessica?"

"I think you're all fools—but that's easy for me to say; I'm sitting up here above you, staring down."

"Jessica!" Tony called out again.

"Let him in," Tom said to the servant.

When the door opened Tony burst in and Tom almost smiled to see the man he had become—Tony looked so much like him. But Tony wasn't even looking at him; he ran over to his mother.

"I came back and saw your car outside. Why are you crying? What's happened here?"

But Jelly was speechless.

Then, looking up, Tony saw Tom standing at the bottom of the staircase. His hands were at his sides and he was staring open-faced at his son.

"Who is this? Mr. Street?" Tony took a step closer. His eyes flared open, then he looked away as if what he was thinking was too bizarre. "Are you . . . Mr. Street?"

"Shall I help you, Father?" Jessica said from the top of the stairs.

Tony's head snapped up, his eyes searching the gallery for her. "Jessica? Is that you?" He ran to the staircase, and she appeared on the top step. "What's happened?"

"Tony," Jelly said, "this is your—"

"No," Jessica snapped. "You can't do it that way. It has to be done easily—he has to be told a story."

"What are all of you talking about?" Tony said as he raced up the staircase.

"Look at that man," Jessica said, pointing down at Tom. "Don't you know him?"

Tony looked down at Tom.

"No—is that your father, Jess?"

"Yes. I saw the look in your eyes when you first saw him. What were you thinking?"

"He looked . . . oh, Jessica, what are you saying? Who is he?"

"I told you he's my father."

"But he looks like—" Tony couldn't finish.

"Don't hide from it, Tony," Jessica said sadly, now holding on to him. "It's all right. It wasn't our fault."

Tony pulled away from her and ran down the stairs to stand in front of Tom.

"Antony," Tom said, reaching out to him.

But Tony, his mouth open in horror, his eyes flooded with tears, stared up at the face, then backed away.

"Oh, my God," he said. "This couldn't be." His eyes darted to Jelly. "Oh, my God, oh, my God."

"They said he was dead," she was saying.

"Antony, I had reasons."

Tony took another step backward.

"You're mad," Tony said. "You're madness itself." He

looked over at Jessica, who was now on the bottom step of the staircase. "Jessica, what have I done to you?"

"Antony, you can't blame yourself," Tom said helplessly.

But Tony's hands flailed out at him. "Don't talk to me! I was right to hate you all those years. You've ruined my life!"

"No," Jessica said. "Don't be foolish. Don't give him that much power over your life."

Tony's fist flew up at Tom's face, but Tom blocked it and held it fiercely, and for a moment the two men were tied to each other by a bond of hatred and love that neither could break.

"I know you hate me and you want to hurt me, but I won't let you," Tom whispered.

Tony pulled back his hand and ran out of the house.

Jelly ran after him.

Tom and Jessica were left standing alone in the half light.

"I feel sorry for you," she said. "But then again I always have. I think it's good that having this house has not made you any happier. If it had, I would detest you."

"I'll close the house up. I'll have it torn down. We'll go back to France. Come back with me, Jessica."

"No, no, no, no—I don't want to see you for a long time," she said slowly as she began to climb the stairs. "All I want is some money."

"You can have as much as you want."

"Good. I'll want a lot."

"But where will you go?"

"Away from you, Father. I want to get away from your extraordinary life."

Something inside Tom collapsed as he watched her turn and walk up the stairs. He felt numb, and he welcomed the numbness. It spread out from his heart until it infused his body with a sense of weightlessness. He was adrift. No one was left, nothing held him—no comfort, no pain, no feeling. That was the price he had paid, and it was extraordinary enough because it had been so unexpected.

Chapter
Eighty

JESSICA LEFT THE house that night. Tom left for Paris the next day, after ordering that the mansion on Fifth Avenue be torn down.

The events that had taken place in New York took their toll. Tom had aged ten years in a few short months, and adding to his malaise was the atmosphere in Paris. A testy peace was holding Europe together, little else.

By day he worked at the office on the rue Lafayette. At night, at home, he saw no one.

The cultured-pearl suit against Paul Jenks and his Japanese partners continued, and Tom was called upon to testify. Asked if he or anyone else could tell the difference between the Japanese pearls and natural pearls, Tom stunned the courtroom by successfully making the correct choice in ten separate tests.

"The reason is not so stupefying," he told the packed courtroom. "The Japanese pearl, what I choose to call the cultured pearl, often lacks a sufficient amount of pearl substance—what we call nacre. The color is different. If you look very closely, you can see the mother-of-pearl nucleus at the center—it's almost like a shadow. It doesn't take an expert to see some of these things, but it is that small percentage of cultured pearls that look so remarkably like natural pearls that I worry about. How easy it will be to substitute one for the other and still charge the natural pearl rate. It is for this reason alone that you must consider our suit."

But the case continued to drag on, and seeing that it would not be settled easily, Tom underwrote the development of an X-ray machine to detect the mother-of-pearl nucleus. Within months, the firm of Jean Perrin and Sons succeeded in producing it.

Tom sat alone in his huge apartment feeling himself grow brittle. He made money—more of it than he had ever made, for pearls were scarce and he seemed to own outright or control the entire world supply.

Then in early June he received word that David Nasis wanted to meet him.

At first Tom said no, but Nasis was persistent. In one week he called fifteen times from London.

"What could it hurt? He's an old friend," Blisky said in the office one day.

"That's exactly what could hurt the most. Tell him I'm not here."

"He won't believe me. He knows you're here."

"Tell him I'm dead."

"That, I think, we are all beginning to believe."

A week later Tom was at home on a rainy, unseasonably cold night. A servant came in and handed Tom an envelope, which, he said, a gentleman had just delivered.

Tom jumped from his seat when he saw what was inside.

It was Margot's ring—the black pearl—perfectly beautiful, untouched, as if she'd just taken it off her finger.

He raced to the front door to chase after the messenger, but found Nasis waiting there with an awkward smile, which dissolved as soon as he saw Tom's face. Although they had done business, they had not seen each other in years and the mask was a shock to Nasis. Rather than remain gawking, he smiled again and his tone of voice became familiar, almost glib.

"D-d-did you think I was trying to contact you for n-n-no reason at all?"

Tom was dumbfounded.

"Well, w-w-won't you invite me in?"

"What? Yes, yes, of course," he said, holding open the door. "Where did you get the ring?"

"All in g-g-good t-t-time. You know how l-l-long it t-t-takes me to s-s-say anything, and it's so dank and cold for a s-s-spring night. Do you think I could have some b-b-brandy?"

"Come into the library—I've got a fire going."

In the library, Nasis stood with his back to the fireplace.

Tom poured the brandy, handed him a snifter, and stared down at the pearl ring.

"You've found him, haven't you?"

Nasis sipped his drink.

"Impuls-s-siveness was always your best and worst f-f-feature, Tom. L-l-look what it's gotten you," he said, indicating the large mahogany-paneled room. He put the snifter on the mantel. "I've heard about what's happened t-t-to you. Jessica told m-m-me."

"You've seen her?"

"Last w-w-week in London."

"Is she still there?"

"She's g-g-gone back to the States. Can't seem to f-f-find a place to s-s-settle. She looks so m-m-much like Margot. I could have almost f-f-fallen in love all o-o-over again. I tried telling her that it w-w-wasn't your f-f-fault. I think she knows th-th-that, and that she'll come back in time."

Tom stared at the ring again.

"The r-r-ring came into my p-p-possession while Jessica was in London. I th-th-thought of giving it to her, but . . . it wasn't mine to g-g-give. It's yours, Tom. I b-b-bought it back for you."

"He is alive, isn't he?"

"If you call it living. About th-th-three weeks ago a poor old Jewish merchant with whom I s-s-sometimes trade came to me and said that he was thinking of acquiring a b-b-black pearl ring, one of the most beautiful b-b-black pearls he'd ever seen. But he couldn't buy it on his own—he w-w-wanted a partner. Of course I said I wanted to see it, and he said it w-w-would take a day or two. The man who owned it w-w-was living up in Norfolk and the merchant had to go up there to fetch it b-b-because the man was too s-s-sick to bring it down to London."

"It's Jenks."

"The m-m-merchant brought me this. I recognized it immediately and b-b-bought it."

"Tell me where he is."

"The old peddlar was s-s-sworn to s-s-secrecy, but I p-p-paid him well enough. He says the man who s-s-sold

400

him the ring is deathly ill—almost paralyzed, and blind. I-ve d-d-done my r-r-research," Nasis said, drawing nearer to Tom, his voice dropping. "One of the l-l-late forms of syphilis is called t-t-tabes dorsalis, also called locomotor at-t-taxia . . . crippling occurs, and blindness and m-m-madness."

Tom's face was flushed with rage and excitement. "Shall we kill him together?" he said fiercely.

"Hatred certainly s-s-seems to have b-b-brought you back to l-l-life."

"He deserves to die. Tell me where he is and we'll do it together."

Nasis straightened and his eye fell on a photograph of Margot that was in a frame on the mantel.

"I'm going to be m-m-married," he said. "I don't love her the way I loved Margot, but I feel free of all this h-h-hatred for the first time in many years."

"Let me have him, and I'll free myself. I've never asked you for anything, Nasis, but now I'm begging you—give him to me."

Nasis turned toward the hearth.

"Look what he's done to me, Nasis. I've lost everything I ever loved. Let me have him, Nasis. Let me kill him."

Nasis looked up at Tom's disfigured face, then back down at the fire.

"He calls himself Lord Tellstone. He l-l-lives in a dilapidated mansion in Great Yarmouth, on the eastern c-c-coast."

"Thank you, Nasis."

"I d-d-don't know that you should thank me—this hatred of yours may be the v-v-very thing that destroys you."

Chapter
Eighty-one

ON THE BOAT crossing the Channel, Tom kept feeling for his gun, which he'd wrapped in a scarf that had belonged to Margot. It was as if she were holding it—and they would both have their revenge.

Racing across the English countryside, her homeland, Tom's head was pressed against the train window. The surroundings were lush. Stone walls crisscrossed the hills. It was a calm and sequestered place that reminded him of Margot's placid eyes and knowing smile. The people sitting in his compartment had the appearance of having a place in the world. He wanted to plead his case for murder with them. Would they encourage him? Would she have wanted revenge as much as he?

When the train reached the coast and he saw the gray expanse of water stretching out beyond the cliffs, Tom remembered being adrift in the lifeboat with Jenks. He could have strangled him then or watched him die slowly of hunger and thirst. Something Jenks had said came back now to haunt him.

"We're alike, you and me—we survived."

It was true—the hatred that lay at the center of Jenks's being was now nestled in Tom's heart. It had to be killed off or it would overtake him completely. He would do it quickly this time. He saw how it would happen—he would pull the trigger, Jenks would fall. He would breathe deeply, finally free of Jenks's contagion.

The town of Great Yarmouth was covered in clouds and mist and a chill rain.

During the half hour it took him to walk to the mansion,

Tom kept feeling for the gun. It spurred him on, warmed him.

Standing on a spit of land that jutted out into the sea like a long crooked finger, the house was now gray and dim, but it looked as if it had once been outlandish, built by some native son who'd gone off and made a fortune, then returned to show his once scornful neighbors how well he'd done.

It had a central dome and two towers, all of wood; a good wind would blow it down one day. The gates had rusted and were flung open like a pair of palsied arms. The drive was overgrown.

Tom pushed open the front door, which was ajar, and walked into a dusty hallway. There was not a sound. The rooms nearby were empty save for some tattered furniture.

Suddenly there was a pounding from above.

Pulling out the gun, Tom climbed a back stairway and heard more pounding and some muttering. The voice was raspy and thick. The smell of feces and urine hung in the air. Rounding a corner, the gun held out in front of himself, Tom walked slowly along, peering into the rooms on either side of the hall. Empty. Then, at a corner room, he stopped and listened. The pounding had ceased. Someone was talking.

"Let me piss—cut open my bladder. Let me piss."

It was Jenks.

Tom stepped into the open doorway.

Jenks's head snapped around. His eyes were glazed over, even paler than Tom remembered. They looked like opaque white glass.

"Who's there?"

Tom said nothing.

Jenks stood in a corner, wearing a robe which hung open. Underneath, he was naked, and one hand held his flaccid penis. He was trying to urinate on a wall. Reaching up, he banged on the wall with his fist.

"Piss! Let me piss!"

His head looked oversized because his body was so wasted. His hair was white and matted, and his skin, scaled and reddened, hung loosely on his sharp bones. He shivered, then walked shakily toward the door. His legs had become twisted and bowed, and he groaned with each step.

At the door he sniffed the air, like an animal.

"Who's there?"

Tom held the gun near Jenks's head.

"That you, Paul? What you doing back here?"

Jenks's eyes were trained on an indistinct point. His twitching hand reached out to paw the air. Tom took a step backward. Jenks's head jerked to the left.

"Who is it?" He took a painful step. "There's no money if that's why you've come." He batted the air. Tom moved in front of him, and Jenks turned his head to the right. "There's no money, no piss, no piss, no money—"

"Jenks!" Tom called out.

Jenks smiled knowingly.

"Oh, I know that voice. I know it. I know it. I know it." Turning slowly, his opaque eyes grappled with the darkness. "Is it you?"

He began walking toward Tom. He reached out and touched the unscarred half of Tom's face.

"Tracked me down," he said. "Knew you would."

He hurled himself away from Tom, fell and landed with a thud, then began crawling toward a door, but the pain was too intense.

Tom knelt above him, training the gun on him.

"Oooh, I'm in more pain than I was on that boat. And you, you damn fool, saved my life." Jenks laughed. "Just want to do away with me now, don't you?

"I was always the blackest part of your soul, Tom—the blackness you could never come to terms with. You still don't understand it. It's why you kept me alive. I fascinated you. Your twin, almost—out in the world on our own with nothing but our wits. Set free, weren't we? Castoffs from a sinking, fiery ship. I like to see the world as that ship, and we pushed off and saved our necks from the dwindling evil world.

"I couldn't have survived without you, Tom. Didn't you ever wonder why you let me survive? Without me, you didn't look so good. The very first time, on that dock with the midget, the way you came at me—all indignation and anger—not so much different than me! We were both made of impulse and anger. You just got the clean end of things, boyzo. If only I'd been born in your clean bed . . . how I hate you for having that clean bed." He lay on the floor, panting. "Now I'm infection and disease. Every inch of me—" He groaned. "Such pain—I could die."

His twitching hand reached up, touched Tom's leg, then his hand. Finally, Jenks felt the gun and pulled it toward himself.

"I want to die now, Tom. Can't stand this pain any longer. I brought you here to do it. Sold her ring to the old Jew, told him to sell it to you or Nasis. Knew you would come —Nasis is such a coward. You kill me, Tom. Fulfill your destiny and mine. Kill all the evil in the world. Hold the gun to my head and shoot me. I want to die. I want you to do it. Kill me now, Tom. Kill me."

Tom's finger was poised on the trigger. In another moment he'd be free.

"I infected her because I wanted to leave a little of myself inside her. Kill me for that, Tom. Kill me."

Tom shook off Jenks's hand, then brought the gun barrel down to Jenks's head and placed it squarely against his left temple.

"That's it—send me off like a rocket; here one minute, gone the next."

Tom's hand shook.

"Don't go soft on me. Kill me!" Jenks hissed.

Tom closed his eyes. *By fighting him, you've become him.* Margot's words to him before he left for Arabia—

"Do it, Tom. Do it now!"

He'd never willfully killed anyone.

"Kill me now!"

At the last moment Tom thought about what Nasis had said—that by killing Jenks, he might also destroy himself. What good would his revenge do?

Tom raised the barrel just above Jenks's head and fired.

Jenks was jolted by the sound and screamed. His hands pawed at the floor. "What did you do? Are we dead? Am I dead?"

Tom rose slowly. It was as if the brutal sound of the shot had awakened him from a dream.

"Don't leave me here like this," Jenks called out. "I want to die. Kill me!"

"All in its time," Tom said, "all in its proper place." And turning, he walked out of the room.

Epilogue

Redeemed

Chapter Eighty-two

IN THE EARLY summer of 1914 Mia de Costa went to London with Diaghilev to open the Ballet Russe's English season, which was a triumph. In July, she returned to Paris, where the mood was growing more and more frantic as rumors of war flared.

At the end of July she invited her old friend and former lover Gustave Laurent and his new wife to her apartment to hear Gustave's new work—he'd begun composing in the last year or so.

She sat spellbound, listening to his dissonant music, which was half charming, almost lulling—half grainy and sober. Suddenly a servant rushed into the music room to announce that Austria had just declared war on Serbia.

"Thank God there will be war!" Laurent called out.

And Mia, closing her eyes, said, yes—it was good to have it finally be here.

On August third Germany declared war on France and everyone poured into the streets to celebrate.

Mia joined a parade that was winding around the Place de la Concorde. She was lifted up and placed upon a white horse. People were running alongside throwing roses, screaming joyously. People had been panting for war—well, not for war exactly, but for a glorious, operatic version of war. They envisioned men dressed in plumes and gold braid, unsullied by wounds or death.

At the entrance to the Ritz Mia thought she saw Jessica Street. She turned and called out to her, but Jessica, if it was Jessica, walked off and was lost in the crowd.

By the end of August, offstage battles were creeping closer. One could hear bombs dropping, and refugees, having fled their homes in Belgium, wandered Paris in rags. The Grand Palais and several schools were turned into hospitals. Cinemas and cafés were closed. The grand boulevards were deserted. Paris was dark, as if a black net had been thrown over it.

At night Mia watched aerial bombardments from the terrace of her apartment as electric beacons swept the skies like glittering needles piercing the darkness. The world was suddenly steeped in danger and death, and the romance of war withered with each passing day.

By October Mia was using her Mercedes as an ambulance to carry the wounded into the center of the city from the railway stations. She worked for hours on end, and at night she slept dreamlessly. She was numb with exhaustion and fear. Her world, a world of beauty and art, was collapsing more quickly than she could have imagined.

Early in the morning on the last Sunday in October, a servant shook her awake and said that someone was waiting to see her.

"At this hour? Who is it?"

"Her name is Susan Aspinall."

"I don't know her. Tell her to come back later."

"I've already told her, madame. She won't leave."

"Oh, all right. Tell her I'll be with her in a moment."

Stepping into slippers and pulling on a robe, Mia left her room and walked down the chilly corridor to a small mauve and green sitting room. When she opened the door and looked at the young woman, she thought she recognized her.

"Miss Aspinall?"

"Yes, Madame de Costa," Susan said, walking toward her. "It's so nice of you to see me."

The girl was lovely in spite of what she had done to herself. She was dressed in dowdy, dark clothes. Her hair was particularly unattractive, pulled back in a tight chignon.

"Have we met before?" Mia asked.

"No, but I believe you're a good friend of my half-sister, Jessica Street."

"Half-sister? I didn't know Jessica had a half-sister."

"Yes, my father was married in New York years before he married Margot Vale."

"And I thought I knew him well. He never said anything

about another family." Mia found herself trembling. She didn't like talking about either Tom or Jessica.

"If you've come looking for Jessica, I think you've made a mistake. I haven't seen her in years."

"I know that. She's told me a great deal about you."

"You've seen her?"

"A month or two ago in New York."

"We didn't part the best of friends."

"She loves you dearly, Madame de Costa."

Mia's eyes brightened. "Did she say that?"

"Yes. She told me all about her life with you."

"I did what I thought was right for her and . . ."

"And my father—yes, I'm sure you did. That's why I've come to see you. I'm trying to find my father."

"Find him? In Paris?"

"Yes. Jessica didn't know where he was. She'd heard he was in Bombay, and it took me forever to get through to a Mr. Jhaveris down there. He assures me that my father isn't in Bombay."

"Have you seen Blisky?"

"Blisky will only say that my father has suffered enough, that he should be left alone, and that he isn't in Paris."

"Why do you think I know? I haven't seen your father in a very long time."

"Jessica told me that she was sure you were the one person he would have been in touch with. She said that he loved you very much."

Mia walked to a window. Outside, the boulevard was as gray as a cadaver. "Jessica was always a bit of a romantic when it came to her father and me. Is she well? What's happened to her?"

Susan told Mia the story of what had happened to all of them in New York.

Mia's eyes filled with tears. "Perhaps Blisky's right; Tom has suffered enough and made the rest of you suffer. My God! One part of his life has been so glorious—the other such hell."

Susan joined Mia at the window. "That's why I've come to see him," she said quietly. "Can you help me find him?"

"You risked your life coming to France now."

"It doesn't matter. I have to see him. I missed him in New

York—I know he would have seen me there if he could."
Susan began crying. "You don't understand what it would
mean to him—everyone's deserted him. He's got no one."

Mia put her arms around the girl. "Mean to him or to
you, my dear?"

"I need to help him now and be helped by him."

"Oh, my poor dear girl, don't cry."

"I need his blessing to go out and live my life. It's as if I'm
still in mourning for him—I can help him, Madame de
Costa. I know I can."

"Not with tears, I'm afraid. I think he's shed more than
his share."

"No, I only let down my guard with you because I know
how much he meant to you. I'm planning to be very good
with him. I won't collapse. He won't have to take care of
me."

Mia smiled. "What will you be for him? What the English
say—very brave?"

"I want to forgive him—no one else has. My brother
hates him, my mother blames him, Jessica blames him
—even you do, I think. I just want to forgive him."

Mia stared warmly at Susan and stroked her cheek. "Yes,
that's the right thing to do for him." She paused for a
moment. "There is a place you can look. It's where I first
saw him, a château he owns in a little town near Paris called
Chaumontel."

"You think he's there?"

"If I were he, I would be—it's one of the most beautiful
places I've ever seen."

Susan grabbed Mia's hand and kissed it. "Thank you,
Madame de Costa."

Mia blushed. "You're doing what I tried to do years ago. I
wanted to help him."

Susan turned to get her bag and shawl.

"But you can't go looking like this," Mia said.

Susan looked down at her clothes. "What's wrong with
the way I look?"

"You said it yourself, my dear. You're dressed as if you're
in mourning. You should be wearing something young and
pretty—he likes that. And your hair . . ." Mia began walking around Susan, seeing what could be done.

"My mother hates the way I wear my hair."

"But it's so much easier hearing it from me, isn't it?" Mia placed her arm around Susan's waist. "Come, let's dress you up—I have something that might be perfect for you."

An hour later Susan was standing in the front hall wearing a light wool berry-colored suit that had been designed for Mia by Paul Poiret, Mia had brushed Susan's hair and arranged it in a loose, wavy style. Susan kept primping.

"Now leave it alone—it looks fine."

"It does or I do? I feel as if it is wearing me."

"No, it's you. You're radiant."

"I hope he's there."

"I hope so, too. He deserves to see you this way."

"Jessica was right. You did love him, didn't you?"

Mia smiled sadly. "Yes, very much."

"Then you have to tell him."

Mia blushed. "Now, you've got your directions."

"Yes, I take the train to Chaumontel from the Gare du Nord."

"And ask anyone there—they'll know the house."

"Thank you, thank you so much," Súsan said, and then left.

Mia walked back to her bedroom and took out the pink pearl necklace that Tom had designed for her.

She sat down at the vanity and held the necklace up to her throat. The pearls felt warm to the touch and seemed to brighten as she slipped them on. He'd always said they needed to be worn to keep their soft lustre—and suddenly she felt that perhaps she didn't have to feel so sad every time she thought about him.

Chapter
Eighty-three

HE WAS LIVING alone in the little chateau, but he was not as desolate as he'd been when Mia first saw him. He spent his time reading, and writing a journal, which he was much too modest to call a biography, although it did have to do with his early life and all his adventures.

He was writing when Susan appeared at the front gate in a taxi. He knew immediately who she was—she looked so much like Jelly, and also like his mother. She had that same look in her eyes. You could see the desire for adventure, and the stifling wariness that held it in check.

Susan was tentative at first, then so much like the little girl who had once come running up to him calling, "Papa, Papa," to tell him her latest story.

They sat in the garden and talked and laughed. She was glad to find out that he, too, had hated the dreaded Aberdeen. She sat rapt as he told her all about his adventures onboard *Medusa,* on the atoll in the South Seas, and in India.

"I want to go out into the world," she said when he paused to take a breath.

"You should do it. Don't be scared of it."

"You're not sorry you made your choices."

"What difference would it make?" he said impulsively, then thought about his choice to spare Jenks and free himself of his own hatred. "That's not true. The only thing we're measured by is the quality of our choices. But tell me what you mean by wanting to go out into the world."

"I want to break free."

"Margot wanted that—I did, too."

"I want something extraordinary in my life. There's time to be settled, isn't there?"

"So I'm finding," he said with a smile.

"You amaze me—I thought I'd find a lost, sad shell of a man."

"Are you disappointed?"

"A little. I wanted to save you."

"How?"

"To forgive you," she said, then stopped. "I do forgive you for leaving us. I forgive you because you did what you had to do, and you're human and fallible."

The garden was bathed in a golden light as the sun set, and a light breeze blew across the terrace. Tom shivered. The breeze carried the scent of burning leaves and reminded him of something ineffable, perhaps only of cooler, shorter days to come. He looked at Susan and smiled.

"You have saved me."

She had tears in her eyes.

"I'm frightened, Papa," she said, although he thought it was said with little conviction, more to see how, or if, he would respond.

Leaning over, he held her. "May I stay with you?" she asked.

"For as long as you like."

"And will you kick me out when it's time for me to leave so I can go out and live my life?"

"Yes, I'll know just the right time."

"Oh, Papa, I didn't want to cry—I didn't want to be the little girl anymore."

"Sh, it's all right. Everything's all right now."

She stayed with him for two weeks and then, without his saying anything, she decided it was time to go. She wanted to leave Europe and America behind. She was heading to India to see if she could get a job teaching there, although she wasn't sure that was what she wanted to do with the rest of her life. He gave her the keys to the house on the Malabar Hill and a letter of introduction to Jhaveris and to the Maharaj Rana of Dholpur.

When the day of her departure arrived and they were at the station waiting for the train, Tom gave her Margot's black pearl. He told her the story of how the pearl had accumulated all the love of each of its owners and how it would protect her and how much Margot would have wanted her to have it. Susan slipped it on. It fit perfectly, as if it had been meant for her all along. And as her train pulled out, she waved to him from her seat, then stared down in wonder at the pearl, as if it were a star she would follow.

After the train left Tom was alone on the platform, feeling more lonely than he had before she'd arrived; she'd brought back to him the feeling of what it was like to love and be loved.

But, reconciled to being alone, he went back to his daily routines—reading, writing in his journal, doing some business—although with the war, there were very few pearls being bought or sold. Then one day a servant came up to his study and said that a woman was waiting to see him in the garden.

When he walked downstairs and saw that it was Mia, he was so pleased to see her, he just stood there staring at her.

She had turned and was holding her hand out to him.

"Tom, there's so much between us," she said so quickly that he didn't know if she meant history or the charged atmosphere between them. There were so many possibilities —there were love and hope, those most triumphant of all of life's convictions.

Hope is the only thing that ever frees us from the past, he thought as he reached out to take her hand.

September, 1986
New York City

416

Acknowledgments

LUSTRE is a work of fiction. To the best of my knowledge all of the characters in it are of my own invention. Many people and organizations help with the writing of a book like this, and I'd like to thank those who generously gave of their time and information:

The New York Public Library, New York City.
The South Street Seaport Museum, New York, City.
The British Council Library of Sri Lanka, Colombo, Sri Lanka.
The National Museum of Sri Lanka, Colombo, Sri Lanka.
The David Sasoon Library, Bombay, India.

Sydny Weinberg Miner, Rena Wolner, Bill Gros, Richard Reuter, Maurice Shire, Frederick Ward, Mark Tague, Hubert Rosenthal, Jacques Rosenthal, Coco Chaze, Julius Cohen, Michael Coan, Norman Bowers, John McHugh, E. Sadler Morgan, Gille Artur, Hugo Teutra, Thierry Graffe, Sherry Morse Maccabee, Mere Raina Faura, Jean-Claude Girard, Ernest D. Reuter, Ken Butler, Ralph Esmerian, Penny Proddow, Benjamin Zucker, Rachelle Epstein, Jimmy Chow, Priscilla Chen, Moussa Naseem, Fazli Saleem, Rodney S. L. Jonklaas, Dr. Hiran Jayewardene, Herbert Gunaratne, Arthur C. Clarke, Pravin M. Nanavati, Mahendra Jhaveri, Fatehchand C. Karani, Modhukar Keni, M. R. Bhave, and Henry Morrison.

Bibliography

STUDENTS OF THE pearl trade will forgive me for having tampered with some facts; my intent was to evoke history rather than report it. The Ceylon fisheries of the 1890s were some of the worst in that area's history. Because of the necessities of my plot, I transposed the rich fisheries of the early twentieth century to the 1890s. Also, shark charmers were outlawed by the British after 1885, but I could not resist them. I used the following books, articles, and films to tell my story as accurately as possible.

Allen, Charles. *Plain Tales from the Raj.* London: Century Publishing Co., Ltd. in association with Andre Deutsch Ltd. and the British Broadcasting System, London, 1975.

Allen, Charles, and Dwivedi, Sharada. *Lives of the Indian Princes.* New York: Crown Publishers, Inc., 1984.

Bagnis, Raymond. *Underwater Guide to Tahiti.* Papeete, Tahiti: Les Editions du Pacifique, 1983.

Becke, Louis. *South Sea Supercargo.* Brisbane, Australia: The Jacaranda Press.

Blanch, Lesley. *The Wilder Shores of Love.* New York City: Carroll and Graf Publishers, Inc., 1954, 1982.

Byron, John. *Photographs of New York Interiors at the Turn of the Century.* New York: Dover Publications, 1976.

Conrad, Joseph. *Sea Stories, Youth and Typhoon*. London: Granada Publishing Ltd., 1984.

Creighton, Margaret S. *Dogwatch and Liberty Days*. Salem, Mass.: The Peabody Museum of Salem, 1982.

Dodd, Edward. *Polynesian Seafaring*. New York: Dodd, Mead and Company, 1972.

Emory, Kenneth. *Material Culture of the Tuamotu Archipelago*. Honolulu, Hawaii: Pacific Anthropological Records #22, Department of Anthropology, Berenice Pauahi Bishop Museum, 1975.

Fizdale, Robert, and Gold, Arthur. *Misia*. New York: Morrow Quill Paperback, 1981.

Girouard, Mark. *Life in an English Country House*. Middlesex, England: Penguin Books, 1980.

Glick, Joel, and Lorusso, Julia. *Healing Stones, The Therapeutic Use of Gems and Minerals*. Albuquerque, New Mexico: Brotherhood of Life, 1976.

Hale, Oron J. *The Great Illusion*. New York: Harper Touchbooks, 1971.

Isaacs, Thelma. *Gemstones, Crystals and Healing*. Black Mountain, North Carolina: Lorien House, 1982.

Kornitzer, Louis. *The Pearl Trader*. New York: Sheridan House, 1937.

Kunz, George Frederick. *The Magic of Jewels and Charms*. New York: J. B. Lippincott Company, 1914.

Kunz, George Frederick. *Shakespeare and Precious Stones*. New York: J. B. Lippincott Company, 1916.

Kunz, George Frederick, and Stevenson, Charles Hugh. *The

Book of the Pearl. New York: The Century Company, 1908.

Langdon, Robert. *Tahiti, Island of Love.* Syndey: Pacific Publications, 1968.

Lubbock, Basil. *Bully Hayes, South Seas Pirate.* London: M. Hopkinson, Ltd., 1931.

Miles, A. Graham. *A Fisherman's Breeze.* New York: Brentano's Publishing, 1924.

Nadelhoffer, Hans. *Cartier, Jewelers Extraordinary.* New York: Harry N. Abrams, Inc., 1984.

Pace, Edward. *The Nineteenth Century, The Contradictions of Progress.* New York: Bonanza Books, Inc., 1985.

Picton, B. *Living Corals.* Papeete, Tahiti: Les Editions du Pacifique, 1980.

Porzelt, Paul. *The Metropolitan Club of New York.* New York: Rizzoli, Inc., 1982.

Richard, C. *Shells of Tahiti.* Papeete, Tahiti: Les Editions du Pacifique, 1984.

Richardson, Wally. *The Spiritual Value of Gemstones.* Marina Del Rey: DeVorss and Company, 1984.

Rosenthal, Leonard. *The Pearl Hunter.* New York: Harry Schuman and Company, 1952.

Schmitt, Lou A. *All Hands Aloft.* Berkley: Howell-North Books, 1965.

Sinclair, David. *Dynasty: The Astors and Their Times.* New York: Beaufort Books, Inc., 1984.

Sitwell, Nigel. "The Queen of Gems Comes Back," *Smithsonian Magazine,* Vol. 15, No. 10, January 1985.

Skinner, Cornelia Otis. *Madame Sarah*. Boston: Houghton Mifflin, 1967.

Tindall, Gillian. *City of Gold*. London: Temple Smith, 1982.

Trout, Jo Franklin. "The Oil Kingdoms," a documentary produced by Pacific Productions, Washington, D.C., 1985.

Villiers, Allan J. *The Sea in Ships*. New York: William Morrow and Company, 1933.

Villiers, Allan J. *The War with The Cape*. New York: Charles Scribner and Sons, 1971.

Wallace, Frederick William. *Wooden Ships and Iron Men*. London: Hodder and Stroughton, 1932.

Ward, Fred. "The Pearl," *National Geographic Magazine*, Vol. 168, No. 2, August 1985.

Zucker, Benjamin. *Gems and Jewels, a Connoisseur's Guide*. New York: Thames and Hudson, 1984.